"BATTEN DOWN THE HATCHES!"

William Ridley and the Celtic Cross is a great and exciting story, but it's far more than that. This book will teach you history, touch your heart and bring laughter and tears. But, maybe more importantly, it will remind you that behind everyday life, there is a supernatural battle in which all believers are involved. Read this book and remember...you'll be glad you did!

Dr. Steve Brown - Author & Founder Key Life Network
www.KeyLife.org

I have known Connie for many years & she lives her life for the Glory of GOD. In Connie's book, she has brought out the beauty of Jesus and the blessing of knowing Him. In and through our broken and blessed times, we can know the Lord's help and guidance in all our different ways. God bless you.

Rev. Gordon Thomson - Faith Mission Director for Scotland
www.FaithMission.org

Do you like to read about the works of God in history? Do you like to immerse yourself in a gospel adventure? Do you have an inquiring imagination and do you like to see Christ triumph? Then I would highly recommend Connie's book; *William Ridley and the Celtic Cross.*

It is a book filled with adventure for the young Christian, as well as good reading for the enquirer among you. An excellent mixture of spiritual realities and teenage trials. Lose yourself in William Ridley's adventures as you think about some of the most important issues we all face.

Brian Lowrie ~ CEO MaD Ministries, Scotland
www.MaDinScotland.com

WILLIAM RIDLEY AND THE CELTIC CROSS

WILLIAM RIDLEY AND THE CELTIC CROSS

CONNIE MACLEOD

Kerusso

Foreword

Richard Pratt is a friend of mine and an Old Testament scholar. A number of years ago he wrote a popular book titled, He Gave Us Stories. That's what God did.

The Bible is, of course, a book containing propositional truth. It is a world view that teaches, explains and proclaims the way the world was created and why it was created. But the Bible is more than that. It is also a book of true stories where God speaks powerfully about his creation and to those he created.

Connie MacLeod has written a wonderful story. If you like stories, you'll like William Ridley and the Celtic Cross and of course, a good story is a gift. But if you read the book and only enjoy the story, you'll miss something important.

This is not just a story. It's a myth in the old sense of the word "myth." A myth is a true story, but the truth is deeper than the story. In this book you can not only enjoy the story, if you look deeper, you'll see the universal "true truth" about a supernatural world many of us ignore, the "true truth" about evil and its reality, the "true truth" about a battle in which we're all engaged and the "true truth" about a God who is sovereign, good and kind.

And most of all, you'll read the "true truth" about your own place in God's story.

We live in a time where many people are without an anchor. There're so many questions: Who am I? Why was I created and why do I exist? What is all of this about? Is there a God and, if there is, does he care? And, maybe the most important question,

"Does he care for me?"

When Albert Camus, the French existentialist philosopher, said that the only question thinking people need to ask is whether or not they should commit suicide, he was talking about the loss of meaning and, with the loss of meaning, we lose everything that's important. The only meaning becomes what one decides is meaningful, and it doesn't matter if one's meaning is collecting soda cans or building a hospital. In the end, it doesn't matter. It's the refrain found in Charles Kingsley's poem that men must work and women must weep, and "the sooner it's over, the sooner to sleep." That's a world view (or, maybe the lack of one) that is dark, scary and so very sad.

What if there is more than that? What if the message of the Bible and this book is true? What if there is meaning? What if you were created for an exciting purpose? What if the story of God's love incarnate in a baby in a manger, the message of forgiveness in the cross and the good news of eternal life is all true?

It is!

There really is an anchor and William Ridley and the Celtic Cross is, underneath the exciting story of a battle, the profound truth to which Scripture calls us. It is the good news that there really is a God, that he really does care and that he sent his son as a sacrifice for us. It is the good news about meaning and the good news that mercy, grace and forgiveness are built into the very fabric of the universe.

Sometimes we forget and it takes a story to remind us.

Just as William Ridley was given a silver Celtic Cross and told to be the defender of the faith, and just as he was told to hold fast and not fear, you, as it were, can have the Celtic Cross, be a defender of the faith and need not fear. That's why you were born!

Enjoy the incredible story you are about to read. But don't miss the "soft sound of sandaled feet" of the story. It's Jesus and he calls you to be his own!

Dr. Steve Brown

Contents

Preface

S ome people are born with a propensity for greatness, called to impossible feats of valour, others to more nefarious deeds, or fame and fortune...but most are simply called to the everyday struggles, tinctured with tiny miracles, the stuff the world takes no notice of.

Yet, these seemingly small events shape the course of eternity.

Do not think your life is small, ordinary, or of no consequence. Every breath you take is a feat of victory as life's purpose is worked out a little more each day.

Here is one such story...

I

Tantallon Castle

*T*was *Autumn 1987.* The day began with an overwhelming sense of anticipation, then by nightfall, an unyielding longing to return to Tantallon Castle. We'd only just turned the key in her heavily nailed oaken door, signifying visiting hours had come to a close; for care of this historical sandstone gem, perched atop sea drenched cliffs, belonged to my parents, Magnus and AnnaLee Ridley. As an eight-year-old budding historian, this ancient medieval curtain wall and her many rooms have played host to brilliant adventures beside a restless ocean in the cradle of Scotland's turbulent past.

"Don't be long, William." Da pointed to dark clouds gathering offshore, "Storm's coming."

"Aye, Da." I called o'er my shoulder, "I'll be along soon." He shot me a doubtful look as I hurried back inside, fingers bumbling down the corridor, over the reddish stone, as though I could reach back in time to become part of Tantallon, and she, in return, transferred a sandy pink residue onto each of my fingers.

Upon entering the Great Hall, slivers of moonlight filtered through remnants of walls that long ago boasted a roaring hearth, elegant courtiers, lively music, and savoury aromas from kingly feasts. But all that came to a crashing halt during the "Rough Wooing," Henry VIII's rather rude way of securing influence over Scotland by arranging a marriage between his son, Edward, and the wean, Mary Queen of Scots.

"Easily distracted!" I could almost hear Mum teasing as I spied my most prized possession. Though dull-edged, my wooden sword was a cracker. Da carved it himself! An essential part of any adventure, now lying in the recesses of the hall where earlier I'd felled a dragon. In the cool night air, I knelt to pick it up, the moonlight shimmering o'er me like a halo, and I watched my breath cascade into gossamer swirls, matching the rhythmic Firth lashing the rocks below. Then it came again... that unrelenting sense of expectation. Something was about to happen!

Holding my breath, even the waves hushed in reverence, and every drop of anticipation led to this very moment. Rising slowly into this sacred ring of light, mingled with the wind and my heartbeat, I heard a voice....

"William! Hold Fast!"

Startled, I looked about the ancient bastion. Had I imagined it? No, twas real, audible, at least to me. Then the thought occurred, "God? Was that you?"

Da would call this a mountaintop moment, one to draw upon for courage, for as keepers of Tantallon and Da, pastor to a small fellowship, our family was well acquainted with troubles. But cloistered in my beloved Tantallon, I savoured the moment.

In the distance, thunder rumbled, and the rush of wind caused a handful of dried leaves to dance around the hall. Then, out of the pale night, a silver moth lit upon my sleeve. Its delicate feet gripped against the currents as I whispered, "Hello! Not to worry.

You're safe here." On closer inspection, I complimented, "Look how beautifully God painted you!"

As if saying thank you, its powdery wings fluttered up and down, then lifted by a gust, the tiny visitor disappeared into the darkness.

"Och! Must get home." I scolded myself when the temperature took a sudden plummet. Twas more than the approaching storm, and instantly, my soul was seized with a terrifying dread. Something evil hurtling towards me pierced the darkness with a shriek so vile, even the creeping things of the night recoiled in fear. A foul stench filled my nostrils, and I stood, trembling...

From the dungeon passageway, burning, soulless eyes, set deep in an ashen face, peered from the shadows, and my body went icy cold as it scrunched its leathered face and let out another terrifying wail. Every fibre of my being strained to scream, but paralysed with fear, a tiny gasp was all I could muster.

Glaring, it sniffed the air, which began to pulse with electricity. Every hair on my head, neck, and arms came to attention, but twas too late to dive for cover. The castle ground shook as a bolt of lightning split the night in a shower of sparks, with thunder so explosive, you'd nae hear the scream escaping my lips. The untamed winds summoned even darker storm clouds that rolled across the moon, cloaking the room in darkness, and I shivered.

With a deafening roar, the demon bore down in full charge. Frozen in its path, no knight of Tantallon could have proved braver as I did the only thing I knew to defend myself. Hefting my sword as though it were made of the finest folded steel, I stepped into the charging foe. With too much momentum to alter course, it impaled itself upon the wooden blade when lightning crackled, engulfing the demon and felling us both to the ground.

Exhaling ragged breaths, I stared, for this was no imaginary dragon. It whimpered as I drew near, then knelt beside it, "What-ever manner of creature you are, you've come fae a horrid existence." Tilting its head, the way curious dogs sometimes do, it quieted as I spoke, "May the Lord relieve your anguish."

It stared in wonder as a tear cascaded down my cheek, then, falling free, landed upon its own. Recoiling, it took one last gasping breath, then vanished like a handful of dust in the wind.

Once more, I found myself alone in the Great Hall, wondering, "What on earth was that?" Then inside my head, or maybe in my heart, I heard again...

"William, hold fast!"

What comfort those words brought, replenishing my strength and my wits. And while the horrible dread had passed, the slight odor of sulphur lingered. Letting go a large sigh, I reached to reclaim my sullied sword, but it too began a transformation. A pale blue light shimmered across the blade, followed by tiny shards of lightning that grew so brilliant, I shielded my eyes, falling back on my heels and into a deep, peaceful sleep.

...When I woke, it seemed a lifetime had passed. The wind whistled through the ancient spires, and I stretched my arms high above my head. "Och," I groaned. "Late again!"

My eyes darted about the room, searching for my sword, nowhere to be seen, yet in its place lay a silver Celtic Cross on a braided leather cord. The steely blue length shimmered in the waning light, and as I took hold of it, thunder rumbled across the heavens. Spinning it back and forth, I discovered it had no seams, only a smithy's mark akin to a broadsword. After tying the ruddy leather around my neck, I pressed the metal to my skin when, from somewhere far above, a raindrop descended, landing on my cheek. Gazing heavenward, again I heard that unmistakable voice...

"William. Ye shall be a defender of the faith!"

2

Chosen

W "illiam! Where are ye?"

"Here Da!"

Exceedingly strong from working round the castle and rowing our dinghy to the Bass, Da made powerful strides through the gathering storm, cutting a formidable silhouette as he entered the Great Hall.

"Yer mum's worried half to death!" Jumping up, I clung to him as he chuckled, "Sleepyhead. Told ye not to dilly-dally!"

With a crack of thunder, the skies erupted, flinging torrents of icy droplets upon our heads. "Och!" I yelled, "That stings!"

"Aye!" Da winced, gathering me into his arms, then bolted towards our cottage at the foot of the castle grounds. Bursting through the door, the stormy blast dispersed an aromatic vapour of mince and tatties, along with Mum's anxious thoughts.

"There's my lads! Come, let's get ye warmed up."

The blazing hearth threw lively shadows on the stone and mortar walls, while Mum wrapped us in warm towels, rubbing my head till I thought it might pop off my shoulders. Then, with a kiss to Da's cheek, she sat beside him, and we thanked God for our meal.

"Pass the tatties to yer mum," Da grinned at her. "Our bairn was sleeping like a lamb up there, ta' castle."

"William, how do you manage that? Oh!" She jumped as a sudden blast of thunder rattled the windows. "Amidst thunder and lightning, no less? Ye had us worried!"

"Sorry, Mum. I did nae mean to cause ye worry."

"Well..." she smiled. "Yer safe now. Although I do wonder what you lads find so fascinating up there?" Glancing at the grins spreading across our faces, Mum rolled her eyes. "Alright then, keep your boyish secrets, but I cannae stand for supper to get cold. Eat!"

"And after all this," Da took a bite, glancing sideways, "still no sword?"

"Och, Da! Mum! Yer nae gonna believe this!"

"A bite of supper first," Da advised, "then ye can tell us all about it."

"Mmm!" An oversized bite of the tasty meal warmed my insides as I began, "Well...God says I'm to be a defender of the faith!"

My parents looked first at each other, then, crossing her arms, Mum lifted a finger to her lip and raised an eyebrow, her way of saying, 'You've got my attention; go on!'

"So," Da queried, "how exactly did the Lord convey this message?"

Throughout dinner, Mum and Da listened as I explained every detail, but before they could respond, I blurted, "I know it sounds daft! And surely twas a dream, but...I cannae explain this!" Pulling the cross from beneath my shirt, it shimmered in the glow of the hearth.

Mum sat back, "Och, child! Some of us have to see before we dare believe. You must've been scared out of your wits!"

"Och!" I patted her hand. "At first I could barely breathe. Felt like something was standing on my chest; my lips couldn't form a sound. But then, twas as if God was standing with me, whispering the scriptures you taught, that we wrestle not with flesh and blood but with the forces of evil. When the demon charged, I called on Jesus, and He defended me. And...He knew my name! He called me by name!"

"Oh, my dear William, of course He knows your name...and every hair on your precious wee head." Mum started weeping, so Da pulled up beside her, wrapping her in his arms as she continued, "The day you were born, Satan tried to take ye from us."

"Blue ya were!" Da added.

"Aye, the cord wrapped so tightly about your neck. Twas like tug of war: the Enemy on one end, The Almighty on the other. But by God's grace, yer here and..." Mum paused. "He spoke to me that morning too."

"He did?" I asked with expectation, "What, what did God say?"

"'This one's to be a warrior.'" She smiled, "Twas true; ye had to fight for yer very first breath!"

Da grasped Mum's hand. "Aye, both yer mum and ye had to fight for yer lives that day. I'd never prayed harder nor been more fearful."

"Once the danger passed," she continued, "we prayed ye'd not get mixed up with ruffians... but I understand now. Yer to be a different type of warrior, for God's kingdom."

"For we are his workmanship, created in Christ Jesus for good works, which God prepared beforehand that we should walk in them." Ephesians 2:10

"Wow!" My mind churned, over and over, "But, Da! What does all this mean?"

"I believe... God let you see something important, Will. This world tis a hard place; not everyone has good intentions. Some folk, if they could get away with something, even if it caused harm, would." Voicing my displeasure with a deep exhale, Da continued, "Tis the way of the world, son. This demon, dream or real, is like folk bound up in darkness. While ye stood bravely against it, your pity shows ye to be a soul of great mercy. That's a gift, son, only God can give ye."

"Truly!" Mum snorted, "Had I been there, I'd have skewered the beast and wished him happy on his way to Hades!"

"And the loveliest wielder of a claymore ye'd be, dearest!" Laughter eased the tension as Da set another brick of peat on the fire. "Ye'd ne'er expect yer fairest Mum to be so fierce a warrior, but..."

She completed his sentence. "There's no lass fiercer, then she, protecting her bairns!"

Though my parents' playful banter made me smile, I still wondered, "But why, Da? Why would God choose me for something so, so... enormous?"

"Ye'd not be the first in our family to ask that."

"What do ye mean?"

"When yer ancestor, Magnus of Orkney, was pressed aboard a British warship, he certainly didn't wake up that morning thinking he'd been chosen."

"What was he chosen for?"

"Adventure!" We giggled, as Da explained, "And a new life in a new country. After two years, his ship docked off the coast of Maine, and for faithful service, he was sent ashore to gather provisions. From thence, he ran, as far and as fast as his feet would carry him. Though many a night he spent hungry and lonely, by God's grace, he built a new life. With his Scottish bride, Susannah, they rallied to the lot they'd been dealt, their children flourished, they earned respect from the native peoples, and he founded the town's first fellowship. His testimony to the mighty God who had protected and guided him inspired many to trust the Lord."

"Is that who yer named after?"

"Aye," Da chuckled, "but thankfully, the dinghy's as close as I get to a warship!"

"Aye! But let's not forget our connection with royalty!" Mum said, peaking my curiosity. "Bishop, Nicholas Ridley!"

"Bishop? Sounds important…" Twas more a question than a statement.

"Ridley," Da responded, "taught Henry VIII and common folk from the Bible, *in English*, that we're saved by Christ's grace alone…not by anything we do or purchase. But, when Henry's daughter Mary came to power, she and the religious leaders declared that illegal."

"But why?" I stared in disbelief. "People need to hear that, so they have hope!"

"Well," Da continued, "some folk cannae see that truth and dinnae want others to either."

"That's horrible!" I gasped.

"Tis!" He nodded. "But worse, she earned the nickname "Bloody Mary" by having nearly 300 men, women, and children burned alive for their faith, Ridley and his friend Hugh Latimer among them."

I shuddered, and Mum drew me close as we listened.

"On the morning of 16 October 1555, they ascended the pyre that would take their lives. Nicholas comforted a weeping woman, 'Though my breakfast may be somewhat sharp, my supper will be more pleasant and sweet.' Then Latimer was heard over the crowd, 'Be of good cheer, Ridley. We shall this day, by God's grace, light up such a candle in England, as, I trust, will ne'er be put out!'"

"But they were about to die in the flames!" I blurted, "Where does courage like that come from?"

"They had surety of where they were going, and whatever we face on account of the Gospel, God provides the strength. But even after death, Ridley and Latimer inspired a flood of hope. Many, many people were saved."

After a moment, I asked, "Do you think… God could use me that way?"

Mum hugged me tighter as Da answered, "Time will tell Will. Time will tell."

3

In Magnus' Steps

With no trace of the previous evening's storm, the Firth lapped the strand around Tantallon, while beneath the thatch of our cottage I stretched my arms high, yawning, waking, and remembering! With a gasp, I touched the cross around my neck, which confirmed, this at least, had not been a dream.

Immediately my brain whirred through the night's events, then flopping back into my pillow, examining my curious new treasure, I sighed, trying to recall God's voice.

"Well, Lord, I dinnae ken what a defender of the faith does, but like my ancestors, I hope to share what an amazing God you are, so folk'll trust in You!"

After breakfast, Da and I headed for Tantallon. I loved tagging along and helping, everything from picking up trash to providing unofficial guided tours. The work was interesting; I usually learned something, and be it good conversation or reflecting on the view, this time with Da meant the world to me.

Ascending the grassy knoll, we heard the excited chatter of tourists from the car park below. Warm weather had them cropping up like daffodils, especially on sunny days like this.

"Amazing how folk are drawn to Scotland and her history! A wee bit like coming home."

"Ye think so, Da?"

"Tis what I've heard." A smile crossed his face. "I'm sure my namesake come fae Orkney would agree...if he'd had the chance to return!"

"He must have ached for Scotland." I sighed, "Can't imagine e'er being that far away, in a land ye don't know, no friends, no family."

"Aye, for a time. Till he and Susannah began a family of their own."

Pondering that, I asked, "Da? Do you think God was mad at the naval officers?"

"What for?"

"Well," I continued, "they changed Magnus' life, completely against his will. I think that would make God angry."

"A fair question, one we'll nae have an answer to till we meet Him."

"I know, Da, but if God really loved Magnus, why would he let something so hurtful happen to him?"

Da drew upon what he knew best: "The wisest man on earth once said, 'In his heart, a man plans his course, but the LORD determines his steps.'"

My face mimicked my words, "I don't understand."

"Twould appear," he grinned, "if God wanted Magnus to go to America, he'd no more choice in the matter than Jonah did in going to Nineveh! But truth be told, he did accomplish what he set out to do."

"He did?"

"Aye!" Da nodded. "He made his way in life, and a good one too. And as for the officers, they did what they believed to be their duty, which apparently was part of God's bigger plan. So, I suppose, we'll have to grant them a good measure of grace."

Crossing my arms, I sighed, "Aye, Da. I suppose yer right."

With one massive hand, Da ruffled my hair, and we shared another laugh in the morning breeze.

People often said we were carbon copies, me, "A shadow of the taller, strapping man." Mum likened our hair to Raven's feathers, and our eyes, to the pale green crest of a wave before it dives back into the sea. When she'd whisper in Da's ear how handsome she found him, his ruddy complexion blushed redder still. And while his limbs held massive strength, he used them often to embrace and encourage those he loved.

Today, we Ridley men would wield that strength by trimming the verge around this enormous structure, starting out back where the morning sun was warming the lush carpet of green. Tis the fine detail most folk ne'er notice, unless, of course, it's been left undone.

Crossing the drawbridge, we entered the inner court when suddenly, I froze. Then a violent shudder raced through my entire being. Da crouched down, placing a hand on each of my shoulders. "Tis alright, Will, I'm here." Then, taking my hand, he led up to the skeletal remains of the Great Hall. "Now, tell me again...what happened?"

Pointing in the direction of the dungeon, I whispered o'er the laughter of tourists exploring the passageway, "That's where I first saw the demon...ne'er heard a sound like that before."

"The beastie's gone now." Da confirmed, "There's naught to fear."

Reaching for his hand, I led to the centre of the room. "And this is where it fell and dis..." I looked up, "...disappeared!"

As the morning sun streamed in all around us, Da repeated his assurance, "Done and dusted. Literally!" He smiled, "And not so frightening in the light of day, eh?"

Grasping the cross about my neck, I nodded. *Have I not commanded you? Be strong and courageous. Do not be frightened, for the LORD your God is with you wherever you go.*

"Aye," Da nodded, "that He is!"

Then stepping into the brilliant sunbeam, I lifted my face with a smile that consumed my whole being and spoke into the light, "And right here, tis where I heard God speak!"

Da stood watching, "I'm proud of ye, son. Your faith is growing."

We both knew you couldn't put God in a box. Da'd preached on water turned to wine, the raging sea calmed, the dead brought back to life, e'ry miracle demonstrating that Jesus is God. We'd heard of angels standing guard, preventing evil men from attacking, but ne'er, ne'er had we expected something like this in our lives.

Facing him, no words could convey what my heart and searching eyes ached to know. No matter how crazy it seemed, I needed to know he believed me, "Da?"

He blew out a big breath. "We'll ne'er fully understand God's ways. But I believe this event, tis preparation, and God'll supply what needs knowing when the time comes." I nodded as he added, "Instead of focusing on the Enemy, trust in God's protection and continue praying for His wisdom."

"Thanks, Da. That's good advice...for any situation."

"Aye." He patted my back, "Now, take good care of that cross. Don't imagine ye'll find its like anywhere!"

4

❧

Curious Visitors

We'd just finished trimming when a family erupted in dispute over a historical placard. With Da's permission, I approached, "Tis too lovely a day for cannon fire!"

Quieting, the family stared as a girl about my age curtsied, "Aye, tis lovely!" Then, resuming an American accent, she giggled, "But you have a funny way of saying hello!"

Hostilities quelled, I spent the afternoon as tour guide to the lass, her brother, and parents. Living here, I'd learnt more about the castle than most historians and always enjoyed sharing with an appreciative audience.

"Tantallon's built on the promontory, meaning she's shielded on three sides by the sea. Braw battle tactics! And those walls," I pointed upwards, "provided soldiers a view for miles around. When we head up, I'll show ye something even more intriguing."

Young Tommy plied, "What's that?"

"Some say... Tis Mary Queen of Scots footprint in the walkway!"

Captivated, they followed through to the gatehouse, where I

14

explained how the Douglas clan defended Tantallon from this position. While describing various deterrents, Tommy pointed above our heads and began shouting, "There! That's the spot!" He whirled towards me, "Have you seen the ghost? It was up there, wearing one of those frilly neck things!"

"Tommy!" His da broke in, "You know that's nonsense!"

"William?" Tommy demanded an answer.

"Uh, thankfully," I stammered, "I cannae say I've e'er seen it."

"Told ya, no ghosts!" The little girl smiled as her father rolled his eyes. "Honestly! That Loch Monster and Fairies...figments of someone's imagination to boost tourism!"

"But, Dad!" Tommy protested, "There's a photograph in the magazine you bought for Rohan!" His da yawned, then Tommy glared at me, "Really, William? The least you could do is pretend it's the ghost of an escaped prisoner! People would eat that up."

"Oh! Let's just add credence to something that doesn't exist! Besides," the man pointed at me, "*he* deals in historical facts, not...hocus-pocus."

This flippant dismissal of his son's curiosity distressed me, plus, after last night, I knew the spiritual realm existed, but dare I explain?

"Oh, Henry. Relax!" The Mrs. interjected, "You promised to do something fun with the kids, so stop spoiling it." He forced a smile as his wife continued, "Apologies, William. While some in our party are less appreciative, Rohan and I are fascinated with your tour. Aren't we sweetheart?"

All eyes turned towards the lass who curtsied again, "Tis an historic event! And Mom and I should be quite pleased if you'd continue."

"Tis alright, lass." I smiled, "Tantallon's seen her share of battles. So, ye could say we've added another page to her history!"

"Oh!" She chimed back, "I like that!"

The lassies chattered away as I led up the spiral stairs, "Mind yer step!" Then, bidding the breathless visitors onto the walkway, I watched as they savoured a deep draught of fresh sea air, marvelling at the view before them.

Dodging a low swooping gull, Henry exclaimed, "Now this... this view alone is worth the price of admission!"

"I'm glad ye see it from my perspective, sir!"

He spat out a cheeky, "You're a bit short to see anything from my perspective!"

Poking his side, the Mrs. emphasised her words, "Oh, hey, biiiig spender! Here's a fact! The price of admission for all four of us doesn't even come close to one of your green fees!" She smiled in his face, "You... are just... plain.... *Rude!*"

"Yes, dear! You're absolutely right." Clearing his throat, he placed an arm around her shoulder and stammered, "Sorry, William. And I'll tell ya something: despite your lack of years, you're a knowledge-able guide."

"No worries." I smiled as they gazed across the water, certain this momentary state of contentment didnae happen often in this family.

"So, what's with the rock out there?" Tommy asked.

"That's Bass Rock! Our friends tend the lighthouse, and it has nearly as much history as Tantallon!"

Tommy chuckled, "You must count your lucky stars to live in a place like this!"

"Well," I thought a moment, "I've ne'er considered stars lucky, but I do thank the One who made them, pretty much e'ry day!"

Henry raised an eyebrow, then lifted his daughter onto his shoulders, "Here ya go, princess! Behold our kingdom, for your papa, the King of Golf!"

After a moment, Rohan queried, "Daddy? Don't you have to win games to be king?"

His wife chuckled, and with a reddening face, he answered, "Uh, yes, honey, I was speaking figuratively."

Rohan nodded as though she knew what he meant, then asked, "What's figure...fig, figa, what you just said?"

"Ah..." he stammered. "It means, if Daddy were King of Golf, Mommy would be Queen, and far as you can see, would be ours."

"Fit for royalty!" The Mrs. beamed a lovely smile.

"That's just what the 1st Earl of Douglas said... although he was a right scoundrel! Murdered his godfather to acquire these lands and title, then passed them to his illegitimate son, George, who became the Earl of Angus."

Tommy chimed, "Now there's a mouthful!"

"Dad?" Rohan tugged his sleeve, "What does illii...eeli..what he just said mean?"

"Em...Oh, look!" Henry diverted, "That section over there's in pretty sad shape. Was it weather or battle that broke down the walls?"

"Mostly battle! The Earl wisnae only a scoundrel; he was an ambitious schemer, duly noted by King James the IV and his son, James V. In 1491, then again in 1528, they repaid his treason by hammering Tantallon with crossbows and culverins."

"What's a culverin?" Tommy asked.

"Em...a type of long barrel cannon. There's one downstairs."

"Cannons!" The Mrs. exclaimed, "Must have made a horrendous racket!"

"Aye! Shook the very ground, though they barely scratched the wall we're standing on, being it's a sturdy 12-foot thick."

Tommy patted the stone, "Built to last!"

"Aye," I nodded. "Brilliant defence! She held in 1639 during the First Bishops' War, but twas Oliver Cromwell's invasion in 1651 caused the devastation to the family apartments across the way."

"How do you remember all those names and dates and battles?"

Tommy seemed puzzled. "I mean, you're like my sister!"

I shrugged, "I find history fascinating; to know who stood here before us, why they succeeded or failed, and what they left behind can be used as a guide map to steer our own course."

"Humph!" Tommy sneered. Then, descending into the Great Hall, he surged forward, swooping around the shadowy room, circling us, "This'd be the perfect place for a horror movie!"

"Och!" I thought, "If he only knew!"

Suddenly halting in front of his sister, he donned a sinister tone. "We'll call it, Rohan meets the ghost of Tantallon." Pressing his face close to hers, he hissed, "And she was never heard from again!"

Backing away, Rohan began crying, till her father chided, "Tommy, stop scaring your sister!" Putting an arm around her, he continued, "I've told you time and time again, there's no such thing! Ghosts, devils, demons... it's nonsense made up by people who want to make a buck selling movie tickets!"

"Sir!" The urge to explain completely overwhelmed me: "I cannae speak for movie makers, but I can honestly tell you, the devil and demons exist!"

Rohan let out a gasp, while Tommy and his mom both exclaimed, "Really?"

Exhaling deeply, Henry looked away. "Oh, for Pete's sake!"

"So," Tommy demanded, "why didn't you back me up on the ghost?"

"Technically..." I explained, "it's nae a ghost!"

"What?" Tommy countered.

Henry began to object, but with a stern look from his wife, he threw up a hand. "Fine, go ahead!"

I took a deep breath. "A very long time ago, God created everything, including angels to deliver messages and serve Him. There're probably millions, but only three are mentioned by name in the Bible. There's Gabriel, who told Mary she was going to have baby

Jesus; Michael, the captain of God's army, and the most beautiful of all the angels, Lucifer, as he was called in the Hebrew language."

"Never heard that one before!" Tommy quipped.

"That's because he's better known as Satan."

The Mrs. gasped, "Satan!"

I nodded. "He grew so proud of his beauty, he wanted to be worshipped in place of God. So, he convinced one third of the angels to side with him, and they went to war, but they lost and got thrown out of heaven. Sometimes, they appear in human form, like in the picture ye mentioned. But when they show their true selves, they're terrifying. They're nae ghosts; they're demons! And one of Satan's biggest lies is to make us think they dinnae exist!"

"There! Told you so," Tommy crowed.

Henry responded with nervous laughter, "Now you're creeping me out, son!"

His wife countered, "How intriguing, William! What else do you know about...these things?"

Rohan looked frightened, so I soothed, "Well, most importantly, if Jesus is on our side, we have nae to fear from them. He's a great protector, and nothing... not armies, not demons, not even Satan are match for God Himself! I suppose what we should really fear..." Henry's head snapped up, "is spending eternity without God's love and protection!"

Henry snorted, "Did someone put you up to saying this?"

"No! But..." I chanced sharing the previous night's events, and the family listened more intently than they had all afternoon as I recounted the demon, the lightning, and God's message, revaling the Celtic Cross from beneath my shirt.

Tommy and Rohan stared wide-eyed, then, after a moment, Henry roared with laughter, "Ah, you Scots, you love a good story! Betcha, I can buy an exact replica in the gift shop, and frankly, son, if you're a warrior... " raising his arms in mock Egyptian form, he snickered,

"I'm King Tut!"

"Nah!" Tommy joined in. "He's just, what do you guys say?" flapping his arms, "Away with the Fairies!"

Evidently, the men were unconvinced. Their laughter stung, and surely my face reflected what I felt deep in my heart...a crushing sadness at their disbelief. Taking a deep breath, I smiled but said no more.

The rising wind off the Firth seemed to snicker at me, and the joy I so readily found at my beloved Tantallon drained from my spirit until the Mrs. called out, "Thanks so much, William!"

But her words were usurped by a darker voice, taunting, "Defender of the faith, are ye? Then why doesn't this family believe in your Jesus?"

It would be the first of many such attacks and a test of faith as the real battle raged in the heavenlies! So consumed by these dark thoughts, I nearly missed Rohan waving farewell while her mum led her off by the other hand.

5

The Two Ps

I'd ne'er had trouble sleeping, but this night was a fitful tossing and turning, like turbulent waves, a continuous rolling back and forth. And no matter how I placed myself in my comfy bed, I could-nae relax. Shadows on the wall seemed to be fighting each other, and every time I closed my eyes to shut them out, I'd hear the horrible roar of that demon. Wrestling free of the covers, I sat bolt upright, grasping my cross, nae because a piece of metal would protect me but as a reminder that the battle belongs to the one who hung upon it. Then I spoke into the darkness, "In Jesus name, be gone!"

My pounding heart began to ease back from full throttle, and I wondered, had I really heard something? After all, it'd been a long, hot day; those tourists weren't very nice, well, the man and his son, plus we hadn't slept much the night before. If my mind had been playing tricks on me, I knew a sure way to refocus. Lying back, I stared at the ceiling and began humming a song Mum played after dinner... one of my favourites...

"Abide with me... fast falls the even tide

The darkness deepens; Lord with me, abide.
When other helpers fail and comforts flee,
Help of the helpless, O abide with me..."

Those ancient words were the very comfort I needed. Exhaling, I smiled into the darkness, then before completing the next verse, I fell fast asleep.

Raindrops pelted our cottage, splatting on the windows and spilling down like great big tears while a tempest whistled through the shutters, but inside, Mum hummed along with the radio as she tucked scones into the oven. She loved lively, Celtic reels she and Da could dance to, and her cheery demeanour brightened the dreich day as we set out chairs and well-worn songbooks for our soon-to-arrive guests. With a playful grin and a kiss to her cheek, Da withdrew to his study to pray and finish preparing the morning's message.

Shortly after, Mum and Miss Norah welcomed Papa G, the Johnstons, and MacLeans into our comfortable parlour. These were good folk, checking throughout the week in case someone needed a hand, a lift to the village, or just a blether and a cuppa.

Ditching their soggy cloaks and wellies in the mud room, Papa G thumbed through the hymnal, flashing a jolly smile, "'Standing on the Promises' is a good one!"

While Mum played the intro on the old upright, the Cromyns hurried in, shaking the rain from their hair and clothes. There was no censure for arriving past the hour, instead, they were greeted with hugs and smiles as side by side we sang praises!

The depth of gratitude emanating from these broken souls would make no sense to someone who'd ne'er met Jesus, but each voice lifted a childlike adoration for our loving God who'd delivered them from terrible trials.

Years ago, Miss Norah married a wealthy man whose temper put her in the hospital more than once! When she asked their minister for help, in return for hefty deposits in the collection plate, he sided with her now ex-husband. People usually blame God when stuff like that happens, but Miss Norah'd be the first to say, "Twasn't God's doing; twas two very lost men, defiling His name, and one day, they'll answer to Him!"

Mr. Girard's name is Gabriel, like the angel, but we call him "Papa G." He and Margot couldnae have children, but they took to Mum and Da like their very own bairns. Her paintings hang in art galleries all around the world, but my favourite resides over our fireplace, capturing Tantallon's rosy hues, and if ye look real close, ye'll see Da, Mum and I painted in it!

Papa G's favourite story is her commission to paint a French duke's portrait. Though royal titles had been abolished, some families kept up appearances by having each other immortalised on canvass. Twas an honour for Margot; however, the impatient duke kept peeking o'er her shoulder, and noticing a dab of paint on her cheek, he tried to wipe it off. Upon slapping his hand, the room erupted in chaos, for striking a peer was a big offence, but all was forgiven when she married him. You see, Papa G was the duke! And though his family made him choose between wealth and privilege, or Margot, he ne'er saw it as a sacrifice; in fact, he says life with Margot in their seaside cottage is the biggest blessing ever.

But last year, Margot took ill, and in less than three weeks, she was gone. Papa G knows she's waiting for him in heaven, but he really misses her and gets teary eyed talking about her. No one in our fellowship has been untouched by grief or loss, but nae matter the storm, something powerful holds us together... Faith!

Miss Norah suggested, "All Heaven Declares," and whilst Mum lifted as close to an angelic voice this side of heaven as yer likely to hear, Da joined his deep, bass tones to our singing. Such beautiful music, rich in God's promises, filled my soul with joy, and as the last strains faded, we stood in awe of God's powerful, loving embrace.

"What beautiful worship!" Da paused, "God truly is good..."

Everyone replied, "All the time!"

"Right!" He smirked. "Now let's take a look at Nahum. This Old Testament book has only three chapters focused on God's impending wrath for Assyria and its capital, Nineveh. Now, mind you, in 722 BC, these bully boys slaughtered most of Israel's Northern Kingdom, torturing and enslaving any survivors. So when Nahum came along, sometime between 660 and 630 B.C., the Southern Kingdom called Judah feared they were next on Assyria's hit list, but God had other plans!

"The first eight verses pretty much sum up the gist of the entire book: God's impending destruction for Israel's enemies. However, the more important message is encouragement for His people: *'The Lord is Good, a stronghold in the day of trouble.'* While these words were written centuries ago to the nation of Israel, they still hold true today for God's people among every tribe, tongue, and nation.

"Many preachers might deliver a fire and brimstone, come to Jesus, turn or burn, and scare the jeepers out of ye, so ye'll say a prayer and think that's all there is to getting saved message from this, but that would paint God as a bitter, vengeful monster. While He doesn't excuse the guilty, more importantly, notice God's nature throughout Nahum and other books of the Bible: *'The Lord is slow to anger and great in power...'* Nahum 1:3 And *'God wishes that none should perish, but all should come to repentance.'* 2 Pet 3:9"

"However, the triumph of Good or Evil requires one or the other to be destroyed. One of them must go, because if the end for the vilest of humanity is the same as for the kindest person we know, something is very wrong, and we should be offended by that. So, alongside someone like Hitler, it's easy to think *I'm not that bad;* however, I'd be making the wrong comparison. Indeed, when we stand before Jesus, whom in fact is perfect, no matter how many good deeds we've done, our sinfulness becomes crystal clear.

"C.S. Lewis once said, 'Hell is a monument to man's freedom!'

'Twas ne'er intended for mankind, but when sin came into the world, everything changed. God's law requires justice, but herein lies the evidence of His great mercy and love for us. Without it, we'd ne'er know our desperate need for redemption, nor the fathomless depths of His forgiveness. The Law and our inability to keep it are what drive us to repent, and ultimately to Jesus!

"So, the message for everyone is this: if we're truly sorry for our sin and believe we are forgiven, with absolutely no conditions and that God will never be angry with us again, we learn to enter His throne room with boldness because we're clothed in the righteousness of Christ. And faith of this magnitude produces amazing results!

"First, we'll be filled with such joy; we'll laugh, dance, sing, and rejoice! Maybe even learn those Ceilidh steps!" Everyone, especially Mum, had a laugh, for Da's left-footedness at the Ceilidh was known far and wide.

"Not only this," Da lowered his voice, "we become dangerous to the Enemy, because when you're this free, you don't care what people think, which leads to speaking truth with great power and love! When you've died and been resurrected, nothing intimidates you. You begin to understand justice, and that's when the book of Nahum begins to make sense. My beloved family, we hold in our hands and our hearts the gift of salvation that this broken world is so desperately in need of...so be bold to share that good news!"

Concluding, Da quoted C.S. Lewis again, "'Love is hard as nails, driven through the hands and feet of the one who loved us.' And that, my dear brothers and sisters, would be Jesus! Now you think about that... Amen!"

Together, we formed a huddle, giving thanks and prayers for our community, then shared encouraging happenings from the week. But all the while, I kept fidgeting, wondering, should I mention what happened at the castle? What if they laugh at me, like those tourists? Plus, those scones Mum baked smelt awfully good...

A flood of reasons to remain silent poured into my brain, until Da's words replayed in my mind, "We become dangerous to the Enemy... you don't care what people think... speaking truth with great power and love!" The echo launched a transfusion of courage that surged through my entire being.

"Anything ye'd like to add, William?" Da asked.

With newfound confidence, I shared my extraordinary experience, drawing out my cross for all to see. Some stared with awe, others with curiosity, and while we all knew God's ways sometimes have no explanation, some expressed doubts.

"Could God be testing *our* faith?" Mr. Cromyn asked.

Da answered, "Well, the cross is real enough."

"Magnus!" Mr. Johnston shook his head. "Children are prone to stories, and William has a vivid imagination, but... as a respected pastor..." He searched for Da's reaction, "How can ye let him weave such a tale?"

"As ye say, William's imagination is lively," Da shrugged, "but the Bible is filled with supernatural events."

"So, yer saying you believe him?" Mr. Johnston challenged.

Flashing a smile in my direction, Da nodded, "Aye!"

The whistling kettle announced tea and sandwiches, along with Mum's tasty scones, while conversations turned to football and the upcoming Ceilidh. But disheartened, I sat alone in the window seat, gazing out on the dreary day till Mum arrived with tea and cucumber sandwiches.

"Penny for yer thoughts!"

Looking up, I answered, "God is...big!"

"Aye, William. That He is." Mom settled in across the table, and after a moment added, "Mysterious too!" We stared at Tantallon in silence till she asked, "Anything else on yer mind?"

Releasing a heavy sigh, I offered, "I'm not sure what He wants me to do."

Lifting her mug, Mum took a sip. "Ye know, even folks who've not had an encounter like yours, wonder the same thing! So, perhaps..." She paused, piquing my curiosity, "He simply wants you to savour the experience and..." she paused again, "Wait."

"Wait?" I blurted, "Wait for what?"

"His timing."

"Oh," I replied, looking less than excited.

"God's preparing you for something. He does that when hearts are willing, some in bigger ways than others." She patted my hand. "I know waiting is dull, but when God calls, ye'll see, ye'll know what to do."

I wrinkled my brow. "Sounds like you've had experience waiting, Mum."

As her laughter spilled into the kitchen, Papa G approached, "Laughter is the music of heaven! And here..." he held up his plate of scones, "is food baked by an angel!"

Toasting Papa G, Mum patted the seat beside her, and he slid across the well-worn fabric, "I simply knew the Lord had something special for you, my darlings." Taking my hand, he said, "Now, I shall pray especially for you, William, for a calling from God is often accompanied by turbulent events."

"Thanks, Papa G! After all that's happened, I'm gonna need those prayers." I eyed him with concern, "But I dinnae ken why a demon would bother me? I'm just a lad."

Mum answered, "The Enemy doesn't play fair."

"Old slewfoot uses fear to keep you quiet and discouraged." Papa G whispered, "Now this may sound strange, but you should find that encouraging!"

"Really?" I asked.

Nodding, he confirmed, "When the Enemy takes an interest, God Himself has something very important for you to do. So, remember, two Ps are absolutely essential!"

"Two Ps? What are they?"

Leaning closer, Papa G shared his wisdom, "Prayer and patience! Talk to God about everything, but wait for His direction... Like Isaiah said, *'they who wait upon the LORD shall renew their strength and mount up with wings like eagles!'* "

Staring open-mouthed, I thought surely God gave Papa G that message, which Mum punctuated with a wink and a smile!

6

Good Science

The weekend was full... full of adventures, full of tourists, and full of time with folk I loved, but today was Monday, in particular, early Monday morning. Da and Mum were chatting over porridge, whilst I, already full of breakfast, gathered books and hurried to catch the bus. With a kiss on Mum's cheek, a hug to Da, and waves out the door, I stepped into the dawning day. The warmth of the sun, stealing frost from the crunchy grass, made it sparkle like a million tiny diamonds, and drawing the crisp air deep into my lungs, I spoke into the morning, "I am thankful to live here, Lord!" Then, glancing towards Tantallon, I shook my head, "Lucky stars. Humph!"

Long before it came into view, our aging bus could be heard chugging up the lane, then halting with an unsettling groan. Mr. Pete swung the squeaky door open with his familiar greeting, memorised and mouthed by each student as he beckoned, "Good morning, William; find a seat. Get a move on, lad, so we can too!"

Halfway down the aisle, the coach jolted back into motion, and

I plopped into the seat beside my mates, Huw Mortimer and Keith Cromyn. Rolling our eyes, we dived into conversation centred on Mr. Tinley's assignment.

"Good Science..." our teacher explained, "does not begin with preconceived notions which attempt to twist evidence to prove them. Rather, it's in observing firsthand, weighing tangible evidence, then presenting, to the best of our knowledge, the most logical conclusion."

First up to share his findings was Huw, who suffers an intense fascination with lions and tigers; however, there simply were none to be found in the borders of Scotland. So, turning to their closest relative, his aptly named cat, Simba, became his observable example.

"I'd been mucking stalls when Simba disappeared into the hayloft. After a mighty scuttle, I heard a wee chirp, which led me to believe my miniature lion had disposed of a mouse! However, she reappeared dragging a sorry-looking, long-feathered bird, dropped it at my feet, and purred triumphantly, expecting praise for her gift.

"What I observed is a cat of any size disnae distinguish between suitable prey and what we'd consider off limits. Plus, what I assumed was the riddance of a pest was in fact the depletion of the pheasant population.

"In closing, I'd like to add, though a domesticated feline, Simba retains the traits of her tribal sisters. As lionesses in the wild do the hunting, presenting their catch to the alpha male, Simba instinctively brought her catch... to me!" Enjoying the attention, Huw took a bow to the left, then to the right.

A few lads groaned, "Aw, Huw...that's lame!"

Clearing his throat, Mr. Tinley pointed out, "Class, that's actually a good assessment. While it appeared to Huw's ears Simba had caught a mouse, to his eyes she proved otherwise, hence the phrase, 'Seeing is believing.' Also, noting Simba's lioness-like instincts was quite clever. Well done!" Satisfied his presentation was a success,

Huw grinned all the way back to his seat.

Next up was North Berwick's detective prodigy, Keith Cromyn, with a much darker topic. He'd been spying!

"Oh dear!" Mr. Tinley exclaimed.

"It's okay, Mr. Tinley." Keith prefaced his report with, "I've changed the names of the parties involved to protect the innocent!" Then he began an interesting tale.

"I'd long suspected my neighbour of cruelty to his wife. They'd had arguments before, but last Friday was the big one! The ruckus began with shouting, dishes breaking, uproar, and crying, then all went absolutely silent. Fearing for the lady's safety, I had to investigate. With a plate of fresh baked biscuits for entrance, I chapped their door once, twice, then, about to try again, Mr. X opened the door.

"Inviting me in, discretely, I looked for signs of a struggle, or at least a few broken plates!" Keith addressed Mr. Tinley, "I detected none. Just then, Mrs. X wafted into the room, offering milk to go with the treats, as though nothing were amiss." Grasping his chin, Keith continued, "All smiles; they enquired after my parents and how I was doing in my studies. As we munched the bickies, investigative acumen could no longer wait to be satisfied."

"Implying nothing in particular, I queried... I couldn't help overhear your conversation earlier... Then the strangest thing happened. Mr. and Mrs. X began laughing. Truth be told, it was a dodgy telly program they watched, and both being hard of hearing, they turned it up, loudly! My suspicions, thankfully, came to naught, and we had a pleasant afternoon. What I discovered is I have lovely neighbours, and for my own part, tis possible my deductions were influenced by an overly serious study of Hercule Poirot and Sherlock Holmes!"

Straightaway, our class burst into chatter, until Mr. Tinley brought us to order, "Excellent Keith, a lesson well worth remembering. Suspicions can lead us to believe the worst of a person when they might be innocent, or the opposite might be true. Both Keith and

Huw assumed something other than what they later observed."

"Remember, fact will always unearth the truth if we are willing to look for it. And very wise introspective that reading or watching telly can colour our view of daily events."

Everyone applauded Keith until Mr. Tinley added, "One word of caution though. If you believe someone's in danger, never go alone; ask an adult you trust to go along." Thanking Keith, Mr. Tinley then called on Hector Menteith.

Dragging his feet, Hector moved forward, groaning, "I didn't do it!"

Mr. Tinley looked disappointed. "Your assignment?"

"Well, that, and everybody'll find out sooner or later, but it wisnae me!"

Mr. Tinley waited, but Hector remained silent until he was prompted, "The fire on the moor?"

"Aye," he groaned. "I was watching with my mates, but I didn't start it!"

"People can be fascinated by a blaze, Hector, but that doesn't mean they started it." Hector lifted his head as Mr. Tinley asked, "So, in keeping with our assignment, what did you observe that night?"

Hector sighed, "When the wind picked up, the flames began to spread because oxygen fuels fire, right?"

"Aye, good!" Mr. Tinley encouraged, "What else?"

"Wind...can change a fire's direction...quickly!" Mr. Tinley nodded as Hector continued, "There's something comforting about the glow of fire; that's why I got close. But people showed up, shouting and pointing at us, so we ran. But honest, I didn't start it!" Clearly upset, Hector headed back to his seat.

Mr. Tinley spoke, "The people who shouted at you are a perfect example of bad science, Hector. Without visual evidence, they assumed you'd set the fire. That's wrong, and I hope we'll glean wisdom from the situation."

"Don't worry, Hector." Siobhan MacDoone patted his arm. "We believe you!"

Hector returned her kindness with a slight smile.

"Siobhan!" Mr. Tinley chirped, "Come along then, we'll hear from you."

Looking stunned, she gulped, then cleared her throat. "I'm sorry, Mr. Tinley. I... completely forgot; I've got nothing to share."

Siobhan always had an opinion, sometimes two, on everything and everyone and, up till now, had ne'er been at a loss for words, which had Mr. Tinley looking puzzled. "Em, thank you for your honesty. However, I'd still like you to come before the class."

Standing, she grimaced, "You're not gonna make me write on the board a hundred times, are ye?"

"No." He grinned, "But this assignment *is* one of your fortes, so I'd like you to give it a go anyway." She sighed as he continued, "Think on everything you've heard today, then suggest one thing that isn't what it seems."

Looking about the room, Siobhan crossed her arms when a huge grin engulfed her face. "Well, Mr. Tinley, not that I'm complaining, but one could say, you're not a fair teacher."

"I see." He nodded. "And what brings you to this supposition?"

"Huw and Keith have obviously put time and effort into their assignment, but Hector," she motioned, "while I believe he didn't start the fire, and I did not. Despite that, you've allowed us to by-pass the work. Like I said, I'm not complaining, but you can't be a fair teacher if you offer double standards. Correct me if *that's* not what it seems!"

Mr. Tinley chuckled. "Occasionally, I've been lenient; however, answer me this. Does leniency equate to unfair treatment?"

Now Siobhan looked puzzled. "I don't understand."

"If I'd asked you to create something and you showed up empty handed, that would be a failure. Yes?" She nodded as he continued,

"However, my instructions for this assignment were to observe, then report on something that wasn't what it seemed. Before you answered, had you thoroughly considered what you believed to be fact?"

"I did."

"And, when prompted, did both you and Hector share your findings?"

She rolled her eyes. "Aye, Mr. Tinley."

"Therefore, might we conclude, there's been no unjust treatment here, only ample opportunity to complete your assignment?"

Tilting her head, she replied, "Fair enough!"

The entire class let go a collective sigh of relief as Siobhan, who'd often sidetracked us with incessant debate, simply let the matter rest.

"Very good then! You may return to your seat." Moving forward, Mr. Tinley glanced about the room, then called, "Master Ridley, what've you to share with us today?"

Though my original assignment had been prepared for over a week, twas nothing compared to what happened at Tantallon! So, reshuffling my thoughts, I drew the cross from beneath my shirt and held it up. "Knowing my family, you'd imagine this cross was a gift from Mum and Da. Or, judging from its Celtic design, a souvenir from Tantallon's gift shop, but in truth, it has a much bigger story."

7

The Iliad & The Bible

Mr. Tinley and our class sat riveted as I described the demon, the lightning strike, finding the cross, and hearing God's voice.

"This epic tale, I suppose, has far more a beginning than an end. You see, there really is a battle between good and evil, but with Jesus, we don't have to be afraid because He protects us. And while finding this cross is remarkable, what's even more remarkable, is God's using it to tell you He loves you and wants you to know Him!"

Perfectly timed, the bell marked the end of class, but no one budged until Mr. Tinley quick-stepped to the front, "Interesting thoughts to ponder class. We'll continue tomorrow."

As everyone shuffled out, Mr. Tinley asked me to stay a moment. Approaching his desk, he asked, "May I see the cross?" Examining it, he seemed fascinated. "Your father's a pastor, is he not?

"Aye."

"No doubt, he's taught you stories from the Bible. I know a few myself, but..." He chuckled, "What you've shared is...quite sensational!"

My heart sank. "You don't believe me, do you, Mr. Tinley?"

"You've always been an honest lad..." Then, folding his hands, he smiled, "But something this, ehm, extraordinary, I'm afraid might cause ye trouble."

I chuckled, "It already has."

"Oh? What happened?"

"I told some tourists at the castle, and they made fun of me."

"So," he raised an eyebrow, "what did you do?"

I shrugged, "I let them."

Mr. Tinley's face curled into a gentle smile. "Well, I admire your tenacity. It takes courage to share your beliefs, but be advised, not everyone will share your enthusiasm."

Like the Wallace and Bruce statues, Huw and Keith flanked the school entrance, and no sooner had my feet touched the yard, did Mr. Tinley's warning ring true. Our classmates surrounded us.

"What did it feel like being so close to lightning?"

"What did the demon look like?"

"Were you scared?"

But one timid query that sang out above all others belonged to Lilly Alcott: "What does God's voice sound like?"

Of all their questions, Lilly's pleased me most, but the thought lasted only a moment as Siobhan and others began pushing in, pawing at my neck, trying to get a glimpse of the cross.

Huw and Keith jumped in-between, "Give him room to breathe!"

"Well," I motioned with my hands, "right before the lightning hit, the hair on my neck and arms stood straight up! The creature was boggin, the filthiest stink you can imagine, and yeah, at first, I was really scared, but God protected me."

Jimmy Laverm hollered, "What about your sword?"

I shrugged, "No idea, but look, there's a sword engraved on the cross!" Pointing it out, I smiled at Lilly, "And God's voice...wow! It's hard to explain, but the same way you know your mum or da's voice, I knew it was Him!"

Lilly's eyes twinkled with delight until Hector overshadowed our excited group, "William, you're such a liar; you made this whole thing up cause ye live near a castle!"

His friend Seth taunted, "Yeah, that thing's probably from the gift shop!"

"No, look!" I protested, "It's really, really special!"

Siobhan snorted, "Does your lucky charm protect from real people, or just imaginary demons?"

Their laughter hurt and puzzled me. All I wanted to do was show them God's love, but instead, Seth shoved me up against Hector, who pushed me back towards Seth. Some kids began shouting for us to fight, and Hector, who ne'er needed a reason, landed a fist in my midsection, knocking me to the ground. As I gasped for air, he snorted, "Not much of a defender on your bum there, are ye Ridley?"

Forcing his way to the centre of the crowd, Headmaster Baffle bellowed, "What is going on here?"

Ushering me into the oversized chair in front of his desk, he scowled, "William, I'm surprised! Fighting is quite out of character for you." Raising one bushy eyebrow, he asked, "Care to explain?" Catching my breath, and halfway through my defence, Mr. Baffle held up a hand, "Tut, tut! There will be no more of this God non-sense at school. You see the commotion it stirs up!"

"But Mr. Baffle!" I protested.

Wagging his finger, our Headmaster ushered me out, then sum-moned Hector and Seth, "Come in, lads, we need to chat!"

"It seems..." Mr. Tinley gazed across our curious faces the follow-ing day, "We've had a bit of a Biblical fracas!" Over our eruption of giggles, he stated, "Yet, after some debate, Mr. Baffle agrees, we might continue a *peaceful* search for a 'good science' hypothesis."

Despite a few groans, we were soon discussing the Red Sea parting, Jesus walking on water, and my experience at the castle.

"How can you believe that stuff?" Seth rolled his eyes. "Like God flooding the whole earth?"

"If He didn't," Aisling Kerr defended, "how did Noah's Ark end up on Mount Ararat?"

"Och! Quit yer havering Aisling." Siobhan chided, "You can't be that foolish!"

Ignoring them, Jimmy grinned, "What I want to know is how did Jesus turn water into wine?"

Mr. Tinley intervened, prompting us to dig deeper. "Young master Ridley has brought us an interesting query. Scientifically speaking, faith and who we understand God to be, or not, is something each of us must wrestle. Apart from William, none of us can prove these events took place, simply because we didn't see them with our own eyes. However, ancient writings like the Bible and Homer's Iliad have helped archaeologists in their search for answers."

Hector protested, "Since when do archaeologists consult the Bible?"

"When digging for lost cities! Ancient books provide clues and information about the topography and history, so when all those elements line up, scientists know they're looking at the actual site of said history. What they find there is yet another story."

"Mr. Tinley..." Keith questioned, "What's the Iliad?"

"In ancient Greek, it means 'Poem of Troy.' Homer's mythology from 8 BC, recounting the Trojan war."

"So," he countered, "was the Trojan War real or a myth?"

"While Troy was in fact an actual city, the nearly invincible Achilles; the Trojan Princes, Hector and Paris; Sparta's king Menelaus and his wife Helen, were most likely fabricated. Being daughter of the Greek god Zeus, Helen's beauty captivated, as they say, 'Hers was the face that launched a thousand ships!'"

Jimmy questioned, "What does that mean?"

"Aphrodite promised Helen to Paris as a reward, *if* he'd declare her the most beautiful goddess of all; however, when he whisked Helen away from Sparta, Menelaus and those thousand ships sailed after them to war."

"Whoa, Mr. Tinley!" Siobhan interrupted, "That's a lot of information!"

"Tis!" He agreed, "And there's more! During ten bloody years, Achilles murdered Hector, then dragged his body around the walls of Troy behind his chariot." We oohed and aah-ed as Mr. Tinley related each scene: "To avenge his brother, Paris kills Achilles, then the Greeks sneak inside the walls of Troy by hiding inside a wooden horse built from their ships. The unsuspecting Trojans, including Paris, are murdered and the city burnt to the ground."

Aisling snorted, "Sounds like a soap!"

"Aye!" Mr. Tinley chuckled, "Multiple plot twists and subplots too, so filled with supernatural twists and turns it would rival any modern fiction novel! Only the ending varies depending on which of the hundred or so translations you read. Makes one wonder, which version is Homer's original work."

Hector raised his hand. "They're probably too old to tell, but aren't there loads of versions of the Bible too?"

"Yeah!" Jimmy blurted, "I've heard folk can't even agree on which one to read."

"Excellent lads! Now you're getting to the root of good science!" Hector sat a little taller as Mr. Tinley continued, "Unlike Homer's work, the Bible was written over many centuries by a variety of authors, and yet, each book retains its integrity alongside the original manuscripts. In the middle ages, copying it into English could get you burned alive, but by 1611, King James VI of Scotland authorised a translation in the English of that period. Over two hundred years later, a shepherd boy discovered the Dead Sea Scrolls. These parchments, though a thousand years older, matched the original biblical texts, *word for word!* Considering we couldn't pass a simple sentence around the room without it getting all higgledy-piggledy, might suggest divine intervention!"

Digesting the information, we nodded as Mr. Tinley continued, "Another great discovery concerning translation of ancient tongues was the Rosetta Stone."

"I know!" Allie chirped. "It helps to understand old wall scribbles."

"Exactly Allie! Like Egyptian hieroglyphs. It was found in 1799 on the western side of the Nile, bearing three distinct scripts, Hieroglyphic, Greek, and Demotic."

"Right then!" Keith called out, "What's Demotic?"

"Another good question, Keith!" Mr. Tinley explained, "Demotic is the everyday language, spoken by the common man in Greece and Egypt. It was thought completely lost, until this key piece of history unlocked them. You see, the men who followed Jesus, being fishermen, would have recorded their stories in this everyday tongue. And, by 1822, Jean-Francois Champollion deciphered the Rosetta Stone hieroglyphs, providing more accurate translations of the sections written in demotic. Are you with me, class?"

We all responded with a big, "Yes, Mr. Tinley!"

"Excellent!" He continued, "Now, I know that's a lot of information, but it's good to stretch our brains, and doubly important to seek truth in whatever field we study. In years to come, more evidence may arise, and indeed, if the Bible is true, then God *is* able to part the Red Sea, change water into wine, Jimmy, and much more than we can possibly imagine—maybe even exchange William's sword for a silver cross! On these events, you yourself must wrestle, till you discover truth...and that my young friends is *good science!*"

After a moment of contemplation, the bell rang, and class was dismissed to converse outside, this time with a newfound respect for the science of faith!

8

Of Bass Rock

A powerful tempest churned beneath our boat, flinging chilly salt spray o'er the bow and dappling our faces as Da rowed towards Bass Rock. Even more exhilarating was a glimpse of dolphins, schools of fish, and sometimes whales bursting from the depths, then diving back beneath the waves. If one longed for excitement, the Firth never disappointed!

Twas our monthly delivery of supplies, and as our heavily laden vessel approached the dock, slipping beneath the towering shadow of the Bass, I exhaled, "Sure makes a lad feel small!"

"Aye, Will." Tossing a line about the pylon, Da looked up, "That it does."

The enormous stone jutting from the Firth is noteworthy not only for its sheer mass, but for the colonies of sea birds blanketing the terrain and three interesting gentlemen whom I call "Keepers of the Rock."

Ioan Ramsay, born in the nearby hamlet, Auldhame, along with Andy and Drew MacCreamhain, brothers from the Outer Hebrides, tend the lighthouse, each well aware that this bastion of illumination conceals a plethora of dark secrets! O'er a hot cuppa and fresh baked treats, compliments of Mum, we exchanged news from the mainland for stories of auld.

"According to legend, the Bass was a gift from King Malcolm III to the noble Lauder family!" Mr. Ramsay measured out his words, "So, naturally... the Lauder crest... bears a gannet." Along with Bass lore, he could name every species nesting in the craggy cliffs, then, with a scratch to his wild head of hair, he clucked, "Truth be told, tis the winged creatures are the real lairds of this island!"

A huge gull punctuated his statement by swooping towards the window with a loud squawk. Da chuckled, "Looks like someone agrees with ye Ioan!"

As it battered the glass, Andy snorted, "Och! Daft bird!"

"Now then." Mr. Ramsay smiled, opening an aged journal, "Blind Harry says here, Sir Robert de Lawdre fought at Stirling Bridge."

"Did he know Wallace?" I chirped loudly.

"Even better, lad," Mr. Ramsay leaned forward. "He was aide-de-camp to Wallace, and believing so surely in the cause, he risked losing the Bass by fighting alongside him."

"What amazing times..." I gasped, "shaping our history. And what stories *they* must have shared!"

Drew frowned, "Bloody stories, I imagine!"

Andy squawked, "Now, that's 'Captain of the Bass' territory!"

"Who's that?" I asked.

"A Lauder from the darker annals of history! Turned the fortress into a prison." Andy leaned forward, "Especially enjoyed torturing Jacobites and Covenanters."

"Forty men..." Drew held up a finger, "perished at his hand, and who's to say the many more because of the abysmal treatment!"

"But not all!" Mr. Ramsay interjected, "Once, four of James Stuart's supporters escaped and took over the island!"

"That was daring!" I exclaimed.

"Aye!" Mr. Ramsay nodded. "And with aid from France, they held the Bass three years for the 'Old Pretender.' Wasn't till a blockade starved them into negotiating, so cleverly, mind you they sailed away free men!"

After lunch, Mr. Ramsay fed my ever increasing appetite for history by leading up a rugged path to what's left of a 15th century chapel. "Twas named to honour Baldred, who retreated to the Bass in the 700s."

I ran my hand over the moss-aged wall. "He must have been a curious sort, living out here by himself."

"Probably tired of religious bickering and politics." Mr. Ramsay cupped a hand to his mouth, "That'd cause any man to become a hermit!"

"Well, hopefully, he enjoyed his own company!"

Mr. Ramsay chuckled, "And lots of eggs from our feathered friends."

"Now that's convenient!"

"Tis!" He motioned, "And the land's fertile for crops, plenty grazing for sheep and, wonder upon wonders, a fresh water well!"

"Really?" Then I remembered, "What about the tunnel under the Bass?"

"Mm..." Mr. Ramsay hesitated, "What about it?"

"Well..." I chose my words carefully: "I've been thinking. Vikings or Pirates could have hidden treasure in there. Will ye take me to see it?"

"Afraid not, lad. Take my word, nothing to be seen in there, cept' the incoming tide!"

"But..."

Mr. Ramsay's expression alone confirmed there'd be no budging on his decision.

"Fair enough," I sighed.

This peculiar way of halting a conversation often presented itself when I most wanted answers, then turning towards the cottage, Mr. Ramsay softened, "Don't wander far. Tea's in twenty minutes."

While exploring the remnants of the chapel, I stared back at Tantallon. From this distance, she looked miniature, then suddenly, that daft gull reappeared, flapping all about my head. Scurrying to safety, I dashed through the door as the bird hit the window with a thud.

Mr. Ramsay chuckled, "William one, bird nil!"

Though his words were joyful, his expression carried a shadow, so forgetting the bird, I said softly, "You look sad, Mr. Ramsay. You alright?"

His face curled into a smile. "I was thinking of me mother."

"Oh... You're missing her." He nodded, then I asked, "What was she like?"

He sighed, "Wish I knew. She..." he paused, "disappeared when I was young. Afterwards, Da sent me to Uncle Frasier here on the Bass."

"Did he...e'er find her?"

"Don't know." He shrugged, "Ne'er saw him again neither, not even when Uncle passed." As a tear escaped down his weathered cheek, I reached to wipe it. Surprised, he gathered his composure, concluding, "But twas long ago." There were so many questions I wanted to ask, or at least say something comforting, but Mr. Ramsay turned the topic, "So, what are they teaching you at school nowadays?"

Keen to see his joy return, I chattered about Mr. Tinley's *good science* project. He laughed about Mr. and Mrs. X and the dodgy telly show, then listened as I described my encounter at Tantallon. At the sight of my cross, Mr. Ramsay sat bolt upright. "What's yer da to say about this?"

Just in from the lighthouse with Drew and Andy, Da offered, "The Lord works in mysterious ways, Ioan, and we've not seen hide nor hair of that sword I carved for him."

"Aye, Magnus, but...the message?" He queried, "Defender of the faith?"

Dropping a handful of spoons with a clatter, Andy let out a nervous giggle.

"That's..." Magnus paused, "yet to be determined."

"Hmm..." Mr. Ramsay nodded.

Over a tasty meal, Da and the lads talked lots and laughed more, but my thoughts kept drifting to Mr. Ramsay's absent parents, Hector and someone dearer, till I found myself speaking my thoughts, "This world's not as safe as I thought!"

"Indeed!" Mr. Ramsay agreed.

Andy chimed, "What makes ye say that sprite?"

With everyone staring, I stammered, "Well... it's safe enough here and at home, but not everyone's lives are like that."

Drew furrowed his brow. "Spot on wee man!"

"People need hope," my voice wavered, "now!"

Da enquired, "Anyone in particular?"

"Well, for starters... Lilly."

In a room of puzzled faces, Mr. Ramsay raised an eyebrow, "Lilly?"

"Lilly Alcott." I nodded. "A girl in my class."

"Ooo!" Andy teased, "William's got a girlfriend!"

"No Andy!" I flashed him a stern look. "She wanted to know what God's voice sounded like! It's really important to her, because her da is..."

"Gerald and Rose's girl." Da finished my sentence.

"Aye. I can still see her in front of the class when she told us..."

"My da, well, everyone in town knows his name, but people don't *really* know who he is." Snickering erupted at the back of the room where Lilly directed her gaze. "I've heard people say he's a drunk, but I know something they don't. Cept' for Mum and me; he's lost folks, and despite the drink, he's a kind heart."

Hector and Seth snorted, but Mr. Tinley shushed them, then encouraged, "Please, Lilly, continue."

"He tells me stories about the Grand Canyon, how its colours change as the sun moves across the sky, and one day he'll row Mum and me down the rapids of the crystal-blue Colorado River! Then, we'll drive to the Pacific Ocean and go surfing!"

With sweeping hand motions, she explained, "Da says you wait for a wave, then paddle like mad till it lifts your board up. Suddenly, you're riding an untamed water horse, becoming one with the ocean as it spills over and over, filling your ears with the rush of waves. The way he tells it, I feel like I'm right there, in beautiful, faraway places!"

"He also loved fishing with his folks on a boat called 'The Rambler.' But one stormy morning, they chugged out into the Firth," her voice quieted, "and ne'er came back. So, he lived with aunties and uncles, but his real family was Eddie Drexler. They became besties, did everything together: football, darts, learning to drive... in fact, they had a double wedding! Da married Mum, and Eddie married her best friend, Bess. And weren't they surprised a week later when navy officers arrived to *collect* them. Apparently, after a visit to the pub, they'd signed up to explore exotic places aboard the HMS Glasgow.

"Their first duty station was the pink sand beaches of Bermuda, where they had a jolly night ashore, but when re-boarding, sailors had to ask permission to cross the quarterdeck. So, Eddie gave the watchman a grand salute as Da hollered, 'Permission to cross the pa-ti-o, Dah-Dee-O!'"

By now, our whole class was giggling, and a tiny laugh escaped Lilly's lips as she added, "Da and Eddie were chuffed, even though it earned them a night in the brig!"

"They wrote Mum and Bess to say how honoured they were to do their bit for home and country, and their ship was sound, so they'd no need to worry. But near the Falkland Islands, bombers attacked. Though all the planes were shot down, one launched a bomb that cut clean through Glasgow's engine room, then out the hull at the water line! Twas a miracle it didn't explode, and Da and Eddie were right there when it happened. Da was cut up, but Eddie..."

Lilly's voice trembled, "Da's best mate in the whole world died beside him. Bess blamed Da, said it should've been him, and sometimes, I think he wishes that too. So, drinking helps him forget, not because he's bad, but because his heart is broken, and he doesn't know how to fix it. Maybe that's not as big a discovery as the others found Mr. Tinley, but that's how I see it."

Our teacher let go a heavy sigh as Lilly returned to her seat. "I'm so sorry, Lilly... Sorry your Da lost his folks, his best mate, and got blamed for what wasn't his fault. We can't keep people from saying mean things," Hector and Seth shifted in their seats as Mr. Tinley continued, "But you know the truth, and yer Da, sharing his stories, honours their memories. Be sure to thank him for his and Eddie's service to our country!"

Sitting taller, Lilly beamed a smile to brighten the dreich day, "I will."

"And," he grinned, "you'll have to tell us about your adventures when you get back from the Grand Canyon! Deal?"

Lilly nodded with a big smile, "Deal, Mr. Tinley!"

Even Hector, who rarely had a kind word for anyone, said, "That was brave, Lilly!" Then he whispered, "My da drinks too."

"I ne'er thought about folks drinking before, but that could explain Mr. Menteith shouting the horrible things he does at Hector." Drew and Andy dropped their heads. "But why? Why would people do that?"

"Like Lilly said," Mr. Ramsay sighed, "people are broken, William. They need fixin', and it seems God's given ye eyes to see."

Da added, "And a heart to do something about it."

"How can *I* fix them?"

Drew and Andy looked up as Da said, "Ye might offer a gesture of friendship."

Mr. Ramsay rubbed his beard, "Is Hector the same lad who punched ye?"

"Aye, but," I defended, "maybe, like Da says, he just needs a friend."

"Should be his da first!" Andy quipped.

Mr. Ramsay returned, "I fear a man cannae give what he's never received."

"Aye Ioan." Da pointed out, "Words have power...to build up or destroy. One kind word can make a huge difference to encourage or heal.

What would that sound like? I wondered, and more importantly, would Hector listen? He'd bullied almost everyone, but Lilly's story softened him. So, after class the next week, I acted on Da's suggestion.

"Hector!"

"What do you want?" He sneered.

"I thought, maybe...you might like to join me and Huw and Keith for a game after school sometime."

Pulling his head back in surprise, he eyed me with suspicion, then after a moment said, "I'll think on it, Ridley!"

That was the start of events that would shake our tiny village to the core.

9

Seige the Castle

After school, Keith, Huw, and I clambered down the dunes to walk along the water's edge. This was our preferred path to Tantallon, tracks sticking fast in the crunchy sand and revelling in the warmth of the sun. In the distance, otters chirped and frolicked, warming their upturned tummies and bobbing in the gentle motion of the waves. Same as us, skimming stones across the sparkling water; they hadn't a care in the world.

Nearing the castle, we commenced bringing Tantallon's legendary events to life, me as James IV, and Huw and Keith acting the ancient Douglases, taunting from the inner court, "Siege all ye will, but we'll ne'er yield to yer raggedy line of pretenders!"

A longer-legged Keith passed Huw in a race to the top of the tower directly above the fortress gate. This vantage point offered a superior position o'er the armies of King James IV and James V, to whom the Red Douglas clan refused to swear fealty, unless, of course, it proved profitable. For in those days, power teetered back and forth upon the edge of a sword, alliances, and the strength of castle walls. Assuming the Douglas stance, Huw and Keith planned on besting a king with imaginary crossbows and verbal taunts.

On the outer court, behind a time-crusted cannon aimed at the battlement where volleys of arrows would have rained down, I ignited the fuse and bellowed, "Fiiii...re!"

As my pretend cannon ball blasted across the moat towards Tantallon, Huw hollered down, "Worst shot of the century! Is that all ye can muster?"

Peeking o'er the ancient gun, I volleyed, "What do you mean 'worst shot of the century?' It went square up the middle!"

"For a well-educated king," Keith returned verbal fire, "ye cannae hit the broad side of a castle!"

Thankfully for Tantallon, neither James IV nor V were able to make a dent in her sandstone skirts either. But the scales were about to tip. Emerging from the moat, Da zigzagged across the outer courtyard, avoiding a pretend hail of arrows.

"Double the guard!" Huw crowed, "The sharpshooter's arrived!"

Peering down the gun barrel, he suggested, "Bring her up a bit, yer Majesty?"

After a few more volleys, Da scooped me up, tucked me neath his arm, and hollered, "Shall I launch this one up, or do ye surrender?"

Conferring with Huw, Keith drew a hanky from his sleeve and waved it, "Cannon fire we can endure, but against this, she'll never hold! We cede the castle!"

From my ridiculous upside-down position, I waved a finger, "Cessation of hostilities have been duly noted!"

Tumbling onto the grass, Da boomed, "Football on the inner court!" Immediately, Keith and Huw scrambled down the spiral steps, tricky business, steep as they are, while I raced Da over the moat. Clambering into the Keep, we halted with a start as Hector Menteith stepped from the shadows.

None of us truly expected Hector to accept my invite, and

shadowed by his towering presence, I wondered, had I done the right thing?

"William," Da broke the tension. "Who's your friend?"

Before I could answer, Hector introduced himself, adding, "And you must be Mr. Ridley."

"Aye." Da stuck out his hand, "Welcome to Tantallon!"

Taken aback, Hector stuck out his hand, "William invited me... to play football."

"Brilliant!" I beamed, "We're just starting."

Though timid at first, the amusement peeled away any semblance of shyness, and we played hard, passing the ball, kicks and spills, laughter and blether, making goals, and falling into heaps on the fresh-scented grass. Twas the first time I think any of us'd e'er heard Hector Menteith laugh.

"It's braw you joined us, Hector!" I encouraged.

"I wasn't sure... ye know, ye'd let me play, but," he paused, "thank you!"

Huw chimed, "You should play all the time."

"Aye," Keith agreed, "we can always use another player!"

"I'd like that. And," Hector stammered, "Mr. Ridley, tis the first time anyone's Da played football with me, or any game for that matter." He softened, "My da's not like you."

"Och lad, not every man's sporty."

"True, but the way ye act with William and these numpties, you... you actually like being with them. My da's always angry," he paused, "mostly with me."

Da put a hand on his shoulder. "People get angry for all sorts of reasons, Hector, and if I had to guess, I'd say it's not you he's angry with. I could talk with him if ye like."

"No, please!" Hector pleaded, "He'd be furious. You cannae."

It pained me to see the fear on Hector's face, but Da reassured, "You've my word! But if ye change yer mind, or e'er need help, the offer stands." As Hector nodded, Da added, "And I'll tell ye something. You've a heavenly Father who loves you very much!"

Our new friend shook his head with a huff, "Easier to believe when folk act like you, but soon as I get home, Da will erase that thought."

When Da was young, he'd gotten into mischief, but always with the security of his parents love and wisdom. The lack of, causing Hector's suffering, tugged at his heart, "Earthly parents don't always get things right, Hector. In fact, we often fail miserably."

"Ya got that right!" Hector retorted, but my sudden gasp prompted a hasty, "No disrespect meant, sir."

"None taken." Da smiled, "But despite our failures, if we humbly admit our faults, bonds can be restored, and God is faithful to forgive and help us do better."

Hector seemed to be weighing Da's words, then taking a deep breath, he turned to me, "William, I owe you an apology. I'm sorry I punched you after Tinley's class."

His apology stunned near as much as his punch, and I stammered, "Thanks, Hector. That took courage and means a lot to hear ye say it." I offered my hand, "Friends?"

Clasping my hand, Hector nodded, "Friends!"

"Good." I smiled, "We'll nae speak of it again."

"See?" Hector reeled, "That's what I mean, how easily you get over something really bad! I wanted to hurt you, William!"

"But you don't anymore, do you?"

"No." He shook his head. "I'm just surprised, that's all."

"God forgives us," Da reassured, "so we try to honor him by doing the same."

Hector sighed, "Can I ask ye something?"

"Aye."

"If there is a God who loves me," his voice trembled, "why does he let my Da tell me I'm worthless or wish I'd ne'er been born?

How can people treat you so bad, ye think horrible thoughts about yourself?"

Da reeled, "A parent should never, ever say that! But even if they do, you must believe; that's not the truth!" He pressed, "Ye hear me, Hector?"

Hector's eyes moistened as he nodded.

"You are fearfully and wonderfully made, knit together inside your mum by the God who made the universe." One sole tear escaped down Hector's flushed cheek as Da continued, "He made you in His image, completely unique, which makes you absolutely priceless!" Da sighed, "I'm so sorry yer da cannae see that right now, but God loves you. His love never wavers...that you can trust!"

Drawing Hector into a hug, our new friend said, "Thanks, Mr. Ridley." Then breaking free, he sputtered, "I'll see ye," then hurried o'er the dunes out of sight.

Our walk to the cottage was hopeful as we agreed to keep encouraging our new friend. Then piling inside, the lot of us swooned from the aroma of roast lamb and veg bathed in rosemary and thyme as Mum sang out, "Wash your hands, lads! You too, husband!"

Da replied by planting a big kiss on Mum's cheek. Over tea we blethered about the braw weather, playful otters, and how pleased everyone was to see Hector.

"Tis a lovely thing you did, inviting him." Mum smiled. "Ye know anything about his family?"

Keith said, "Not much; tis the first time we've really spoken."

"Aye." I looked to my friends for confirmation, "Don't think we've e'er seen his mum."

"The only thing we know about Mr. Menteith," Huw added, "is he roars like a lion. We've all heard him bellowing at Hector!"

Keith added, "Aye! Fightening!"

"Hector's ne'er said, but," I looked at my friends, "We're pretty sure Mr. Menteith beats him."

Mum looked horrified, then Keith offered, "Maybe that's why Hector bullies everyone. If he swings first..." he shrugged.

"We cannae assume that, lads," Da offered, "but let's make it our mission to help, any way we can."

Mum held out her hands, "Let's start by praying for Hector and his da to come to know God's love."

Huw added, "And to hear Hector laugh more!"

In the weeks to follow, Hector showed up often, and over time, milk and biscuits, our conversations grew deeper. While he rarely spoke about his family, he often noted, "Your da's strong but kind! And yer mum's a good cook and sings pretty!"

"When did you hear Mum sing?"

The corners of his mouth twitched, "Outside yer cottage...Sunday!"

"Och, lad," Mum sighed, "you should've come in. You ne'er need an invite."

Hector looked down at his feet. "I'll have tae think about that."

"Bring your folks too!" She encouraged.

Hector froze. "Da'd ne'er come, and Mum... She and my brother died. We'd have been twins, but now it's just Da and me. He ne'er talks about them."

We all gasped, and Mum squeezed Hector's hand. "I'm so sorry, Hector!"

Looking back and forth at Mum and Da, he trailed off, "I just wish..."

"What son," Da plied, "what do you wish?"

"I wish they hadn't died, and that Da wasn't angry, and that he'd talk with me, like you do with William."

Tears were streaming down Mum's face as she wrapped him in her arms. "Oh, dear lad! Maybe that's why the Lord brought ye to us."

Accepting her hug, he regained composure, then addressed Da, "I've ne'er seen what you have in my Da, but I'm starting to believe it has something to do with this... God, you all go on about."

Da nodded. "Only God could give you that wisdom, Hector. He's a mighty friend who'll lead, guide, and protect ye!"

Hector shook his head. "You see? The way you talk about Him, like He's an actual person, like He's your friend...how do ye know He's really there?"

Long into the evening, we shared about Jesus. I told him, "He speaks to us in the Bible, in songs, sometimes through things people say, and in the sky, the sea, the mountains, and creation all around us."

Huw added, "And you can talk to God anytime. Folks call it prayer, but tis conversation with someone who's always there to listen!"

"Maybe that's why old Pete grumbles under his breath." Hector snorted, "He's praying to get through the bus ride with us!"

Giggling, Mum set a hearty snack before us. Then munching biscuits and gulping down milk, four growing boys huddled, deep in conversation about creation and the mysteries of the universe. We all had questions... some with answers, some without.

Keith and Huw were reaching for more biscuits when Hector leaned in, looked me in the eyes, and whispered, "So what really happened at Tantallon that night?"

Searching for any sign of untruth, Hector listened. Though he had doubts, the cross was solid enough, and fascinated, he ran his fingers across the shiny metal, "Tis a mystery!"

Since my encounter at Tantallon, I'd been praying for the people of Alba and the rescuing of their souls. And now before me sat one of Scotland's very own sons, desperately in need of God's touch. With all my heart, I prayed that somehow my story would be enough to fill Hector with true hope.

10

A Ceilidh Luau

The days were growing longer, school finally let out for summer and the village was buzzing with excitement. Why? Because Papa G and his friends had spent much of their youth exploring the South Pacific and to cheer him, they proposed a visit to Samoa and Mo'orea. While that would've been an adventure ne'er to forget, his grieving heart wasn't ready. So, they arranged to bring Polynesia to Papa G!

Stepping across a tartan and heathered Brig o' Doon bridge, fragrant flowers of red, yellow, pink, and white adorned lush green vines woven into latticed arches, while ocean surf and bird songs beckoned those passing beneath to the very first Ceilidh Luau.

Inside, torches bathed tiki statues atop sugary sand and murals of tattooed natives paddling kayaks over turquoise water, smoking volcanoes, and exotic ladies on sun drenched-beaches in a golden light. Add to this an aromatic feast, plus an entire dance troupe flown in for the evening, and speculation ran wild over the cost of this extravagant gift.

Joining Huw and Keith, we checked out the tiki carvings, then headed for the stage where Hector'd been helping the band load in. He told us, "They're called Blue Horses!"

"Hmm," Huw grimaced, "ne'er seen a blue horse before."

"Ye'd nae want to either!" Hector whispered, "Comes from the Kelpies rising out of the Clyde!"

Taking a stage-side view, we watched their set-up. Musicians tuned, plugging cords into instruments, while others repeated, "Check, check, check" into microphones for a man twisting knobs on a board with lots of coloured lights.

All the while, a steady stream of kilted men, women in floral dresses, and scads of children flowed in, captivated by the sights and sounds that soon gave way to Ceilidh tunes. The lively reels were braw, and we lads watched couples twirling across the floor, especially amused by my da. For some reason, he could memorise the Bible, but never the dance steps! Utterly hopeless, he twirled left instead of right, back instead of forward, bumping into other couples, thankfully all good sports, and if only for Mum's sake, he kept trying.

"Yer rubbish at the dance man!" Keith's Da called across the floor, "How does yer Mrs. put up with ye?"

Da only grinned, bumping his way through the song, but Mum defended, "Aye, Sir Cromyn, but he's cracking at bringing me daffies!"

Another turn round the floor, and his Mrs. clucked, "Puts you to shame, dear! Have ye naught to say for yer'self?"

Answering in the dance, Hal Cromyn swung her round into a deep dip, then planted a kiss on his wife's thoroughly surprised face!

When the applause faded, Blue Horses began an instrumental led by the fiddle and penny whistle. The couples responded to the haunting tune, like dancers atop a music box, moving in perfect symmetry. And while the room spun round them, Da and Mum held close, whispering, laughing, and gazing into each other's eyes as though nothing else in the world existed.

I too stood admiring someone across the room. Lilly and her mum glimmered in matching dresses, and her face curled into a dazzling smile as Mr. Alcott, looking a bit sozzled, swept his wife out onto the dance floor.

Keith slapped my shoulder. "You look a bit dazed, Will!"

Ignoring his comment, I moved towards Lilly, entirely caught up in the dancing, when suddenly she turned and spoke, "Feasgar breagha, William!"

"Aye!" Discovered, my face flushed with heat. "Tis a lovely evening, and you look very pretty, Lilly!"

"Thank you! Da bought Mum and I matching muumuus!" She spun round, showing off her flowery new dress, then tapping a flower behind her ear, she asked, "Do you think I look Hawaiian?"

Surprised, I stammered, "Well, I, yes, yes, very Hawaiian!" Satisfied, she turned back to watch the dancers. I whispered over the music, "I've heard the waves in Hawaii are enormous!"

"Aye!" She bubbled with excitement. "There's a beach called Peáhi, where Da says the waves are twice the height of Tantallon!"

"Really?"

She smiled and nodded.

"Braw!" Twas all I could think to say. Again, turning our gaze towards the whirling couples, I remarked, "Your folks dance well together."

"Aye, they do!" She sighed as they waltzed past, then furrowing her brow, she added, "Though yer da seems to have a bit of trouble there."

Unable to hold back a laugh, I held out my hand, "Will ye dance with me, Lilly?"

With a nod, we joined hands, each taking a deep breath, making our first turn round the floor, when the fiddle and penny whistle held out the last, lingering note of the song.

While couples reshuffled, I stood facing Lilly, hands still clasped, barely breathing. Time had stopped...till her da whispered in my ear, "Son, dancing means moving your feet!" Over much chatter, the band announced the next song, and Mr. Alcott called over his shoulder, "Watch how it's done," then skipped off with his daughter.

My hands were still midair when Mrs. Alcott, not to be left in want of a partner, came to my rescue. "Well, William, shall we give it a whirl?" And that's how I came to learn the Cumberland Square!

Four couples faced into a square. When the music started, the dancers at 12 and 6 o'clock sashayed hand in hand to the centre, men crossing back-to-back. Stepping around each other, the lassies crossed back-to-back and all returned to start positions. These steps were then danced by the couples at 3 and 9 o'clock. Next, the starting couples moved centre, pressing palms high in the air, circling clockwise for 8 counts, then reversing, circling counterclockwise. As they returned to start positions, the other couples repeated this circular bit, some locking arms around the waist, and the bravest lassies lifted their feet as the lads swung em round.

"Whee!" Lilly squealed with delight when Mr. and Mrs. Alcott lifted us in the spin, and we all laughed! After dancing the sequence a time or two, twas easy, even for Da, who, to Mum's great delight, was finally able to remember all the steps! His achievement did not go unnoticed, as the entire room erupted in three cheers for Da!

The fab Blue Horses took a bow and a well-earned break, providing the dancers a breather and hungry guests time to sample the sumptuous tropical feast. Ne'er had I tasted such delicious pineapple! Then, with dishes cleared, the lights dimmed, and the biggest man I'd e'er seen appeared, blowing into a conch shell. The strange trumpeting was followed by tribal shouts and loud rhythmic drumming that stopped Lilly in her tracks alongside me.

We both blushed as bare chested men and Polynesian lassies in naught but grass skirts, bikini tops, and colourful headdresses strutted by to take centre stage! Their dramatic entrance mesmerised as they moved their bodies to the fevered drumming, then with a shout, all came to a sensational halt and the room erupted in applause.

Amid our cheers, a large, brown skinned woman with a hearty laugh and friendly smile stepped into the spotlight, greeting everyone with a long, held out, "Alooooooo....ha!"

After a few tries, the guests got the hang of it, returning her greeting, then listened as she spoke of island culture. I immediately felt connected to this woman, as taken with her island as I am with Scotland! But Lilly, too shy to cross to her folks on the other side of the dance floor, looked around, fidgeting. Patting my chair, she sat beside me, beaming a smile so consuming, I jumped when the Hawaiian lady asked, "Do you know how to hula?"

"Certainly not!" I fired back, which brought hearty laughter from the gathering.

Getting acquainted, she purred, "Well, Cousin William, I'm Cousin Lita, because we're all cousins on the islands... I'm going to teach you about hula!"

Though fascinated with her rhythmic speaking, I stared wide-eyed, mouth hung open, wondering what exactly she meant by that!

"But first..." her melodious voice sang out, "Tonight's celebration opens with the beautiful welcome song from the mysterious land of Samoa."

"Faauta o le mea" filled the room with an island symphony comprised solely of men and women's voices! Joyful harmonies seemed to flutter from heaven, blending perfectly with deep bass notes that reverberated in my tummy, mesmerising and resulting in more applause.

Then Cousin Lita explained, "Samoans are known as the 'Happy People' which our warriors are about to demonstrate in the Samoan Slap Dance."

Twisting and turning, the men stomped and slapped their bodies all in rhythm, singing with such effervescent joy that everyone in the room was swaying along. Then, the mood darkened as tattooed warriors charged centre stage, bulging their eyes, sticking out tongues, and chanting in a strange tongue. Their deep shouts crested, and with one loud roar, the men froze like terrifying statues.

Cousin Lita explained, "The Maori pre-battle challenge, Haka, was intended to intimidate an enemy, something like your highland bagpipes!"

Intimidating it was, but short lived as the ladies reappeared in Maori skirts and headpieces. Sweet harmonies lilted over quick strummed guitars as they twirled cords with pompoms in intricate patterns. The men joined, clapping and stomping, tossing percussive shakers back and forth, everyone yipping with joy as they sang. This cultural celebration was unlike anything I'd ever seen, and Papa G nodded with a knowing look.

"Each movement in hula," Cousin Lita demonstrated, "by the hand, wrist, foot, or hips tells a story. This traditional Hawaiian dance whispers of handsome Ohi'a and beautiful Lehua. The moment their eyes met, they fell deeply in love, and he won her hand in marriage. Together, they cherished every sunrise and sunset, until one day, while Ohi'a was working in the fields, the alluring Pele came down from the volcano. Smitten with the handsome young man, she was determined to have him, but he ignored her advances. Then, as she did every day, Lehua brought Ohi'a his midday meal. At the sight of his beautiful wife, Ohi'a's face lit up with love, but when Pele saw them together, she flew into a jealous rage. Dropping her human disguise, she changed into a pillar of fire and struck Ohi'a, turning him into a twisted, ugly tree. Lehua fell to her knees and pleaded with Pele to change her too, so she could be beside her husband. But Pele's selfish heart was harder than lava tempered by the Hawaiian surf, and she left the girl to weep. This angered the other gods, who took pity on Lehua, transforming her into a beautiful, crimson flower."

"To this day," she concluded, "the Ohi'a Lehua tree, a gnarly trunk with beautiful red blossoms, grows on the slopes of the volcano, but you must never pick one. For doing so separates the couple, which causes their tears to rain down upon the island."

The dancers retold the fable, spinning round, pressing their hands up, then down, and as the music took a final upward slide, the ladies stretched their arms, fingertips, and gaze towards heaven.

As the applause faded, Miss Parker stood up and crowed, "That's all very interesting for the men, but where've ye put the hula boys?"

Shaking a hand with pinky and thumb extended, Cousin Lita called back, "Hang loose girl!" Aside to the audience, she said, "I see every town has one wicked wahini!"

Miss Parker, enjoying the attention, took a bow, first to the left, then to the right.

"However," Lita continued, "Polynesian women are known for their *quiet* beauty."

Sheepishly, Miss Parker looked side to side, then sat down.

"But occasionally a thunderous one..."

Acting out Cousin Lita's commentary, a Hula girl grabbed the ear of a male dancer and led him across the stage, chirping, "Nag, nag, nag, nag!"

"...wakes the slumbering volcano god," Lita concluded, "who must be appeased." Looking frightened, the girl released the warrior's ear, who crossed his arms with a smug look. "Listen!" She asked, "Do you hear a rumble?"

With that, every light in the room, save the tikis, went out. The drums began pounding a deep tribal rhythm, and muscular, bare-footed warriors charged in from either side of the vine-wrapped arches, carrying torches that lit up the room. On the dance floor, they twirled the flaming batons, tossing them back and forth while chanting to beating drums. Excitement built as they circled round one dancer, spinning four flaming ends round his body, over his head, and even rested one on his tongue! Kneeling centre stage, he bent backwards until his shoulders touched the floor, then passed the burning torches beneath his body. The heat was intense, and spectators gasped as the fire dancer rose from the floor. Tossing the torches high above him, he spun around, dropped to the floor, then caught the flaming batons as the drumming came to a raucous halt!

Jumping to his feet, Papa G applauded, elbowing me with a huge smile.

"Wow!" Lilly and I exclaimed as the room erupted with another rousing round of appreciation.

After braving the intense heat, the men went to mop off while Cousin Lita sang "Pearly Shells," encouraging us to sing along. Then the troupe, led by "Big Ed," demonstrated Hawaiian net fishing in a dance called the Hukilau.

I whispered to Papa G, "They make fishing look easy!"

"Apparently," he replied, "Hawaiian fish jump right into the net!"

Crossing his arms, Da added, "That'd ne'er work on the Firth!"

Mid laugh, hula girls lassoed Papa G and his friends with flower wreaths, leading them centre stage, all save one. Cousin Lita teased, "Is there no brave Scotsman to dance with our island beauty? Cousin William?"

In an instant, I was standing beside Papa G, the girls wrapping us in grass skirts, mine nearly as long as I was tall, while Cousin Lita rallied, "Let's have a hand for our brave warriors in their Island Kilts!"

Ne'er dreaming I'd be on stage, my nerves kicked in until Papa G winked, "In such cases, you simply have to 'hang loose' and have fun." The drums began a slow percussive rhythm, and he swayed his hips to the beat, "See Will? Nothing to it!" But as the tempo increased, the fevered pitch left a red-faced Papa G and friends laughing too hard to keep up!

The Hawaiian show was a brilliant success, and strangely enough, Blue Horses' music flowed together seamlessly. Huw & Keith finally worked up the courage to beg a partner for the next dance, and while they waited for the music to begin, I headed towards Lilly, but so had Hector!

Colliding in front of her, we stood staring while the band began the reel.

"Well..." He glared at me, "Now what?"

For Lilly's sake and Hector's, I gave a gentleman's bow, then watched as they joined the couples gliding across the floor. Consoling myself with a smile from Lilly, I was convinced twas the right thing to do. Hector was smiling, and all my friends were enjoying the dance. The whole of North Berwick seemed to be caught up in the lively tune when everything came to a screeching halt...

11

Angels or Demons

Toppling the floral archway, Mr. Menteith bellowed a fury of unrepeatable words, then shouted above the music, "Hector, you lazy wretch! Where are ye?"

Shaking a vine from his arm, Hector's da ploughed a swath through the middle of the dancers. Drunk past his senses, he swung at anyone in his path until the men, including Big Ed and the Hawaiian dancers, surrounded him. The band stopped, and the room went silent as Mr. Menteith eyed this circle of guardians in stunned confusion.

Punching the air, he bellowed, "Where's Ridley?" Like a wild thing, he whirled around, "Come out, ye coward! I'll teach ye to poison my son against me."

Stepping forward, Da replied, "I'm here, Nate. Calm yer'self."

Irritated further, he strutted back and forth, wagging his head, "Oh, Nate, calm yer'self! Trust the Lord, and everything'll be fine. Next ye'll be giving us a sermon, preacher man!"

"Tis the Ceilidh Nate." Da breathed, "Folk are here to enjoy them-

65

selves. Come have a seat; we'll talk."

Nate snapped back, "Ain't nothing I want to hear from the likes o you!"

"Surely we can work this out, just," Da cleared his throat, "tell me what's got ye so angry."

"Ye think I don't know what yer about?" Nate snorted, "Filling my lad's head with thoughts about God. As though yer God could love him better than his own father!"

"Oh Nate, God loves ye too, if ye'd just let Him."

Nate huffed, searing his gaze on Da. "Ye mingin eejit, ain't nae such thing. In fact, I'll prove what trusting God gets ye right now." Thrusting his fist into the air, he growled, "I dare him to stop me!"

Instantly, Nate took a running lunge at Da when the strangest thing happened. In midair, his arm twisted behind his back! The harder he resisted, the more restrained he became. Thrashing back and forth, he spun round, hollering at Big Ed to turn him loose. Everyone stared, for something was clearly holding him back, but what?

As Mr. Menteith's anger burned hotter, so did the hampering of his movements; then, with a loud popping sound, his mouth clamped shut while his face revolted in frightening contortions. Tossing his head side to side, he strained to speak, but all that filtered through his clenched lips were muffled shrieks! It seemed he'd explode, for his face turned brilliant red and his body shook in convulsions, till, at last, he collapsed in a heap on the dance floor.

"Nate." Da put a hand on his shoulder. "Ye alright?"

Looking shattered, all he could do was nod.

Hal Cromyn asked, "Can ye stand?"

Painfully aware of his predicament, Nate reached out while Da and the others helped him to his feet. In the awkward silence, one of the Hawaiian men shouted, "What's wrong with you? You got an evil spirit or something?"

Looking horrified, Nate's eyes darted round the room. Braving the brunt of his da's embarrassing conduct, Hector made way through the crowd to stand before him. After a long moment, Hector sighed, then, averting his gaze, whispered, "Da, we should go."

Helping him past the ruined decorations, Da and Hal drove them home, where except for an overstuffed couch and a grandfather clock, the Menteith parlour was bare.

Nate entered, rubbing his temples. "I've a headache. Think I need to lay down."

As his knees buckled, Da and Hal caught Nate by the arms, then helped him to bed. No sooner had they removed his shoes, he fell into a dead sleep and began snoring. Staring at his da, Hector covered his face, then fled out the front door, where he began to sob deep, desperate tears of grief for a situation he saw no way out of.

Taking a quilt from the couch, Da draped it over Hector's shoulders and embraced him as he wept. After a time, he urged, "Come back inside, lad."

Around the kitchen table, Da said, "It's nae easy when folk we love harm themselves...and others in the process."

Straightening his posture, Hector sighed, "I appreciate your help getting us home, Mr. Ridley, Mr. Cromyn, but you should go back to your families and the dance."

Da shook his head. "Tis alright, lad, they'll understand."

"They might," he continued, "but if Da wakes, he'll be angry, and I cannae say what he's likely to do."

Mr. Cromyn replied, "Well, I imagine a king-size headache will quell some of his anger."

"Och..." Hector rolled his eyes. "You only saw a wee bit. I wish it weren't so, but that's how he is. I'm really sorry."

"Yer not responsible for your da's actions, so you've nae need to apologize." Da consoled, "And please don't worry, we'll figure this out together."

"What on earth can ye possibly do?"

Showing more wisdom than the man who lay fast asleep inside, Da smiled at the lad, "For starters, we'll put the kettle on."

Sifting through the cupboards, he found cocoa powder and poured a cup for Hector. Though anxious his da might wake, he took the hot brew and sat quietly. The ticking clock grew louder, then pierced the night with a chime, causing Hector to jump, "I don't know how we'll pay for the things Da ruined."

Mr. Cromyn patted his shoulder. "Not to worry, lad. They served a bigger purpose, alerting folk to your da's need for help."

"Well, at least he didn't hit anyone tonight." Thinking back on what he'd seen, Hector added, "Thankfully that huge man held him back."

Hal enquired, "What man?"

Hector pointed towards Da, "The man who stepped out from behind Mr. Ridley."

"You mean Big Ed?" Da asked.

"No." Hector furrowed his brow, "Taller than him. And, thankfully, he covered Da's mouth, so you didn't hear what he normally goes on about... But please don't e'er tell him I said that!"

Da and Hal stared, looking puzzled.

Hector urged, "Don't tell me you didn't see him!"

Shaking their heads in the negative, Da reassured, "I cannae say I did...but you obviously saw someone."

"If ye remember," Hal mused, "Nate did dare God to stop him."

Hector raised an eyebrow. "So, what are you saying?"

"Maybe," Hal whispered, "God sent an angel."

"Pfft! An angel?" Hector quipped, "Nah, this lad was big. Real as you and me. But his hair was..." He searched for the word "shining. Ye know, shimmery, sort of. And smiling, like he enjoyed what he was doing!"

Da exhaled, "The main thing is no one got hurt. Now you could do with some rest, son."

Son! The word struck Hector with a deep sense of peace, quieting his soul as he sipped down the last bit of cocoa. Handing Da his mug, he curled up on the sofa and sighed, "Must be nice to have a Da like you."

"The way you handled yourself tonight," Da's voice wavered, "any man would be proud to call you his son."

Hector managed a tiny thank you, then added, "You know, I teased William about the thing at the castle, but you believed him, and I think you believe me too."

"I do, because some things..." Da shrugged, "have no earthly explanation."

Hector offered, "Could've been part of the band."

"Well," Da soothed, "whoever he was, he protected even yer Da."

"Aye," Hal agreed. "Now, ye should get some sleep, lad."

Laying back on an oversized pillow that welcomed his small head and abundance of thoughts, Hector smiled, then, after a long moment, exhaled, "Good night!"

Returning his smile as the clock chimed again, Da brushed the hair from his forehead, and in a few minutes, Hector drifted off into a deep sleep.

Back at the hall, murmurs swirled about, threatening to end the evening on an anxious note until Cousin Lita began singing. Her voice was soon joined by two, three, and then the rest of the performers in a soothing melody that washed away the tension, like waves carrying sorrows out to sea. Blue Horses followed with a pretty instrumental, then a jolly reel that got folks dancing again. But for the last song, all the musicians combined talents on "Aloha Oi," which means, "Until We Meet Again."

A peaceful hush descended upon the room, and Cousin Lita brought the evening to a close with a farewell, "Alooooo-ha!" As the dancers retired to the sound of swishing grass skirts, she called out,

"Cousin William! If you ever come to Hawaii, you come see me, OK?" Winking, she added, "And bring that big handsome Papa G with you!"

Running over, I hugged her, trying not to cry, "Aloha Oi Cousin Lita!"

Wrapping me in her arms, she sang out, "Aloha Oi, Warrior William!"

Cousin Lita couldn't have known what God had said, yet she called me, "Warrior!" And though we'd only met hours ago, through stories, dances, and songs, I felt a deep connection to her and the dancers, who'd soon be far, far away, and I wondered if we would ever meet again.

Standing beside Papa G, we stared after them, and he whispered, "I know what you're feeling, Will. I'll miss them too."

As the lights came up, folks tidied the hall and the kitchen, the band packed up, and several men formed a huddle discussing what might be done about Nate Menteith.

"I agree, Magnus," Papa G added, "for the lad's sake, something should be done."

"Tis a family matter!" Another man shouted, "Not our business to push in!"

"It couldn't hurt to talk," Hal offered.

"So, then," Da asked, "who'll go with me in the morning?"

Listening to their debate, my anxious thoughts diverted when Lilly scampered over. Taking a deep breath, she announced, "I didn't get to say it earlier, but thank you for the dance, William Ridley!"

Before I could reply, she stood on tiptoe and kissed my cheek. Gazing at her, I stammered, "You're welcome, Lilly. Twas a lot of fun!"

She nodded, smiling, till her mum called, "Lilly, time to go!"

With a curtsy, she tapped her fingertips to her throat, saying, "I believe!"

Running off to join her folks, we waved across the hall, and the silliest of grins broke out across my face. While revelling in happy thoughts, Keith poked my ribs. Then he and Huw, in clunky trainers, curtsied, bumping into each other, blowing kisses and cooing, "Nighty, night, William!"

I suppose I should've been embarrassed, but their teasing only made me grin wider. Rolling my eyes, I shook my head. "I'm ne'er going to hear the end of this!"

Twas half one when we reached home, Mum resting her head on Da's shoulder, he with his arm around her. They tucked me in with a kiss and a wish for sweet dreams, but who could sleep with the evening's events swirling around in their brain? Laying in my cosy bed, staring at the ceiling, I thanked God for Mum and Da and this wonderful night. I prayed for Papa G and Cousin Lita, still amazed she called me Warrior, and for all the dancers, for safe travel, hoping we would see each other again. And though I didn't know how, I asked God to help Hector and his da. Like the cross around my neck, what happened tonight was a mystery, and I continued to wonder what God meant by "Defender of the Faith."

Somewhere amid those thoughts, sleep transported me to the most perfect of dreams. Cousin Lita sang sweet lullabies, happy couples danced reels, and I hovered o'er turquoise blue waves till once again I became captivated by the sweetness of Lilly's smiling face and soft kiss to my cheek.

12

Mischief

For weeks after the Ceilidh, anywhere Papa G and his friends went, folk offered to buy them a cuppa or something stronger just to blether about Polynesia. Their rather unusual gift inspired lots of lively conversations, like Miss Parker melting, word by word, expressing extreme gratitude for the chance to have met the "handsome, tanned, muscular warriors." Of course, the men were just as chuffed recalling the beautiful hula girls.

Tea shops, markets, street corners, and pubs resounded with tales of fire dancing and amusing attempts at hula, prompting "KG," code for King George, to shout, "Hey, Gabe! Show em how it's really done!"

Initially, Papa G feigned reluctance, but soon enough, he'd treat the crowd to his celebrated version of the hula. Along with KG, "Flyboy Flynn," and Cyril, whose nickname was to remain a mystery, they laughed like schoolboys sharing their island adventures.

Spry for his years, Cyril spouted, "One time, in the cool, damp caves of Rurutu, Flyboy was *filage de fils*, how you say, spinning tales, as we explored. Gabe so *absorbé*, hits his head on the stalactite, which reverberated so loud, we thought sure the ceiling would come down on us."

"*Absurdité!*" Papa G spun his finger in the air. "Twas the stars circling my head!"

"*Oui!*" KG smiled. "He lay in the cave dreaming of Tahitian girls!"

"No help from you three!" Papa G retorted, "When I opened my eyes, they're like little birds, peering down at me, so I ask, 'What are you staring at!?'"

I loved their stories, but even more, hearing Papa G laugh again.

Miss Parker recollected, "Shame about Nate Menteith though!"

At the mention of his name, an uneasy silence encompassed the room, as though Nate's angry shadow had barged back in. And while the celebrated foursome had stories a plenty, murmurs regarding the incident and mysterious man with shining hair resounded.

"Twas fairy mischief, I tell ye!" Molly Cameron noted, "Ye saw it, plain as I did. Nate wisnae able to open his mouth!"

"Fairies mademoiselle?" KG chuckled, shaking his head.

"Twas that big Hawaiian!" Mr. Alcott chided, "Most of ye were too sozzled to know the difference!"

"Och Gerald!" Molly countered, "Yer one to talk?"

The conversation continued to bubble, yet no one seemed bothered that Nate, nor Hector were anywhere to be seen. Three weeks had passed, and though Da and others had stopped by, the Menteith home remained dark, the occupants missing. So, Keith, Huw, and I set out to pay a visit of our own.

The shed door hung wide open, but the garden, much in need of attention, was vacant. Putting fear aside, Huw rang the bell. As we waited, all remained eerily quiet. Ringing again, this time Keith flapped the letter slot, but the only reply came from a powerful gust of wind that swung the shed door closed with a bang.

Huw shifted uneasily, "That was weird!"

"Tut! Twas the wind, Huw!" Unfazed, Keith asked, "Can ye see inside?"

"Don't know." I waved, "...follow me." Gathering beneath the front window, on tiptoe, I pressed my nose to the glass and peered into the darkened room.

Keith repeated, "See anything?"

Shushing him, I turned back, where a single pane of glass was all that separated me from Nate Menteith's growling face. "Get off my property or I'll whip ye like the cursed dogs ye are!"

Bolting from the yard, we ran without looking back, but in a manner of speaking, Mr. Menteith reached home before we did. Hanging up the phone, Mum tried to hide her tears as we burst into the cottage. Shaken, she asked, "William, what happened with Mr. Menteith?"

"We wanted to see Hector," I explained, "but he chased us. I'm sorry."

Keith and Huw echoed, "Yeah, really sorry, Mrs. Ridley."

"Och, lads," Mum reassured, "Mr. Menteith's anger's not your fault. He needs help."

"But Mrs. Ridley!" Keith blurted, "What if... what if he's done something bad to Hector? We haven't seen him in *three* weeks!"

With Nate's threats still hot in her ears, Mum commanded, "I know you're anxious, as am I, but the men are handling this. Now, you mustn't go there again." Looking sad, she added, "Promise me!"

Needing no further enticement, Huw and I nodded vigorously, but Keith offered a lighthearted "Um-hum" with fingers crossed behind his back. When Mum turned to answer the phone, Huw poked his side.

Catching his breath, Keith whispered, "What? You know I could never promise *not to investigate!*"

Gathering in the window seat, Huw whispered back, "Keith, this isn't like having cookies with Mr. and Mrs. X!"

"I know, but Hector's our friend." He urged, "We should do something!"

I countered, "We just did, and look what happened!"

Keith's eyes grew wide. "Exactly! You saw how crazy Mr. Menteith was! Imagine living with that! And what if he's got Hector tied up somewhere?"

I sighed, "That's exactly why our Das need to handle this."

With a tray of milk and bickies, Mum sat down beside us and whispered, "What's all the whispering about?"

Looking sheepishly at each other, Keith fessed up, "I had my fingers crossed."

Mum furrowed her brow. "You had your fingers crossed?"

"Aye, Mrs. Ridley, em..." He paused, "When you asked us to promise we'd stay away from Hector's... I had my fingers crossed."

"Oh. I see." She folded her hands. "So, you think it wise to go back, all on your own?"

Rolling his eyes, Keith sighed, "Huw and William were just making that very same point. I'm just worried about Hector, and I think we should investigate. Seriously, Mrs. Ridley, doesn't anyone care about him?"

"Of course we care about Hector and his da! But we care about keeping you safe too, so ye mustn't go there."

Huw gave Keith another poke, "Told ya!"

"Hector'll come round when he's ready," Mum advised, "and letting things cool down a bit will go easier for him at home."

Glancing at each other, Keith surmised, "We made things worse, didn't we?"

"I daresay it didn't help." Mum patted his hand. "I know that's the last thing ye'd want, but Mr. Menteith phoned both your mums."

"Oh dear!" Huw groaned, "Is Mum angry?"

"No, she's not, nor is your mum, Keith." She chuckled, "Although she wisnae surprised." Understanding our good intentions had gone amiss, we listened as Mum continued, "Unfortunately for Hector, this has been going on for some time, but plans are in motion to help them. So..." Looking at Keith, she requested, "Without crossing fingers, promise me you'll stay clear of Hector's." This time, we all agreed as Da appeared in the doorway. Looking up, Mum asked, "What news?"

Da shook his head. "Hal and I spoke with an Inspector McFayden. All he said was, Nate regrets his actions. He's away to sort things and we need to respect their privacy."

Gasping in disbelief, we realized there wisnae more anyone could do except pray.

"Right then," Da sighed. "Who's for a row to the Bass?"

13

Prisoners of Note

The sound of water rushing beneath the boat and sunshine sparkling on the Firth eased our worries as the dinghy glided further and further from shore. Pulling long, powerful strokes, Da pointed with his chin, "Look, someone's waving!"

A small, ginger-haired figure at the water's edge caused my heart-beat to quicken. So, when Huw confirmed, "That's Lilly!" I jumped to my feet, waving back.

"Sit down, lover boy," Keith hollered, "or ye'll have us all in the water!"

Holding back a smirk, Da continued rowing as I plunked down on the wooden seat.

Huw began to crow, "Nighty Ni..."

"Don't even think about saying that!" I cut him off lightning fast.

"Did I miss something?" Da queried.

"Well, Mr. Ridley," Keith cleared his throat, "only if you consider William's first kiss with Lilly Alcott *something*."

I gasped as Huw pointed at me, "Did he forget to mention that?"

Da shot me an incredulous look as Huw and Keith burst into laughter. "You and Lilly Alcott, eh?" He nodded with a cheeky grin.

"Twas nothing, Da, just Lilly thanked me for dancing." I took a deep breath, "And she kissed me," pointing to my cheek, "Here! And of course my best friends are never going to let me forget it!"

"*Ev-ver!*" Keith snorted, and he and Huw giggled till the boat started pitching back and forth.

"Okay!" I retorted, "Now who's rocking the boat?"

The welcome distraction came courtesy of a passing school of fish. Tonnes of flapping tails and gills brought the Firth to a furious boil, and out of the upheaval, a huge specimen sprang skyward, then flopped down at Huw's feet!

"Will ye look at that?" Da marvelled.

Immediately, Huw snatched the fish and tossed it back into the water. We stared, gobsmacked, til he slapped his forehead. "Och, I cannae believe I did that!"

Pulling up the oars, Da chuckled, "Best not to mention that on a fishing CV!"

We watched the fish leaping and skimming across the sparkling deep until a furiously flapping trio leapt from the water, and all in succession, landed with three smacks on the deck. Da shouted, "Time to Hukilau lads! Grab the net!"

Due to its remote location, The Bass didn't get many visitors, so Andy, Drew, and Mr. Ramsay were chuffed to welcome the lads and possibly the easiest lunch e'er caught! Over a mid-day meal, they fielded question after question about the lighthouse and former prison.

Ever the detective, Keith enquired, "So, who was the most famous prisoner, and what'd he do?"

Mr. Ramsay rubbed his whiskered chin. "Spose' it depends on who you ask, but in my opinion, that'd be Alexander Peden."

"Who was he?" We asked in tandem.

Ioan enlightened our inquisitive minds: "Peden was an Ayrshire lad, born in the 1600s, who became a pastor... known for," he searched for the right word, "*predicting* things."

"Predicting?" Keith interrupted. "Like Nostradamus, necromancer sort of stuff?"

Mr. Ramsay lifted a finger, "An interesting question, Keith, the answer depending entirely on the power behind it."

"Ooo!" Huw piped up, "What does that mean, Mr. Ramsay?"

"It means not all fortune tellers are fake," he leaned closer, "because the real ones get their power from the dark one... Yet, men like Peden related messages from God."

"But how can you tell the difference?" Keith's curiosity churned, "How do you know *who's* voice they're listening to?"

Huw thumped Keith on the head, "You ask too many questions!"

"Och...Easy lad!" Mr. Ramsay chided.

Keith shook it off, smiling, "How do you think I got so smart?"

With a sideways look, Huw snorted, "Okay, so how do you tell the difference?"

"Well, since you mentioned Nostradamus, we'll compare. In the 1500s, wealthy patrons, even royals, like Catherine of Medici, paid huge sums for his counsel. Though his predictions were vague, in the French Court, he gained wealth and influence over state and Catherine's personal affairs. Peden, on the other hand, named specific people and events, which came to pass, but ne'er used his gift for favors."

Huw joked, "So, he didn't charge a fiver?"

"Definitely not. But more than prophecy, Peden was a man of prayer. And God provided miraculous answers."

"So," Keith threw up his hands, "what happened?"

"When Charles II reclaimed the throne, he ordered ministers to use only the Book of Common Prayer for worship, presented as an act of," Ioan winked his fingers, "religious uniformity."

Huw asked, "Was that so bad?"

"Sounds good, doesn't it?" Mr. Ramsay sighed, "But in reality, Charles had banned preaching from the Bible. Anyone who did became an enemy to his crown."

"But if a pastor doesn't teach from the Bible," I protested, "what's the point?"

"In a word, William, control! Under threat of death, Peden and thousands of pastors were forced to resign."

"Resign?" Keith blurted, "What happened to their people?"

"Charles ordered them to attend religious meetings led by men who didn't know the Bible nor care to. E'er heard of wolves in sheep's clothing?"

"Aye!" We all acknowledged.

"Anyone resisting was imprisoned...or shot." We lads gasped as he continued, "But Alexander took to the road. Behind a mask and wig, he ministered, preaching repentance and salvation. In turn, folk fed and protected him; some even wore masks to confuse the soldiers, buying Peden time to escape."

"Superbly mysterious!" Keith chirped.

"With grim consequences," I added, "if he got caught!"

"Aye! But he escaped, time and time again!" Mr. Ramsay recounted, "One night, soldiers were tipped off to their gathering. Twas death for certain! As folk scattered into the night, Alexander prayed for God to throw His cloak over them."

"And did He?" Huw asked.

Mr. Ramsay grinned, "So thick a Scots mist descended, covering the lot of em, the soldiers rode right by as though they were invisible!" He nodded at our amazed faces. "But after 10 years on the run, he was holding a conventicle."

"A what?" Keith quizzed.

"Exactly what I asked!" Mr. Ramsay confirmed, "A meeting, considered unlawful because they were worshipping Jesus."

"Och," I reeled, "That's horrible!"

Keith quipped, "That'd put a damper on Sundays!"

"Then what happened?" Huw urged, "At the... conventicle?"

"A Major Cockburn arrested everyone, sentenced Peden to four and a quarter years on the Bass, plus fifteen months more in the Edinburgh Tollbooth!"

"Did he..." I hesitated, "survive?"

"If he did, twas a miracle!" Huw ran a finger across his throat, sticking out his tongue. "Sassenachs were brutal to prisoners."

Augmenting his statement, Keith pretended to yank on a noose about his neck.

Shaking his head, Mr. Ramsay chuckled, "True enough, lads. The Governor of the Bass was an evil piece of work, but a man's days are in God's hands, not his captors."

Huw quipped, "He sounds quite jolly!"

"Jolly aye," Mr. Ramsay shuddered, "when torturing prisoners! Those he particularly disliked went to the dungeon, deathly cold from sea spray. And to make things worse, he placed a levy on everything the poor souls ate or drank."

"But they were prisoners!" I worried, "What if they couldn't pay?"

"They were fed bits of salted fish...makes ye mighty thirsty...but no water."

Keith blurted, "Ye cannae survive without water!"

"Aye!" Drawing close, Mr. Ramsay hushed his voice, "So, they foraged for rock puddles, most so riddled with birdie excrement, twas easier taken sucked through porridge oats."

"Eeew!" We exclaimed in disgust.

"But the worst," he punctuated by retrieving a book from the shelf, "was the solitary confine."

Keith pointed, "What's that?"

"This lad is a record of all those unfortunate souls held on the Bass, and something I discovered tucked inside the pages." Holding a yellowish document, he grinned, "A letter penned by Peden hisself!"

Our jaws dropped, marvelling at the time worn document. Then Huw said, "Amazing, it's still in one piece, but can ye read it?"

Keith took a closer look. "The hand's hard to make out."

"But," I smiled at Mr. Ramsay, "I bet ye know every word it says!"

With a dapper smile, Mr. Ramsay cleared his throat, then put voice to Peden's words, penned in his darkest days upon the Bass...

" *'We are close shut up in our chambers, not permitted to converse, diet, worship together, but conducted out by two at once in the day to breathe in the open air. Envying with reverence the birds their freedom...'* "

"There's something here I've not been able to make out, but he continues, '*...provoking and calling on us to bless him for the most common mercies, and again close shut up, day and night to hear only the sighs and groans of our fellow prisoners. I return to thank you for your seasonable supply, as evidence of your love of him and your affectionate remembrance of us. Persuade yourself, you are in our remembrance, though not so deep as we in yours - and grace be to all them that love our Lord Jesus Christ in that sincerity. So prayith your unworthy and affectionate well-wisher in bonds - A. P.'* "

"He was like Paul..." I exclaimed, "in prison for telling people about Jesus!"

"Aye, lad... much like Paul, and many others after him!"

"Did he e'er get off the Bass?"

"Aye Keith," Mr. Ramsay related, "only to find he and 60 other Covenanters were further sentenced to banishment."

Huw gasped, "That's so unfair!"

Keith rubbed his chin. "Where'd they send em?"

"Sold as slaves to wealthy plantation owners in the colonies. Don't teach ye that in history, do they? But when the captain of the American vessel heard they'd been banished for their faith..." Mr. Ramsay baited our curiosity, "He let em all go!"

"Whoa!" Huw exhaled. "Bet they took a long holiday after that!"

Keith and I stared at Huw, but Mr. Ramsay smiled, "Not Peden. Despite danger and all he'd been through, he pressed on."

"So," Keith remained curious, "what'd he predict, exactly?"

"That he," Mr. Ramsay folded his hands, "and those sentenced to banishment would be released."

Keith snorted, "Clearly coincidence!"

"Well... One might call it...providence." Mr. Ramsay considered what he was about to say: "His most infamous prediction came on John Brown's wedding day, in a message for the bride, *'Your John's a good man, but ye'll nae enjoy him long. Prize his company and keep linen to wrap his body, for it'll be bloody.'* "

"Och!" Huw grumbled, "What happened to congratulations?"

"Something tells me he was horribly right." I muttered.

"Three years later, John missed one of those government meetings." He continued, "When the soldiers arrived, they told him to pray, for he was about to meet his maker. Instead, he shared the gospel with them."

"And?" Keith demanded.

"They murdered him in front of his wife and bairns."

Huw gasped, "Pure evil!"

After a moment, Keith asked, "Was there no way to alter his prophecy?"

Mr. Ramsay scratched his beard. "John knew that day would come, as did his wife. Throughout history, good men and women have given their lives so others might hear the Gospel and be saved from God's wrath."

"Only God," I thought out loud, "could give faith of that..."

Keith interrupted, "Did they kill Peden too?"

"No, laddie," Mr. Ramsay continued, "but twas less than a year later, weary and ill, Alexander Peden stepped into eternity."

Furrowing his brow, Huw groaned as Keith quipped, "At least

they didn't murder him."

"True, although King Charles ordered his corpse dug up and hung from the gallows."

"That's absurd!" I exclaimed.

Huw added, "And he called Peden a fanatic?"

"Why on earth," Keith scowled, "would you hang a man who's already dead?"

Mr. Ramsay exhaled, "When folk are blinded by hate, logic rarely surfaces."

"But why do people hate the Gospel so much?" I asked, "If they disagree, why not walk away? Why kill the messenger?"

"Because..." This time, Da answered, "God's perfect light exposes our dark deeds. That makes people angry; they want to blot out that light."

Waiting for that truth to sink in, Mr. Ramsay clapped his hands. "Right then! Time for a walkabout!"

With a whistle, Max, his blue-eyed border collie, leapt up and burst out into the sunshine. A welcome rush of sea air urged us up the steep green incline while Max ran energetic rings around our group, pausing only to nosey the scads of bird nests dotting the landscape. With the wind whipping through our clothes, Mr. Ramsay cautioned, "Stay clear the edge, lads! No safety nets here."

Max's darting back and forth startled the dozy feathered residents, who surged onto the blustery currents. The multitude of flapping wings sounded like a mighty war bird, and we ducked as this squadron let go sticky white bombs of retaliation for the fright Max'd given. Wagging his tail in triumph, Mr. Ramsay praised, "Good boy Max!" Then, holding up a hand, he ordered, "Stay!"

Getting down on his tummy, Ioan led us in a crawl towards the clifftop nests, "Careful lads." Not having grasped the concept of stay, Max wriggled right alongside, licking our faces and ears as we engaged in the tricky business of pilfering eggs. Tricky, not only in warding off puppy kisses, but keeping an eye on the birds who nae appreciate ye nicking from their nests!

Back at the lighthouse, Andy and Drew welcomed our inquisitive trio. Excited chatter echoed through the spiral tower as we wound our way to the upper landing, where Andy handed out harnesses.

Keith questioned, "What are these for?"

Clipping to the inside railing, Drew smiled, "Snap in and ye'll see!"

Unbolting the door, Andy called over his shoulder, "Brace your-selves!"

With a turn of the latch, the door blew open, crashing hard against the interior ironworks. Instantly, the full force of ragged wind that carried gulls and gannets high above the Bass rippled through and tugged at our clothes. Taking no notice, Drew and Andy stepped onto the ledge while we lads peered out.

"It's quite safe." Drew beckoned, and one by one, we stepped out onto the blustery perch.

Leaning headlong into the wind, we whooped with excitement. Then, hanging our heads over the rails, we watched the white capped waves battering the rocks below and shouted at the top of our lungs, "Hello! Mr. Ridley, Mr. Ramsay! Up here!"

Andy chuckled, "They'll nae hear ye o'er this wind!"

"Nice view though, eh?" Drew smiled, pleased by our delight.

"Brilliant!" Huw replied, "Simply brilliant!"

Keith followed, "You really get to do this every day?"

"Aye!" Flexing his biceps, Andy grinned, "How else do ye think we keep so strong and fit?" Then straight to their work, Drew and Andy answered countless questions while we peered over their shoulders and out towards the horizon.

14

Message in a Bottle

"Best day of summer yet!" Huw shouted into the wind atop Tantallon.

"Aye," Keith nodded. "Mr. Ramsay's stories were braw! Who'd have thought there'd be so much to investigate on a rock?"

"What about the lighthouse?" Huw added, "Fabby view from the top and snatching eggs right outta the bird's nests!"

"Plus fish jumping right into the boat!" I smiled, "Have ye e'er seen that before?"

Keith grinned at Huw, "Still cannae believe you threw that first one back!"

"Och!" He slapped his head. "Can we just forget that?"

We continued chatting like magpies till a familiar voice rang out, "Behold! I'm come to defend Tantallon with yous!"

Shading my eyes, I breathed, "Lilly?"

Haloed by the sun, she replied, "Aye! Tis if ye'll let a girl join." Clad in a billowy sea green gown, wielding a tinfoil sword behind a shield she'd fashioned from cardboard and tartan, Lilly's long red locks shimmered in the sun. Then she lowered her voice, *"I can fight off ole Longshanks too!"*

Keith and Huw jumped to their feet, recapping their curtsy routine, chuckling, "Milady!"

"Knights aren't supposed to curtsy!" She corrected, "They bow." Demonstrating the knightly art, she swirled her hand, "Like this!" Unaware they were mimicking her, I smiled at Lilly's attempt to sort these goofy lads who began laughing so hard, they broke into snorts. With a big sigh, she said to me, "I can see my services are sorely needed here!"

"In that case..." Keith addressed her, "You *may*... join us..."

"Excellent," she replied in haste.

"Not so fast!" She raised an eyebrow as he explained, "As long as you do something useful, like teach courtly dancing or kiss a frog and turn him into a prince...um."

As Keith paused, Huw rushed towards Lilly, bellowing, "And plead for mercy when we hang you over the castle wall!" Mid-stride, he tripped over a protruding stone and landed flat on his face at her feet.

Stepping next to Lilly, I defended, "Ne'er mess with the lady of the castle, Huw; it always goes badly!"

Scrambling to his feet and dusting off, Lilly crossed her arms, asking sweetly, "Are you alright?"

Before Huw could reply, Keith poked his tummy, "Aye, he's fine. That's just his idea of courtly dancing!"

"Oh!" Looking bewildered, she pronounced, "Well, as a matter of fact, I dance the Farandole quite well." Demonstrating, she took a few sweeping steps, "And I can make parchment for official decrees!"

Looking beaten, Huw grumbled, "That only covers the first part!"

In the wink of an eye, Lilly pecked Huw and Keith on their cheeks, then stepped back. While they wiped their faces in surprise, she huffed, "Well, I've kissed two frogs," then looking in my direction, her voice softened, "and one boy, but he was already a prince!"

I stammered as Huw and Keith crowed, "Ooooh...Lilly and William sitting in a tree, K, I, S, S, I, N, G, first comes love, then comes marriage..."

Face flushing, I groaned, but Lilly countered, "Well then, that makes me the Lady of Tantallon, and history proves they only hang you over the wall if you annoy the royal in residence, which, by your own declaration lads, would be me! So, best be on your smartest behaviour!"

Keith and Huw had met their match in this tiny warrior princess, until a huge breeze whipped past, wrapping those billowy sleeves completely around her head. By the time she worked her way out, we were laughing so hard, we could barely breathe!

Lilly fit right in and never let Huw nor Keith get the upper hand when teasing. Over summer, romping along the cool blue water's edge, there was scarce a day we didn't spend together, reenacting history, crowning a monarch, feasting in the Great Hall, or pleading for mercy in the dungeon, all quite amusing for Tantallon guests.

"William!" Keith said, pretending to be a Hollywood producer, "More determination on your brow for the charge!" Or, putting an arm around her shoulder, "Lilly darling, if you're going to act the part of 'damsel in distress,' you'll need one of those pointy caps with the scarfy thing!"

"Is that a technical term?" she chided.

"No Keith!" Huw quipped, "Lilly brought a sword. Make her a shield maiden. She can defend the castle! Fire the cannons."

"Cannons!" She scrunched up her nose. "They're filthy. And, with all that gunpowder and smoke, I'll get my dress dirty!"

"What about aiding the cause?" I asked, "Defending the castle at all costs?"

Lilly pursed her lips. "Well, what if, for today, I want to be Queen of a quiet castle?"

"Then Milady, you must command! Like this…" Huw bowed, using as gruff a voice as he could muster, "Down peasants!"

Glancing haughtily down her nose, she purred, "Thank you Hadley," then batted her eyelashes, "What time will you be serving tea?"

Lilly raced us lads up and down passageways and staircases, and with a knack for sword play and surprise attacks, she could match wooden blades with any of us. Plus, her copious questions rivalled even Keith's curiosity.

"Where are all the secret passageways?"

"Not telling you!" Keith teased her.

While we hadn't actually discovered any, we did find bits of pottery and one very old button. But Lilly's favourite place was the Great Hall. I often found her there, early mornings, before Keith and Huw arrived, face lifted to the sky with her eyes closed.

"Good Morning, fair maiden!"

"Oh!" Lilly caught her breath. "Good morning, Sir William! I…um, I thought, if I stood here long enough, God might speak to me too." Twas one of many reasons I was so fond of Lilly.

On dreich days, our noisy foursome clumped together in the cottage window seat, researching and planning adventures. Scouring old maps and the Ridley family book, we read about ancestors, some encompassing chapters of perils or intriguing situations, while others warranted only a name between dates, the one on which they entered the world and the other upon which they'd left it.

Lilly was fascinated by Magnus. "What an adventure he had, sailing the ocean and escaping to freedom!"

Huw added, "Likely dodging bullets in the process!"

"I wonder what he and Susannah looked like?" She smiled at me, "He must've loved her dearly!"

While smiling back, Keith teased, "Um…like anyone we know?"

Huw ignored our banter, "They sure had lots of children back in those days."

Lilly sighed, "Must be nice to have a house full of brothers and sisters."

"Why?" Keith teased, "Isn't hanging out with us enough?" Grabbing her round the neck, he started rubbing the top of her head.

"Cease!" She cried, squirming out of his grip, retaliating with tickling, which Huw and I joined in on.

Besides laughter, we shared a deep interest in all things historical. Having studied the Book of Kells, Lilly perfected her own fancy script to adorn paper she'd drench in coffee that, when dried, passed rather well as ancient parchment. On them, we each penned a message, as was customary, in rhyme, producing something of a treasure map. The document was then rolled and squeezed into a dark blue bottle gifted from the local inn, then set afloat on the Firth. As this would be our last dispatch of summer, Lilly unrolled her finest, golden parchment yet.

Praising her image of Tantallon atop a cliff, with ample room for our jottings, Keith took pen in hand, "Lilly Angelo! Ye sure we should write on this?"

"Oh, aye curious one!" She placed her hands on her hips. "Just make it memorable!"

"As you wish, Milady!" Keith rolled his eyes, then wrote...

> *'You've come upon this bottled quest*
> *Because it sailed and sought you out,*
> *Your charge this day before ye rest*
> *Is place a smile on someone's snout!'*
> *Best Regards,*
> *Keith Cromyn*

"Snout?" Huw mocked, "Nice touch Keith!"

"Och!" Keith sputtered, handing him the pen. "Here, let's see you do better!"

Huw had given previous thought to his message, scribbling fast as he spoke each word,

> *'If ye who finds this bottled wish,*
> *are chuffed as though ye'd caught a great big fish…'*

Keith peered over his shoulder. "Would that be the one you tossed back in the water?"

"Hush Keith," Lilly giggled, "let him finish!"

"As I was writing…"

> *'…as though ye'd caught a great big fish,*
> *give wings to your dreams abundant in measure,*
> *for every day's a wonderful adventure to treasure!*
> *Huw Mortimer ~ 1987'*

"Aww!" Lilly gushed, "Sounds like a greeting card, Huw!"

Keith snorted, "Especially that part about the fish!"

"OK, OK!" Huw's face flushed. "A lad can make a mistake, but you do realize, whoever finds this will have to *fish* it out of the water!"

Despite groans and rolling eyes, Huw passed the pen to Lilly, who diverted, "You go next, Will."

Pressing the pen to her hand, I replied, "Ladies first, Lil… you have a go!"

"Ooooh, William," cooed Keith. "So gallant!"

Lilly shot me a brilliant smile, "All right then, but you can't see till I'm done." She waited till we stepped back far enough to accommodate her wish. Then, biting the end of the pen, she looked up and chirped, "No peeking!"

From the agreed distance, we watched Lilly tilt her head, one side to the other, till she began scratching down letters like an ancient scribe, the pen furiously adorning the paper. Keith, unable to abide an inactive brain, blurted, "Must be something very special to take *all* this time!"

Scarcely looking up, she waved her hand before her face, "Shh!" After a few more minutes, she set the pen down. "Okay, you can look now!"

Gathering round, we marvelled, not only at Lilly's words but her artwork...

> *'From this castle I'd travel upon water horse waves,*
> *like this wee note that's tread o'er oceans some days.*
> *Though it journeys to places I've not yet explored,*
> *perhaps we shall meet upon some distant shore.*
> *Till then, may merry songs fly on wings like a dove*
> *bringing joy from Tantallon CC4 with love!*
> *Lilly Alcott'*

"Lil," Huw praised, "tis brilliant! Love the horse head coming out of the waves!"

Tracing the picture with my finger, I breathed, "The dove's feathers have so much detail, ye can almost feel their softness."

Keith offered, "I like the twig in its beak, morphing into music notes; that's braw!"

Lilly blushed at our praise. "Your artwork's wonderful, Lilly, and I think you've summed up what we've been trying to say."

Huw and Keith um-hummed agreement.

"One question though." Everyone stared as I asked, "What's CC4?"

Scribbling alongside her words, Lilly filled the open space with a replica of what I'd been wearing around my neck... a Celtic Cross!

"Now there's a clever lassie!" Keith spouted.

Still admiring her artistry, Huw murmured, "What about you, Will?"

I shrugged, "What can I add to that?"

"Aw, come on!" Keith urged, "Certainly you have something to share!"

"Maybe, but I'm rubbish at rhyming."

"Don't be a wimp!" Huw countered, "Just think of something that ties all this together."

"Like a treasure map!" Lilly encouraged.

"Hmm. There's really only one treasure that matters." Newly

Inspired, I spoke as I wrote,

> *"I'm one tiny voice... on this great planet, Earth,*
> *yet... bestowed with a gift of immeasurable worth..."*

Hovering over my shoulder, Keith blurted in my ear, "I like that!"

Startled, I recoiled as Lilly placed a hand on his shoulder. "Let him breathe Keith!"

I continued,

> *"If you're travelling the world in life's uneasy quest,*
> *heavy laden with burdens, soul weary for rest*
> *trust God for great wonders, the Ancient of Days*
> *let Him love you forever and teach you His ways.*
> *There's no greater hope for the world than God's Son*
> *for eternity rests not on us, but on what Jesus has done.*
> *The messenger simply delivers the Word.*
> *Now it's up to the hearer to heed what you've heard.*
> *William Ridley ~ Defender of the Faith ~ 27.8.87"*

As I laid down the pen, Lilly exclaimed, "William, that's beautiful!"

"What do you mean, you can't rhyme?" Huw mussed my hair, "That's perfect!"

Keith tapped his fingers on the parchment. "Though I'd ne'er do it, I like the way ye tell people about Jesus."

"Thanks Keith." I replied, looking o'er my shoulder, "But that's partly why we're here."

Lilly asked, "You think so?"

"Well yeah, Jesus told us to. And besides, He loves us so much, I cannae help it. I want everyone to know about Him."

"Oh!" Lilly looked perplexed. "Is Jesus..." She searched for the right word, "nice?"

Staring at each face, I blurted, "Fathoms better than nice Lil! Jesus is the bright morning star, creator of everything, He's...He's God!"

"Did he create those thousands of shades of blue in the ocean?"

"Aye," I nodded, "and in the sky too!"

"They are beautiful! So, I suppose, Jesus is too." Then, with a giggle, she asked, "Who do ye think'll find our bottle?"

"And where'll it go?" Huw added, "Be braw to put a camera inside and get underwater pictures."

"Aye!" I chirped, "Like Jacques Cousteau!"

"Just make sure to put an address in there," Keith reminded, "so whoever finds it can trace it back to us!"

Before rolling up the weathered paper, Mum took a Polaroid, then sealed the tube with a big dollop of melted wax. Pressing a hand carved Saltire seal into the middle of the crimson puddle, Keith made it goop out the sides, then we blew on the setting wax. Over milk and oaties, Mum complimented our project, then snapped another photograph as we slipped the document inside its inky blue container. Message ready for dispatch, she called out the door as we trod down the well-worn path to Tantallon, "Not too close to the edge now!"

Each deep in thought, we made a regal procession across the drawbridge, through the Keep, and down to the cliff's edge above the water. The wind picked up slightly as Huw handed the bottle to Keith, who passed it to me, and I, in turn, placed it in Lilly's small hand. The honour of releasing our last message of summer fell to our shield maiden.

Holding the bottle above her head, we raised our swords in salute, then pressing a hand to the glass, we repeated the secret oath, "Tantallon Four, hope and good cheer, Alba forever, safe journey, no fear!"

Stepping back, we provided ample room for the toss when a ray of sunlight pierced the clouds, pouring through the bottle and casting an ocean blue hue upon Lilly's face. Drinking in the celestial light, she giggled, bestowing an impish smile on each of us, then with all her might, she cast the bottle headlong out over the water.

End o'er end, o'er end, it spun, and we held our breath as it made the long journey down to the Firth. As it splashed down bottom first, we stood in silence, shoulder to shoulder, watching it bob in the sparkling waves. Then, blending into the thousand shades of blue, the bottle carrying our happy tidings disappeared beyond the waves.

15

Free Fall

Wisdom. My friends and I found it to be a key, unlatching doors we never knew existed, like an explorer's map guiding and illuminating life's most fantastical mysteries. So, when the last rays of August sun dipped below the horizon, we welcomed fresh new morsels of knowledge from teachers who enjoyed challenging our intellect!

"Word has it... Mr. Tinley's planning something!"

"He's always planning something, Sherlock!" Huw fired back.

"Any idea what?" I asked.

Keith crossed his arms, grinning, "Can't tell ye."

"Och, Keith!" Lilly threw up her hands. "For once, can't ye just spit it out?"

"Alright!" Taken aback, he said, "Nighttime...astronomy labs."

Our excited chatter startled the new bus driver on her maiden voyage, who also had buckets of dark, dreary rain to contend with. And while downpours remained constant, changes awaited our jolly group, the first being Hector's height! He'd grown at least two, maybe even three inches taller! Only what seemed braw to us twas a sore reminder of being surrounded by students two years his junior. Even his clothes declared the breach as last year's smart looking blazer strained to cover his longer limbs.

"Hector!" I waved as he boarded the bus, yanking on his sleeves, "Tis great to see you!" Acknowledging with only a nod, I added, "We all missed you this summer!"

"Aye!" Keith's curiosity flowed, "Where'd ye go?"

Furrowing his brow, he puzzled, "You missed...?" He might've shared something of his mysterious time away, but stopping mid-sentence, he turned towards the window and sighed, "Och, nowhere, just away. You know?"

I didn't know, but I was glad to see him, so I chattered on, "Mr. Tinley's got a telescope...to take us stargazing!"

Hector glanced sideways, raising an eyebrow at Huw, who added, "He said there's something very special we'll get to see!"

Huffing, he replied, "Lucky you!"

"You'll see it too, Hector!" Lilly chimed, "In astronomy class."

Continuing to gaze out the window, Hector offered no response, so I changed the subject, "Can ye join us for football today?"

Pointing to the steady pelting rain, he snorted, "In all this? Are ye daft?"

Just then, our driver jammed the brakes to avoid a sheep that dashed into the road, causing an eruption of squeals as students gripped chair backs to keep their seats. All except Hector, who rolled out into the aisle, hollering, "I'm injured! I'm injured!"

The woman at the wheel turned in horror as he rolled side to side, the way footballers do when they're either really hurt, or in his case, just faking it! Brakes applied, Mrs. Sherry ran towards Hector, who gave Lilly a cheeky wink, then whispered, "Thanks, Ridley, but I'm a bit busy right now!"

As our driver leaned o'er him, Hector jumped up, clasped her hands in his and asked in a husky voice, "May I have this dance?"

Completely unnerved, Mrs. Sherry staggered back as far as the constraints of the aisle would allow. "Young man!" She directed, "You take your seat right now, and I'll nae report your cheek!"

With a mischievous grin, he did as she asked, but as she walked forward, Hector swaggered his head, mimicking, "Take your seat young man, and I'll nae report your cheek!"

While almost everyone laughed, Hector's rude behaviour upset me, my friends, and especially our new driver. Wherever he'd gone, he'd returned with a dark sense of humour, attracting an audience hungry for whatever prank he'd pull next.

"Hey Jimmy!" Hector distracted our mate who'd been fumbling through his rucksack and stuck out his foot, so Jimmy tumbled into the aisle.

Clearly annoyed, Jimmy quipped, "Why can't you just be normal?"

"Cause it's fun to watch the mighty fall!"

"Oh really!" He retaliated, "Like yer da stumbling into the Ceilidh? You have to admit, he looked daft wrapped in flowers, punching at the air!"

While students erupted in laughter, a fierce look crossed Hector's face, and he whirled around, "What're ye gawking at?"

Jimmy shrugged, "The mighty falling?"

Hector's smouldering glance silenced any further comment, and from that moment, he shut down. None of us knew what to say or how to help, but at every opportunity, I invited him to visit. "Come on, Hector, it'll be fun. Remember?"

But he'd sigh, make a face, and then an excuse, "I'm busy today. Besides," he added, "I'm too old to play with kiddies!"

Truth be told, my home life ate at Hector's soul. Deep down, he yearned for what every lad needs... a da he can trust.

"I don't know why you're so worried about him, Will." Huw chided.

"Because he's our friend!" I sighed, "That's worth something."

Keith played with a plate of chips, "Ye expect too much."

"What's that mean?"

"We tried, remember?" Huw folded his arms, "Made old Nate meaner than ever."

"But..." I began to defend.

"The lad's got issues, Will." Keith grimaced, "And much as ye'd like, ye can't save everyone!"

With autumn turned to winter, temperatures plummeted and visitors to Tantallon grew thin, like warm breath in the frosty air. This also meant crossings to the Bass would be o'er high seas and through fierce winds. However, Mr. Ramsay had sorted a Christmas surprise with the lads from the boating basin.

After attaching an outboard motor to our stern, they waved, "Safe journey, Magnus!" as we sped out across the icy Firth.

The steady humming engine churned up a frothy wake and provided ease of docking in the turbulent waters. Anticipating our arrival, the keepers clamoured down the steep passageway, stopping short at the dock's edge.

"Ahoy lads!" Drew waved.

As Da prepared to toss a line, Andy halted, "Whoa! Not so fast."

"Eh? What's this?" Da smirked as our boat bobbed in the chop.

"Docking levies for Ridleys!" Drew pointed, "The motor, ye know...pay up!"

Rolling his eyes, Da tossed the line at Drew's head, who secured it to the dock with Mr. Ramsay. Bundled in thick woven clothing, long beard, and tousled hair, he took on the mantle of a Hebridean St. Nicholas and gave us a warm, welcoming hug.

The aroma of coffee brewing on the hob and a basket of Mum's fresh baked scones gathered hungry lads around the table, while Andy filled our mugs and Mr. Ramsay gave thanks for the food and safe passage.

"A fine gift!" Da exclaimed, "Can't thank ye enough!"

"Did ye see how fast we crossed the Firth?" I chirped.

Andy grinned, "Wish I could've seen ye'r faces when the marina lads arrived!"

Rubbing his usually sore from the row over biceps, Da chuckled, "Ye know, a man could get used to this! Really, thank you!"

Mr. Ramsay smiled, "Tis we who should be thanking you. If not for your faithful deliveries, we'd be in a sorry state!"

Shaking his head, Da gave Mr. Ramsay a hug, "Ioan! Andy... Drew. Truly a generous gift that'll be well used!"

"Oh Magnus, one thing." Andy held up a finger. "We'll be borrowing it time to time, so you don't go getting soft in the arms!"

Drew responded with a slap to the back of his brother's head, "Och, for goodness sakes!"

After finishing his coffee and shaking loose the crumbs caught in his beard, Mr. Ramsay retrieved a package from the window ledge. Without a word, he placed it in front of me.

"For me?" I asked in wonder.

With three nods to the affirmative, I unwrapped the vintage paper, finding a carved oaken box. The grainy lid bore Tantallon and the Bass, but in place of the lighthouse was a Celtic cross beaming across the Firth!

Turning it about, I exclaimed, "It's beautiful!"

"I carved the Bass!" Drew blurted.

"Aye!" Andy thumped his arm. "But I carved Tantallon!"

Mr. Ramsay rolled his eyes. "We all put a hand to it, to remind ye what a bright spot you are when ye visit!"

"Aww, thank you!" I repeated, "Thank you so much! This must have taken ages to carve!"

Drew chimed, "Time's something we've plenty of here on the Bass!"

"Look Da," I marvelled, "Tantallon, the Bass, and rays of light around the cross. It's brilliant!"

The men beamed as I hugged each of them, then Da and I presented our dear friends with gifts as well. Andy and Drew were chuffed with foul weather breeches and slickers, but for Mr. Ramsay, we'd found a second-hand, golden pocket watch. The off-white face boasted large Roman numerals, and the cover displayed a sprawling oak etched o'er a lakeside cottage and tiny boat. Watching in expectation, Mr. Ramsay unwrapped our small token.

At first, he said nothing, simply staring at the timepiece, and for a moment, I thought he was displeased. But holding it up by the chain, spinning it back and forth, he exclaimed, "Well, glory be! This is Uncle Frasier's old watch!"

"Jings!" Da exclaimed, "Really?"

"How can ye tell?" I asked.

"Here!" Mr. Ramsay pointed to initials below the boat, "I. F. I. This belonged to my grandfather, Ioan. He passed it to Uncle Frasier, who had all our initials carved in it... said one day it'd come to me. But when he passed, they took him away afore I remembered twas still in his pocket." He breathed, "Ne'er thought I'd see this again."

"A little Peden must've rubbed off on Uncle Frasier."

"Eh Magnus?"

"He did say it'd come back to ye."

"That he did!" Mr. Ramsay had tears in his eyes. "Thank ye, Magnus, William! Ye've no idea how precious a gift this is. In fact," he added, "you'd nae have known, but today would've been Uncle's 90th birthday!"

"Och!" Andy snorted, "The most peculiar things happen when you get together!"

For the most part, the Keeper's only contact with the outside world were our monthly supply runs, so conversation centred around North Berwick happenings, sports, and a wee bit of politics. Despite the plight of miners and print workers, Margaret Thatcher won a third term as prime minister, which had nae happened since the 1820s. Plus Rangers won their first league title in years, though Andy kept his crowing to a minimum, mindful of Drew lamenting Celtic's trophy-less season. On the confines of the Bass, team loyalties were honoured in good natured fun, occasionally ending with one brother in a headlock till the other shouted, "Uncle!"

But before sports talk turned physical, Andy declared, "There's a lens needs replacing!"

"All right, all right," Drew agreed, "but before we hoist ourselves into peril at sea, I wanna hear about those hula girls again!"

"Nae brother!" Andy chided, "Ye've already got yourself a lassie."

To my bewildered stare, Drew grinned a wide, toothy grin, "Aye, and I'll be travelling back with Magnus and the lad here to the mainland." As I looked for Da's confirmation, he continued, "Tae ask her to marry me...for Christmas!"

"Ah!" Andy's jaw dropped open.

Mr. Ramsay stared, "Golly be, Drew, when were ye gonna tell us?"

With a cheeky grin, he tilted his head. "Just did!"

"Well, what's her name?" I questioned, "Is she ta live here on the Bass?"

Andy piped, "Depends on if she's fool enough to marry this wimp!"

Drew retorted, "Her name's Abigail, and yes, she'll be coming to the Bass...tis if she can put up with the likes of these salty dogs!"

Mr. Ramsay laughed, "This day's just full of surprises!"

Just then, a fierce current raced down the chimney, threatening to quench the fire, and the cosy room took a chill as the shutters rattled and the wind howled, but our Christmas spirit would not be dampened by weather nor wind. With his deep bass voice, Mr. Ramsay began singing, "Joy to the World," and in harmonies, we sang every carol or bit of one we could remember, drowning out the noisy tempest.

After our concert, I tagged along with Andy and Drew as they wound their way up the spiral tower with a lens replacement and fittings. Twas no easy task, for Da had to hoist the delicate bundle up the narrow centre of the tower at precisely the same speed we were climbing to keep it from banging the railings. Tis the same bucket and pulleys used to haul supplies and fuel for the original paraffin lamps, which also kept one from making the oft precarious climb more often than necessary.

"Don't stop now, Will!" Andy urged through the deafening howl that paused my ascent, but after a few more spirals, we reached the uppermost landing.

The outer door, though bolted tightly, groaned against its hinges, and I could feel the tower sway as the wind buffeted her from off the sea.

"Hold tight the railing!" Drew warned, "It's blowing a hoolie up here, and the weather maiden delights in surprises."

"No worries, I'll nae let go!"

"Weather maiden?" Andy grumbled, "More like a banshee!"

In all this wind, we were to haul the Fresnel replacement from the gallery deck, up a ladder to the widow's walk, then through a tiny hatch into the lantern room. So, before going further, Andy harnessed us up, clipping our safety lines to the railing.

Then, unbolting the old iron door, Drew called o'er his shoulder, "Stand clear!"

The mighty force he unleashed was both intimidating and exhilarating, and had we not braced for it, I'd have been knocked off my feet! But since Andy and Drew had climbed aloft many times in far rougher weather, this excursion promised to be as exciting as it was successful.

Cradling the swathed lens, Andy stepped onto the ledge, followed by Drew, who helped steady him. As we scurried up the ladder, Andy called over the tempest, "How's this for excitement?"

"Brilliant!" The wind tossed my words back in my face as I shouted, "Absolutely brilliant!"

Once the lens room hatch was opened, Drew climbed inside, lifting me up behind him. From there, I watched a wind battered Andy pass the lens to Drew, then, quick as a whip, hoist himself up after it. Surprisingly, despite the icy wind, I found it quite warm inside the glass enclosure.

Drew tugged at the neck of his jumper, "Almost tropical in here!"

"Aye, tis warm." I agreed.

"Warm enough for a luau! Eh Will?" Andy winked, poking my side, "Hear you're pretty good at hula dancing!"

"Don't know about that, Andy," I snorted, "but I've just the thing for your Christmas."

He scrunched up his face, "What's rain gear got to do with hula?"

Reaching into my pocket, I presented another gift. "You'll see!"

Unwrapping a Hula Girl puppet, Andy threw his head back with a laugh.

"Papa G sent her along to cheer ya up!"

The doll, wearing a swishy grass skirt, was held together by rubber bands, perched atop a spring-loaded pedestal. Pressing several times, Andy figured how to make her dance without collapsing, then Drew began singing, "Tiny Bubbles!" Between the heat, Andy's dancing doll, Drew's off-key singing, and me tapping a rhythm on the metal flooring, we'd our very own hula show.

We laughed so hard, Andy chided, "Okay, enough, you're fogging up the glass!"

The snug space prevented me getting a close-up view of the replacement, so I gazed across the Firth on my beloved Tantallon. Monstrous foamy waves lashed the rocks beneath while snow swirled around her ancient spires. How many times, I mused, had Peden gazed upon her majestic frame and how different it looked from the day Lilly tossed our bottled message onto the waves. Where in the world had it gone, I wondered, when a sudden sway of the tower pitched me forward, bumping my nose against the cold glass. At the same time, metal clanked on metal, and Drew let out with a cuss.

"This constant swaying is not helping!" Andy exclaimed.

"Hey Will." Drew waved me over, "Lend us a wee hand."

He literally meant a wee hand, for the fittings had dropped between the flooring plates. "Easy-peasy," I smiled, retrieving the bits. "Good thing you brought me along, huh?"

Andy responded by ruffling my already windblown head of hair. With the new lens in place and one more dance from his hula doll, we prepared for the icy blast awaiting us.

While lighthouses were designed for mariners' safety, less thought was given to those tending them, so checking tethers, Andy opened the chute, "Here we go again."

Easing down, his legs swung like banners in the sustaining wind, until he braced his feet against the railing. Then dropping to the encircling grate, he stood square, grabbing for the old lens. After setting it down, he turned back towards Drew, who lowered me through the hatchway. With feet flailing in the wind, still short of Andy's reach, I raised my arms to slip down lower, but a sudden gust blew my body sideways.

"Hold on, William!" Drew bellowed.

But the wind increased, and though we clung with all our might, my sweaty hands were ripped from his grasp. Immediately, Andy lunged up to catch me, but his body slammed against the railing with a thud, and the howling gale swept me over the edge.

The world shifted into slow motion; Andy's lips were moving, but sound was jumbled, and for a split second, I hung suspended in mid-air. Millimetres from his outstretched arms, desperately grasping the sky between us, our eyes locked, but what frightened me most twas the look of horror overtaking Andy's face.

Simultaneously, time and gravity kicked in, and I plummeted. The rush of icy wind and whirling snow bit into my cheeks as I hurtled downwards alongside the weathered tower. Pain seared my flesh as

I scraped along the stony exterior, and grasping the safety rope, the nylon cord ripped away bits of skin as it zipped through my palms. Then, with a gasp, my descent came to an abrupt halt as my bodyweight jerked against my tether. Dangling in the wind, I found myself literally at the end of my rope!

Far above, Andy and Drew were shouting something, trying to hoist me back up. Perhaps it was the snow, but their faces paled of colour, watching helpless as the wind swung me further out, opposite the tower, when something unexpected happened.

In the midst of this very real peril, an overwhelming sense of peace enveloped me. My body relaxed, and my heart stopped racing. Twas as though I'd stepped outside myself, watching from afar. The wind and chaos ceased, and I heard Mum's voice in my head, *"Twas a tug of war, the Enemy on one side, the Almighty on the other..."*

Against every instinct, I let go of the rope, put a hand to the cross around my neck, closed my eyes, and prayed, "Jesus, please help me!"

In the eye of this storm, I felt His mighty presence, the way I did at the castle. I had no idea what would happen, but dangling o'er the rocky shore, I was absolutely fearless.

Twas Drew's frantic, *"Push off! Push off! Push off!"* that reclaimed my attention. From far above, he was aware that the violent winds were about to slam my body against the lighthouse. Without hesitation, I obeyed, pressing my feet out in front of me to soften the impact. But as my toe nicked the side of the tower, a huge updraft pushed me sideways, then upwards, while Drew and Andy scrambled to reel in the excess rope before it could pull taught again. In an act of sheer will, Andy hung over the edge, as arm over arm, the brothers reeled me in, and with one last heave, yanked me up over the side, where we collapsed in a heap on the metal grating.

Immediately, Andy wrenched open the lighthouse door, dragging us inside, fighting hard to close and bolt it behind us. The wind, still howling, continued a ferocious assault, pressing the door hard against its hinges, but none of us said a word. We simply breathed, chests heaving, eyes darting back and forth.

With a tearful sob, Andy broke down, "I was so afraid you were going to die!" Then he slapped his brother, "Drew, why'd you let him go?"

"I didn't mean to." Drew's voice sounded ragged. "The wind, our hands were sweaty! Oh, William, please forgive me!"

"Drew!" I pleaded, "Twasn't your fault, nor Andy's! None of us could've held on against that wind!"

Andy was shaking. "Are you hurt? Did you break anything?"

"Och!" My hands began to sting. "Maybe a little rope burn."

Drew stared at my bloody palms, "Ow! That looks painful."

Andy began sobbing, "I'm sorry! I'm so sorry, William! All I can see is you falling away, and I couldn't stop it!"

"Andy, it's okay." I gave bold reassurance, "Listen...this wisnae your fault!"

"No, no! I never should have brought you up here today. I should have known better with this wind. How could I face your da, or mum if, if...?" He couldn't speak it, and remembering Mum's tears not long ago, the thought of her being grieved by my harm sobered my thoughts.

"I'm not afraid to die, Andy, but I understand you and everyone who loves me would be grieved if..." I breathed, "things had gone differently."

Shaking his head, Andy exhaled, "I'm just glad you're safe now!"

Attempting to lighten the air, I joked, "I did tell Mr. Ramsay if the wind was right; I could fly like one of his gannets!"

"William, that's not funny!" Drew clucked, "I was so scared, I think I'm gonna have to change my trousers!"

Sharing a collective grin, Da cleared the top step, lungs heaving with a fearful look in his eyes, "What's all the shouting up here?"

Thinking fast, I blurted, "Drew was gonna toss Andy's hula girl in the oil bucket!" Andy rolled his eyes; Drew slapped a palm to his forehead, and we all released a huge sigh of relief.

Da and Mr. Ramsay patched up my hands and wrapped my side where a small swath of skin had ripped away as we talked over what happened.

Andy kept blaming himself, but Da assured, "If there were blame, t'would be solely mine. I allowed William to go up with ye."

"Aye," Andy sobbed, "but you did nae see him falling!"

Putting an arm around his shoulder, Da steadied, "It's not your fault. Okay?" Andy simply nodded as Da added, "You either Drew!"

Mr. Ramsay added, "Aye, lads, you're *all* safe now, and that's all what matters."

"Will's our Bass cat, got nine lives. Er..." Drew's face curled into a grin, "Well, eight now!"

Rolling my eyes, I soothed, "Either way would've been alright, cause I'd be with Jesus, although...I would miss you all very much."

Da hugged me closer, "Yer not going anywhere now, son."

"But Da, ye said ye'rself, every man's days are numbered by God."

An emotional nod sufficed as his agreement.

"Well, that's for certain," Mr. Ramsay's eyes twinkled, "but knowing the outcome, how'd it feel to be flapping away like a gannet?"

"It happened so fast," I rattled on, "but twas *so* exciting!"

A loud gasp and clatter in the kitchen had Da on his feet. "Drew, ye alright?"

"Look!" We gasped as he produced the cable that had been my lifeline. The section they'd tied to the rail had worn so thin, twas no more than a thread!

"Because he holds fast to me in love, I will deliver him; I will protect him because he knows my name. When he calls to me, I will answer him; I will be with him in trouble; I will rescue him and honor him." ~ Psalm 91: 14-15

16

The Real Gift

After exhausting every possible detail of the mishap, Mr. Ramsay redirected, "You lads must be famished!"

Before the chaos ensued, he'd been preparing a Christmas feast of fresh fish, baked veg, roasted potatoes, and home baked bread with slabs of tasty butter. After a heaping portion of thanks to the Keeper o' our days for my life, this abundance of food, and cherished family, we ate. In seconds, Drew and Andy attacked their dinner, cutlery clanking, scraping plates, smacking lips, and slurping down Irn-Bru in-between bites.

"Best not to get your fingers in the way when these lads are hungry!" Mr. Ramsay nodded in their direction.

Momentarily, the brothers looked up, then returned to the task at hand with renewed gusto. When all was consumed, we sat back, satisfied smiles crossing our faces, while Mr. Ramsay headed back to the hob to pour coffee. But for me, he'd prepared a piping hot mug of pressed apple juice with a real cinnamon stick!

With full tummies and lighter hearts, Drew gushed about Miss

Abigail, how pretty and smart she is, and how they'd courted via letters over the past two years. "You get to know someone deeply by what they write...or don't." With a dreamy look, he sighed, "I can almost hear her voice when I read her words."

"You, sly pup!" Andy retorted.

Mr. Ramsay clucked, "And ne'er a word!"

Drew simply smiled, then we topped off our evening telling stories into the wee hours until I couldn't hold back a yawn.

"Yer wee head's not big enough to make a yawn that size!" Andy teased.

After a time, conversation quieted and a hush fell over the room, with naught left to hear but the crackling hearth. The warmth of the fire bathed the room in soothing golden light, and the burning peat lulled us into a dreamy state. We gazed, like folk do at ocean waves, quieted, comforted in the flickering glow, until one exploding ember, popping sparks across the room, roused me from my dozy state.

"Right then," Da gave a wee nudge, "away to yer bed, son."

I loved the safety of Da's strength as he picked me up and carried me to the waiting featherbed. Mr. Ramsay lifted the heavy duvet, where I snuggled beneath the folds, cosy, warm, and protected from the howling tempest outside. In this snug room, no more than a closet's worth of space, I rested as Da smoothed the hair from my brow. Then, just before the last bit of lamp light disappeared behind the heavy oaken door, Mr. Ramsay whispered, "Sleep tight, lad!"

At first light, we readied for the chilly trip across the Firth. Drew was eager to get ashore, but before climbing aboard, Andy hugged his brother, "Don't know why she would, but here's to Miss Abigail saying, Yes!"

Drew patted his back. "If she doesnae, we've still got Ioan to cook for us!"

"Och!" Mr. Ramsay shook his head. "Poor lass, has no idea what she's getting herself into!"

With farewell hugs, we wished Andy and Mr. Ramsay a 'Happy Christmas!' as they helped us cast off. I longed for them to come too, but then there'd be no one to light the beacon. So, to the hum of the engine, we waved, watching them grow smaller and smaller through the still strong wind that caused millions of snowflakes to swirl around us like playful fairies. Some landed on my nose and eyelashes or attached themselves to the ice crystals on deck, sparkling in the early morning light. It might have been multiple layers of clothing, or Drew's excitement heading towards his bride to be, or Da and I getting back to Mum at the cottage, but despite the icy wind, snow, and waves, we all felt quite warm.

Mum'd already been baking and cleaning for the scads of visitors we'd host in the next fortnight. She'd also fixed up a room for Drew, who would stay with us until the wedding. Affectionately known as the *Fezziwiggs* of North Berwick, Mum and Da had our cottage so festive, twas like a Dickens' novel come to life. A hand-picked fragrant spruce stood beside the hearth, covered in baubles and heirloom ornaments passed down from the first keepers of this cottage. Tiny golden lights entwined within the branches added a warm glow to our parlour, intensifying the piney fragrance.

The mahogany mantle displayed Great Auntie Glee's knitted manger scene, and like a bow atop a package, Da hung a pinecone and holly berry wreath on our front door. He'd also strung a sprig of mistletoe between the kitchen and parlour so he could swipe a kiss as Mum bustled between rooms. Christmas sparkled in every corner of our home, but the finishing touch was a single white candle in the window...a beacon for anyone who'd lost their way, and to serve as reminder that the true light of the world had come, offering hope to this hurting world!

Today, Miss Norah and Mum were baking cookies, pies, and the all-important Christmas pudding, infusing the entire house with wonderful aromas, keeping Keith, Huw, Lilly, and I close underfoot as they moved about the kitchen. We lads helped Mum squeeze bowls of cookie dough from an aluminium press into green wreaths, golden stars, and red poinsettias, while Lilly and Miss Norah twisted rolls of red and white dough into candy cane shapes, all topped with sugary sprinkles.

When the pans were safe in the oven, Miss Norah cloaked the pudding in a linen wrapper. "I remember," she mused, "making Christmas pudding with my mum, and if they could be had, placing oranges in our stockings o'er the fireplace. Twas the only source of heat we had back then!"

"Miss Norah?" Lilly asked, "Why'd your mum fill stockings instead of Santa?"

"Oh..." She stammered, "Em."

In the silence, Lilly searched from face to face, "Did I say something wrong?"

"No!" She responded quickly, "Not at all, dear; my mum was helping Santa, like one of his elves."

Her answer contented Lilly, until Huw burst out laughing. "What?" She chided, "What's so funny?"

Huw snorted, "Nothing, Lilly; I just didn't know you still believed in Santa."

Mum gasped, and a wide-eyed Keith poked him in the side.

"What's not to believe Huw? He lives at the North Pole with Mrs. Claus and the elves, puts toys under your tree and travels the world by sleigh and flying rein..." Stopping mid-sentence, she turned, "William! *You* believe in Santa, don't you?"

"Uh..." My prolonged silence spoke volumes, causing her lovely blue eyes to well up with tears.

"Lilly." Mum patted the stool beside her, "Come sit by me."

Staying put, she snorted, "Well, if it's bad news, I'd rather hear it from William!"

"Oh Lilly...," With all eyes on me again, I took a deep breath. "Um, Christmas...as we know is a very special time, full of traditions, like baking cookies, decorating trees, carolling, sleigh riding, um...and people add to the fun of those traditions with stories." Lilly stared as I continued, "Some of those stories are true, while others are...more for fun."

"You mean like Frosty?" Lilly held up a hand, "Cause snowmen don't really come to life and dance!"

"Exactly!" I breathed a sigh of relief. "Em, Frosty, and the Grinch, those kinds of stories are fun. They make you feel good, and some-times they have a message, but like you said, they're not real." Staring into her watery eyes, I bit my bottom lip. "Lilly, I'm sorry, but Santa's a story parents tell their children, because..." I halted, "Well, I don't actually know why, because eventually everyone finds out he's more an idea than a person; he isn't... real."

There, I'd said it, and now was only afraid of how Lilly would take the news.

"Ugh!" Lilly sighed heavily, "I knew it; I just knew it!"

"You did?" I asked.

"Aye! Da tells lots of stories, so I know when he's fibbing, and lately, it's all been about Santa. Well, that's, that's..."

"Devious and deliberately wrong!" Keith stuck a finger in the air. "Just imagine how upsetting it is for children to find out there's no Santa...that we've been lied to!"

"Right, you are, Keith!" Mum nodded. "I cried for three days when I found out."

"So did I, AnnaLee! Oh, I'm afraid it's true, Lilly. I'm so sorry dear. Here," Miss Norah beckoned, "we'll have a cry together."

"I'm not going to cry!" Lilly huffed, "This is a relief. Now I don't have to lose sleep worrying about a man in a fur suit getting covered in soot. Imagine cleaning soot out of fur? Nightmare! Or worse, what if, being a little plump, he got stuck in a chimney and roasted?

You don't know how I worried about that!"

"So..." I proceeded, "you're okay with this?"

"Oh, aye!" With that, she licked her spoon clean of batter.

Huw, Keith, and I glanced back and forth until Mum cleared her throat, "Why don't you find a game to play while the cookies are baking?"

In the parlour, wonderful aromas of baking goodies wafted in as we plunked down puzzle pieces on the rug by the fireplace. Lilly and Keith were sorting end pieces and matching colours when Huw jumped up, "I nearly forgot, *A Charlie Brown Christmas* is on to-day!" Crossing the room, he flipped the telly switch, and a tiny dot appeared center screen, which before long displayed the colourful cartoon in whole.

Lilly commented on Sally's '*naturally curly hair.*' "I always wanted curly hair, but I don't suppose you can ask for that for Christmas."

"No, Lil, nor big brothers or little sisters either," Keith replied with a wink.

"Right lads." She jumped up as Schroeder began playing piano. "On your feet! Time to dance the Snoopy song!"

Groaning, we agreed, long as she vowed never to tell anyone! Bopping our heads side to side, we mimicked the characters till we fell over amid peals of laughter. Then quieting, we listened to Linus's speech...

"And there were in the same country shepherds, abiding in the fields keeping watch o'er their flock by night, and lo, the angel of the Lord came upon them. And the glory of the Lord shone round about them, and they were sore afraid. And the angel said unto them, 'Fear not, for behold, I bring you tidings of great joy that will be for all people. For unto you is born this day, in the city of David, a Saviour, who is Christ the Lord. And this shall be a sign unto you: ye shall find the babe wrapped in swaddling clothes and lying in a manger.' And suddenly there was with the angel, a multitude of the heavenly host praising God, and saying, Glory to God in the highest, and on earth peace, goodwill toward men! That's what Christmas is all about, Charlie Brown."

During commercials, Huw added, "And the shepherds did go to Bethlehem, fast as go could go, where they found Mary and Joseph, with baby Jesus in a manger just like angels said. And they were so chuffed, they told everybody!"

"So," Lilly set down her puzzle piece, "what do ye think the angels looked like?"

Her eyes got wide as Keith described, "They'd have been at least ten feet tall, with huge wings that could carry them great distances, faster than eagles!"

"I bet they wear beautiful white gowns," she added, "that look like spider webs!"

"What?" Keith reeled, "Why spider webs?"

"Uh, Keith! Because they glisten in the light!" He rolled his eyes as Lilly asked, "Ye think they have curly hair?"

"Never pondered that before, but logically...it must be straight!"

"Why straight?" Huw asked.

"Angel hair pasta!" Keith threw up his hands. "Straight as it gets!"

"Uh!" Huw groaned, "Why didn't I think of that?"

"Although it gets squiggly when boiled," she grinned, "so maybe it's both."

"Straight or curly," I added, "they'd have been frightening!"

"My angel wouldn't be scary!" Lilly countered, "She'd have shiny silver wings and curly yellow hair. Da says in stories you can make characters any way you like!"

"But Lilly!" I blurted, "This is a true story; this one really happened...that's why we celebrate Christmas."

"What on earth does Linus and angels and shepherds and a baby in a manger have to do with presents?"

I hated always being the serious one, but I wanted Lilly to

understand, "Well, Christmas is when people who love God cele-brate the greatest gift the world has ever been given... Jesus."

"So," she raised an eyebrow, "Jesus is the gift?"

"Exactly!"

"How's that?"

"Okay," I said, "When Jesus was a bairn, wise men travelled far across the desert, bringing gifts of gold because they knew he was the king of all kings."

"And spices like frankincense and myrrh," Keith added, "used to prepare a body for burial...in those days."

"Okay, that's weird," Lilly stared, "but why all the fuss? What did Jesus do that makes him the greatest gift? Like, how is he better than my da, or a puppy? Cause that's what I'm hoping for in case you were looking for ideas."

"Well, for starters," I chuckled, "Jesus is God!"

"But I thought God was in heaven."

"He is Lilly! But when He looked down on the earth and saw how bad things were, He knew people needed to be rescued. So, He came as baby Jesus, lived in a human body, and when He became a man, He spoke about His coming kingdom.

"...Our rescue required one sinless sacrifice; that's why Jesus is called the Lamb of God. He suffered a horrible death, but after three days, He rose from the grave! Now He lives in Heaven, but one day He's coming back to fix this broken world. His people will love one another and honour Jesus because God deserves that."

"Sounds like a good plan, but," she questioned, "if Jesus is God and he left Heaven, who took care of things while he was away?"

"That's the thing about God," I said, "He's everywhere at once."

"Well, William, that's confusing and impossible; no one can be in two places at once!"

"Absolutely Lilly, people cannae...but God can."

She crossed her arms. "How?"

I giggled, "Braw question, but one I don't have the answer for. I guess, if we understood everything about God, He wouldn't be God."

"Yeah," Huw added, "some things we have to take on faith."

"So Christmas," I concluded, "while it's not the exact day Jesus was born, is His birthday party."

"Great!" Lilly huffed, throwing her arms up, "Just great!"

"What, what's wrong?" I asked.

"First there's no Santa, and now you're telling me Christmas isn't Jesus' birthday! *Anything else* you want to spring on me today?"

Keith and Huw rolled on the floor laughing while I held my head in my hands, "Actually, this is great news!"

With hands on her hips, Lilly demanded, "Astonish me!"

My friends listened as I continued, "Jesus promised to come back and make everything perfect... no sorrow, no sickness, no death, no tears."

She raised an eyebrow. "That *would* take an act of God!"

"Aye!" I smiled, "So, while we wait on Him, we give Christmas gifts, like the wise men did, as a reflection of our love for God, and for each other. And deep inside, you feel the anticipation!"

"The what?"

"You know..." Huw explained, "That feeling something's about to happen, you don't know what, you just know it's gonna be good?"

Lilly wrinkled up her nose. "Oh, aye. It's true, people seem much nicer at Christmas, maybe because of," she chewed on the new word, "anticipation, for gifts, or cards, or visits from folk we haven't seen all year, or just spending time with Mum and Da." She whispered, "Especially when they're not fighting."

"I like Christmas Eve best!" Keith clarified, "the excitement before opening presents, and wondering what goodies I'll find in my stocking!"

"Ugh!" Huw groaned, "*I'm not going to let this dog's commercialism ruin my Christmas!* It's definitely sledging, playing in the snow and hot chocolate to warm you up." Pausing, he added, "What about you, Will? What's your favourite part of Christmas?"

"Oh!" I tried to put my immensity of thoughts into words: "All of it, the joy, visits from folk, the music, the crisp cold air, the food, smiles from strangers, stories of unexpected kindness, but most of all," I breathed, "God's presence. He just feels closer at Christmas, and I love being near Him. There's nothing like it in the whole world. Jesus really *is* the best gift ever!"

The Peanuts cast punctuated my statement, shouting, *"Merry Christmas, Charlie Brown!"* Then we joined them singing, "Hark the Herald Angels Sing." Even Da and Drew, just in from chopping fire-wood sang along.

After the baking was done, Mom and Miss Norah joined us in the parlour. Gathered round the piano, Miss Norah sang, "The Christmas Song," then Da and Mum joined voices on, "Sleigh Ride," and I added my famous horse whistle at the end, when there came a chap at the door.

Ernie, our postie, arrived with a package and a handful of cards to add to those already strung around the room. There were greetings in an array of forest animals, snow covered villages, skaters, bustling streets, manger scenes, and Victorian homes, windows aglow with holiday preparations, and while thumbing through the newest batch, Mum called, "William! There's something for you!"

Rushing over with my friends, Mum handed me a rosy red envelope with *"ALOHA WILLIAM!"* written across the flap!

"Well, open it!" Lilly urged.

As I turned it over, Keith crowed, "No wait!"

"Why?" I asked.

"This Lilly," after a long pause, he said, "is what anticipation feels like!"

"Och!" She huffed, messing his curly head of hair.

Sparkling with seashells and palm trees underneath a starry sky, it read, 'Abundant Aloha for a Merry Christmas!' Cousin Lita had drawn a smiling tiki and wrote, "Mahalo, Warrior William!" In fact, all the dancers signed their names, including Big Ed, who added, "Hang loose hula boy! Someday you'll be a fire dancer!"

17

Culcreuch Proposal

The whole of Berwick glittered with lights, decorations, and excitement, all fading in the rearview mirror as Da drove us to a wee town snuggled in the Campsie Fells. Drew was too nervous to appreciate the beauty of Fintry and its snow-covered hills, for he'd been concentrating on what he'd say to Abigail. Having no idea he was off the Bass, when the door opened, she let out a squeal of delight and threw her arms around Drew's neck!

She had long chestnut coloured hair and pale brown eyes that sparkled as she called back inside, "Mum, Da, you'll nae believe who's standing on our doorstep!"

In an instant, a stern looking man appeared, filling the archway above his head. "Ah Drew!" Mr. Milsom's furrowed brow softened, and his long face curled into a smile. "We thought we might see you! Get yourself in, and bring your friends."

Getting acquainted over a pot of tea, George and Annie Milsom filled up on Tantallon history and Drew's vivid picture of everyday life as a keeper on the Bass.

"That's fascinating!" Annie exclaimed, "Makes our wee village seem a bit dull."

Mum chuckled, "We could well do with a lull in the adventure department!"

"Oh, aye." George leaned in, "We heard about your fall, William!"

"Wildest ride I've e'er been on!"

Drew patted my arm. "I'm just thankful he's still here to tell the tale!"

While capturing everyone's attention with the perils of hanging over the side of a lighthouse, Drew and George headed to the kitchen. The outcome of his request clear as both men rejoined us, grinning, Drew the widest. But when all eyes settled on him, he stammered, "Go on then."

"What are you two up to?" Abi asked with a smile.

Leaning over, Drew whispered, "Care to join me for a wee walk?"

Glancing at her da, who nodded approval, Abi jumped to her feet.

George explained, "Young folk need time for courting."

"That's what my Great Auntie Glee used to say," Mum gushed, "about my Magnus."

Da nearly choked on his tea. "As I remember, Auntie Glee wasn't so gleeful about me courting you."

Mum chuckled, "Aye, but ye won her over with your sweet words and handfuls of pinched daffodils."

"Pinched?" He blurted, "Och, never pinched lass, only gathered from an obliging field, where they were in the plenty! Always made her smile."

"Aye. Twas fun to watch you two!"

Da grinned at Mum, "Why is it women like to see men sweat?"

We laughed a lot that afternoon, then Mr. Milsom winked at his wife as Abi and Drew bundled up and headed out the door.

Hand in hand, they turned down the frost covered lane to Culcreuch Castle, where ancient trees stood watch on either side and sheep bunching tightly searched for nibbles in the snow dusted fields. The only sound was their footsteps on the crunchy white ground till Drew remarked, "Tis peaceful here, like out ta lighthouse."

"Tis." Abi smiled, pausing a moment, "And I imagine it's quite pretty on the Firth."

"Aye, tis pretty... like you," he added quickly, "and quiet."

In the distance, a ewe lifted her head, bleating into the frosty afternoon, and Abi giggled at his nervous response, "Our town crier agrees!" Then she added, "With only open mics and long walks for entertainment, I'm willing to venture the Bass isn't much different from Fintry."

"Sure, Ioan's concerts are always entertaining! But the Firth," he exclaimed, "Oh, the mighty sea!"

Abi sighed, "I've loved your letters, the way you describe the sights and sounds. I can hardly wait to see it!"

"I've been looking forward to showing it to you!" Drew's face beamed, for he adored Abi, savouring her words and noticing each delicate feature on her lovely face.

Upon reaching the castle, he unlatched the ancient door, and they stepped inside. Making way past a clump of chatty visitors, they ducked beneath the low-hanging stag-horn chandelier, drawing near the roaring fire. Taking Abi's coat, he nestled her into an oversized tartan armchair overlooking the parlour, and she sang out, "Oh, I do love this room! It's filled with history and memories; warms ye right up!"

"Remember our first date here?" Drew grinned.

"Oh, aye! How could I forget? You stood up and sang, 'My Girl' right in the middle of tea!"

He whispered, "You'll always be my girl!" Be it the heat from the fire or Drew's remark, Abi's face blushed crimson as he continued, "And of all the days we've spent here, I'll remember this one more than any other."

"Really?" She looked puzzled. "What's so special about today?"

There and then, wrapped in the golden glow of the hearth, Drew took a deep breath, then knelt down before her. "I'm not romantic, Abi, but I do love ye. And I can't offer much in the way of a home, cept' the view is quite spectacular, and most likely we'll never be wealthy, but if you'll be my wife..."

Abi put a hand over her quivering lips while her sparkly brown eyes welled up with tears. By now, the crowd had quieted, and all eyes were on them as Drew tugged his collar, "It's a little warm in here." Then taking her hand in his, he asked, "Abi, will you... will you marry me?"

Happy tears rolled down her rosy cheeks, and she nodded vigorously, "Aye Drew. Aye! I'll marry you... I love you so much!" Leaning forward, she threw her arms around his neck, and the crowd erupted in applause as they kissed before the fire.

"Ugh..." That's all Mum and Abi talked about all the way back to North Berwick. I never realised how important every little detail of what they wore, or what they said and how they said it, and what Drew said when she said yes, and what the people did when she said yes, and what they talked about on the walk back to the farmhouse could be, and besides, who can remember all those details?

"Eh-hem," Lilly chided, "I know someone who remembers e'ry detail about a certain castle, all the battles fought there, all the people who lived there, and when they were born or came to visit... so maybe it's not just a girl thing!"

Lilly did have a point, and during Christmas break, she discovered one very important detail that was missing! Along with a multitude of visitors to a nearby cathedral, we admired the grandeur of high stone arches, heraldic standards, plaques and statues recalling chivalrous knights, and massive sunlit, stained-glass windows. Voices echoed throughout the cavernous interior and people pointed to and fro until we came to the nativity scene.

"What's wrong Lil?" Keith asked, placing a hand on her shoulder.

Looking distraught, she whispered, "Call the police!"

Alerting a nearby officer, she pointed, "See! Linus said, I'd find the baby in a manger, but He's gone!"

Kneeling beside Lilly, he inspected the scene, then soft as his gruff voice could, he whispered, "I see what you mean, lassie, but tis only the 19th." She stared back until he clarified, "Jesus ain't been born yet!"

"Oh," she nodded, prompting a great deal of interesting conversation.

Be it quaint, tucked away villages, or bustling city streets, buildings and archways glistened with tinsel and lights, animated characters bedecked storefront windows, and Christmas carols wafted through the crisp winter air. Bairns pressed their faces to toy shop windows, dreaming of something marvellous under their tree come Christmas morn, and their unbridled delight spilled over to passersby, making this, as the song says, the most wonderful time of year!

Besides shopping, Mum and Da had two extra special reasons for venturing into Edinburgh... Drew and Abi.

Rings and wedding clothes were top of the list, so we made a day of it. After choosing simple silver Celtic bands, the ladies headed in one direction, gents in another, to meet up at the Christmas market in-between. Our eyes feasted upon delight after delight, all the latest bits and bobs, gadgets, and had-to-haves, none of which anyone needed, but still we enjoyed the seemingly endless display.

Drew selected a weathered tartan for his kilt, topped with a white embroidered sark. From head down to his ghillie brogues, looking every bit the strapping young Scotsman, he asked, "Ye think Abi'll like it?"

"Aye lad!" Da nodded. "Ye better stand ready to catch her. One look at ye in your wedding clothes and she's like to swoon!"

Unaccustomed to attention, Drew blushed at his handsome reflection, then sighed, "Just wish Andy and Ioan could be here."

After paying the clerk, there was still one thing left to acquire. Shopping had birthed in us a huge appetite, so we made our way to a crowded chippy! From a cramped window seat, we chattered away, watching people scurrying to and fro and wondering what Mum, Abi, and Annie were whispering about because they kept bursting into giggles.

Our tummies were actually sore from laughing when we stepped back into the bustle. A dusting of snow began to fall over the softly lit ancient city, and tiny flakes swirled round about us, carried on the wind, dancing in circles on the pavement before coming to rest on a thin blanket of white. Looking up into the snowy night sky, to my ever-present friend, I whispered, "Thank you, Jesus, for this blessing of time together!"

As Christmas Eve dawned, I bounded out of bed and accompanied Da on the watery trek to the Bass to deliver another surprise. Two lads from the engine shop volunteered to cover beacon lighting duties, allowing a gob-smacked Andy and Mr. Ramsay to attend the wedding! With quick thinking, Da arranged a kilt and sark for Andy, who made a dapper best man, and Mr. Ramsay, full of surprises, donned a kilt of his own.

He smiled, "Tis not every day this plaid comes out into society!"

His weathered hair resembled the red highland coos, with wispy silver strands woven here and there, and after a trim, Mum had him looking quite smart. Then Da took the lads on one last-minute run to town.

Abi and her mum were at Miss Norah's, and one could only imagine the giggles with all those ladies in one room, amid yards and yards of white meshy fabric I'd caught a glimpse of in the chippy. While Mum was tearing around the cottage looking for Abi's hairpins, the flowers arrived, now covering the parlour and foyer. Then the photographer carried in an array of bags and stands, followed by the caterer, with huge plates of meats, cheeses, salads, and all the trimmings.

Besides Andy, Ioan, and the Milsoms, Drew and Abi had little family between them, but plenty of well-wishers began to fill our home. Keith and Huw arrived with their folks, then Papa G and the MacLeans, and to my great delight, Lilly and her folks joined us too. Though a bit tight on space, peals of laughter, interesting conversations, and jolly company proved this would be a braw celebration!

Our parlour, in all its Christmas finery, lit by the roaring hearth, threw light and shadows past a bejewelled tree onto every corner and archway decked in pine branches, holly, and wedding flowers. Adding to the glow were seven hand-dipped candles atop an ancient candelabra from Tantallon's store of artifacts. The ornate branches each held a candle, tallest in the middle, with three sloping downwards on each side. As the tiny flames danced, Da announced that this Christmas Eve would be a wee bit different. We'd not only be celebrating the birth of our Lord, Jesus, but joining Drew and Abi together in marriage.

The men, including me, wore smart black jackets and tartan kilts, all standing beside Drew, who looked a proper Scottish groom, patiently waiting up front. And the ladies resembled finely wrapped gifts in shades of red and black velvet, with gold, tartan, and rose trimmings. As folks took their seats, a hush fell over the room, and Mum began playing the "Bridal March" on the old upright, signalling all to stand. As Abi and her Da emerged from the kitchen, all eyes turned towards the bride.

Abi was radiant in a shimmery white gown, trimmed with sparkly bits, pearly beads, and a sash of tartan draped across her shoulder. That, she would exchange for Drew's family plaid as they repeated the ancient tradition of hand binding, along with vows and rings, which I got to carry down the aisle, and yes, they had to kiss again!

Everyone cheered, and the very first thing they did as husband and wife was worship the Lord as we sang "Oh, Come All Ye Faithful." Then in the soft light, we listened as Mum played a new song about God's "Plan" for Mary and Joseph and redemption for all His people.

After Da shared the real Christmas story, while pouring a cup of wine and breaking a fresh loaf of bread, he explained God's plan of salvation, beginning with Jesus stepping down into human history as fully God, yet fully man, living a sinless life, and so becoming the only worthy sacrifice to pardon our sins. The bread and the wine are reminders that Jesus gave himself to be crucified and took the punishment we deserve. But through repentance, God transfers His goodness, so when He looks down on us, instead of our sin, He sees us covered in Jesus' righteousness and loves us as His sons and daughters. Without repentance, salvation is impossible, leaving an eternal chasm between us and God. So, if you hadn't trusted Christ as Saviour, Da warned to let the bread and cup pass, but for those who believed, he asked we search our hearts and ask God's forgiveness for our wrongs. Then together, we shared the bread and wine as Mum played "Silent Night," which was prettier than I ever remember.

Amid the shimmering candlelit room, bathed in God's mighty presence, I treasured the moment, the way I did when He spoke at Tantallon. In my thoughts, I thanked Him that I lived to see Drew and Abi get married, that Mr. Ramsay was comforted by Uncle Frasier's watch resting in his pocket, and for Mum and Da loving me and each other so well. I prayed for Drew and Abi holding hands, gazing at each other, that the Lord would bless them in their new life together.

Then I prayed especially for Lilly, who now knew there was no Santa but instead that Jesus is real and that He really loves her. My thoughts were so deep, I jumped as Mum began playing "Joy to the World!" We sang with such exuberance, we'd have woke the neighbours if we had any, but we simply couldn't help the joy spilling from our hearts and our faces. It was Christmas, the village bells were chiming, Drew and Abi were kissing…again, and on this stellar, starry night, we had truly been touched by the awesome presence of Jesus!

18

A Verdant Visit

Ding, ding, ding, ding, ding... Andy claimed our attention by dinging his fork on the edge of his glass so he might take up the best man's duty of toasting. With all eyes in his direction, he stammered, "I, I've a...few words for the bride and groom."

Drew volleyed back, "Aye, that's what I'm afraid of!"

With a hearty laugh, Andy relaxed, "Firstly, on this happiest of occasions, we thank God for bringing us all together. To my good brother Drew, I pray ye'll honour and cherish this beautiful lady, for the precious treasure you've been given. Listen to her heart with patience and respond with tenderness.... Maybe snore a wee bit softer." Drew rolled his eyes as Andy continued, "And to Abi, my lovely new sister-in-law, as you come to know my brother the way I do, I pray yer respect for his honest and good character will grow to rival the heights of the Fintry Hills ye've been born to. May ye love him beyond his many, many, *many* foibles, knowing yer now part of and protected by *our* family." He paused, "And for your new life on the Bass, may the good Lord grant ye the patience to put up with the lot of us!" Drew raised his glass, "To Drew and Abi! Long life and happy ever afters!"

Joining Andy, we raised our glasses in kind, "To Drew and Abi, Happy Ever After!"

The remainder of the evening we feasted on a banquet fit for a king and an entire court, with no lack of Christmas and Ceilidh tunes, danced to in every free space available! Then, from the inner fold of his ghillie hose, Drew retrieved his sgian dubh and carved out the first slice of wedding cake for his bride. Miss Norah and Mum had outdone themselves, covering the three-tiered tower of confection in creamy white icing, trimmed with sprigs of holly and heather! Yet all the fancy details and festivities couldn't hold the couple any longer. After feeding each other the sweet cake, Drew and Abi set off for a honeymoon at Papa G's seaside cottage, while he, Andy, and Mr. Ramsay bunked at our house for a Merry Christmas indeed!

After so much excitement, I thought sleep would be difficult to come by, but no sooner had I closed my eyes did I slip into a glorious dream. Soaring through the clouds, I was carried on wings of eagles across the heavens, catching glimpses of indescribable beauty! Then, ever so gently, set down in my room, where every nook and corner glistened, for above my bed, an enormous chandelier hung suspended by a single strand of golden light. I studied the strand and exquisite crystals, sparkling like diamonds, when suddenly they were swallowed up by something even more wonderful. A portal from Heaven opened, and a lush green vine engulfed the fixture in foliage, with no beginning nor end that I could discern. Then, from within the greenery, a man's face appeared, kind and gentle, and to my great surprise, he smiled! I couldn't help but stare, and then he spoke.

"I'm three sixteen!"

Pulling my head back, I scrunched my face up in question until he spoke again, *"But you know me as John 3:16!"*

"Oh!" A huge smile crossed my face. "Now I get it!" Then, as quickly as he appeared, the smiling vine man ungrew himself back up into heaven. His words filled my heart to nearly bursting with joy. It felt warm and safe, like when your folks tuck you in and kiss you goodnight, yet something much deeper. This fathomless awe and overwhelming sense of God's love made me laugh out loud, till I realised I was fully awake, sitting upright in my bed. I'll not tell my classmates, for most didn't believe me, and some even got angry when I spoke of God's love, but that didn't matter now. I got to glimpse God's merriment at my gob smacked face! Other than folks in Bible days, I'd never known anyone who'd experienced such unique connections with the Lord. And next to my carved box from the keepers, this was the best Christmas gift ever!

Despite little sleep, my fantastic dream gave me wings, and I bounded out of bed, off to the kitchen, where Papa G and Mr. Ramsay were already chatting over a hot cuppa. Sliding sideways into the room, I sang out, "Happy Christmas!"

They returned my greeting with hugs and laughter, then I listened to their stories, for these men were so dear, I simply loved the sound of their voices. However, my speedy entrance announced I had something to share, especially when I began with, "You're nae gonna believe this!"

There was safety in sharing with Mr. Ramsay and Papa G... never a worry they'd nae believe, for they'd lived long enough to know God does amazing things, plus our ensuing discussions always proved interesting.

Papa G smiled, "The Lord surely chose an interesting way of communicating!"

"Reminds us," Mr. Ramsay added, "to expect the unexpected."

"God must love to surprise us!" I giggled, "I bet it makes Him smile!"

"Aye lad," Papa G nodded. "I'm sure it does."

All too soon, time begged the return of Mr. Ramsay and a some-what sleepy Andy to the Bass, and to our delight, Mum joined us too. The shop lads had nae problem with the beacon but were much relieved to see us. As soon as we reached the upper landing, the front door flew open, and they shouted, "Happy Christmas!"

This cottage had been Mr. Ramsay's safe haven since he was a lad, and leading inside, he seemed relieved to be home. While Mum's basket of baking and wedding leftovers delighted the shop lads, he put the kettle on for tea. Then, setting out mugs, he placed the only cup and saucer the Bass possessed, painted with a lassie in a field of daffodils before Mum.

"Found this in a charity shop yesterday. It's got yer name on it, AnnaLee, anytime yer o'er."

"How thoughtful, Ioan!" Mum said, "Reminds me of my mum. She always said tea tasted best in a china cup."

"And how like ye, my love," Da added, "enraptured with daffodils!"

"For my part...I've always thought tea tasted better in a comfy seat...next to a glowing hearth..." Stirring up a handful of coals, Mr. Ramsay completed his thought, "With friends!" Instantly, the flames jumped to attention, adding warmth and a golden glow to the room.

Holding hands with Da, Mum sipped her tea, remarking, "William loves the wee box ye carved for him. Tis a treasure, the love ye have for him...and this place!"

Mr. Ramsay gazed in my direction. "Just a wee something to remember us by." He shrugged, "They don't stay young forever, and visiting the Bass may dull in time."

"Mr. Ramsay!" I insisted, "I'll always come visit ye here on the Bass! Ye've nae need to worry for that!"

"I'd like that...very much, William."

Mum glanced around, "A girl could be quite comfy here."

"I hope so!" Mr. Ramsay smiled, "We've ne'er had a lass to stay with us."

"Well," Mum replied, "Abi couldn't want for a warmer welcome. The room you've set up for her and Drew is lovely." And to Mr. Ramsay's delight, Mum brought along girly things for each room to help Abi feel more settled.

"It may take time to adjust to the confines of the rock." Ioan added, "Especially if yer used to long walks about the country."

"Och," Mum replied, "There's room enough to walk about, and," looking towards Da, "a trip ashore when needed. In any case, ne'er underestimate the power of love to change difficult into doable!"

"As you and I, my lass, are living proof!" Da raised his mug, "Here! Here!"

Our visit was short, so the shop lads might enjoy the rest of Christmas day with their families. The sun warming the chilly air made our crossing pleasant, and on a day so glorious, even the sea otters seemed to be celebrating as they frolicked in the waves.

Papa G provided the lads a lift home in his royal blue Citroen DS. The perfect car for a deposed French duke, boasting fine classic lines and just a hint of mystery. We waved as they rolled down the drive, the engine's purr fading around the snowy bend.

Now, twas time for our own celebration. Our home was always open, folk stopping for a cuppa, tourists in search of directions, or our church family in need of prayer, a meal, or counsel. So, I cherished this rare day all to ourselves.

Da cuddled Mum on our cosy parlour couch, "We've certainly had an eventful year!"

"Aye!" She sighed, "Drew and Abi married, a Hawaiian luau, and yer very first successful Ceilidh dance!"

"Brilliant, Da!"

"Now there," he chuckled, "twas a thing to be seen! Along with Will's flying lesson."

"Och!" Mum shuddered, "Don't remind me!"

Da pulled her closer, "By God's grace, Ioan and Andy made it o'er for the wedding, plus yer first trip to the Bass in years!"

They shared sleepy smiles as I held up my cross, "And this interesting blessing!"

"Aye! God's doing something wonderful." Da paused, "As He always is."

Rolling upside-down on the carpet, I chuckled when Mum asked, "What's brewing in that noggin of yours?"

"I'm just...happy!" I rolled back upright. "It's been the best year ever, and I got to share it with everyone I love! Plus, I had the most amazing dream last night! I flew through the clouds, then a man's face appeared in a vine, and when he spoke, I knew it was Jesus!"

"Jesus in a vine? Intriguing!" Da asked, "How'd you know it was Him?"

"Because... He said, 'I'm 3, 16, but you know me as John 3:16!' Then the vine disappeared back up into heaven!"

"Now that's unique!" Da chuckled.

"I don't know why He does, because I'm nobody special, but I love it when God speaks to me!" Mum and Da shared that concerned look acquired the night my cross appeared, so I asked, "Did I say something wrong?"

"No." Mum shook her head. "Except ye are very special! And we're as amazed as you are."

"Only..." Da added, "we know from experience, mountain top moments are often followed by difficulties. There's purpose in every thing God does, so whatever lies ahead, ye need to remember how He's spoken to you and how dearly He loves you..."

"*And* how dearly we love you!" Mum completed Da's thought. "Don't e'er let anyone cause you to doubt that." After a moment, she prompted, "Okay?"

I nodded. "Aye, I'll remember." My parents knew what they were talking about, as I would soon discover. Life didn't always make sense; hurts ran deep, and doubts could be overpowering. So by revisiting these events and holding to God's promises, He would supply my courage and strength. Plus, the Celtic Cross around my neck daily reminded the Lord had chosen me for something. What He might ask of me remained unclear, but when He did, would I be ready?

19

꧁

Stargazing

In a flash, Christmas was over, Abi and Drew left for the Bass, and Huw, Lilly, and I found ourselves once again travellers aboard Mrs. Sherry's coach. Bouncing down the lane, jolly voices filled the air, until all chatter, along with the gears, ground to a halt as Keith hobbled aboard, propped up on crutches, foot in a cast reaching half-way up his calf.

Helping him into a seat, Mrs. Sherry set us back in motion, and Keith called back, "Tell ya when we get to school!"

But it nae took that long, as his ill-fated incident was passed from stem to stern. While navigating a swath of evergreens, Keith's sled hit a patch of ice, sending him tumbling off into the wood, snapping his ankle like a twig! Bad news for any lad bent on becoming a footballer, but on the bright side, he'd have more time to investigate the latest unsolved crimes.

"I really don't understand Keith." Lilly sighed, "Why must you dabble in murders and maleficence? Isn't there enough of that on telly?"

136

"Well, Lilly," he began, "as usual, you're right. However, by study-ing the perpetrators' methods, I become better equipped to discover *'who done it!'* Thereby, bringing more criminals to justice and, in turn, cutting down the copious number of crimes on telly!"

"That'll never fly!" Huw cited, "People are *way* too fascinated by that stuff!"

I offered, "Huw does have a point, Lil!"

"I suppose...but," she grimaced, "digging around in body parts and all, that's just...morbid!" Delivering a maniacal laugh between our heads, Lilly teased, "Speaking of unsolved mysteries, Huw's a live one!"

"Aye!" I joked, "He could peel back centuries of macabre, maybe even discover the identity of Jack the Ripper!"

"Matter of fact," Keith held up a finger, "in Jack's day, a man was heard near the crime scenes, laughing in the same crazed manner, suggesting a derangement or some sort of mental instability!"

"Tough crowd!" Huw huffed in response, then plopping down cross-legged on the ground, he pouted, "I could ask Mr. X to kick your other ankle, Keith!"

"Och, relax, Huw, we're just joking." Keith snickered, "We know you have issues!"

Snorting in protest, Huw jumped to his feet, and rubbing his knuckles into Keith's curly brown head, he grimaced, "Broken ankle or not, take it back!"

Lilly jumped backwards, "Is this what unrepressed anger looks like?"

Looking on, I teased, "Apparently!"

In a flash, Keith felled Huw to the ground at the point of his crutch. "It'll do ye nae good to struggle; I've been studying the way of the ninja...in case one needed to defend oneself!"

With the rubbery end of the crutch in his tummy, Huw began to laugh, pleading, "OK...OK, I give up. Quit tickling me!"

With a smug look, Keith gave one last nudge, releasing Huw.

"You two are like Clouseau and Kato!" Huw stared blankly, till I added, "You know, the Pink Panther?"

Keith acknowledged with a tilt of his head, "I'm quicker!"

Instantly, Huw poked Keith in the side, causing another eruption of giggles.

"Hey!" I redirected, "Mr. Tinley has our first night lab planned."

Keith spouted, "When?"

"I should think you," Lilly teased, "of all people, would have sussed that out by now!"

"I know when..." Huw purred, "And what!" Our sudden attention startled him. "Well, that is, I overheard Mr. Tinley saying, in a fortnight, apparently, we'll be staring up at Saturn and her rings! Hasn't been this close in decades. Quite the scoop, ye know!"

The date, oddly enough, fell upon the Ides of March. While this was not a particularly good day to be Caesar, it was a great evening to be an astronomy student. Away from artificial light, Tantallon's front court provided the perfect stage for excited stargazers to glimpse the heavenly expanse above.

As Mr. Tinley situated the telescope, students milled round, enjoying music spilling from a portable radio. Most of the girls were singing along to something called, "American Pie." Their faces formed wispy breaths around the curious lyrics, and I wondered what they could possibly mean.

When it concluded, Lilly declared, "That's the longest recorded song in history. A full 8 and a half minutes!"

"No, it's not!" She whirled towards Hector, who countered, "It's "In-a-gadda dah vida."

"That's not music!" Siobhan huffed, "Just noise, so that doesn't count!"

Huw countered, "What about all the great classical compositions?"

A multitude of mixed opinions stoked tempers in the chilly night, until Mr. Tinley rallied, "Alright ladies and gents. Time to refocus." Pointing up, he concluded, "On Space! So, what do we know about Saturn?"

Jimmy sang out, "It's the 6th planet from the Sun, with enormous rings of gas that circle the entire planet!"

"Excellent Jimmy, you've done a bit of homework!"

Enjoying the praise, Jimmy smiled until Hector whispered, "Homework, nothin. A gaseous little wimp always recognises his superior!"

"Hector!" Mr. Tinley shushed the quibble. "Now, let's do a bit of comparison. Who can tell me the make-up of the Earth's atmosphere?"

Keith responded, "Primarily oxygen and nitrogen."

"Good Keith! With the perfect ratio of these elements, to support human life."

Lilly added, "We're also the perfect distance from the sun!"

"Excellent Lilly! If we were a fraction closer, the sun's intense heat would burn us to a crisp! Yet a fraction further away, and the Earth would freeze over." Waiting for the information to sink in, he added, "But Saturn, on the other hand, is a massive ball of hydrogen and helium."

Jimmy called out, "The stuff inside balloons that makes you talk funny!"

"Aye, Jimmy, but why?"

Keith offered, "It has something to do with the density or weight of the gas, right?"

"You're on to something!" Mr. Tinley explained, "Helium is lighter than air, so when your voice travels through it, the higher-pitched tones are amplified, while the lower tones are reduced."

Siobhan raised the tone of her voice, "Causing us to sound like Alvin and the chipmunks!"

"Aye," our teacher smirked, "but too much is definitely not healthy.

Reduces oxygen to the brain. In fact...best not to do that." Mr. Tinley cleared his throat. "Now, at 900 million miles from the Sun, give or take, Saturn is cold and desolate, yet a fascinating beauty. And thanks to the invention of the telescope, tonight we'll bridge that distance."

"OK, OK, so why are we still chatting?" Hector fussed, "It's cold out here. When are we going to see this thing?"

"Patience, Hector, she's worth waiting for!" Hector crossed his arms as our teacher continued, "Anyone remember how large the Earth is?" After a few mumbles and shrugs, he refreshed our memories, "Approximately 7,917 miles at the equator."

Hector asked, "So, what does that mean exactly, Mr. T?"

"It means..." Mr. Tinley drew this out: "You'd have to drive a constant speed of 50 miles per hour for 21 days to complete one trip around the Earth!"

"Impossible, Mr. Tinley!" Siobhan quipped, "You'd have to stop for petrol!"

"And the toilet!" Jimmy giggled.

"Right you are," he added, "but that's only to provide perspective. For as big as the Earth is, Saturn's diameter, 74,897 miles, and rings that stretch out twice that distance completely dwarf our planet!"

Leaning on his crutch, Keith questioned, "So, how big is that, really?"

"It's so big, Keith, it would take 764 planet Earths to make one Saturn. But then we're comparing apples to oranges, because Earth is the only planet that can sustain human life."

Siobhan interjected, "What about extra terrestrials?"

"That Siobhan, I have no answer for... yet." Mr. Tinley grinned, "So, while Saturn's big, our Sun is even bigger. It would take 1,300,000 Earths to equal the mass of our Sun." He waited for the information to sink in, adding, "Yet, alongside Canis Majoris, the "Big Dog" star, our Sun would look like a speck of dust! The universe is amazingly huge!"

Amid astonished gasps and clucks of disbelief, Mr. Tinley seemed pleased to see us weighing and measuring the data. "Yet, there's order to our solar system, rules and laws that govern its rotation and keep us in constant motion. Has it ever occurred to you, when you spin a ball, eventually it comes to a stop, yet the Earth and the entire universe continue to rotate, century after century after century? If they ever stopped, planets would collide, and life as we know it would cease to exist. So, we should ask how these complex systems were made. And, what keeps them in constant motion?"

"Ugh!" Hector threw his head back in disgust. "Enough with the grand thoughts! Are we gonna see this thing, or not?"

"Aye." Mr. Tinley smiled, "And I dare ye nae to be impressed!"

Peering through the telescope, over a gazillion miles of space, Saturn spun silently across the vastness of our galaxy. Siobhan exclaimed, "It reminds me of a kaleidoscope! Except instead of waltzing colours, Saturn is performing an elegant dance in shades of grey."

"Fascinating," I breathed, staring in silent wonder and trying to comprehend the enormous size of this tiny orb spinning across an ocean of space.

My classmates grew impatient. "Let someone else have a look, William!"

No sooner had I stepped back to oblige when the leather braid of my cross hooked on the tripod and yanked me down. My cheekbone hit the eyepiece with such force, I literally saw stars. Grabbing my shoulder, Mr. Tinley steadied me and helped untether my cross as Lilly dashed to my side.

Nudging us out of the way, Hector sneered, "You ever think God's trying to tell ya something, Ridley? Like, it's my turn!"

"No!" Jimmy shouted, "It's mine."

"Easy lads!" Mr. Tinley calmed, "Saturn's not going anywhere and everyone'll have a turn." He stepped back, "Ye look a bit shaky, William, ye alright?"

Dazed, I nodded in the affirmative, adding, "Ladies first fellas, let Lilly go next!"

"Aw yeah!" Huw snorted, "He's fine, Mr. Tinley!"

Lilly rolled her eyes, then shot me a smile as the lads beckoned her towards the telescope. On tiptoe, she marvelled, "That's remarkable, Mr. Tinley! But it wouldn't be much fun driving around those rings; they're quite flat, and that would get boring!"

Jimmy quipped, "Not if there's a meteor shower while you're driving Lil!"

Our laughter and warm breath swirled in the cool evening, then Mr. Tinley offered the eyepiece to Hector, "Take a look, lad."

Sauntering up, he peered through the glass. "I don't see anything!" He whirled back, "Where is this blasted bit of cosmic dust?"

"Here." Mr. Tinley realigned the scope, then bid Hector to take his place, "Now, see what you make of this!"

The spectacular sight awed even Hector, who breathed, "You weren't kidding! I can really see it!" He gazed intently, "So tiny, but there's the rings, just like ye said. Saturn is magnificent!"

Hector'd completely forgot himself, but turning towards our elated teacher and classmates, he faltered, "I mean, I saw it, but I don't know what you're all going on about. You can't even see the color of the planet. At least in photographs, it's a little more lifelike."

Stepping away from the telescope, Hector receded into the shadows, which made me sad. For quick as a meteor screeching across the sky, his joy faded, but this evening would be memorable for two reasons. The blue and purple rings surfacing on my cheek would rival Saturn's, and Hector's glimmer of joy birthed a bright new idea.

20

Battle with the Devil

Admit it or not, Hector'd been fascinated by what he'd seen through the telescope, so with a little coaxing, he helped me calculate distances between planets, ratios of atmospheric gases, counting moons of planets and discovering heaps about our galaxy. And beneath that tough exterior, I discovered Hector had a sense of humour.

"Nice shiner, Ridley!"

"Thanks!" I winced. "Well worth it, don't ye think?"

Hector nodded. "Almost makes up for not seeing Saturn in colour!"

"That was pretty braw!"

"Hmm," he added, "be nice to see more stuff like that."

"Aye! Oh, um... by the way, Mum and Da said to come by anytime."

At the mention of my folks, Hector's countenance fell. "Ah, I can't. Least not today."

That became Hector's usual response, but I kept asking until a strange look crossed his face. Twasn't anger or exasperation, but more like sadness, and from then on he began avoiding me.

"Why try so hard, Will?" Keith didn't understand, "If Hector doesn't want to be friends, why pester him?"

"Aye," Huw sputtered. "Given half the chance, he'd knock ye down again, easy!"

"I see it more as investing, not pestering, and honestly, if our das acted like Mr. Menteith, wouldn't you want a friend to help?"

"Do what ye like, Will," Keith grimaced. "All I'm sayin is, ye cannae save the whole world!"

How, I wondered, could something so important be of so little interest to my friends? Sure, Hector's da needed help, but more than anything, I prayed for one tiny window into Hector's soul, where our heavenly Father's overwhelming love and tender touch of mercy would restore his hope!

So even though he ignored me, I waved anyway. But after class today, things changed. Hector lowered his head like a charging bull, pushing and shoving his way through the crowd, backing me into a corner. "What is it with you, Ridley?"

"What do you mean?"

"I don't get you; I've been dodging you for weeks, and you just won't quit. What is it you want from me?"

Thinking it should have been evident, I stammered, "Uh, I..."

"Uh?" He snorted, towering over me, "You're never at a loss for words, Ridley. Why are you being so nice? What *do* you want?"

"I just...want to be your friend." The words stunned him as I explained, "I've been praying for you and for your da, a lot actually, and with things being what they are, I thought you could use a friend."

Searching my eyes, he remained silent, then softened, "Look, William..." I smiled because he actually used my name. "I appreciate what you and your parents have done for me, especially after the Ceilidh."

"Is yer da any better?"

Hector chuckled, "He's not like your da Will. Okay? We don't cosy up and talk it out till everything's better."

"I'm really sorry."

He drew in a deep breath, "He has been kinder lately, but he misses Mum, and my little brother. There's no room for..." He stopped mid-sentence, then furrowed his brow. "William, some things a lad has to work out on his own. Ye understand?"

We stared for a moment. I didn't understand, but with a nod, I lied. As he turned and walked away, immediately I felt angry at myself for not saying something wiser or finding a way to help. But no, instead I nodded, and Hector walked away. Before he'd even slipped round the corner, anxiety gripped my entire being.

The assault began with a voice taunting in my head, "Who do you think you are? You don't know Hector well enough to speak to him about something so personal. He's never gonna want to know your God now. He thinks you're a whacked-out Jesus freak, and he's probably laughing at you right now!"

My insides were in turmoil, second guessing everything I'd said or hadn't said. For nearly an hour this chaos tormented my soul, making me sick to my stomach and gasping for air until I cried out, "Lord, I'm so sorry. I've completely messed this up!"

Instantly, I felt God's presence, heard that familiar voice, who spoke into and obliterated the consuming darkness, "Why are you in turmoil? I set up that meeting; you delivered the message; now stop worrying; the rest is up to me!"

It felt like the weight of the world had been lifted, and with a huge sigh, I headed home. Da would be at Tantallon, so I hiked up to the inner close and sat on the wall beside where he'd been working.

"He's not coming?" As I shook my head, Da asked, "You okay?"

Sucking in a jagged breath, I held my head in my hands, explaining the voices. "Da, people are gonna think I'm crazy! You must think

I'm crazy! But I heard them, and I felt so condemned it made me ill. How is that possible?"

"And so..." Da looked troubled. "It begins."

"What do ye mean?"

"We're in a battle, Will... like the war movies we've seen, only not with guns or earthly weapons. It's a spiritual assault with well-crafted strategy, wrestling for souls, and the enemy ne'er fights fair. Of course, he wants you to doubt yourself, so ye'll focus on the attack and hesitate to share your faith. But God reassured you in the midst of that battle."

"He did!"

"Did you think," Da softened, "being a *Defender of the Faith* would be easy?"

"Honestly," I shrugged, "I had no idea what it would be like... I just ne'er imagined I'd feel so powerless."

Da put a hand on my shoulder. "Ah, but feelings cannae be trusted! Your words, son, and especially your prayers *are* powerful, so don't you ever give up. God draws whom He will. Our job is to plant the seeds, and like He told you, the rest is up to Him."

Da's encouragement was exactly what I needed, and as the last visitor crossed the moat bridge, we stopped to pray for Hector, his da, our family, and for protection, then together we closed Tantallon's ancient door and headed home.

Mum also hadn't been feeling well, yet she prepared a lovely evening tea, then soon after welcomed our Wednesday study group. Without mentioning her ills, she served coffees, teas, sandwiches, and biscuits. Despite countless reasons that might have prevented our gathering, we all showed up, drinking deeply from the refreshing well of God's word. As the evening grew late, my thoughts lightened, and I headed off for a peaceful night's sleep.

But, after praying, I fell into a miry realm of dreams, driving Papa G's Citroen along a wide, sandy beach where people were milling around, going about their lives with no thought to anything around them. Coming to a stop, I got out and stood on the running board, scanning the horizon, searching, and calling out for Mum. Then, without warning, the full moon shot up from below the left horizon. Its trail of light blasted across the sky in a matter of seconds, and I was certain this was the end of the world, but no one noticed. Frightened for their souls, I dropped to my knees, crying out as loud as I could, "People, get ready; Jesus is coming!" And still, despite my pleading, they ignored me, continuing on their way. Then instantly, I woke in a cold sweat.

"William!" Mum rushed into my room, "What's the matter?"

Shaking, I sobbed, "Mum, my dream twas so real... people need to know Jesus is coming, but they wouldn't listen! They just kept walking around like they couldn't hear me."

"Shh!" Mum rocked me in her arms. "Tis alright, Will. Tis alright."

Catching my breath, I huffed, "Not much of a warrior, am I?"

Taking me by the shoulders, she smiled, "I think you're the bravest lad in all of Scotland!" My expression begged her reassurance, "Remember Elijah?"

"A little," I exhaled.

"He had the same concern; people were being led to destruction. So, he challenged the prophets of Baal to a showdown...to prove who's god was real. They begged their wooden statue all day to consume their offering, but when nothing happened, the crowd laughed, and Elijah joked, 'Is your god asleep?' Then he doused his offering with four huge jars of water, not once or twice, but three times, so even the trenches beneath the altar were filled, then Elijah said, 'Lord, show these people that You alone are God! Restore their faith in You!'

"You know what happened?" Shaking my head, she smiled, "The heavens brought down such a blast of fire; it consumed not only the offering but the wood, the stones, the dust beneath it, and every last drop of water! God's spectacular display restored the people's faith and they bowed and worshipped Him!"

"Wow," I said as the effects of my dream wore off.

"However," Mum continued, "not everyone was impressed. These horrible men were friends of the king's wife, Jezebel, and when she heard they'd been exposed as frauds and put to the sword, she was furious. She vowed before the day was out to hunt Elijah down and kill him too."

I groaned, "That's how I've been feeling, hunted."

"Sometimes," Mum hugged me tighter, "even that's part of God's plan."

"Really?" I asked, "So, what happened next?"

"Elijah fled to the wilderness."

"Then what?"

"He stopped on a mountain, and God asked, 'What are you doing here Elijah?' After explaining, God stirred up a mighty wind, an earthquake, and huge fire that broke the mountain into bits. Then God asked Elijah again, 'What are you doing here?' At this point, any answer probably seemed silly, so God refreshed him and sent him back to finish what he was called to do." Mum smiled, "Sometimes we need a reminder of who we're serving."

"So...even the godliest men can be frightened and discouraged." Mum nodded as I continued, "It's good to know I'm not alone."

Pressing her hands to my face, Mum reassured, "You're ne'er alone, son. God is always with you! I believe He's giving you dreams, like He did for Joseph, to prepare you, because people *are* wandering about without God in their lives. And you may be the one to point them in the right direction!"

"I want God to save Hector and his da." I sighed, "But I don't know what else to do."

Mum pulled me close, "Two Ps! Remember? Prayer and patience." She grew serious. "There'll be days ye weep for folk to turn to Jesus;

some will ignore, maybe even hate you for it, but you must trust the Lord. He'll ne'er leave you nor lose a single soul He intends to save."

Little by little, God was revealing what "Defender of the Faith" meant. It was hard, with big doubts and bad dreams, accusations, and enemy attacks when I least expected. Yet at the same time, there was love and encouragement from Mum and Da, our church family, in His glorious landscape and from God Himself. All I had to do was touch the cross around my neck, or remember the green 3:16 encounter! Like Mum said, I wasn't alone, but for this kind of battle, there was only one way to prepare, and that was getting deep into God's Word.

I began reading the Book of John from start to finish, at least a dozen times, and each time God revealed something new. First, I discovered the opening, "In the beginning was the Word," mirrors the first sentence of Genesis, "In the beginning God created the heavens and the earth!" As I read again, "In the beginning was the Word, and the Word was with God, and the Word was God!" And further, "the Word became flesh and dwelt among us," the meaning became clear: that Jesus is the Word, the 'logos,' as it was first written in Greek. He spoke, creating everything, and it all belongs to Him! Jesus kept telling people He was the way to eternal life, *I Am the way*, *I Am* the truth, and every time He answered the religious leaders' questions with, 'I Am,' he was telling them, 'I Am, The Great I Am,' the very God that spoke to Moses from the burning bush, the one who was with the Father in glory before the world existed. He knew who He was, and He knew what He had to do. He told His disciples how He had to go away, but not to lose heart, that He would always be with them, and their sorrow would turn to joy. He was crucified because He kept claiming to be God! Three days after this brutal end, just as He said, Jesus appeared, alive, before hundreds of people who saw Him, ate with Him, and spoke with Him. Because of His great love for His people, He didn't leave us without comfort; He sent His Spirit to breathe new life into our souls, to give us hope for the tough days we would endure, to lift our heads and wipe our tears, because He truly does love us that much!

These were huge revelations, and Da was breathless answering my many questions. We blethered for hours, studying, and the more I learned, the more I wanted to share. But that's when things started getting dodgy, with more opposition than I could write down in a library's worth of volumes. It was crazy, like suddenly I had a target on my head. Simple tasks became near impossible with obstacles at every turn, making me late for almost everything. Friends and teachers misheard my words, reacting as though I'd said something nasty, and the more I tried to defend myself, the worse it got!

But God says to be strong and courageous. Hundreds of times He's commanded, *"Do not fear!"* Yet we linger before untravelled roads or choices to be made because the unknown is frightening to human nature, which, above all, desires to be in control of pretty much everything. Surely, the truest test of character is handing your life's control over to God. While we'll ne'er be alone, we'll go toe-to-toe with a formidable enemy, and if our faith is not genuine, we'll be devastated when life turns upside down. And, when, not if, is a solid guarantee!

Seeing my struggles increase, Da continued to arm me for battle. "Proceed onto this field knowing we wrestle 'not with flesh and blood, but against cosmic powers, over this present darkness, against the spiritual forces of evil in the heavenly places.' " And believe me, what started appearing nightly, and sometimes in broad daylight, proved it!

Demons attack in many ways to frighten and keep you from your purpose. In fact, Satan knows the Bible better than most Christians, along with our weak spots. If there be a chink in our armour, he'll find it, then pick away till we're nearly destroyed. Mortals have not a breath of hope against that kind of evil. Worse yet, most people don't believe Satan exists, although they'll pay dearly to see his work in darkened theaters, to be frightened out of their wits! The devil's nae a cute little fella dressed in red with a pitchfork, and he has no control over hell either! He's a fallen angel on his way to destruction, so full of hate, he'll take as many as he can deceive along with him.

"But Da," I needed detail. "Why is Satan allowed to mess with God's people?"

"Long ago," Da recounted the history of the ages, "God created a hierarchy of angels to serve Him. The Cherubim, like the ones atop the Ark of the Covenant...large, winged servants..."

"Wait! I thought Cherubim were chubby babies, like on Valentine cards."

"Interestingly, no," Da chuckled. "They're a bit more formidable, armed with flaming swords, and tasked with guarding the tree of life."

"There's something ye don't see every day!"

"Aye," Da continued, "There's also Seraphim. They're mentioned twice in the Bible, as six winged, pure, passionate worshippers that attend God around His throne."

"How many angels are there?"

"Millions, I imagine, but as ye know, God only mentions a few by name. Gabriel, who spoke to Mary and Zacharias, foretelling the births of Jesus and His cousin, John the Baptist."

"Aye, I remember." I added, "I'd love to meet Gabriel! Although...he might be scary in person!"

"Most assuredly!" Da nodded. "Nearly every mention of encounters with angels says people fall down as if dead! Imagine Michael leading God's armies; he must be fearsome!"

"He'd have to be! But...if everything was meant to be perfect, why did God need warrior angels?"

Da raised an eyebrow, "What do you think?"

"Well... He knew what was going to happen."

"Exactly!"

"Because..." I added, "He'd created another angel, the most beautiful of all the heavenly beings."

Da whispered, "The ancient dragon! So prideful, he wanted God's glory and to be worshipped. So, war arose in heaven. In one of the greatest battles of all time, Michael and his angels took up arms against Satan. And though the devil and a third of the angels fought, they were outmatched. Michael led the heavenly host in victory, and Satan, along with the defeated angels, were cast down from heaven."

I nodded. "So they were..."

"Cursed...and knowing their time is short, demons roam the earth seething with hatred for everything that God loves, taking every opportunity to cause chaos and despair. The Bible says the dragon became furious and went off to make war with those who keep God's commandments and hold to the testimony of Jesus. So strategically, he seized one opportune moment that would change the course of human history." Da paused, "Because of man's first sin, eating a piece of fruit that God said not to, *we* handed dominion of the earth over to Satan."

"But people often blame God for the bad Satan tempts people to do!"

"Aye, they'll do Will, because that piece of fruit came stuffed with a deadly lie. One bite, and bam! Humans became enslaved, abused, depressed, and deceived. While Adam and Eve didn't die instantly, they died spiritually, and human relationship with God was forever changed. If not restrained, Satan would destroy every living thing. His goal is to lead folk far enough away from the truth that they'll miss God's glorious salvation and suffer his same terrible, unavoidable, eternal fate."

"But why would he care?"

"Because Satan hates God. And what's the worst thing a man can do to hurt another?" I shook my head as Da answered himself, "He attacks their children, their families."

"But why Da? Why does God allow him to hurt people?"

"I don't know, but somehow, someway, our struggles play a bigger role in eternity, and every breath God chooses to grant us is precious. Much the same way Jesus suffered to provide salvation, our suffering accomplishes God's perfect will for our lives. It doesn't always make sense, but tis those very trials that drive us to the saving arms of Jesus."

21

Armour and Tactics

"Dinner's on the table, lads!"

Mum's invitation and the aroma of something tasty was a welcome break from our heavy conversation, apparently etched on our faces as we sat down.

"A moment please," she held up a finger, then dashed from the room.

Da and I shared a puzzled look when a billowy figure appeared in the doorway. Concealed beneath a black, floor-length cloak and lacy veil, Mum groaned, "Alas. I'm so sorry."

Sitting bolt upright, Da squeezed one bicep, then the other, asking, "Did someone die?"

Mum's veil puffed up and down as she spoke, "Well, pfft, you two looked, pfft, so wretchedly glum, pfft, I thought..." she took a dramatic pause, "pfft, surely, God must have died!"

"Och!" Da gasped, "Wife! Ye cheeky, wee sprite! I'm so relieved. Thought I'd died and hadn't the sense to keel over!"

Lifting her veil, she flashed a huge smile. "Are ye better then, husband?"

"Come here, ye daft woman!" With a hearty laugh, he encircled her waist, "Give us a kiss!" Relieved to see our spirits lift, she did, then wrapped Da and I in a great big hug beneath that enormous cape.

My parents laughed often, and twas a joy to watch them amuse each other, but supper awaited. Relinquishing the cloak, Mum served us piping hot haggis, eggs, and toast with gravy while recalling one of Tantallon's visitors.

"Oof, this poor woman was in an awful state; hardly took a breath, going on about the architect's lack of foresight."

Da asked, "She was displeased with Tantallon?"

"Oh, aye," Mum continued, "so distressed, I had to help her to the bench." Mum cupped a hand to the side of her mouth, "Nae used to walking much!"

"So, what was the matter?" Da asked.

"Well," Mum sighed, "when I asked, she eyed me like I was daft, then started waving her arms, 'Haven't you noticed? Every castle... *Every castle* you go to is on a hill! You always have to climb a hill or cross some difficult barrier to get to them!'"

"She wasn't serious...was she?" I asked.

Mum nodded, acting out the lady's indignation. "'Honestly!' she huffed. 'How could builders of such magnificent structures have so little regard for people who travel halfway round the world to see them?'"

Da chuckled, "What'd ye say to her?"

Pursing her lips and arching her brows, she replied, "Not a word. Not one word!"

"Well," Da offered, "in defence of Tantallon's architects, they had nae idea a defensible position would be so inconvenient for 20th-century visitors."

"Aye!" Mum added, "Those pesky battle tactics!"

With lighter hearts and fuller tummies, Da and I continued

our study.

"It says here, 'Put on the whole armour of God.' "

Holding his stomach, Da groaned, "God's gonna have to get me a bigger suit if yer mum keeps feeding us so!"

"Me too!"

Together, we read, *"Stand therefore, having fastened on the belt of truth, and having put on the breastplate of righteousness, and, as shoes for your feet, having put on the readiness given by the gospel of peace. In all circumstances, take up the shield of faith, with which you can extinguish all the flaming darts of the evil one; and take the helmet of salvation, and the sword of the Spirit, which is the Word of God, praying at all times in the Spirit, with all prayer and supplication." Ephesians 6:14-18*

"Will?" A blank stare wasn't the reaction Da was expecting.

While I heard the words, my brain wouldn't absorb them. "Now I know what David felt like trying on Saul's armour!"

"How's that?"

"Twas too big. Armour is made for knights, men trained for war, and I know these words are important, but I don't understand them or how I'll ever be strong enough to wear the armour."

"That's just it, Will! God doesn't expect us to do this on our own. And He'll not send us into battle without protection. So..." He paused, "What's the best way to eat an elephant?"

Together we chimed, "One bite at a time!"

"Right then." Da began, "Let's start with the Belt."

"Truth has to do with God's Word, right?"

"Exactly!" He explained, "It's knowing what God said and trusting it, no matter what lies others tempt us to believe. Satan tricked Eve by twisting the truth. The more she considered his question, 'Did God say...' the easier it became to doubt God's goodness. If we're not grounded in His Word, it's easy to be deceived."

"Oh, aye!" I exclaimed, "That makes sense."

"The Breastplate of Righteousness is our integrity, living an honourable life. The world knows when God's people fall short, and worse, we dishonor the Lord. Yet, a man who wears it faithfully, will see God work mightily."

Stretching my legs out, I wiggled my feet. "What about the shoes?"

"Interesting allegory! Both the shoes and shield trace back to ancient times. If a soldier's feet or legs were wounded, he could nae stand to resist a foe nor flee if the fight went badly. Our shoes are the unshakeable foundation of hope in the Living God! Being supernaturally rescued by Him should be so evident in how we live, that people ask, 'What's different about you?'"

Rolling my eyes, I snorted, "I've heard that before!"

"We all have a unique story to share, so others can be saved." Da added, "Some will embrace God with joy, others will reject Him, but if we're faithful, they can ne'er say they haven't been told."

"Ye take a bashin' in God's army, huh, Da?"

"As you've seen." Da shook his head. "Some attacks were so crafty, ne'er saw them coming."

"Like what?"

"Och!" He sighed, "Someday I'll tell ye, but same as the Romans soaked their shields in water before battle, we must prepare."

"What did soaking do, besides make them heavier?"

"It prevented burning arrows from setting them aflame."

"So, faith is an extra measure of protection?"

"Aye! For times when flaming arrows cover the sky so thick, you cannae see the light of day. Which is why we need The Helmet of Salvation! Because no matter what befalls us here, our eternal home is in heaven, and nothing, absolutely nothing, can separate us from God's love!" Da tapped my shoulder. "All this armour is defensive, but our one offensive, the thing Satan cannae withstand, is The Sword of the Spirit."

"Which is?"

"The Word of God! So sharp it can pierce a man to the very soul, or cause the enemy to flee in terror. When we study or pray, Satan and his minions know and do their best to keep us distracted or discouraged. But ultimately, the battle belongs to Jesus, and with faith in His Word, covered by a shield of prayer, God equips us to contend with the powers of darkness! What the world considers ridiculous resounds mightily in the spiritual realm." Da chuckled, "Ye'd nae think Miss Norah a shield maiden, but every time she prays, demons shudder! Prayer is that powerful!"

"Miss Norah, a shield maiden!" I smiled, "That's braw!"

"Okay." Da closed the Bible, "Enough for one night."

"Thanks, Da!" I yawned, stretching my arms up high, "That's a lot easier to understand."

"Yer welcome Will." Wearily, he rose, kissing my head, then stopped at the door, "God's armour is always available, but you have to put it on for it to work..." He smiled, "daily!"

There was so much to take in, and the more I studied, the more demons attacked. I'd wake up in the wee hours, sensing evil approaching from a vast distance, yet within seconds, twas in the room with me. I was so frightened; I couldn't breathe or speak. They choked me, and sometimes I could see their terrifying faces or smell the stench of sulphur. Fear overpowered, but somewhere in the depths of my soul, if I could simply think, 'In Jesus' name be gone,' instantly, they vanished. Of course, my heart needed a while longer to quit pounding, but this night, after our wonderful time of study, the enemy relented. Armour is good!

The following morning, Mum prepared to join us at the Bass! She knew Abi could do with a woman's company, but after breakfast, she got dizzy and her face went pale.

"Och, tis nothing," she declared, "I'm fine."

"Um," Da felt her forehead, "not today, my darlin' lass." Scooping her into his arms, he placed Mum on the settee and stroked her hair, "Ye'll fair better resting here."

Mum would gladly have braved the trip but relented, "My knight in shining armour. Ye know I love ye!"

"Aye!" Tucking her in with her journal and a hot cuppa, Da reminded, "But don't be fussing o'er the house. Rest!"

"I will." She smiled, then pointed to the mantle, "Oh, I nearly forgot!"

Picking up a package wrapped in pink ribbons and sparkly bits, Da gave it a wee shake,."For Abi?"

"Aye!"

With a kiss to her forehead, Da whispered, "Back in a wee while."

"See to it, husband!" She chided, "And keep that safe and dry!"

"As you wish, dearest wife!"

Churning up a foamy wake, Da guided our vessel o'er the sparkling blue water. The warmth of the sun soaked into our tired bones, and before long, we docked at the Bass.

Swinging the door wide, Mr. Ramsay sang out, "So good to see you lads!"

Without hesitation, I ran to his waiting arms, but Abi protested, "Hey wee man, what about your best girl?" Arms out wide, she picked me up and swung me round, "I do believe you've grown!"

"You think so?" I giggled.

"Alright then!" Da countered, "Where's my hug?"

As she snuggled into Da's embrace, Andy shook his head. "Pfft! Glad ye got that out of your systems!" Instantly, Drew grabbed his brother round the neck, rubbing his head till Andy hollered, "Quit!"

Shaking her head with a laugh, Abi gazed towards the door, then at the daffodil cup Mr. Ramsay had set out. "Did AnnaLee not come with ye?"

"I'm sorry, lass, she wisnae well today, but," Da produced the glittery pink gift, "she sent this for ye."

"Oh, how kind!" Then Abi reminded several times, "Please be sure to thank AnnaLee!"

Andy added, "Aye, and hope she's feeling better soon!"

Once supplies were toted up from the dock, Mr. Ramsay put the kettle on while Abi served a savoury sea bass with potato and leek soup on a table of dainty napkins and more silverware than we knew what to do with.

"This is tasty, Abi!" I complimented, downing the soup.

Returning a smile, she listened to Da and Mr. Ramsay's conversation as the hungry brothers wasted no time scoffing down every bit of food set before them.

Then wiping a sleeve across his mouth, Andy let out a loud belch, followed by a yelp. Looking up from his empty plate, he glared at his brother, who'd poked his side. "What?"

Drew chided, "Mind yer manners; there's a lady!"

"Aw, hen," Andy looked sad. "I'm sorry, just appreciating the tasty meal ye made!"

"Tis alright, Andy," she waved her hand, "still getting used to living here. It's a bit different than Fintry."

"Aye." Da offered, "Takes time getting used to!"

Drew patted her hand to reassure, but Abi pulled away, covering her trembling lip., "I just... I miss my mum!"

As she ran off sobbing, Drew snapped at Andy, "Now see what ye've gone and done!"

"Me?" Andy threw up his hands. "What've I to do with her Mum?"

With a heaving sigh, Drew followed to their room, where we could hear Abi crying. Biting my lip, I looked at Mr. Ramsay as Max ran to their door and sat like a sentry.

With furrowed brow, Andy gathered dishes and headed for the kitchen,."I didn't mean to upset her, Ioan!" As her sobbing grew louder, he groaned, "It tears me up to hear her cry!"

Then Max began whimpering. Laying flat, he covered his furry ears with his paws, and Da noted, "You're nae the only one!"

"Och, Max!" Andy clucked, "Dog knows how to make a fella feel even worse!"

"Tis not yer' fault, lad." Mr. Ramsay soothed, "She'll be right as rain. Just give it time."

"Ioan's right." Da reinforced, "The Bass is a big change for Abi, away from home and her folks. She expected AnnaLee, and you three lads, much as ye love her, are a sorry replacement for girl time."

"Girl time?" I asked, "What's that?"

Da smiled, "Something men'll ne'er understand, women talking their hearts out, examining situations from every possible angle, not to find a solution, but to discover how they feel about it!"

"Huh?" That sounded impossibly deep.

Mr. Ramsay chuckled, and before long the sobs faded, then Abi and Drew, with his arm encircling her waist, emerged in better spirits. Her sparkly brown eyes were red and puffy from crying, but her countenance was tender. "I'm so sorry! I didn't mean to spoil your visit, Magnus."

"Aw lass, nothing's spoilt!" Da crossed the room and wrapped her in a hug, "In fact, we're mighty impressed with that spread ye put out, eh lads?"

"Brilliant sea bass!" Ioan chirped.

"Aye!" Andy rallied, "Three cheers for Abi!" And we all shouted, 'Hooray!'

Blushing from the attention, Da took Abi's hands in his, "Ye see lass, I know a thing or two about a wife missing her mum, intensified by living way out here." She nodded as Da addressed her and Drew, "Now why don't you two have a think about it, and if ye like, we'll get ye back to the mainland for a visit."

"Really?" She bounced with joy!

"Aye lass!"

Somehow, Mum wasn't one bit surprised. Anticipating our arrival, she'd set tea things in the parlour and fussed o'er the newlyweds, tucking Abi under a blanket, "Let's get ye warmed up, lass!"

Mum and Abi both looked revived, but after a second cuppa, Abi was anxious to call her folks, and from the other room, her soft conversation erupted into squeals of delight.

"Mum and Da'll be here in the morning!"

Mum brushed Abi's windblown hair from her eyes. "That'll be lovely."

"Well, lovebirds," Da offered, "let's get ye settled in Will's room."

After supper, Da and Drew chatted on one side of the parlour, while Abi and Mum huddled on the other. Heads together, they whispered, then burst into hushed laughter!

"Is that what ye call 'girl time'?"

"Aye, Will." Da smiled, "Something like that."

The fresh air and our run to the Bass, provided a deep yearning for a comfy spot to lay my head. Safe beneath the covers, I snuggled close to Mum, expecting to drift right off, but tired as I was, sleep wouldn't come.

I lay on my right, then shifted to the left, but a feather in the mattress kept poking me. I flipped onto my tummy and sighed because the pillow wrapped around my head and made it hard to breathe.

"Sweet dreams, Will." Mum said softly.

"You too, Mum," I echoed, rolling onto my back.

For a few minutes, I lay there, listening to the sound of my parents' soft, steady breathing, lulling me into a dreamy state, but just as I began to doze, Da began to snore. Twasn't loud, but it startled me, and my mind zeroed in on the sound, amplified in my ears, till it became my sole focus.

Yawning, I stared at the ceiling, making faces, then shadow puppets when Da stirred. Motionless, I held my breath until he resumed his light snores. Tired as I was and not being able to sleep seemed unfair, irritating even, so I eased out of bed and headed for the kitchen. Opening the fridge, a bottle of jam toppled out. As it hurtled towards the floor, I extended my leg to block the fall, and it landed a direct hit to my big right toe!

"Ow!" I stifled a yell, trying not to wake anyone, then rubbed my smarting toe. After pouring a glass of milk, I sipped down the cool liquid, but my leg and foot began to twinge. Clenching tighter and tighter, my toes curled completely under my foot with a pain so violent, it dropped me to the floor. Hard as I tried to wrench my toes back into place, it felt as though something stronger was fighting me. The pain seared through my foot, and all I could do was call out, "Lord, help me! Please, Jesus, make it stop." Then, quick as it began, my toes returned to their rightful places.

Completely awake now, I hobbled to the parlour settee, wrapping myself in the blanket Mum had left for Abi. Gazing at the red coals, still popping out tiny yellow flames in the hearth, I rubbed my toes, thankful that sleep finally felt near. I prayed for Abi and Drew, my folks, Hector, Miss Norah, Papa G, friends at school, and for Mr. Ramsay, Andy, and Max on the Bass. Then I smiled and said an extra prayer for Lilly and her folks too.

Letting go a contented sigh, I teetered on the edge of sleep, but suddenly, my eyes flew open. "Great!" I huffed, peering around the darkened room, "I'm just not going to sleep tonight."

Instantly, fear gripped my soul! Demons had frightened me before, but this felt a million times more evil, speeding towards me faster than anything known to man could move. And it was in the room, drawing near the sofa.

My breath was ragged, words, thoughts wouldn't come, and I was too terrified to roll over and see what it was. I quaked at the revolting inward hissing, and then it spoke, not audibly, but in my thoughts, "Turn around and face your fear!"

Before I could think, words spilt out, "I don't have to look at pestilence!" Faster than lightning, it slammed my shoulder into the sofa, and I cried, "In Jesus' name be gone!"

My heart was pounding and my shoulder ached, but I thanked the

Lord for His protection as I lay there, wrestling with my thoughts. Regaining composure, for a long while, I listened to the silence, but something still felt wrong. This cheeky devil had returned, standing silent, lurking in the shadows.

Without fear, I spoke into the darkness, "Jesus rebuke you!" and instantly, it was gone. If I told anyone, they'd think me crazy, but I'm sure this attack twas Satan himself!

The question is, why?

22

Demon Trouble

Despite many prayers, the attacks continued night, after night after night. The lack of sleep began taking a toll on my studies and had me nodding off in class. Often a quick bob of my head went unnoticed, but when teachers had to wake me, our class discovered a great new source of amusement!

"Feeling a wee bit wabbit, Will?" Aisling snickered.

"Hey, Cinder-fella!" Hector teased, "Step-monster, keeping ye up late to clean the castle?"

Dare I explain? No, they'd ne'er understand, so I smiled back, sleepy-eyed as they laughed. On the bright side, I lacked enough energy to care, convincing myself twas a sign of maturity. But one thing I couldn't avoid was Huw, Lilly, and Keith's sleuthing. When they pressed for answers, my vague excuses disappointed, not to mention Hector'd been hinting he knew something they didn't.

Up till now, we'd kept no secrets from each other, but this would frighten Lilly, plus if word got out, the teasing would likely be worse than the attacks. Half the school already thought I was daft and

165

more than losing sleep, I feared losing my friends. Who'd want to be friends with a boy who talks to God and gets harassed by demons? No, for now, this would remain my secret; however, silence played right into the enemy's strategy!

After napping in class again, Lilly and Huw cornered me.

"Will! You look like a half-shorn sheep in the rain!"

"Thanks Huw!" I huffed, "Nice of you to notice."

"Actually," Lilly intervened, "what Huw meant is...we're worried about you, Will!"

"Oh!" I tried to remain calm. "I'm sorry, please don't worry. It's late-night studying, that's all."

Lilly put a hand on my shoulder. "You shouldn't let that keep you from resting; you'll get sick."

Huw quipped, "Or fall over and break your head!"

"I rather like your new nickname," catching up, Keith teased, "Cinder-fella!"

"I have been called worse, ye know!"

Huw retorted, "It's not funny, Will."

"I know. And I really am thankful you've all been sticking up for me."

"So..." Keith pressed, "What's the problem?"

"I know it sounds ridiculous, but I cannae sleep, so I've been studying, because..." I rolled my eyes. "I cannae sleep! So, might as well be productive." While those things were true, they weren't the whole truth.

"Yeah," Huw poked my side, "you keep saying that. You know, maybe if you closed your books and then your eyes, you'd get different results!"

I exhaled, "Maybe!"

But Hector's niggling had Keith's brain churning, "William, if you're tired enough to fall asleep in class, then you should be able to go home and get a good night's sleep."

I snorted, "I wish!"

He crossed his arms. "We're friends, right?"

"Aye! Of course!"

"Friends help each other when they're overwhelmed. So, what can we do to help you? Hmm?"

"Oh...uh," I glanced around. "Know any good lullabies?"

"Really Will?" Keith snapped, "What are you hiding?"

"What do you mean?"

"Could it be this late-night studying is for your *secret project*? The one Hector knows about, but you won't tell your friends!"

Trying to keep my eyes open, I yawned, "Keith, I have absolutely no idea what you're talking about."

"Yeah?" He fired back, "Convince me!"

"I don't know what you want me to say. I'm...exhausted!"

"I'm sorry, I'm not buying that." Keith pointed his finger in my face, "When the body's tired, you lay down, close your eyes, and off to sleep ye go. Solved!" I yawned again as he demanded, "Why won't you tell us what's going on?"

"Because," I yawned again, "there's nothing '*going on*."

Drawing out his words, Keith challenged, "What about the project? Hector said..."

I cut him off, "There's no project."

"There!" He crowed, "From your own lips, The *Snow* Project!"

"No," I corrected, 'There's *no* project, not snow! Why won't you believe me?"

"This is so unlike you, Will," Keith began pacing, "keeping stuff from your friends!"

His incessant questioning annoyed me, but keeping secrets ate at my conscience until I remembered hearing once, to avoid answering a question, ask one back!

I tried a lighter tone, "What makes you think I'm keeping something from you?"

"Because you're a horrible liar, Will Ridley, and I haven't been learning detective skills these past years for nothing." His hands flew up and down. "Your whole person is screaming something's wrong, but your lips are zipped! What... is... wrong?"

Exhaustion, jet fuelled cranky, and I threw my hands up. "If my person is screaming it's because you're badgering me! So, stop it. I'm not one of your silly petri dishes that needs micro-scoping for answers!"

"Silly?" He snorted, "Really? Silly? Look at you! You're falling apart; won't let your friends help, and I'm the one who's silly?" He quieted, "Well, William Ridley, be silly on your own. I'm not wasting another breath on you!" Grabbing Huw by the sleeve, he turned and stomped off with Huw close behind.

Exasperated, I stared after them, "What just happened? Where're they going?" It hurt to see Keith so upset, but I was too tired to think. Searching Lilly's eyes for understanding, she shrugged and began to turn away.

"You're leaving too?"

Lilly drew a deep breath. "Keith has a bent for the dramatic, and he'll get over it, but he's right, you know. You're not yourself, Will, and I miss the old you! Before you got all..." she hesitated, "churchy."

"Churchy?" I baulked.

She brushed my cheek with her hand. "Let us know when you're back, okay?"

Lilly trotted away, leaving me to wallow in my bruised feelings and exhaustion. Slumping down against the wall, their words kept replaying in my ears, but what could I do? They believed Hector, and my vague replies added to their distrust, plus Lilly calling me "churchy" hit a nerve. While their concern was genuine, I wondered. What would be worse, losing my friends because they think I'm lying or because I told them the truth? Consumed in dark thoughts, the blaring bus horn startled me.

"Get a move on, William!" Mrs. Sherry hollered, "There's a storm coming!"

Indeed, there was a storm approaching. As clouds gathered and rain began to fall, I climbed aboard the coach. Looking for a seat, my merry friends turned their backs to me, and for the first time since we'd met, we would ride home apart. Plus, Hector pushed in alongside them, chit-chatting like best pals. After all the times I invited him to join us, this hurt even more.

Head down, I made way to the back of the bus, avoiding curious stares. Humiliation danced about me a second time today, which made me angry— angry at the demons for causing this, and, though I didn't want to admit it, angry at God for allowing it.

The wind picked up, the rain fell harder, and the ride home seemed longer than ever as my friends laughter and conversation pulsed in my ears. I fought the feeling that they were laughing at me, then chugging to a stop, I trudged down the aisle, past their backs, to the open door. Before climbing down into the dreich day, I took a last look over my shoulder. Would she? Yes, Lilly's eyes met mine, but Hector grabbed her chin, turning her attention back to their group. Rejection completed in full!

As the bus lurched forward, bequeathing faint laughter in its wake, the slanting rain pelted my head. My mud soaked wellies turned each trudging step into a marathon's worth of energy expended, and by the time I reached our cottage, I was soaked through. I didn't want to talk, dry off, or even eat a snack. The first and only thing I could wrap my mind around was going straight to my bed. Surely after a nap, a talk with Da would provide a solution.

Lacing my dripping coat over a wall peg, I headed towards my room, through the parlour, when panic ripped the weariness from my being. Mum was lying face down on the floor!

"Mum! Mum!" I dropped to her side, trying to wake her.

It took every ounce of strength to turn her over and the jolt made her gasp for air. Her breathing was sporadic, and putting a pillow under her head, I dialled for help. A man spoke distinctly, calming me while discerning Mum's condition and our location. He kept talking, but I had to let Da know, yet I couldn't leave Mum. I patted her hand, speaking gently until the ambulance arrived. Medics jumped into action, placing Mum on a stretcher, asking questions as they placed an oxygen mask on her face.

I kept asking, "Is she gonna be alright?"

The lights and sirens brought Da sprinting through the pelting rain from Tantallon, and in a flash, we were in the car, speeding behind them to hospital.

Mum was hooked by wires and tubes to machines— the kind of things you see on telly, when someone's really sick. The nurses were kind, but we were frightened, praying the Lord would let her live. Not knowing what was wrong, Da protested as they escorted us out of the emergency room so the medics could do whatever it was they were doing.

The ticking clock got louder and louder as we waited, and all kinds of medical staff rushed back and forth, so we prayed. We always prayed, and we knew God heard us, and when we were all prayed out, we sang. Da's deep, rich voice began, Amazing Grace...first softly, then a little louder. Joining in, folks in the waiting area turned to look at us, then one by one, they began singing too. It was our heartfelt prayer, lifted heavenward, and God heard each voice crying out from that huddled bunch of folk waiting on news of loved ones.

When the doc finally approached, he looked grim. "Mr. Ridley, your wife is weak, but stable."

"What happened?

"It appears," he explained, "she's suffered a seizure."

"A seizure?" Da repeated.

"Um, and a contusion near the temple, from her fall. In that respect, at least, she was lucky." Da exhaled a deep sigh as the doctor continued, "The trauma caused minor bleeding in the brain. So, at present, we're going to monitor her, then run further tests in the morning."

Da stammered, "Will she be alright?"

The doctor's face revealed more than he was saying, "She's well taken care of. We'll let you know more soon as we're able." Rubbing his big hands across his face, Da thanked the doc, then put a strong arm around me as we waited a little longer.

When they led us to Mum's room, Da rushed to her side, covering her hand in his. He whispered something, then brushed her hair back, revealing a hideous purple bruise. I'd never seen Da shake with fear till now.

"She may hear you, but don't expect a response." The doc explained, "We've got her on some pretty strong meds."

Da nodded his thanks, and the doctor hurried off to his next patient. Standing frozen, he waved me over, "It's okay, Will." Together, we pulled up chairs, close to the bed as possible, and talked to Mum, telling her how much we loved her.

Da whispered, "When they're not looking, we're gonna break out of here, run o'er to Tantallon, and pick buckets of daffodils!" But Mum lay still, quiet, eyes closed, machines beeping, so he kept talking.

Da was a strong man, but being unable to protect his precious girl left him undone. As he spoke to her, sometimes things I couldn't hear, tears flowed down his cheeks, and that frightened me. I sat close, holding his hand, listening to the humming machines, and praying for God to make Mum better.

It was midnight when a nurse offered us an empty room beside Mum's, away from the bustle of the bright hallways. She calmed Da's objections, "You'll be more help to her if you're rested. Don't worry, I'll wake you if needed."

After tucking me into the tightly made bed, Da kissed my forehead and whispered, "Try to sleep, son."

"You too, Da!" As he forced a smile, I asked, "Is Mum gonna be okay?"

He sighed, "She's in good hands. The doctor said she's stable and the Lord is good, so not to worry. Hm?"

"Aye," I nodded, trying to encourage him. "I love you, Da!"

"Love you too, Will," came his tired reply.

The light seeping under the door haloed Da as he sat down, head bowed in prayer, when sleep finally washed over me like a tidal wave. In the valley of dreams, I wandered through a dark, murky place, and again, I was looking for Mum. I found her sitting in our cottage window seat. Though in shadow, she was well, and we spoke, but I couldn't make out what she was saying. Suddenly, to my right, a dark figure appeared, filling the doorway and bellowing about his god, Poseidon. His words frightened and confused me until a short, round woman with long, poker straight, pitch black hair caught my attention. Her head teetered side to side as her body wobbled towards us. Stopping in front of me, she lifted her head, revealing a horrifying sight. Twasn't a woman at all, but some wretched, dark spirit that spewed at me, "I hate your family, and I hate your God even more!"

Sitting bolt upright, I cried, "Jesus, save us!"

Immediately, the darkness vanished, and the brilliance of a brand-new day streamed in through half drawn curtains. Gathering my wits, I tumbled out of bed and raced next door, where my fears melted. Mum was sitting up, taking tea with Da, and I couldn't hold back the tears that spilt from my eyes. I was so thankful to see her awake, I called out in a raspy voice, "Mum!"

She reached out her hand, "Oh, William, my love!" Words failed me, so I ran and gave her the best hug possible across the bed rails. Smoothing my ruffled hair, she sighed, "You poor dears, you both look so tired!"

Our wee family clung to each other, tired yes, but the danger had passed, and we thanked the Lord for His goodness. He'd heard our prayers and answered as the monitors and machines, one by one, were taken away, and every test, one after the other, came back clear. The puzzled doctor warned us to continue monitoring Mum's condition, but with no other symptoms, they sent her home.

Sleepily, she smiled at Da. "What's this I hear about pinching daffodils?"

His girl was gonna be fine!

23

Ne'er an Explanation

Miss Norah rallied the troops, taking up kitchen duties, preparing meals, and keeping a close eye on Mum, who wisnae used to people fussing over her.

"Set that kettle down, AnnaLee!" Miss Norah declared.

Weakened, Mum needed no further coaxing, letting us take care of her for a change.

"These scones'll be ready in a jiffy!"

Papa G put his efforts into baking, and the house filled with well wishers, along with Keith, Huw, and Lilly and their folks, bearing flowers and plates of food.

"I felt fine...really." Mum explained, "One minute I was dusting, and the next, I woke in hospital."

Mrs. Alcott gasped, "That must've been terrifying!"

There were a thousand questions about Mum's seizure and all the doctor had to say, which with so little sleep seemed fuzzy. But Da answered, so as the ladies said, they could pray intelligently.

Maybe twas lack of sleep, but that irritated me. "It's not like God doesn't know what needs done!" Yet, their genuine concern guilted my irritable thoughts into silence. Truly, I was thankful for their prayers and comforted seeing Mum tucked neath a blanket, sipping a cuppa, and enjoying the company, though she did look tired. We all looked tired, and she flashed me a sleepy smile.

Keith, Huw, and Lilly, looking ill at ease, huddled in the window seat, where we'd planned so many adventures, and I sighed, dreading the thought of another row. I wasn't ready for it, not today, not with Mum being unwell.

Staying planted on Mum's blanket wrapped feet, she stroked my hair. Twas the safest I'd felt in a long time, until she gave me *the look*— the one that precedes her uncanny discernment of a situation before I've said a word.

"It's okay, Will; I'm not going anywhere. Sort things out with them, hum?" Though I hesitated, she gave a wink, then a wee nudge, and I was up, on my way.

I hated being separated from my friends, and the distance between us felt fathoms longer than the few steps it took to reach them. The timing was horrible, but somehow I had to mend this fracture, yet I had no idea what to say.

Keith spoke first, "Sit down, Will. You look horrible!"

Sliding in beside Lilly, I inhaled as Huw consoled, "Sorry your Mum got sick, Will."

"Thanks," my voice broke, "twas horrible!"

Lilly grabbed my hand. "Oh, William!"

Emptied of strength, I breathed, "But I am glad to see you all."

"Same here." Huw's brow furrowed.

"So, what happened, exactly?" While attempting to piece my thoughts together, Keith jabbed, "Or is that a secret too?"

Lilly slapped his arm. "Keith, that wasn't nice."

Staring at him, I began, "Friday had me gutted. When I got home, I was heading to bed for a long lie in. Instead, I found Mum, face-down on the floor!"

"How frightening!" Lilly said with concern.

Huw asked, "What'd you do?"

"I turned her over, called for help, Da and I followed the ambulance. There were lots of nurses and doctors, all kinds of machines, and questions. They ran dozens of tests, more than they told us about, I think, but the doctor couldn't find anything."

"Strange," Keith raised an eyebrow, "although not for your family, I suppose!"

Then Huw asked, "How'd she get that shiner?"

"Stargazing?" Keith smirked.

"Keith!" Lilly chided, "That looks like it hurts a lot!"

It was painful to see Mum's face so bruised. "She hit the table when she fell. The doctor said she's lucky it wasn't closer to her temple, though it caused bleeding in her brain. So, she needs a lot of rest the next few months."

Huw asked, "Will they do more testing?"

"Not now, but we're to keep her from doing anything strenuous."

"Well, that's not gonna work!" Keith frowned. "Who's gonna feed you?"

"Believe it or not, Keith, Da's a pretty good cook, and between him and Miss Norah, Mum's not getting off that settee, not for the next few weeks anyway."

Looking in our direction, Mum pursed her lips, overwhelmed that all this talk centred on her. I gave a small wave, and she returned a lovely, reassuring smile, the kind that makes everything seem better.

Satisfied, Keith offered, "Well, that's good news."

"Umm..." Catching our attention, Lilly asked softly, "So, how are you, Sleeping Beauty?"

Resting my chin in my hand, I replied, "Well, there's a question!"

She volleyed, "I haven't seen *that* look since the day you told me about Santa Claus." I rubbed my hands o'er my face till Lilly urged,

"Just spit it out; it can't be that bad!"

In my brain, I prayed for the right words— how to tell my friends without losing them or making things worse. But first, I swore them to secrecy, "I mean it. You have to swear you won't say anything to anybody, ever, ever, ever, and I really mean, ever!"

"Okay!" Huw laughed, "We get the picture, Will. What?"

"I'm serious! You cannae speak a word of this to anyone! And no fingers crossed either, Keith!"

"So there *is* a secret!" He leaned closer. "Well, this better be good!"

With nods of agreement, I rubbed my temples, then folded my hands. "First, I want to apologize. You're my friends, and I'm sorry I didn't trust to tell you. And Keith, you're right, I am a horrible liar." I breathed, "It's just, what's happening is frightening, and I didn't want to scare anyone, especially not you, Lil." My friends looked concerned as I continued, "Not to mention, there's a ginormous chance you'll think I'm daft, but this is it."

From the very start to what happened at the hospital, I described the attacks. The lads stared mesmerised, while Lilly's face paled.

"But, at the name of Jesus, they have to leave. So even though demons can be terrifying and keep you from sleeping, you don't have to fear." I emphasised, "Jesus will protect us!"

"Really?" Keith grimaced, "That's it?"

"Aye...I mean, I had to look up pestilence, which means a fatal disease, cause that's what Satan is, a fatal infection of lies and despair."

"Em..." Keith smirked, "Can I just say, you're incredibly weird! The strangest things happen to you, and there's ne'er an explanation."

Huw scoffed, slapping my shoulder. "Ye think?"

"So, alright." Keith prompted, "We forgive you for not saying any-thing. Right?" With nods of approval, he added, "If that was my story, I wouldn't have said anything either. Takes courage to admit being off your nut!"

"Keith!" Lilly defended, "He's not kidding!"

"I didn't say he was. It's just...not something ye hear every day."

"No, it's not." Lilly emphasised, "But I know William's telling the truth!"

"And how would you know..." Huw teased, "Shield Maiden?"

Leaning in closer, she whispered, "Because I've seen one too!"

24

Rebuke & Reunite

Gasping as though we'd been punched, Lilly spared not a single detail. "Last night, I couldn't sleep…"

"Uff!" Keith huffed, "Another insomniac!"

Shooting him an irritated glance, Lilly said, "I was worried about Will, and since he's always talking to God, I thought I'd give it a try."

"Oh, Lil!" I gushed, "That's braw!"

She smiled, "Da has a Bible."

"How on earth did that happen?" Keith quipped.

"It belonged to Eddie! Okay?" She softened, "He left it to Da."

"Oh!" The snark went out of his voice, "Sorry."

"Anyway, I flipped through it, till I came to something called P-salms."

Huw snorted at her pronunciation.

"What?" She demanded.

"Nothing." Huw shook his head.

She sighed, "The words were soothing, and I read at least a dozen pages, though I didn't understand it all. I figured God knew what you needed, and it must have helped, because I felt better. But right before I fell asleep, it felt like someone was watching me!"

"That's creepy," Huw inserted, "but still, nothing like William's *incidents*!"

"Mr. Oh-so impatient," Lilly chided, "that's because I wasn't finished!"

Huw looked away, but Lilly stared until he acknowledged, "My apologies. Please, go on."

"Early this morning, it sounded like the front door opened. Our kitty usually paws the latch to go out, so I didn't think much of it, but then I heard footsteps. Someone *was* in the house, and they were coming up the stairs!"

"Och," Keith groaned, "that would give a fright well enough."

Huw asked, "Did ya get your sword and shield?"

"No, I just sat up, wondering who was there."

Keith prompted, "And?"

"Everything began to look wavy, like opening your eyes underwater." We hung on her words, "Even stranger, what walked into my room looked like..." She let out a tiny breath, "Hector..."

Keith reeled back, snickering, "Hector?"

"Yeah! I couldn't figure out how he'd gotten in, unless Da left the door unlocked."

"Told you he's trouble!" Huw huffed, "Did your Da knock his teeth out?"

"No." She shook her head. "What I'm trying to tell you is, it wasn't Hector."

Huw blurted, "What?"

"Well," Keith demanded, "if it wisnae Hector, who was it?"

"It walked like him, moved like him, wore his uniform, you know how it's too short and he's always pulling at the sleeves?" We nodded, as she continued, "It was doing that...even had dark wavy hair, but covering its face."

Keith asked, "Then what?"

She looked frightened. "It sat beside me."

Huw exhaled, "No!"

"Took my hand, and when it looked at me..."

"What?" Keith blurted, "What'd it look like?"

Lilly shrunk back, "Terrifying! Worse than the scariest movie I've ever seen. There was a horrible stink that burnt the inside of my nose, and I could barely breathe. I thought I was going to die!"

She began sobbing when Keith made a tsk-ing sound, drawing out her name, "Lilly! One bus ride, a cosy wee chat, and you've got a thing for Hector!"

"Keith! Are you crazy? I screamed so loud it woke Mum and Da! Go ask them. I was so frightened I..." Her voice broke, "I couldn't stop crying!"

Keith rolled his eyes, "I'm not sure what you're eating before you go to bed, but I don't want any of it!"

"That's cruel, Keith! Can't you see how upset she is?" His disbelief arched with his brow, but Lilly calmed as I took her hand. "I'm so sorry, Lil. I know how frightening they are."

"Oh come on! You just had a bad dream."

"Absolutely not!" she shot back. "I know what I saw, Keith Cromyn, and it would have frightened even you!"

He avoided our eyes as I asked her, "You okay?"

Lilly nodded, while Huw patted her arm.

I stared at Keith. "Are you wishing you hadn't asked now?"

"No. You know I'd nae have rested till I knew everything. But demons?" He shook his head. "Seriously! Great acting everyone, but the joke's over."

"Keith!" I threw up my hands. "I know it's hard to believe, and if I hadn't seen them myself, I'd be sceptical too, but there's stuff out there that's bigger than us, and it's not all in your forensic books."

"I suppose you're gonna tell me this is Bible stuff, part of your *defender* status."

"Actually, there's a lot about this in the Bible. It says we're not wrestling with flesh and blood, but instead, against the spiritual forces of evil in heavenly places. Charles Spurgeon, one of the best preachers in the world, wrote an entire book on spiritual warfare. I cannae explain it, but when you start telling people about Jesus, it's like...stepping into battle."

Huw and Lilly sighed as Keith sat back, pressing his fingers together, "I'm sorry, Will. I deal in facts, things you can examine, ye know, hold in your hands. This is beyond what a lad like me can comprehend."

I lifted the cross from under my shirt, "What about this? Is this a lie?"

"No." He stammered, "That cross came from somewhere, and Lilly obviously saw something too; it's just, your stories keep getting more..." He clucked, "complicated."

"Yeah, tell me about it!" Releasing a heavy sigh, I said, "You've known me a long time, Keith. Look me in the eyes and ask yourself, am I lying?"

In a matter of moments, Keith had his answer, "No Will. I don't know how, but you're not lying...I'd be able to tell. I've just never seen anything like that...*and* hope to God I never do!"

"Me too! Seriously, I wouldn't wish this on anybody."

Huw added, "But there must be a reason."

Lilly's voice quavered, "For William, aye, but why me? I'm not all churchy like he is!"

"Churchy?" That was the second time she'd called me that.

"You know, talking to people about God, repeating Bible verses." She gasped, "Maybe it showed up because I read from the Bible!"

Keith nodded. "Interesting observation, Lil."

"Yeah." Huw added, "Like opening Pandora's box."

"No!" I protested, "It's nothing like that. You said yourself, Lil, reading Psalms was comforting, remember? Someone's bothered you turned to God's Word for help."

"I hadn't thought about that." She quieted, "But why did it look like Hector? Was God warning me?"

"With his behaviour?" Huw quipped, "I wouldn't think ye'd need a warning."

Keith grinned so wide, he snorted, "Lilly and Hector sitting in a tree..."

Fighting back tears, she stuck a finger in his face. "Keith Cromyn, that is not funny! Did you not hear what we just said?"

"I'm sorry, Lil. It's just, comedy helps when I'm, well, scared." Keith cleared his throat. "Hearing you describe that thing coming up the stairs made the hair on my neck stand straight up!"

"You?" She raised her eyebrows. "Oh digger of bones, student of body parts and heinous crimes, scared?"

"I'm not totally flawless!" Her tiny laugh lightened our spirits. "Besides," Keith added, "it's not the dead ye need to worry about!"

Looking at my friends, I offered, "I think we should pray."

"Really?" Keith asked. "Isn't that what started all this?"

"No!" Huw took Lilly's hand, then mine. "Praying is good! But you start Will."

Closing our eyes, I exhaled, "Lord, it's me, William, and my best friends, Huw, Keith, and Lilly... We were sad to be apart, so first, thank You for bringing us back together."

Everyone 'Um-hummed' as I continued, "And thank you for protecting us from the demons. They are frightening, so please keep them away, unless there's some purpose in it."

Lilly tapped my leg under the table, but I kept my head bowed. "But, God, if you do let them come back, send them to me, not Lilly."

She squeezed my hand and opening an eye, we shared a smile. Then I prayed, "Thank you, Jesus, for loving us, and thank you so much for bringing Mum home!" Everyone um-hummed again, "Please help her get well and look after our families. Heal their hurts and help us find our strength in you." Taking another deep breath, I added, "And God, please help Hector and his da too."

My friends pulled back at his name, but I continued, "Keep us safe, be our shield and defender and make us bold in the face of our enemies. We love you Jesus and ask this in your powerful name."

Then Lilly added, "And please help William get some sleep!"

And we all said, "Amen!"

Our wee foursome had survived this battle, and prayer provided the calm reassurance we needed, along with the pleasure of being reunited.

Meanwhile, Mr. Alcott had questions. "Magnus, I don't like to waste anyone's time, especially when your Mrs. is unwell, but we," he appeared uncomfortable, "we need your advice."

"Sure Gerald." Da responded, "How can I help?"

"This morning, Lilly woke, screaming bloody murder. Horrible dream."

"No, Da." She corrected, "I told ye, twas real!"

"Okay." He soothed, "Just tell Mr. Ridley what happened."

As Lilly explained, Rose added, "Magnus, we don't believe in ghosts, but something *was* in her room!"

"And by God, if it was Hector Menteith," Gerald spouted, "I'm going to thrash him!"

"Twas nae the lad Gerald." Rose touched his hand. "We know that."

"Ye alright, lass?"

Lilly nodded. "I'll be fine, Mr. Ridley, but I don't ever want to see that thing again."

"Of that, I'm certain. But I must ask, are ye..." Da paused, "is Hector bothering ye?"

"No sir. Twasn't him. It was..." She was resolute, "Evil!"

Gerald noted, "We all smelt sulphur."

Rose confirmed, "Aye, very strange."

"I don't mean to frighten you, but it's possible Lilly encountered a demon." With a snort, Gerald and Rose stared open mouthed as Da clarified, "Tis rare, but they are capable of appearing as someone we know. Some might call them ghosts, but they're demons."

Gerald scowled, "So, what does that mean?"

"When God is working in our lives, it's not unusual to experience opposition from the enemy."

Rose asked, "Then, as a pastor, might you ask God to help us?"

"Aye. I'll pray with ye, Rose, but for the record, your prayers are as worthy of God's ears as mine. There's no middleman with Jesus."

"But in that movie," she insisted, "they called a priest."

"Och, Hollywood!" Da baulked, "They make a right mess of things!"

"How so?" Gerald was genuinely interested.

"Jesus alone is our defender, not some man-made rituals or incantations. And sure, a pastor ought to know his Bible, but he's no more holy nor qualified to ask God's help than any other soul crying out in need."

"So, even," Gerald paused, "the lowest of the low can ask God for help?"

"As you see!" Da raised his hand, " 'Amazing Grace' saved even a wretch like me." Gerald's jaw dropped as Da confirmed, "The Lord sees only two types of people, those that love and serve Him, and those that don't. There's common mercy for all, but faith is God's gift, and if it's His will, He grants it, in His time."

A smile crossed Gerald's face. "Ye sound like an old friend of mine."

"Eddie." Rose whispered.

"Aye," he nodded, then sighed, "So what do we do?"

Da offered, "The only way to battle Satan..."

"Satan!" Rose repeated.

"Aye!" Da confirmed, "He's real enough, and the only way to fight him is with faith in God's Word and prayer!"

"Like reciting the 23rd psalm?" Gerald asked.

"Praying through the Psalms is great when we cannae find our own words, but reciting them as though they've some magical power is useless." Da explained, "All God asks is an honest cry from our hearts. That's more precious to Him than a thousand songs or cathedrals built in His honour. And should a demon be so bold as to show up, rebuke it in the name of Jesus."

"Rebuke?" asked Lilly.

"Say, 'In Jesus' name be gone!' The Lord's name is power, and all evil must flee at the mention of His name."

Lilly breathed, "Wish I'd known that this morning, Mr. Ridley!"

A sense of peace enveloped the Alcotts as they prayed with Da for the Lord's guidance and protection. Midway through, Gerald and Lilly each opened an eye, sharing a smile. Things seemed better already.

It would be a long month before Mum was able to get around on her own so, Miss Norah helped us, preparing ice packs for Mum's bruise, keeping her company, and filling our home with tasty meals and joyful conversations.

In the evenings, Da rubbed sweet scented ointment on Mum's temples to help her sleep, and knowing my struggles, did the same for me. Then lifting prayers of thanks and praise, we slept peacefully in God's glorious, healing presence.

Whether it was the fragrance, God's grace, Mum and Da nearby, sheer exhaustion, or a combination, I began sleeping entire nights through without interference. Plus, seeing Mum grow stronger, more like herself, was a great comfort. She played the piano again, and her voice, though weak, filled our home with songs and renewed hope.

With Mum out of danger, life resumed some of its natural pace, but unfortunately, so did my sleeplessness. It crept in as a niggling restlessness, rising to a new level of anxiety, and before long, despite much prayer, the demonic attacks resumed.

"Ugh!"

One great relief was Lilly had been spared any repeat visits. And my friends were no longer cross with me, faithfully keeping my secret, yet eager to hear every detail of the attacks that went on and on and on for the better part of a year. We made a pact to pray for each other nightly, which must have held sway in the heavenlies, for a funny thing happened— the shock value wore off!

Tis been a long time since they darkened my room, but I remember the last visit with utmost clarity. Sleep deprivation had brought me to a breaking point. Fear was replaced by exasperation as I sensed the approach of yet one more foul demonic being. Barely opening an eye, I sighed, "Oh, for Pete's sake! In Jesus' name, be gone!"

Peace! In the quiet of the wee hours, I rolled over and plumped my pillow, then visualised something so comical, I laughed out loud. I could almost see this demoralised gremlin, skulking away, tail between its legs, muttering, *"He wasn't even afraid of me!"*

A satisfied grin crossed my face as I whispered into the darkness, "Jesus always triumphs!"

For reasons I may never know, the enemy had taken an interest in taunting me. Why did God allow this? Maybe as preparation for what lay ahead, but frightening as it was, Jesus let me experience His power firsthand, seeing evil flee at the mention of His name!

He was teaching me to be fearless in the face of dragons and to trust Him as my ever-present refuge. Yet how much I still had to learn.

25

The Talk

8 September 1995 held great significance, for two specific reasons. First, a major theatrical release was about to inspire Scots the world o'er, and second, twas my 16th birthday! Despite anticipation the size of Bass Rock, one thing kept me from bolting out of bed long before the sun lit the morning sky: the sound of my parents' voices. I lay content, listening to their hushed conversation, realising that no matter what this day held, I already had the best birthday gift ever, their love.

They addressed difficult issues, teaching me not just with words but by their actions. I learnt the value of a hard day's work alongside Da, who challenged my mind and nurtured my faith, living by God's word. So, after breakfast, before any festivities, we walked down beside the Firth to have *The Talk!* You know...about the birds and bees. Some parents wait till their children ask or avoid it entirely, but Da knew the importance of tackling this delicate subject.

Gazing out to sea, he folded his hands, then took a deep breath. "How much do you know about... anatomy?"

"Hmmm... We dissected frogs," I answered, "to see how muscles and tendons work."

"Uh, "Da cleared his throat, "I was thinking more along the lines of *human* anatomy."

"Oh! Em," I struggled. "The basics, I guess?"

With care and respect, Da explained that, well, *you know what*, was designed for a husband and wife to enjoy without shame, to bless them with children, and as an expression of their love for God and each other.

"When a man and a woman become one flesh, it's not merely physical, it binds them spiritually. So, despite what you may've heard, this exquisite gift should be saved for your bride alone. That way, there's never more than the two of you in your marriage bed."

"Oh!" I gulped, face flushing crimson as boisterous gulls swooping overhead seemed to be laughing at my embarrassment!

Da comforted, "You'll see someday. And when you become a husband, your role will be to lead, provide for, and protect your wife and family. They come before work or ministry."

"That's a hard balance, Da, even for you!"

"As you well know. The world's filled with broken, needy people, but ye only get one family. If neglected, ye'll have only yourself to blame when it falls apart. No glory for God in that." Da flashed an impish smile. "Yet, a wife who is cherished, feels safe and valued, and cannae help lavishing that love back on her family."

"Like Mum!"

"Aye."

"How do you do it?"

"Grace!" He chuckled, "Ne'er keep secrets. Listen, and look in her eyes when you talk, that builds a close, lasting friendship. Choose your bride wisely, and she'll make you laugh...a lot!" Sharing knowing grins, Da continued, "Mind you're a bit young to be looking for a wife, but a good one, as God says, is one who talks back."

"Hm?"

"I mean that in the best sense. Women have what's called intuition and usually listen closer for God's voice than men, so a wise man considers his wife's input." Studying my reaction, he asked, "What?"

"I couldn't help thinking of Lilly, standing in the Great Hall, waiting for God to speak to her."

"Lilly Alcott, eh?"

"Yeah, Da!" As he raised an eyebrow, I stammered, "I mean, no, not like that, but what you said... reminded me of her."

"I see!" He cleared his throat again. "Now, if you're blessed with children."

"Children!"

"Aye, as we were when you arrived." Da patted my shoulder, "There's no job more important than rearing yer bairns!"

"You really think so, Da?"

"Aye. Some folk traipse around the world, hoping to leave their mark, prove they've accomplished something. But how many, on their last day, would trade all their accolades to be surrounded by a loving family?"

"All of them, I imagine." I added, "If they're being honest."

Da nodded. "Well-loved bairns are the most precious legacy a man can leave behind!"

With a sigh, we gazed out to sea, and the sun bearing down had me aching for a northerly breeze. "Sure is warm today!"

"Tis." He paused. "Now...that's God's way of doing things, but the world's filled with diversions. Every man has a weakness, and be assured, you'll be tempted in yours, but a real man, with God's help, does what's right no matter the cost. After all..." Meeting Da's gaze, I felt an unexpected twinge of guilt: "If sin wasn't pleasurable, it wouldn't be so easy to talk ourselves into, would it?"

Wide eyed, my head twisted side to side, "No!"

"Something wrong?"

I exhaled, "Earlier this week, Hector asked me to join him and his mates. It'd been such a long time since we'd spoken, he caught me off guard."

"Oh? What happened?"

"One of the lads had a magazine..." Da grew concerned as I went on. "I told them it wasn't right; they shouldn't be looking at girls like that, and the Bible says we shouldn't awaken love before its time."

Da stifled a chuckle. "Wisdom yes, but not well received, I imagine."

"Och!" I cringed, remembering, "They called me a Jesus Freak, said love had nothing to do with it."

"Well, they're kind of right... on both counts."

I let out a huge sigh, "Da!"

"What?"

"There's more, but...I don't know how to tell you."

He looked puzzled. "You can tell me anything, Will."

"I know, but," picking my words carefully, I whispered, "One of them shouted I didn't want to look because... because I liked Huw instead."

"Och!" Da snorted, "Nonsense."

"Hector started laughing. Then his mates joined in and everyone was staring, and I didn't want to tell ye Da, because I..." Heaving a sigh, I confessed, "I'm sorry; I wanted to prove them wrong, so I looked!"

Da looked stunned, like he hadn't heard correctly, "What?"

"Twas only a moment!" I defended, "I mean, for once, just once, I wanted to fit in, but it only made me feel worse. I threw it back, then they laughed even harder!"

Da rubbed his chin, thinking. Then instead of the reproof I expected, he offered the blessing of wisdom, "See how easy it is? One split second decision created the shame I see all over your face."

I couldn't look at him, but Da lifted my chin, waiting for me to meet his gaze. "An unwise choice, eh?" I nodded as he continued, "But I understand."

"But…" I grieved, "I'm supposed to be a defender of the faith. How can God use me now?"

"By asking His pardon and remembering the wisdom you're learning from it now." The awful heaviness I'd been hiding lifted as Da reminded, "God has done mighty things through extremely flawed people. Even Moses and David sinned, but God didn't cast them away. He loved them through their shame and continued to mould their character. That's what redemption is all about!" Our eyes locked as he spoke, "He's chosen you, Will, to be His instrument. That's a heavy responsibility for anyone. God knows that, and He'll ne'er leave you nor stop loving you. And neither will I, nor your mum."

If not for our talk, I'd still be thrashing myself for my stupid mistake, bereft of this sweet, overwhelming flood of peace. All I could do was breathe, until another fear arose. "Please don't tell Mum. I couldn't bear it if she knew."

"We love you, Will!" Da comforted, "And there's nothing you cannae share with either of us, but I'll nae tell her. The Lord knows you're sorry, and that's all He asks of anyone."

If there were words to express how thankful I was, I couldn't find them, not only for Da's confidence but for the precious bond between father and son.

"Now, I know ye want to help Hector," Da added, "but ye must be careful. He's not been in a good place for some time. Nor are those lads he goes about with."

"I know Da, I know…"

"Believe me, godly character takes a lifetime to establish, yet only a moment to destroy. Don't think for one second the enemy wouldn't like to take you out of the game! Look how many times he's tried already." Da sighed, "You're young, William, but ye must be wise.

This battle's not for the faint of heart!"

Da's weighty words illuminated how differently I thought and believed than those lads. "You're right Da. After everything went sideways, I said if they felt half the shame I did, they'd repent, but it's like they're blind. They devour with their eyes yet, don't see the damage it does to their soul!"

"Unless God opens their eyes," Da stressed, "they cannae see!" Softening, he reflected, "I know you made a mistake, Will, but I'm glad you told me."

"That's probably the hardest thing I've ever had to do, but thank you, Da, for grace. It won't happen again!" As he patted my shoulder, I confided, "People think I'm strange. They still tease me about the demon and my cross."

"I'm sorry, son, but trust me, I do understand!" Da smiled, "People think I'm strange too, and nothing near as interesting has happened to me!"

A hearty laugh was most welcome, then Da said, "Folk'll always have opinions and rude things to say, but they're not your judge. God is. And if yer brave enough to walk His path, you'll live well, without shame or regret. And even if the entire world forsakes you, Jesus never will."

I nodded, inhaling the fresh sea air. "Da?"

"Aye?"

"Thank you for teaching me, not just with words. You're a good father and, from what I see, an excellent husband!"

He smiled like a toothpaste advert, "I thought this was the talk where I'm to encourage you, my wean!" The noisy gulls laughed o'er head, then he cloaked his words in a tone saved especially for weighty sermon points: "You're growing into a fine, godly young man, William, and I hope ye'll always know how proud I am to call you my son!"

We sat for a long time, listening to the water lap the shore, feeling the breeze and sun shining warm upon our heads. Then, beneath the shadow of Tantallon's walls, a lone tern broke the serenity, splashing into the chilly water after a fish. Da glanced in its direction. "Any questions?"

Over the years, I'd have many, but right now, I wanted very much to know, "How do you know when you've met *the girl*?"

"That, my son," he chuckled, "tis a matter of patience and prayer."

"Aye! The two Ps! The very words Mum and Papa G used the first time God spoke to me at Tantallon."

"Excellent advice..." Da smiled, "especially when it comes to women! If yer patient, being the kind of man a young lady can respect, the Lord will bring her across yer path. And believe me, ye'll know!"

26

Braveheart Birthday

Drew and Abi's wedding had filled our home with joy, and what a happy time it was, but a wife? For me? The thought ne'er crossed my mind, especially when life at home was so comfortable. Twas hard to imagine things would ever change, but they do.

In lieu of adventures at Tantallon, I found myself daydreaming about Lilly, her smile, dancing at the Ceilidh, laughing as the wind wrapped her billowy sleeves around her head, topped by the cheeky look she shot us lads before tossing our message into the Firth. Those memories were precious, yet despite Huw and Keith's teasing, she'd ne'er thought of me as more than her friend. But there she was in my thoughts again, reddish-gold hair sparkling in the sun, deep blue eyes laughing as she envisioned the colourful, arid vastness of the Grand Canyon, or surfing atop the mighty, untamed Pacific waves. Happy thoughts!

But presently, we Tantallon Four simply enjoy each other's company, although sword play has been replaced by verbal jousting about the world around us. Keith continues to investigate every punctilious detail of unsolved crimes and Parliament, causing Lilly to yawn with disinterest, unless the skullduggery happened to be in some exotic location. Huw, ever enchanted with wild grimalkins, delights in tales from the far reaches of Africa, providing a diversity of topics, all well worth a listen. And while my friends' interests carry them far away, my heart, first and foremost, belongs to Scotland, her people, her history, and her future. So, for today's big celebration, Mum and Da arranged an outing to Stirling.

Huw chimed with excitement. "Mr. Gibson couldn't have bestowed a more appropriate birthday gift on anyone, Will!"

"Aye! If I ever see him, I'll have to thank him!"

Mr. Ramsay had shared heroic tales of Willelmus Wallensis who gave his lifeblood for Scotland's freedom. So, standing in the massive queue, we awaited *Braveheart* with great anticipation.

From the stunning Highlands opening, accented by stirring narrative and music, to the epic Claymore slicing through the sky, announcing Scotland's triumph, souls were aflame with patriotism. Coveted over centuries, our beloved Alba was dearly won at the edge of a sword, and despite Hollywood taking liberties with our hero's story, the message was clear. True Scots belong heart and soul to this wild and mysterious land.

During the torture and beheading scene, nearly every lass in the cinema began to weep, so Da pulled Mum close, and Huw and I took Lilly's hands in ours.

"It's okay, Lil," Huw whispered, "tis only a movie!"

"But Huw," she whispered in a croaky voice, "this story's true! And men who stand for what's right get hurt!" Squeezing my hand hard, Lilly rested her head on my shoulder, and those lovely blue eyes wept hot tears, drenching my shirt. How I yearned to pull her close and let her know, if it were in my power, she would have her happy ending.

Outside the cinema, blue skies drenched us in sunlight, and I tilted my head up, drinking in the air, "Pure Alba!"

With a shove, Keith joked, "Acting the part of Wallace, my liege?"

"*This*," I declared, "is the very same fragrance Wallace delighted in, upon returning from abroad!"

Huw clucked, "Which you would recognise from extensive world travel, I suppose?"

"Not exactly," I chirped. "But breathe! This earthy scent, full of peat, gorse, heather...this, my friends, is the fragrance of home!"

"Combined with beautiful landscapes," Lilly humoured, "no wonder Wallace and his compatriots fought so valiantly! And now that you mention it, the air does smell lovely!"

"I think not Will!" Stepping inside the chippy, Huw waved the air towards his face, "Rather, this is the fragrance of Scotland!"

"Fish and chips?" queried Keith.

"Oh, aye!" Huw resounded.

"But Huw!" Mum chirped, "Ye've neglected a steaming haggis."

"Speaking of steaming," Da smirked, "don't forget the invigorating scent of Highland Coos!"

"Oh, Aye, Mr. Ridley." Lilly returned his grin, "Nothing like the scent of freshly pooed fields!"

"Och, you two!" Huw spouted, "That's gross!"

Lilly smiled, nodding up and down as Da chuckled, "All right! On that note, let's get something to eat!"

Over our meal, we discussed each scene, weeding out historical faux pas, yet astonished at the sheer impact the story, music, and scenery'd had on our hearts. Since Mum and Lilly covered their eyes, Huw and Keith filled in the goriest details of the battle scenes, while I noted the Battle of Stirling Bridge was conspicuously lacking a bridge.

"Ye know..." Keith chimed, "the king's treasurer died in that battle. So hated, by *both* sides he was; they flayed his corpse, and Scots and Sassenachs alike took pieces of his hide as souvenirs!"

"EEEEwwww!" Simultaneously, Lilly and Mum squealed, "That's disgusting!"

Enjoying the reaction, he added, "And get this, Wallace used what was left to make a sheath for his sword!"

"Och, lads!" Da exclaimed, "Some things are best left till after lunch. Although ye cannae deny Wallace used brilliant tactics to best a superior military force."

Lilly gushed, "Ye think he had blue eyes like Mel Gibson?"

Huw and Keith groaned, but I suggested, "That's a question for Blind Harry."

"What?" Keith quipped, "Wait! How would he know?"

"Harry didn't have to see," I answered, "to know things."

While he shook his head, Mum chirped, "Isabella's gowns were beautiful!"

"But," Da took Mum's hand, "yer still the loveliest princess I've e'er seen!"

"Aww! That's so sweet, Mr. Ridley!" Lilly smiled as Mum and Da glanced at each other, then asked, "So, what happened to the baby?"

"What baby?" Keith asked.

"This baby!" Huw punched my arm, "He grew up and we're celebrating his birthday!"

Lilly rolled her eyes. "No, the baby the princess had with Wallace!"

"Oh," I countered, "Hollywood was doing what Hollywood does best."

"What do ye mean?"

"Creating a romance between Isabella and Wallace made for a good plot twist, but it ne'er happened."

Lilly seemed gutted. "How can ye be sure?"

"Do the math." Keith interjected, "Princess Isabella was born in 1295. She'd have been ten when Wallace was executed in 1305."

"Oh!" She muttered, "Well, that's disappointing!"

With heads full of Wallace, castle sieges, hidden crown jewels and the pilfered Stone of Destiny, we ventured into Stirling Castle. Overlooking the enormous dining hall, we sat in meticulously carved armchairs, acting the part of lairds and a lady.

From her ancient throne, Lilly decreed, "In celebration of Ridley the Younger's 16th year, we shall dance the *Dashing White Sergeant*." Grabbing my surprised self by the arm, we wafted to the centre of the hall, where we lads imitated her grand sweeping motions, then joined hands, circling left, then right.

Lilly giggled, "You've been practicing!"

Keith counted rhythm as we danced beneath the immense timber canopy, arched o'er walls boasting heraldic tapestries and massive embroidered curtains, drawn back, so sunshine spilt in through stained glass windows. Filling the hall with laughter and a few mis-steps, our merriment halted abruptly when a woman bellowed, "Off with his head!"

Folks milling about the room giggled, but I couldn't help imagining the poor souls who heard that for real... a fleeting thought until Keith ushered us out onto the sunny courtyard.

Our happy chatter reverberated o'er the ancient battlements as we linked arms and trod down the cobbled entrance path. Then one by one, we exited through an ancient wooden portal, greeted on the far side of the castle walls by a red-bearded piper in sark and Breacan an Fheilidh.

Looking every bit the part of a *Braveheart* extra, he entertained the crowd with lively tunes, and the cloth spread at his feet beckoned them to bestow their gratitude in coins, or something more. After a happy reel, applause quieted, and the piper nodded in our direction. Re-filling the bag, the drones bellowed a deep rumbling tone, then a low mournful tune spilt from the chanter. This lone piper playing pibroch completely mesmerised.

After a few minutes, Huw tugged my sleeve, "Come on, Will," yet I couldn't draw myself away from the haunting sound.

"Seriously Ridley!" Keith moaned, "Don't you ever get tired of this stuff?"

"Shh," I hushed, trying not to miss a note.

"Let him be Keith," Lilly chided, "tis his birthday."

It'd been an amazing day, inhaling volumes of Scottish history, but still, I wanted to stay immersed in that sound. It was braw, ancient, and stirred my soul, like the legacy of The Bruce and Wallace!

While I lingered, a man approached, then stood beside me. He glanced over several times, so I acknowledged with a nod when he remarked, "Folk say a piper went missing in the tunnels neath Edinburgh."

"Aye," I whispered, "in the 1700s."

He persisted, "Sometimes they say you can still hear him piping."

"Um." I replied and closed my eyes, not wanting to miss any more of the tune.

Placing a hand on my shoulder, he interrupted again, "Eerie! This tune reminds me of the day he went missing!"

Shooting him a startled look, he flashed a disturbing grin as I removed his hand, "Thanks, thanks for that."

With impeccable timing, Lilly grabbed my arm, "Come on birthday boy, we've to get you home!"

A glorious sunset bathed Tantallon and our jolly party in soft rosy light, then Mum handed me a long glass and pointed towards the Bass. Mr. Ramsay, Andy, Drew, and Abi were waving alongside the biggest birthday card I'd ever seen!

Flapping in the sea breeze, their banner read, '*Co-là-breith math Uilleam!*'

Waving back, I thanked the Lord for my dear friends and this wonderful day. Then, like the finale in a fireworks display, Da handed me one last surprise, a Claidheamh Mor!

"Where did you find this?" I asked with wonder.

"Twas yer mum's doing."

"But yer Da's idea! An heirloom, linking Ridley past, present, and future." Staring in awe at my folks, then at this exquisite sword, Mum added, "Every warrior needs a proper blade."

"Much sturdier than the one I carved for ye." Da noted.

The hilt, carved from animal horn, adorned with Celtic knots, protruded from a long leather scabbard. Unsheathing the blade, it sang a steely song into the wind.

"Careful William!" Mum warned, "It's sharp."

With ample distance between us, I raised the blade above my head, then swung it down and around in figure eights with ease. "This is brilliant! And a piece of our history!"

"May I have a look?"

"Aye, shield maiden!" I replied as Lilly and the lads stepped closer. Together, we examined the fine detail, "Look!" I discovered, "There's a cross on the hilt!"

Mum and Da smiled as Lilly ran her fingers o'er it, "Matches beautifully with yours!"

Keith questioned, "Do ye know where it was forged?"

"And who owned it?" I chimed, "I'd like to know everything about it!"

"And so, you shall!" Mum smiled, "But not on empty stomachs!"

Placing the blade in its sheath, I wrapped Mum and Da in a hug, then, Lilly, Huw, and Keith, wrapped arms around us too!

"Thank you!" Nearly weeping, I repeated, "Thank you all so much!"

As the sun disappeared beyond the horizon, we gathered for tea in the window seat, tinctured with lively conversation, closer examination of the sword, merry singing, and, of course, scrumptious homemade birthday cake.

Just before heading home, Lilly called me aside and whispered, "Happy Birthday, William, Defender of the Faith!" And sweetly, as she did at the Ceilidh, she tapped my cross, rose up on tiptoe, and kissed my cheek.

Immediately, Huw and Keith pointed, squealing, "William and Lilly sitting in a tree, K I S S I N G..."

Rolling her eyes and quick as a whip, she poked the lads in their tummies. They snorted with laughter, responding with clumsy curtsies to the left, to the right, then accidentally banged their heads together with a horrible thud.

Both Huw and Keith hit the carpet, holding their heads, rolling back and forth, so Lilly and I leaned over to help. In a flash, Huw grabbed Lilly's arm, then mine, and we all landed on the floor in a heap, laughing so hard, tears came squeezing out of our eye sockets! I could ne'er have imagined a more braw celebration!

27

❧

Beauties & Bullies

"What planneth the musketeers tomorrow?" Lilly enquired between classes.

"Studying," I mumbled while digging through my rucksack.

"What else would three handsome swashbucklers like us do on a weekend?" Keith donned a big cheesy grin.

Lilly curtsied, "Save me a window seat, d'Artagnan."

"One for all and all for..." Huw stopped short as Seth Parker pushed in-between us.

"William, ye dropped something!"

"What?"

He pointed, "Down there."

Directing my gaze towards 'said something,' Seth shoved me head-first into the wall and Lilly spun round, shouting, "What is wrong with you? Ye dangle-berry!" As he disappeared down the corridor, she sighed, "You okay?"

Holding a smarting wrist, I giggled, "Aye, long as ye ne'er call me a dangle-berry."

"We need to do something about him..." Huw grumbled, "*and* Hector!"

With a wry smile, Keith suggested, "Something inventive!"

"I know you'd ne'er start a fight, Will, but..." Lilly paused, "Just once, I'd love to see you shove those numpties back. See how they like it!"

"Ah, Lil, you know that ne'er solves anything."

"True, but if you stood up to them, maybe they'd quit!"

"Maybe," I said as we moved towards class, "but they've got pack mentality. They see something different, like our friendship, then pick it apart because they're angry or envious. Honestly," I looked in Seth's direction, "I feel sorry for them."

She wrinkled her forehead, "William Ridley! I've ne'er met anyone who thinks like you do."

"And yer not like to!" Huw and Keith both chimed.

Returning their silly grins, I said, "I'll take *that* as a compliment."

Despite Hector and Seth's ongoing jabs, we enjoyed studying together, yet more often laughing so hard we could barely breathe. The year seemed to fly past, then as exams drew near, we trembled under the pressure. While some of us passed by the skin of our teeth, the point was, we passed, marking the start of summer break. But unlike our previous summers at Tantallon, one of us would be missing. Lilly and her mum were off to Skye to visit her Granaidh.

"Och! Don't look so glum lads. I'll write!"

Huw groaned, "Bottled messages take a long time, Lil!"

"Aw, Huw. You look just like Eeyore when you sulk." He rolled his eyes as she teased, "Just keep an eye out for the postie...especially *you* Keith!"

Like Eeny, Meeny, and Miny, minus Moe, we stood side by side, waving as Lilly and her mum drove off, but not before whispering a promise that Da and I would take her to the Bass when she returned. Leaning out the window, she hollered, "I'll hold you to that Will Ridley!"

Eyeing me sheepishly, Keith and Huw offered up what seemed to be their favourite tune, "William and Lilly sitting in a tree..."

There was still plenty to keep a lad busy, tidying the grounds and welcoming guests at Tantallon, providing as much history as a body could stand, while Mum clad in historical gowns entertained with stories and songs. Despite her unexplained malady, she was again her steady, joyful self.

On clear, starry evenings, Da would point up over Tantallon and whisper, "God placed the North Star in the heavens, but He made yer mum to shine even brighter!" For she was his beloved, sparkling jewel. Again, I thought of Lilly.

Keith and Huw had taken posts at North Berwick Lumber Company, stocking, sweeping, clerking, and delivering parcels, all great for building muscles, and earning a few quid to spend on the latest cinema offering. Their appetite for any adventure Hollywood could splash across the screen had them blethering about exotic cars, high-speed chases, beautiful starlets, and surprising plot twists.

All that glitz fascinated Huw. "Can ye believe the outrageous wages they make for doing something so fab? What would a guy do with all that money?"

Keith stifled a laugh. "You'd get face lifts from smiling all the way to the bank! None of that stuff's real anyway."

"Oh, but it is Keith! Actors bring fascinating stories and characters to life...that inspires people." Huw thought a moment, "Hey, I could do that! Plus, if the film were set in Africa, I'd see real lions!"

"Okay Hollywood," Keith simpered, "you do that. I'll settle for making history of my own."

"Well, Keith," I said, "if you get busy solving an enormous crime, Huw can play you in a film about it."

"Och no!" He cringed, messing Huw's hair. "At least find someone handsome to play me!"

"Uh!" Huw's mouth stood agape. "Ye think you're more handsome than me, do ye?"

"Aye," Keith nodded. "I'm the dapper dude!" Raising his eyebrows, he grinned, "Don't ye think?"

Huw stuck a finger down his throat, and we burst into laughter, but our silliness halted when Elaine, our no nonsense postie, headed up the walk. Keith stared with puppy-dog eyes as she handed over a letter addressed to "The Princes of Tantallon Castle."

Normally up and down our drive faster than lightning, today Elaine stopped, studying our faces. "Princes, eh?"

"Aye Milady." Keith puffed out his chest then gave a courtly bow, "At yer service!"

"Hmm." She tilted her head. "And I always thought you were just a bunch of scruffy rascals."

"Och!" Huw protested, "What's that supposed tae mean?"

With a giggle and a wave o'er head, she hurried off as Keith sighed, "She noticed me!"

"Oh, aye Keith! She noticed." I slapped his shoulder. "Ye scruffy rascal!"

"Och no!" He countered, "I'm sure she meant you!"

"Well," I shook the letter, "at least someone thinks we're princes."

"Let me see!" Still brooding, Huw snatched the envelope covered in Lilly's fancy doodles, then sniffed the contents, "Ooooh, smelly paper. Lilly *likes* William!"

I protested, "It's addressed to all of us."

"So," Keith smirked, "what does she say then?"

Glancing sideways at Huw, I took the note, cleared my throat, and began to read.

"Dear William, Huw, and Keith, not that there's any particular order of preference, because you're all as dear to me as any brother could be. I only posted this to William because he's the organised one and will certainly gather you lads together to read this."

"William, more organised than me?" Keith huffed, "Rubbish!"

"Aw Keith," Huw rebounded, "ye know she said that to niggle ye. And she's not here, so ye cannae tease her back. Brilliant!"

Though nearly 300 miles away, Lilly was still capable of irritating our investigative friend. Attempting to hide a smile, I asked, "Shall we continue?"

"Aye," Keith resolved with a thump to the back of my head.

Shrugging off his wallop, I read aloud.

"I hope you're enjoying the summer at Tantallon. I'm missing the warm days by the water and our adventures, but you'll not feel sorry for me as I'm having a few adventures of my own. We lodged our first two nights with cousins in the wee village of Kilmahog, which for larks they call, 'Kill my hog already, will ya!' There may be a dark family secret to that, but I'm nae telling. There's a woollen mill, loads of sheep, mountain trails, and a sweet fragrance in the air William would love.

"Driving up Loch Alsh, we saw fabulous bens and deep blue lochs, plus we took a wee break at Eilean Donan Castle. She's tidier than Tantallon, but not nearly as much fun without you lads.

"It took most of the day to reach Gran's on the north side, but over the bridge, Mum and I were gobsmacked by Skye. She's a marvellous and mysterious lady with winding roads astride breath-taking sea sides and sweeping mountain ranges—the likes I've ne'er seen before. A photograph can't truly capture the beauty of The Old Man of Storr. Gran calls him a stony old grump, peering down at anyone with the audacity to drive past his realm!

"You should see the water here! It's even bluer than the Firth, and so peaceful as it washes over the stoney beach, smoothing and polishing the rocks in the constant back and forth of the waves. And Keith, there's a mysterious abandoned boat called *The Melody*. I'll investigate and write more soon.

"Love to you and your folks, now off to kill-my-hog...

"Lilly"

Her detailed artwork alongside those expressive words helped us envision the sights. And though we missed our friend, we were chuffed to hear she was enjoying herself.

After the reading of the letter, we headed to town, where the cinema offered a western but, more importantly, provided our growing frames with huge helpings of curry chips. Along High Street, we perused charity shops for hidden treasures, like a tweedy deer stalker for Keith and a vintage valise for Huw's journey to Africa.

Amid a row of vintage teapots, Keith pouted, "I'm afraid there's nothing in here for you!"

Then he and Huw began another chorus of 'William and Lilly sitting in a tree...'

"Will you two stop!" I protested, "It's not like that."

But my cheeks only burnt deeper crimson as they teased, "Oh give into it, Will! Any fool can see you're crazy for each other!"

Before I could reply, a herd of brightly attired tourists pushed past, nearly knocking us over.

Huw huffed, "Sasanachs!"

"Shh!" I shushed as the offenders, oblivious to their ill manners, hurried out the door in search of *a real souvenir shop.* Following, twas impossible to miss their debate, whether Wallace had e'er lodged at Tantallon.

"If they weren't so rude," Keith whispered, "they might be enjoying the extensive historical knowledge in that head of yours!"

"Hmm," I nodded, for on the heels of Wallace's screen debut, streams of folk were arriving from nearly everywhere, longing to discover a connection with our national hero. While the increase in traffic and scary driving irritated some locals, I found their enthusiasm for Scotland refreshing! Huw and Keith were equally enthusiastic, especially when they spied two lassies across the street, consulting an atlas.

"Make haste," Keith jabbed Huw, "oh knight in shining armour."

"What?" Huw stared, bewildered.

He pointed, "The damsels need directions!"

"Oh!" he replied.

Keith crossed with Huw close behind, but nearing the pavement, Hector, Seth, and another lad appeared, shoving them back into the street. "Not so fast, lads!"

"Hey!" Huw protested, "Who do you think you are?"

Seth stared him down. "You're about to find out!"

I hurried over, "Aw Huw, let it be."

Incredulously, he huffed, "Did ye see what he did, Will?"

"Aye." Putting a hand on his shoulder, I urged him in the opposite direction, "but not worth getting drawn into."

Seth called after us, "Aw, preacher boy's afraid!"

Something told me not to, but I turned back, "I'm not afraid."

Twas Huw now, urging me to turn away as Seth fumed, "Well, ye should be! No trinket's gonna save ye now!" Stepping closer, he balled his hand into a fist.

Instantly, Hector stepped between us, "I'll handle this!"

While Hector stared me down, Seth backed away.

"Why?" I asked.

Hector's face drew up in question, "Why, what?"

I whispered, "You've got it in you to be something so much better, Hector; why do you run with these lads?"

The third lad shouted, "What's he saying?"

"Nothing to worry you! Told ye, I'll handle this." As they moved off, Hector motioned with his chin, "Get lost, Ridley! For yer own good."

For a long moment, we stared at each other, till I offered, "Yer always welcome to join us."

"Not likely." He scoffed, "Ye know, sometimes...I almost feel sorry for ye, Will."

"For me? How's that?"

Letting go an exasperated sigh, he clucked, "Ye talk to God, pretend there's demons; come on, yer a bit of a nutter!" Rejoining his friends, he called over his shoulder, "And as always, two steps behind!"

As they headed towards the girls, Keith seemed puzzled. "Master Menteith kept Seth from throwing that punch, Will."

"Aye," I stared in their direction. "I believe he did."

"Will wonders never cease?" Huw breathed, "What were you talking about?"

"Erm... A bit of encouragement is all."

"Oh?" Keith's curiosity was up, but a blaring car horn and its driver shouting to clear the road had us scrambling to safety. Looking over his shoulder, Hector put an arm around the girl with the Atlas and winked.

"Cheeky! Keith muttered.

"Och! Enough of them!" Huw groaned, "Come on."

Enjoying the sunshine and fresh air off the Firth, we made our way to the square, where an ancient fountain still commands a noteworthy presence.

"Back in the day," I declared, "this fountain would have been the town crier's podium...where everyone gathered to hear the news."

Keith added, "And likely, lots of gossip!"

"Wonder what passed for a good headline?" Huw asked.

Jumping up on the edge and cupping a hand to my mouth, I shouted, "Meat pies for tuppence! Five a shilling!"

"Wait a minute!" Keith held up a finger. "They'd be cheaper to buy one at a time!"

"Just seeing if you're paying attention."

Huw jumped up alongside me, but at the first strains of *that* song, I outlunged him, "Scotland aligns with France! Edward retaliates!"

Some passersby smiled, while others hardly noticed our antics.

Then Keith asked, "Okay, what happened there?"

"You don't know?"

"Sorry," he shrugged, "not up on *current* events."

"In the late 1200s," I jumped down. "'Sir Longshanks,' as you know, had his eye on Scotland. Berwick on Tweed's where it began."

Huw muttered, "That's in England!"

"Tis now, but back then, Scotland had purchased it from Richard the Lionheart, so he could finance his crusades."

"Well?" Keith queried, "Don't leave us flappin' in the breeze! What happened?"

"Edward ordered every soul massacred, and I quote, 'So the mills could be turned round with the flow of their blood.'"

"Och!" Huw grimaced, "Don't ye know any happy stories, Will?"

"They're still being written!"

"So..." Keith asked, "why Berwick?"

"Location! Berwick was a thriving seaport, rivalled only by London for trade, and Edward meant to have her."

"Yeah, but commandeering wealth is one thing, massacring every soul, that's...insane! What was he *really* after?"

"Now yer thinking! The real prize was Scotland! Balliol made an alliance with France. Nothing more than spit and a handshake, but to Edward, twas an act of war, providing all the reason he needed to invade."

Keith added, "All about power again, right?"

"Unfortunately," I sputtered, "and true to his word, he slaughtered 15,000 men, women, and children."

Huw baulked, "He killed children?"

I nodded. "A few men held out in Red Hall, and one archer, aiming for Longshanks, killed his cousin instead."

Keith bellowed, "Too bad he missed! Could have changed the course of history!"

"True...but Edward's men torched the hall; no one survived."

"But..." Keith questioned, "If there were no survivors, how do you know what happened?"

"Edward's *tactics* traumatised even battle hardened soldiers. Some dared whisper, the only time the king seemed disturbed was watching a woman giving birth being hacked to death by his men."

"Och!" Huw, balled up his face, "Sick!"

"He assumed brutality would demoralise the people and further deprived them of their king, publicly stripping Balliol of his crown, then stole our Stone of Destiny. What he didn't anticipate was igniting the hearts of Scots to rally behind their king. Twas a time for heroes to rise."

"How do you know all this Will?" Huw gestured, "There're no plaques or markers tae mention it."

"Tis our country, our history!" I exclaimed, "It's said ye've only to dig a few feet down and likely come upon human remains."

"No way!" Keith gasped.

"Aye!" I nodded. "Why aren't we taught about what our ancestors endured?"

Keith hesitated, "Because remembering stirs up bad blood."

"But why?" I countered. "You want answers when one person is slain, but this, this was a massacre our history books ignore! Don't those souls have a right to be remembered?"

"Of course they do," he defended, "but it does nae good to quarrel with the past."

"Agreed," I continued, "but shouldn't we honour those who perished and learn from what happened?"

"Aye!" Huw nodded. "Power and riches corrupt, even the best of men can be driven to insane feats to prove a point."

"Like Wallace...sacking York then?"

I sighed with exasperation, "He ne'er sacked York!"

Keith put a hand on my shoulder. "Ye know I'm joking, right?"

After walking a bit further, we plopped down upon well-worn

benches, watching traffic weave through the tourist speckled streets. The noontime bells chimed from the church tower, and the fresh breeze off the water filled our lungs.

"Will?" Huw muttered, staring at the view.

"Aye?"

"You should write a book or start a tour company."

"Hmm." I responded.

More insistent, he continued, "Honestly, with your grasp of Scotland's history, Tantallon, the Wars of Independence, the martyrs in your family, and Wallace, of course, you'd make a fortune!"

"I am passionate about our history; it just makes me sad, so few of us know or care about where we come from. Like Wallace said in the movie, we've no sense of who we are as Scots. These tourists walking about," I motioned in their direction, "they have more zeal for being Scottish than a whole lot of us!"

Huw snorted, "*They* think everyone still runs around in kilts!"

"That was another time," Keith countered, "another era!"

"Yeah, but how?" I asked, "How do we reclaim our heritage, our identity?"

"Face it Will." Keith grinned, "We've been amalgamated!"

"So what to do?" Huw retorted, "Storm Westminster?"

"Och, no!" Keith laughed, "But maybe, just maybe we can rebuild Hadrian's wall."

"Aye," I chuckled, "and if Lilly were here, with her tinfoil sword and shield, she'd have it sorted in a wink!"

Truly, we held no grudge against our English neighbours, yet I longed for my fellow countrymen to remember how far we'd travelled and how far we'd yet to go. So, we sat watching traffic, everyone bustling towards some destination, everyone except us.

After a fortnight, Lilly's second letter arrived, and like children anticipating a bedtime story, we huddled close to read about our little sister's Skye adventure.

"Hello again, dear lads!

"Today I'm writing from the bow of The Melody! The wind is up and even though she's on the shoals, gazing towards the horizon makes it seem she's out to sea. So, ye'll not complain if the paper's rumpled; tis hard to keep it from flapping in this breeze!

"The ship belonged to a local fisherman, but international laws took away his right to fish Scottish waters. Does nae seem fair, but on a brighter note, Gran says she's keen to meet you all and see Tantallon, the Bass and especially Mr. Ramsay. Best provide him fair warning!

"The weather's been atrocious, with howling winds from the Minch and pelting rain. I mean really pelting. Right now it's coming down sideways, but yesterday we explored Kilt Rock! Over time, fierce winds and driving rain sheared pleats into the giant cliffs, hence the name, and rushing streams gush over them, plummeting to the dark blue sea below.

"The view is stunning, and mysterious siren like voices draw you towards the cliff's edge, but the winds are so wild, one doesn't dare approach it! Gran told me twas fairies, but in truth, this eerie sound is the wind singing through the safety rails. The stronger the gust, the louder the song, and, while being pummelled by the wind, the sound seems to pass right through ye!

"Skye is breathtaking, but I miss you lads and so wish you were here. Mum hasn't decided yet, but another week and we may be back in Berwick, and I can hardly wait to hear all about your adventures!

"Sending my love to you and your folks, and off to kill-my-hog... Again!

"Lilly"

While our threesome was jolly, nothing near as exciting was happening. No grand adventures or bottled notes, and with Summer quickly waning, Lilly's third post announcing her return by week's end was happy news indeed.

Lilly and her mum arrived bearing souvenirs gleaned from the beaches of Skye. Ocean polished stones provided a deep grey canvass, drizzled with squiggly white lines and shapes as though an artist had designed them.

"Here Will." Lilly handed me a sizable stone. "This one's for you!"

She beamed as I examined it. "Looks like the midnight sky!"

Running our fingers over the white squiggles, she pointed out, "See? Here's Saturn, and this looks like the North Star."

"Aye, it does!" I motioned to Keith and Huw, "You have to see this."

While they inspected the stone, Lilly placed a smaller one in Keith's hand. "And for our budding sleuth, look for the hidden treasure!"

After a moment, he laughed, "You didn't find this, Lilly; you marked it yourself."

"Well..." She scrunched up her face, "I did help just a bit... but isn't it perfect?"

"Let me see!" Huw pushed in, "What are ye looking at?"

Keith smiled, "It's a spy glass."

I added, "Now that's a perfect Keith souvenir if ever I saw one!"

"Thanks Lilly!" Keith grinned, "That's really sweet!"

"You're welcome," she sighed. "I had such a good time, but I missed you all!"

Feeling overlooked, disappointment clouded Huw's face till Lilly pinched his cheek, "Dear Huw, you're looking just as Eeyore as when Mum and I drove out a few weeks ago."

"Am not!" He shot back.

"Don't worry." She soothed, "I didn't forget you."

Huw's face lit up as she reached into her pocket and handed him a dark brown stone. He stared for a moment, then shook his head, "No way!"

Biting her lip, a smile accompanied her nod. "Tis real as we are.

You can call it your Sea Lion!"

Adding our heads to their huddle, Keith and I gazed at the stone Lilly found, bearing the head of a lion, complete with bushy mane!

Huw gushed, "You're amazing, Lilly!"

I added, "These are absolutely perfect, Lil. Thank you!"

We shared a smile while the lads continued their praise, causing Lilly to blush, "Tis nothing. I missed ye, that's all." Then, with an impish grin, she asked, "So, what'd you get for me?"

I gasped as we stood, wide eyed, stammering, "Er, um..."

"Och! I'm kidding! Did you lads forget how to joke while I was away?"

With sighs of relief, Mum appeared in the nick of time with a finely decorated confection, "It wouldn't be a real welcome home without cake!"

Lilly's jaw dropped in surprise, then, like Quicksilver, she slopped a finger full of gooey icing into her mouth. "Umm, that's lovely, Mrs. Ridley!"

"And lovely to see ye back, lass." Mum gave her a hug, "Three cheers for Lilly come home!"

"Not so fast, young lady!" Suddenly, all attention diverted to a tiny, yet imposing woman standing in our doorway. "I suppose these gentlemen are your friends from Tantallon?"

"Aye, Gran!" She replied.

"Well?" Looking indignant, she snapped, "Introduce us!"

And so she did. Likely Gran MacCrimmon's mischievous streak created sticky situations, but Mrs. Alcott and Lilly, being of the same ilk, held their own with her. Together, these ladies had a force about them, especially Gran, who left no question she intended to see the Bass for herself.

"We should get an early start tomorrow," she smiled at Da, "if that suits."

"Just so happens," Da countered, "supply runs set out at half seven, and we'd be delighted to have you ladies along!"

Gran smiled, Lilly smiled, and I smiled bigger, knowing I'd finally be able to introduce her to my dear friends on the Bass!

28

Lassies on the Bass

Standing at the water's edge with deep furrows in his brow, Gerald Alcott hailed, "Take care of my girls, Magnus! You bring em back safe!"

"I will!" Da assured, "Ye've my word, Gerald."

For good measure, I added, "They're in safe hands, Mr. Alcott."

He gave a nod as we helped his wife and daughter aboard, then Mum called out, "There's room for one more!"

"Nae!" Gerald fired back, "I'll wait here!" Softening, he added, "When de ye s'pose ye'll be back?"

"Long as the mist holds off, back this evening." Da pointed seaward, "But if it thickens, we'll spend the night, and ye can expect us tomorrow afternoon."

"Fair enough," Lilly's Da responded, more tense than he let on.

"Tis alright, Ger," his wife soothed, "we'll be back before ye know it!"

"See to it, Mrs. Ye adventuresome hens are off again!" Holding up a hand, he grinned, "Enjoy yourselves."

Despite her years, Gran hopped aboard the supply laden boat with ease, announcing, "I've always loved the sea, from the time I was a wean." Da offered her a hand while she chattered, "But Mum forbid me going near the boats."

"More likely, twas the fishermen!" Lilly giggled, and Gran winked back.

As Da helped her get settled, Mum lamented, "I'd hoped for blue skies and sunshine; tis so much nicer when the weather cooperates."

"Oh, but Mrs. Ridley," Lilly chirped, "we've heard so much about the Bass, we'd make this trip in a squall if need be!"

"Speak for yer self!" Rose giggled, "We're not all as adventurous as you."

"In any case," Gran shifted about, "we've an able captain, so weigh anchor!"

"Gran," Lilly chided, "the dinghy doesn't have an anchor. That's for big ships."

"I knew that. But ye must allow yer Gran a bit of *leeway*!" She teased, "Get it? Lee-Way?"

Lilly rolled her eyes, and Rose giggled, "Mum, ye wee cheek!"

Gulls often followed our boat looking for handouts, and despite the weather, our passengers delighted in seeing them hovering above, along with an occasional fish popping from the blue grey waves. That is, until one let loose, dropping a huge splat of poo right on Mum's knee.

"Och!" She exclaimed, "Ye cheeky feathered poo bag!"

Da began laughing so hard, he could barely steer the boat. "Feathered poo bag?" He snorted, "Don't believe I've ever heard that expression before."

Wiping the gooey substance from her trousers and holding up a soiled hand, Mum giggled, "Well, love, I could share this bounty from above, then see what ye come up with?"

"Och, wife," Da winced, "not in front of our guests!"

Flashing him a smile, she leaned over to wash her hands in the chilly water, then Lilly chirped, "At least it didn't land in your hair. *That* would be really gross!"

Rose wrinkled her nose. "Happened to me once."

"Eeew, Mum!" Lilly grimaced, "With this lot, we should've brought a brolly!"

"Oh, do tell!" Gran spurted.

"Years ago, Gerald and I took a ferry to Mull, when the crew thought they'd have a laugh." Rose held up a finger. "Water guns...filled with green hand cream...shot into the air above unsuspecting passengers, and what do ye think? One huge glop landed right on top of my head!"

"That wasn't very nice!" Lilly added, "But at least it wasn't poo."

"Aye, true." Rose nodded. "But just imagine how startled we were."

"Oh, how fun!" Gran giggled, "Wish I'd thought of that." Taking in the damp sea air, she gave Lilly a pinch, "This'll put roses in those pretty cheeks. Ye warm enough?"

"Aye Gran," she replied, "How about you?"

She nodded her reply, then poked an elbow in my side, "Ye'r awfully quiet, lad. What do you think of my granddaughter? A beauty, eh?"

"Aw Gran!" My cheeks flushed with colour as Lilly groaned, "You promised you wouldn't embarrass me!"

"Och! Nothing embarrassing, dear, that's fact!" Turning to me, she demanded, "What? Cat got your tongue?"

Taking a deep breath, I pronounced, "No, not at all. In fact, I've always said Lilly is the bonniest girl in Scotland!" Lilly shot me a surprised smile, and I added, "Perhaps the world!"

Gran smiled with satisfaction, "Lad's got good taste, dear."

Now twas Lilly looking out to sea to conceal the rush of color in her cheeks, while Mum and Da shared a cheeky grin. This conversation was thickening nearly as fast as the mist, so thankfully, we pulled up alongside the Bass dock. Before Da could toss a line, Gran blurted, "Well, where is everybody? You told me there'd be handsome, young lads to meet us!"

"Patience," steadied Rose.

"Stay put, ladies," Da instructed, "just till we get the dock lines secure." Then, out of the upper-lying mist, we heard Drew and Andy scurrying down the stone steps.

Gran chided, "About time somebody sent a rescue party!"

"So sorry, we were up lighting the beacon." Then Andy bowed, "Welcome to the Bass fair maidens!"

The girls giggled, and Gran played along, "Enchanted!"

Extending his hand, Drew warned, "Mind your step. Dinghy's bobbing like a cork in this chop."

While Da and Drew assisted the ladies, Andy pointed beyond us, "Glad ye made it in before the fog."

"You and me both!" Da returned.

Everyone safely ashore, Drew bellowed, "Abi'll be chuffed to see ye all!"

"Aye!" Andy ruffled the back of my head. "It's usually just these two sea dogs."

I jested, "Now there's a welcome ye don't get every day!"

Followed by a procession of supply laden lads, Mum led us up to the cottage where Abi and Mr. Ramsay waited with open arms.

"AnnaLee!" Abi squealed, jumping with excitement, "I'm so glad to see you! And William! And all your friends!"

"And what about me?" Da set down his bundle, "Chopped liver now, I suppose?"

While Abi rushed to give Da a hug, Mr. Ramsay wrapped Lilly and I in a welcoming embrace, "Ah, lass, William's told us so much about his beautiful Lilly," then holding her at arm's length, his face curled into a warm smile, "He's spot on! Pleasure to meet ye dear."

"*His Lilly?*" She beamed in my direction, "Is that so?"

"Aye," Mr. Ramsay nodded.

With a curtsy, she returned his greeting, "Tis a pleasure to meet you as well. I've heard so much about your adventures on the Bass, I've been looking forward to this for ages!"

"Honestly, I cannae fathom why he's nae brought ye before now!"

"Oh, William's nae to blame!" Lilly defended, "I'd have come sooner, but Da ne'er allowed it, least not till today. And I'm so glad he did!"

"We all are!" I beamed.

Glancing at Gran taking charge in the kitchen, Lilly whispered, "A certain arrival may have had something to do with it."

"Everything in God's perfect time, I say." Mr. Ramsay chuckled, wrapping us in another hug.

All the while, Gran was investigating and commenting on every nuance of the cottage, especially the misty view from the parlour window. Addressing Abi, she nodded her approval, "Quite the honour to be mistress of such a fine abode!"

Abi offered her a seat. "We're truly blessed in so many ways!"

While we sat down to tea, Mr. Ramsay excused, "I'm terribly sorry, Mrs. MacCrimmon, we've only one proper cup and saucer, which belongs to AnnaLee."

"No worries, Ioan," Mum chirped, "we can make an exception."

"Tis Sally, if ye please!" Gran winked at Mr. Ramsay, "And I'll nae hear of that! MacCrimmon's are hearty stock, so I'll sip a mug like the rest of these sailors!"

Andy raised his mug, "Here! Here!"

The women delighted themselves with what ladies talk about, touring rooms and commenting on all the little niceties Abi'd adorned the cottage with.

"That's tenacity, lass!" Gran declared.

Mum gave Abi a knowing look. "Takes a strong woman to endure the long winters and isolation out here."

"Twas hard at first," Abi admitted, "but now I couldn't imagine living anywhere else." She smiled in his direction, "Drew's the perfect husband..."

"Perfect?" Gran interrupted, snorting, "Just you wait!"

Puzzled, Abi redirected, "Plus, Andy and Ioan make me feel right at home."

Mum gave her a cuddle. "I'm so pleased, lass."

"Oh AnnaLee," she threw her head back. "I don't know what I'd've done if not for your kindness. Ye've helped so much...plus, there's news!"

Relaxing by the hearth, we lads talked sports and events from the mainland until shrieks burst from the adjoining room, followed immediately by peals of laughter.

Poised to run in their direction, I queried, "Should we see if they're alright?"

Da and Mr. Ramsay replied in tandem, "Nah, girl talk!"

Since heavy fog prevented us exploring the Bass as I'd hoped, Andy and Drew provided a lighthouse tour. At the summit, murky skies shrouded the tower, muffling the sea yet amplifying the keepers' voices.

Explaining the workings of the lighthouse, Andy pointed to the golden beam swirling overhead, disappearing into the thick standing mist, "It's just like clockwork!"

Gran exclaimed, "Who'd have thought I'd see a wonder like this at my age!"

"Or make it up that many steps!" Remarked an out of breath Rose.

Mr. Ramsay offered her his hand, "She's been making folks breathless and lighting the Firth since 1902!"

"Fabulous!" Gran took his other arm, "But tell me again, Ioan, how does it all work?"

While Gran held Mr. Ramsay's attention, Lilly stood beside me, peering into the mist. "Is this where you fell from, Will?"

"Aye." I leaned on the railing, pointing up, "We were coming out of the lens house, and you'd not know it by today's weather, but the wind was so fierce, the door was nearly bursting off its hinges. Snatched me right over the side."

She shivered in the chill of the afternoon. "Sounds frightening!"

"Twas at first, but thank God for safety harnesses!" She stared into my eyes for a long, quiet moment, til I asked, "What?"

"I'm just so thankful you're still here. I'd miss you terribly if..." Her eyes filled with tears, "if something had happened to you."

While God had made me bold to share about Him, in matters of the heart, I found myself in uncharted waters. Lilly was my dearest friend, but when I opened my mouth to speak, nothing came out. Then, like magnets, our shoulders gravitated towards each other, and the tiny brush jolted through me like a bolt of lightning, causing us both to catch our breath.

As I studied her face, I found my courage: "My dear shield maiden, not to worry. God still has purpose for me. He's gonna keep me around awhile longer."

"I mean it, Will! You lads are all dear to me, but..." She stressed, "*you* especially."

Biting my lip warmed into another smile, "As you are to me, Lil! And now that we've a moment, there's something I'd like to ask you."

"Really?" She smiled, "Go on."

"I've always..."

Wanting to say this just right, I hesitated when Mr. Ramsay clapped a hand on my shoulder. "Tis a fine mess! Where's our blue skies to show off the breathtaking view?"

Mum responded, "Exactly what I'd hoped for, Ioan!"

Gran grumbled back, "I'd say we had enough breathtaking on the climb up here!"

"Eek!" Rose let out a minuscule squeal when a gannet emerged from the mist. Equally alarmed to find humans in his airspace, the bird responded with one enormous squawk.

Gran swatted the air, "Another cheeky feathered poo bag!"

Alas, my question would have to wait a little longer.

After evening tea, we listened to stories of life on the Bass and detailed answers to Gran's endless questions. All the while, Drew, cuddling Abi, waited for an opportunity to speak, until an astute Mr. Ramsay prompted, "Alright then, out with it, you two!"

"Ye may have guessed, but," Drew grasped Abi's hand, "we're going to be parents!"

"Oh!" I exclaimed, "A baby on the Bass!"

Clinging to Drew's arm, Abi looked radiant. "Aye, we're so excited!"

Lilly gushed, "Your story's so romantic, Abi!"

The girls giggled, and she agreed, "Tis Lilly, but it's not just my story; it belongs to the Bass. And tis only the start!"

While nearly all attention was on the happy couple, Lilly captivated my thoughts. My gaze fixed upon her in the soft evening light, laughing and enjoying herself with the people I loved dearest in the world. Twas a strange and wondrous new feeling, suddenly diverted by handshakes, hugs, and a room bubbling over with excitement as the ladies chattered about baby things.

Amid their happy commotion, Da crossed to the window, peering out into the thick night sky. "Gerald'll be fretting over his girls in this fog." He exhaled, "I'd be if I were him."

"True." Rose agreed, "He's ne'er been easy watching anyone head out to sea." Lilly shot her mum a concerned look, and Rose responded, smoothing her daughter's long, red tresses, "Though we did leave him his favourite meal for tea tonight."

"Well," Gran puffed, "hope he's not fretting too much, or he'll wind up in the pub!"

"Mum!" Rose gasped with embarrassment.

"What?" Gran threw her hands up, "I'm just saying."

"Rose," Mum diverted, "Lilly says you're a fab cook! What'd you make for tea?"

"Oh, uh, a lovely roast, with potato, veg, and loads of gravy." Regaining composure, she smiled, "Ger loves gravy and fresh baked scones with cream and strawberry jam."

"Blessed man," added Mr. Ramsay. "I'm a pushover for a scone with clotted cream."

"Me too!" Andy spouted, "Although difficult to come by here ta Bass."

Drew poked his brother, "What're ye on about? Abi makes brilliant scones, slathered with butter and bramble berry jam. Tastiest you'll find anywhere!"

Abi beamed at his praise, but Andy joked, "Might ye be a wee bit biased?"

"Nae Andy." Abi answered his cheek, "A wise man praises the cook, especially when eating is one of his favourite past times!"

"Now that ye mention it," Da grinned, "Drew does look like he's eating for two!"

As the fire smouldered down to coals, we retired for the evening, and Mr. Ramsay showed the Alcott ladies to the cosy room under the stairs. "Ye should be nice and snug in here. Just call out if ye need anything."

"Thanks, Ioan," the ladies replied, voices growing hushed as they closed themselves in for the night.

Mum and Da took Mr. Ramsay's room, then he covered me with a cedar scented duvet on the tufted parlour couch. As I stretched out, he smiled, "I remember tucking you in as a lad. My, how time flies!"

"I remember too. Shame we cannae stay like that forever."

He let out a laugh. "T'would be nice, Will. Though someday, ye'll have sons of your own to tuck in." The thought was strangely comforting, then he added, "Maybe with someone we know?"

"You mean...Lilly?"

His eyes sparkled. "Well, if not that dear lassie, I'd be mighty surprised."

"Ye think...she likes me?"

He nodded, "I may be an old man, but some things I still see quite clearly!"

I returned his smile, "Thanks... Mr. Ramsay."

"Eh?"

"For the way you've cared for me over the years. I'm truly blessed!"

"As am I, Will. As am I!" Watching the kerosine light follow him down the hall, he called out, "Night lad."

On this moonless night, shrouded in mist and happy memories, sleep came easily. My dreams were filled with good things, happy thoughts, when all at once I sensed a presence. Opening one eye, I caught my breath, discovering Gran MacCrimmon hovering over me.

"Daylight's wasting lad! Ye gonna sleep all day?"

Up like a shot, I found the day just dawning as she offered a hot cuppa, studying me, uncomfortably silent. Sipping the hot liquid, I whispered, "Did ye sleep well?"

She nodded, still staring.

"Looks like clear skies today, sunshine too!"

"Aye," she nodded again.

"If yer up for a trek, Mr. Ramsay'd be happy to show us the island. He's got tonnes of stories about the Bass and all the birds."

"Lovely!" Her countenance lightened as Mr. Ramsay came down the hall.

"Good Morning!" He chirped, "Trust everyone slept well."

"Thank you, Ioan. Best sleep I've had in ages. Tis the fresh air," Gran purred at him, holding out a hot cuppa, "and such *good* company!"

Rubbing his whiskers, he accepted the coffee, blushing a deep crimson. "Em," Mr. Ramsay cleared his throat. "Fancy a walk about the island? Looks a good day for it."

"I'd be delighted!" She replied.

The sun burnt away any lingering mist, and the sky stretched over us like an ocean of blue. Max jumped and yapped, nipping at our heels along the steep pathway, and after a condensed history of the prison and chapel, Mr. Ramsay led us a safe distance from the cliffside.

"Gannets can hit the water at nearly sixty miles an hour when they fish!" Then, pointing out the countless nests, he described how best to pinch a few eggs for breakfast.

"That's a rough way to make an omelette." Gran remarked.

He grinned, "Even harder when the birds realise what yer up tae!"

That afternoon, mindful of her condition, Drew encircled Abi's waist, and they waved from the cottage, "Safe journey!"

Mum gave her one last hug and joined us, navigating the steep passage to the dock. Before Lilly climbed aboard our considerably lighter dinghy, Mr. Ramsay whispered in her ear, and both smiled in my direction. All aboard, the prop churned up the sea, and I sat transfixed on the Bass and dear friends growing smaller and smaller as we hastened towards the mainland.

"I see why you love Mr. Ramsay Will." Lilly had been studying my expression, "He's like the Grandpa I ne'er had."

"He's a good man. Practically raised Andy and Drew, and he's taught me so many things."

Leaning closer, she touched my arm. "I hope ye'll let me come visit him again."

"Anytime ye like Lil. I loved having ye along!" There was such sweetness in her words, and again, I found I couldn't stop gazing at her, "What did he whisper to you, back there?"

An impish smile covered her face as she lowered her voice. "I'll tell ye, but first, what were you going to ask me?"

"Oh! Um..." suddenly aware of Gran's gaze fixed upon us, I whispered, "I was hoping for a little less of an audience."

"Totally understandable!" Then she leaned closer to my ear, but Gran interrupted.

"Away! Away I say!" Rocking the boat, arms flailing, she shouted at a circling gull, "We'll nae have a repeat of what ye left on AnnaLee's knee!"

With a wink, Da mouthed to Mum, "Cheeky, feathered poo bag!"

Under Gran's continued scrutiny, Lilly whispered, "Ask me later."

Nearing the shore, a lone figure waited, in much the same spot we'd left him, making me wonder if Mr. Alcott had budged at all since the previous morning. Waving excitedly, Lilly and her mum covered him with hugs and chatter the moment we stepped ashore. Much relieved, Mr. Alcott gathered his girlies, declining our invite for a cuppa, and like a flash of lightning, they were gone with Gran in tow.

29

⧉

A Precarious Dilemma

Pulling up the drive, the Alcotts met with a surprise.

"For you, Lilly!"

A myriad of thoughts raced through her brain because the same young man who'd bullied her friends stood offering her an armful of flowers.

Hector Menteith smiled, "Heard you were back from Skye."

"Yeah, um..." Lilly stammered, "a day or so."

"Well then," he handed her a bouquet of pink and yellow blooms. "Here's yer official welcome home. Although they're not as pretty as you are!"

As her folks looked on, she smiled, "Thank you, Hector. That's..." Hesitating, she accepted his gift, "very kind of you."

He then held out a daisy, "And a warm welcome to Lilly's Gran!"

Instantly charmed, Gran smiled, "Hector, eh? Well, invite the lad in for tea Lilly!"

Looking at her mum and da, they nodded agreement.

After a full day exploring the Bass and Hector's surprise visit, Lilly yawned, "I don't know about you, Gran, but I'm knackered."

"Umm." She agreed, adding, "He's really quite charming."

"*Mr. Ramsay?*" Lilly teased.

"Aye, Ioan is charming, but I was thinking of Hector. Handsome too!"

Lilly's tone soured, "Oh."

"Oh?" Gran queried, "That's all you've to say about the young man who delivered such lovely flowers?"

"Twas kind of him, although," Lilly squirmed, "I'm a bit astonished."

"Why should his bringing you flowers be astonishing, dear?"

"Not that, Gran. Let's just say, if you knew Hector," she emphasised, "you'd be suspicious."

"Nonsense!" Gran insisted, "He acted the perfect gentleman."

"Acted being the key word here!" Lilly wanted her to understand, "I wouldn't trust Hector far as I could throw him, and neither should you."

Gran snorted, "Why on earth not?"

"Well..." Lilly searched for the right words: "When it suits, he can be charming, but he's bullied almost everyone at school, including William, Huw, and Keith! So, him showing up like that makes me... uneasy."

"Uneasy child? He's a storyteller, like your da, *and* the Hector I used to date. You love that!"

"You never mentioned a Hector?"

"Well, twas years ago, but he still holds a special place in my heart."

Lilly grinned, "you're just full of surprises, Gran!"

"More than ye know...in fact, you should see more of Hector."

"Gran, really," Lilly protested, "you shouldn't encourage..."

She interrupted, "That's why I've invited him for tea tomorrow."

"Gran! What do you think you're doing?"

"Sometimes," she grinned, "young people need encouragement!"

Inciting the opposite effect, Lilly reacted, "I can't believe you did that... I *don't* like Hector like that!"

"Ye didn't mind him bringing flowers."

"He surprised me. And flowers are one thing, Gran, but... I..."

"Hm?"

"If I like anyone... ye know, as more than a friend, tis William."

Gran raised her eyebrow. "That hesitant, tongue-tied pup?"

"He's not tongue-tied," Lilly blushed. "Ye just made him nervous!"

Gran clucked, "The lad didn't have the sense to prepare a welcome home gift!"

"Our trip to the Bass was a fine gift. Besides, he makes me feel safe!"

"Safe?" Gran huffed, "Safe from what young lady?"

"I don't know Gran, but if you knew Hector and William's true natures, we'd not be having this conversation."

"Lilly!" Gran scowled, "Someday you'll learn; feelings are like butterflies; they come and go. You're just being obstinate!"

"No, I'm not!" Lilly reeled, "I just don't understand why you're pushing me towards someone *you* barely know!"

"Told ye," Gran grinned, "young folks need a nudge now and then."

Exasperated, Lilly cried out, "Mum!"

While Gran MacCrimmon was playing matchmaker, I was picking Da's brain.

"I tried to ask her at the lighthouse, then in the boat, but just couldn't find the right moment."

Remaining serious was impossible as Da's face curled into a cheeky grin, "For momentous occasions such as these, one simply needs to create his own perfect timing."

"Aye," I jested, "but how exactly does one do that?"

"A touch of the unexpected." I stared, none the wiser, then Da asked, "Store bought or wildflowers?"

"Daffodils. Definitely daffodils, just like Mum!"

"Then I suggest gathering up a bunch and paying a visit. Tuck a card inside with the question, then wait for her answer."

"Brilliant Da! The card's a great idea, but how long do I wait? Till she reads it, or..." I worried, "What if she says no?"

"Remember our talk at the Firth?"

"Oh," I cringed, "what part?"

"Knowing the right girl?" I nodded as Da continued, "You and Lilly have adored each other since you were weans. Seriously, how many times have Huw and Keith teased you?"

Remembering their curtsies and songs, I chuckled, "Och, I've stopped counting."

Da rallied, "If you don't have your answer before day's end, I'd be mighty surprised."

Taking a deep breath, I chapped the door, and Lilly overflowed as I presented the daffodils, tied with scarlet ribbon over a swath of Ridley tartan. "William, they're beautiful! Thank you!"

"You're welcome. I was hoping you'd like them."

"You know daffies are my favourite!" We both smiled, then extracting the shiny shield shaped card from the blooms, she giggled, "What's this?"

"Um. A proposal of sorts..." Her face wrinkled as I struggled for words, "Em, I mean...what I wanted to ask you."

"Oh!" She smiled, opening the card, and I held my breath as she read,

> *"Though a month lies still before the event,*
> *Please do me the honour of considering my intent*
> *If it please you, my fair and lovely lady,*
> *Join me in dance at the upcoming Ceilidh."*

"William!" She exclaimed, "I don't care what Huw says; yer poetry's beautiful!"

I rolled my eyes, laughing, "Will ye?"

"Aye!" She nodded. "I'd love to! I was hoping that's what you wanted to ask."

Unsure of what to do next, we stood, grinning, till I blurted, "Brilliant! I mean, thank you, Lilly! I'm really excited!"

"Me too!" She whispered.

"What's he doing here?" Gran peered out from behind Lilly.

"Gran, it's William! Remember? He and his folks took us to the Bass."

Scowling at the daffodils, she sneered, "And what of it?"

Exasperated, Lilly groaned, "Och!"

"I was wondering how you ladies enjoyed the trip?"

Gran chirped back, "Lovely excursion, but ye, still haven't answered me."

I was perplexed by her sudden coolness, then Lilly, cradling her bouquet, answered for me, "William brought me daffodils with poetry, *and* he's asked me to the Ceilidh!"

With a sly look, Gran detonated our happy moment, "Well, yer too late, Dearie. She just agreed to go with Hector!"

"What?" We both squawked.

Stepping from behind Gran, Hector grinned, "Aye Ridley, still two steps behind!"

The flowers slipped from Lilly's grasp as she planted her hands on her hips, "I did no such thing, Hector, and ye know it!"

Hector winked, "Don't worry, lass. Gran accepted for ye...we're all set."

"Oh no, we are not!" She protested, "I've just accepted William's invitation...I'm going with him, and that's all there is to it! Matter of fact, you should probably leave." Softening, she added, "Please."

"He'll do no such thing. I've just poured tea, so come inside before it gets cold." Taking his arm, Gran commanded over her shoulder, "Say goodbye to William and don't keep us waiting."

"Och!" Lilly threw her hands in the air as they headed inside, then together, we knelt, gathering flowers. "She'll not have the last word on this, ye can count on that!"

"I'm relieved, Lil, but wow! What have I done to offend your Gran?"

"You haven't offended her, Will, but when she gets a notion, she is determined. However..." she grinned, "being of the same stock, I can be just as headstrong!"

Taking her hand, I helped her up. "Now, why doesn't that surprise me?"

"I'm so sorry, William. I didn't invite Hector. Gran did, without me knowing, because he showed up last night," She rolled her eyes, "with flowers!"

"It's okay, Lil." I shrugged, "You don't owe me any explanation."

"Oh, but I want you to understand!" Her hands waved. "They were together all evening, whispering and laughing. You'd nae think he was the same lad. Then Gran invited him back and Mum and Da didn't say a word! I should have hid! I mean, who is he to ask Gran to accept a Ceilidh invitation for me?"

I shook my head. "I'm so sorry."

"What?" She halted, "Why are you sorry?"

"I'm sorry your family would put you in this position, and that yer Da didn't stand up for ye."

"Oh, he means well." Lilly groaned, "It's just... Gran's sick and Da's afraid if they argue, she'll have a heart attack. So they give in. It's like trying to dodge a hurricane!"

"I do understand, but..." I hesitated.

"What?"

"Ye know, I try ne'er to say anything ill about anyone, but yer Da needs to know what Hector's like, so he can protect you."

"*He knows* Will, but Hector's in there right now putting on such an act; he's got them twisted round his finger." Her brow furrowed. "It feels like a trap."

"Lilly," I touched her cheek, "Princess and defender of Tantallon, you've never bowed to threat before. So, hold fast, and all will turn out well!"

Her jaw dropped. "*That's* what Mr. Ramsay said."

"It is?"

"Aye!" She sighed, "He said I was a rare treasure, and yer brave and true, and no matter what happened, if we held fast, all would turn out well."

"And so it shall!" I nodded, "You'll see."

Gran poked her head out, "Lilly, you're being rude; come in and attend to *your* guest!"

She let out an exasperated sigh, as I encouraged, "No worries fair lass. There's plenty of time to win Gran over."

"That..." she grinned, "will take a miracle!"

"Then, tis good I know someone who's speciality is miracles!" She stared as I took her hand, "Just keep your guard up and know I'm praying for ye."

"Lilly!" Gran's shrill voice pierced the air.

"I've gotta go Will. Thanks again for the lovely time at the Bass, and the daffies! They're beautiful."

"We'll do that again soon!" I called after her, "Oh, and I love the rock! Thanks!"

While Gran kept Lilly busy touring and shopping and pressing her to accept Hector's invite to the Ceilidh, our spirits dampened.

"Ye finally get the nerve to ask Lilly out, and Gran happens!" Keith sputtered, "Horrible luck, Will!"

"Not luck, Keith; it's a test." I added, "And this too will pass."

Huw stood up, grinning, "I say, we storm the castle!" Within minutes, we were walking towards Lilly's, and he mused, "Reminds me of the day Hector's Da chased us. Remember?"

"Ug," I groaned. "How could I forget?"

Keith snickered, "Here's to nae repeating that!"

Nearing her house, Huw whispered, "Think we'll catch a glimpse of the tower captive?" But before we could answer, the front door creaked open and Lilly bounded down the drive.

"I'm so happy to see you, lads!" With a finger to her lips, she spun us round, "Quick! To Tantallon!"

Scurrying down the lane, Keith quipped, "Escaped the castle guard, did ye?"

"Aye!" Lilly let out a laugh. "And I'm desperate for a view of the Firth!"

"Wait a minute." Huw stopped us, "How'd ye get away?"

Pulling us into a huddle, she purred, "Battle tactics. Mum diverted, I ran!"

Dashing far from our worries, we raced up and down Tantallon's ancient stairways, enjoying the last of our summer holiday.

On the castle ramparts, Lilly's long red tresses danced in the wind as she overlooked the Firth. "Oh," she exhaled, "I love it here!"

Huw'd been studying her, "Me too! Reminds me of your first visit, when your sleeves wrapped around your head."

"As I recall," Lilly countered, "you threatened to hang me over the wall. Nice welcome, lads!"

Keith chirped, "Twas the least we could do for a pushy little shield maiden!"

With hands on hips, she teased, "I'm a young lady now," then stuck out her tongue.

"Well, that's real grown up!" Keith chuckled.

In the quiet of the dungeon, far below this sunny afternoon, Huw grew solemn, "Lil, I know you'd rather not think about it, but any ideas on the Ceilidh?"

Looking at her feet, she raised her eyes, "You know by now, William asked me."

Keith grinned ear to ear, "We wondered when you two'd finally get together!"

"Cheeky!" Then, with a longing look, she entreated, "With all my heart, I want to go with you, William, but Mum and Da are pressuring me to give in to Gran."

"I don't get it." Keith questioned, "Why is she so intent on you going with Hector?"

"Her first love was a boy named Hector, but her folks put a stop to it, made her marry someone else. So, maybe she's trying to rewrite history through us."

"Yet," Huw pointed out, "she's doing the same thing to you!"

"Aye, and she makes me feel *so* guilty!" Lilly's eyes pleaded, "But if I don't do what she asks, she might have another heart attack."

Keith exploded, "That's emotional blackmail!"

Crossing the room, I took her hands in mine. "Lil?"

"Aye?" she said softly.

"More than anything, I'd like to take you to the Ceilidh."

"More than anything," she fought back tears, "I want to go with you!"

"Aww," Keith and Huw replied in tandem.

Glancing at my friends, I continued, "But, what if, just this once to keep the peace, you give Gran what she wants?"

She snorted, "You're joking me, right?"

"Hello?" Keith grimaced, "Have you lost your ever lovin' mind?"

"Just listen." My friends stared in disbelief as I offered, "Beneath it all, Gran has a broken heart, and ye'll have nae peace unless she gets her way, right?"

"But William," Lilly protested, "I don't want to go anywhere with Hector. And you of all people, how could you even suggest such a thing?"

Immediately, Huw and Keith rattled off protests of their own.

"Hold on," I stopped them. "You'll nae be going alone."

"What?" Huw and Keith blurted, while Lilly huffed, "I don't understand."

I clarified, "We're the Tantallon 4, right?"

"Aye! Yeah!" They agreed.

"So technically, if Gran accepted on your behalf, she accepted for all of us!" A smile seeped across Lilly's face, and Huw and Keith caught on as I continued, "We shall be yer chaperones. Anywhere you go...we go!"

"Yeah!" Huw stood taller. "Ye'll nae have to be alone with Hector. Not for one moment."

"Brilliant! Absolutely brilliant!" Keith threw up his hands. "Why didn't I think of that?"

"Oh, William," Lilly stammered, "that's a great idea. You know I hate to disappoint Gran, and in a way, even Hector, he's actually been very sweet."

"Well, that's reassuring!" Keith sneered, "Although he wanted to pummell us a few weeks ago."

Lilly gasped, "You never mentioned that!"

"Actually," I corrected, "that was Seth."

"Still not good!" Lilly added. "What if they both show up?"

"Believe me, Lil," I soothed, "between us, and our folks, you'll be well protected."

Running her hand through her hair, she breathed, "This could actually work."

Keith cleared his throat. "There's one thing ye've forgotten, Will."

"What's that?"

He grimaced, "Who's gonna break the news to Hector?"

30

Ceilidh Chaos

By pooling our summer wages and Papa G pulling a few strings, we hired a vintage Rolls Royce to carry us to the Ceilidh. But when it rolled up the lane, this stunner exceeded our wildest expectations.

Beneath a smart black chauffeur's cap, Papa G opened the pearlescent door and beckoned, "*Entrez, s'il vous plaît messieurs.*"

Sinking deep into the scarlet interior, we inhaled the earthy scent of well-kept leather and highly polished wood. Then looking about the salon, Huw exhaled, "Just like Hollywood!"

"Not quite Tarzan." Keith ran his hand over the ribbed interior. "This is the real thing!"

Throwing my head back on the spacious seat, I grinned, "Lilly's gonna be so surprised!"

The thick whitewall tyres made a distinguished crunch on the gravel, announcing our arrival at the Alcott's. And, since it required no confrontation on their part, Gerald and Rose agreed to our alternate plan.

"Now there's a posh ride," he exclaimed. "What year is that?"

Papa G dispensed the particulars of this 1951 Silver Wraith as we oohed and ah-ed over the engine, long classic lines, and vintage dials set in an exquisite teakwood dash. Meanwhile, Mum and Mrs. Alcott peeked inside the coach. "Lilly'll be thrilled!" Rose declared, "And honoured to be escorted by you handsome lads."

"Thanks Mrs., A!" Keith returned, "We aim to please."

"You ne'er give up, do ye laddie?" The commotion drew an irritated Gran outside, "She's going with Hector!"

"Och, for goodness' sake, Sal!" Gerald hushed, "Haud yer weesht!"

Then every head turned as Lilly stepped o'er the threshold wrapped in a flowing pink plaid gown, satin gloves reaching to her elbows and hair curled up in yellow ribbons, baby's breath, and one golden daffy. While her complexion needed no makeup, she complimented her cheeks and lips with a dusting of shimmery pink.

We stared, speechless, until Lilly squealed, "Look at you handsome laddies in your kilts!" A slight breeze caused the pleats in her gown to shimmer as she moved toward us. "And where did you find that car? It's fabulous!" We were as gobsmacked with her as she was with the car, and still staring, she quizzed, "Hello! Anyone out there?"

"Wow Lilly!" Huw broke the silence, "You really are a princess...under all that quirkiness!"

"Thanks Huw." She giggled, spinning around, so the length of the glistening garment flared out. "Like my gown?" Playing with the pleats, she added, "Mum made it!"

"Lilly!" I took her hand, "You're absolutely stunning!" She bit her lip as we held hands, gazing at each other.

"Rose," Mum gushed, "that gown's fit for a queen! I had no idea you were such a talented seamstress."

She smiled at her daughter, "It did turn out quite lovely!"

Gerald sighed, "When did our little girl grow up?"

"Believe it or not, Lil..." Keith admitted, "Ye've rendered us speechless!"

She snorted, "That's not like to last long!"

Though our attire boasted of royalty, we were still our playful selves, and I bowed, "Fair princess of Tantallon, ye must arrive at the ball in style!"

"Ooooh!" she cooed, "and in style we shall be!"

Keith swirled his hand. "Your footmen and coach await!"

"Mademoiselle!" Papa G bowed.

Lilly returned his greeting with a deep curtsy, then threw her hands up in glee, "Oh my gosh! This is fab! Please tell me it doesn't turn into a pumpkin at midnight!"

Just then, Hector, dressed in kilt and Prince Charlie jacket, stepped from the Alcott's front door. Stopping short, he sighed, "What now?"

Lilly hinted, "My courtly brothers in arms, and *our* ride."

"What are you taking about Lil?"

She toyed with her words, "We thought it only fair, since you asked Gran on my behalf..."

We completed her sentence, "That we lads accepted on her behalf."

"No way!" He puffed, "Ye told Gran you'd be happy to go with me!"

"I wasn't finished!" Hector pulled back from her rebuke, "So, since William did ask me first, we all go together, or we don't go at all!"

After a moment, he pointed to the Rolls, "We're going in that?" Lilly nodded eagerly, then looking us over, Hector shrugged, "Alright," offering her his arm, "but I get the first *and* the last dance!"

"Done!" She took his arm with her right, then mine on her left, adding, "And absolutely no fighting lads. I'll dance with all of ye."

Hector gave us a sideways glance, "At least we didn't get dressed up for nothing," then nodded at Papa G. "Nice coach!"

With five of us scrunched into a space made for fewer occupants, we chattered about our posh attire, the vintage auto, and Lilly's gown. Hector even joked, "Outsmarted by three juniors! If this gets out, I'll ne'er hear the end of it."

"No worries, Hector," Huw soothed. "We're all friends here."

"Like when we were lads, remember?" I added.

We smiled, but whether it was the attention, or regrets of lost time, Hector fidgeted, answering, "Yeah, I remember."

While there'd be no Hawaiian dancers or exotic flowers, we were guaranteed a cracking Ceilidh band, so as Papa G opened the door, we piled out in our finery, anticipating what the night might bring.

As promised, Lilly danced the first reel with Hector, and to soothe any hard feelings, the next as well. She followed with Huw, then Keith, then favoured me as we spun round the floor, her gown shimmering in the soft light. And so it went, until our third dance, when she confided, "I saved the best for last!"

The band began a slow take on the "Star of County Down," and from the moment we joined hands, our feet took wings, barely touching the floor.

Mr. Alcott called over, "I see ye've learnt to move your feet, William!"

Little by little, the band quickened the tempo, and we laughed and swirled, faster and faster, round and round the dance floor, till the tune came to a rollicking end. Standing breathless, smiling, anticipating, I looked into Lilly's deep blue eyes and touched her petal soft cheek. Letting out a tiny sigh, she drew closer, pressing her hand to the cross around my neck.

"It's my turn now!" Hector pressed in.

"Wait a minute!" Lilly objected, "I've danced every song since we arrived and could do with a sip of water." She smiled at Hector, "Please?"

"Of course," he stammered. "Should've thought of that, and let me find you a seat." Welcoming his invitation, she settled into the chair as he headed off for refreshments.

Gazing about the room, her eyes sparkled. "Tis an amazing

Ceilidh!"

"Aye, tis." I sat beside her. "But better than the luau?"

"Hmm! The night's young; can't say just yet." Then, kicking off a shoe, she groaned, "Ow! My feet are killing me!"

"Oh, sorry! Who invented high heels anyway?"

"Not sure," she scowled, "but they certainly weren't dancers!"

In the soft light, I studied her face. "Your mum created a master-piece." To her puzzled expression, I confirmed, "You...your gown. It's beautiful."

"Thanks Will." Lilly blushed, smoothing the pleats, "Mum put so much love into it." She glanced back, "You're quite braw yourself, all grown up and handsome."

"Thanks Lil!" Twas my turn to blush.

She looked about, "I'm just so happy everything worked out."

"Aye!" I agreed, "And it's nice to see Hector enjoying himself too, especially with all he goes through at home. I got him to ask your Gran to dance."

"I saw!" Lilly giggled, "Twas so sweet. Ye know, that's what I like about you, Will," she moved closer, "you notice things about people. You care about them. That's rare."

"What kind of man would I be if I didn't care?"

"Eh hum!" Hector stood between us with two glasses of punch. Taking a sip, he handed one to Lilly: "Every queen needs a token food taster to protect the rose!"

She stared as he knelt at her feet. "What are you doing?"

"Never fear my lass," he replied. "Yer safe in my hands, from your head to your toes."

"Nice poetry, Hector!" She complimented, then he removed her other shoe and began to rub her tiny feet. "Oh!" She tensed, with shy surprise, "That's marvelous! You heard me tell William my feet were hurting."

"Nae. The art of observation, some are just born with it." He winked, "Eh Will?" I didn't know how to answer, but Hector filled in the blank, "Two steps, Ridley!"

With those words, the evening shifted. Sitting next to the girl who meant the world to me, I cringed, watching Hector rubbing her feet, capturing her attention, her smiles and her laughter. While they chatted about the dance, the band, even Papa G and the Rolls, I sat silent, wondering what to do. Hector kept rearranging himself, so little by little, Lilly had turned her back to me. Cheeky on his part, but she seemed to be enjoying herself, so I waited.

Before long, Huw and Keith trudged over with heaping plates of food, "Who's hungry?"

Jumping up, Hector grabbed two plates, handing one to Lilly. "Perfect timing, lads!"

There was plenty to go round and our lighthearted banter filled the air, but as we ate, Hector began whispering in Lilly's ear. They laughed, and she whispered back, acting more and more as though we weren't there.

"What..." Keith leaned over, "is going on?"

I shrugged as they resumed a place on the dance floor and Huw, Keith and I watched as the band played a slow, mournful tune called "Molly Bán." The singer's sorrow echoed the ache in my heart as Hector drew Lilly close and sang to her upturned face.

"How can she fall for that?" I huffed.

Huw snorted, "We've the makings of a Shakespearean tragedy here."

Giving him a sideways look, Keith soothed, "No worries, Will. You'll sort it on the next dance."

Sighing heavily, I continued staring, sure my heart would burst, when Siobhan MacDoone took hold of my hand, "William, will ye dance with me?"

Surprised, I stammered, "I...Em..."

"Sure he will!" Huw and Keith answered for me, providing an

encouraging shove in her direction.

Joining her in the dance, my heart was elsewhere, and rude as it was, I couldn't help glancing in their direction. I had no conversation, but Siobhan took pity. "Ye alright, Will?"

Forcing a smile, I lied, "Aye, I'm fine, Siobhan."

"It's a cracker of a band." After a moment, she grimaced, "except for this song!"

I finally laughed, "Yer spot on there."

"Sure yer alright?" She asked again.

"Aye!" I attempted a cheerier tone, "Twas nice of ye to ask me to dance."

"Well, a braw lad like yourself shouldn't be standing on the side lines." She glanced in their direction, "Even if ye are in love with Lilly Alcott."

I choked out, "Is it that obvious?"

"William!" She rolled her eyes. "*And* if ye really liked her, ye wouldn't let Hector weasel his way in."

Those were bold words for a lass I hardly knew, but she did have a point. While considering it, she manoeuvred us into their view, then began twirling the hair at the back of my neck. Instantly swatting her hand like a pesky midge, a voice in my head warned, '*Walk away, now!*'

But before I could think of an excuse, Siobhan gave a wink, drawing out her words, "Or, if ye ever change yer mind..." She grabbed my cross, yanked me forward, and there in the centre of the dance floor, planted a huge kiss on my face.

To say I was shocked would be an understatement, worsening to monumental proportions when Siobhan followed with a stinging slap to my cheek, then strode off across the room. Staring in disbelief, a sea of curious faces stared back as the enormity of what happened began sinking in. Immediately, I wiped my lips with the back of my hand, wishing it might erase what Siobhan'd just done.

Then I saw Lilly.

Shaking, tears spilling down her flushed cheeks. "I don't believe what I just saw, William! How could you?"

"Lilly! *She* kissed me."

"Yeah," she scolded, "well, ye didn't have to kiss her back!"

"I didn't!" I pleaded, "She grabbed my cross and pulled me."

"Really?" Lilly scoffed, "Then why'd she slap you?"

I shook my head. "I don't know!" Hector put a hand on her shoulder as I stammered, "This isn't what it seems, Lil. It's all wrong."

"You got that right!" She huffed, "Don't you ever come near me again, William Ridley. I... I hate you!" Yanking the daffodil from her hair, she threw it at me, then hurried away, sobbing.

Under the weight of angry stares, I knelt to reclaim the crumpled flower. And Hector, towering over me, smiled triumphantly, "Tough luck with the lassies, Will."

I had no words to refute his contempt, and he had no sympathy for my despair. With a snicker, he hurried after Lilly as the room began buzzing with chatter.

Taking action, Da hurried me outside, away from the scathing stares. "You okay?"

Looking up into the night sky, I fought back tears. "No!" I covered my face. "Oh da! I don't even know Siobhan. Why would she do that?"

He put a hand on my shoulder. "What did she say to you?"

"Lilly?"

"No, what's her name again?"

"Siobhan," I sighed, shaking my head, recounting her words. They stung in my ears like the slap to my cheek, "Och, makes no sense."

"Unless..." Da took a deep breath. "She likes you and wanted to make Lilly jealous."

"Well, that certainly worked!" I sputtered, "She hates me now!"

"Will," Da reassured, "you and Lilly have known each other a long time. Rest assured, you'll get this sorted."

Dare I even hope? My heart felt it would burst. My lack of discernment caused Lilly's tears, and I loathed myself for being so naive. What a strange and horrible twist this evening had taken, and Gran MacCrimmon wielded it against me.

"You should've listened to your Gran! If I were you, I'd ne'er see that lad again!" Throwing Lilly's words back at her, she huffed, "Safe indeed!"

The Alcotts left immediately, along with Hector, who grasped Lilly's hand. "Look Lil, I know I'm not your first choice, but if there's anything I can do to help, I'm here. No strings attached, just a friendly shoulder to lean on."

<h1 style="text-align:center">31</h1>

Bad to Worse

Lilly wouldn't even look at me, let alone allow me to explain, and seeing her with Hector the next few weeks increased my agony. Plus, every time I got near her, Siobhan showed up. Despite my protests, she'd grab my arm and gush how happy she was to see me, at least as long as Lilly was in sight. The whole thing stank of sulphur, and though I couldn't prove it, I felt sure Hector had a hand in it. So, all I could do was wait.

After another long fortnight, while staring out the corridor window, Lilly touched my shoulder. Our smiles were tense, but her temper had cooled.

"Hi Will."

"Lilly! I'm so sorry about what happened."

"I've been thinking," she shook her head, "it doesn't make sense."

"I didn't even want to dance with Siobhan, but when she asked, the lads pushed me."

"Hey Willy!" Siobhan called, rounding the corner.

"Go away!" I held up my hand, "Right now!"

Lilly's eyes shimmered with hope, but paying no heed, Siobhan pinched my cheek. "You promised me a movie handsome, so no getting out of that!"

"Stop!" I brushed her hand away. "I did no such thing!"

Commandeering the conversation, she winked, "I love when you play coy, Willy." Then leaning over, she whispered, "Really, Lil, you missed out; he's an amazing kisser!"

"You horrible liar!" I bellowed, but Siobhan's theatricals did their work. "Lilly!" I cried, but she turned and ran as my voice trailed off, "Please come back!"

Siobhan chuckled, then hurried after her, calling, "Paws off, girlie, he's mine!"

As students filled the corridor, I fell hard against the wall, slid down to the floor, and not caring who saw, I wept.

Even Huw and Keith attempted amends, but Lilly pointed out, "Twas you lads who pushed him and Siobhan together in the first place!" Before long, she banished all three of us from her life.

Then somewhere, in the midst of this turmoil, Mr. Ramsay's words resurfaced: "Hold Fast, and all will turn out well." So every waking moment, I prayed, first, asking God to protect Lilly from whatever Hector and her Gran were filling her head with, and second, to bring the truth to light.

After weeks of prayer and encouragement from my folks that this situation had purpose even if I couldn't see it, a glimmer of hope arose. Like a train off its rails, Siobhan pushed past me through the crowded hall and shoved Lilly and Keith into a corner. Instinctively, he followed her out behind our school.

Striding up to Hector, she demanded, "You promised! Twenty quid for helping with your little ruse!"

"Shh Siobhan! You'll have it soon."

"Don't you shush me, Hector Menteith! I need that money now!"

"Why the hurry?" He purred.

She glared at him, "Like you don't know!"

"That was yer doing." Hector huffed, "Besides, you were supposed to charm William. Not my fault you couldn't pull that off!"

"Listen dirtbag!" Siobhan seethed, "I wouldn't be in this mess if you hadn't..."

"Hadn't what?" She whirled around to see Keith waiting for an answer.

Hector choked, "What are you looking at, Spyglass?"

Keith rubbed his chin, "A spider's web."

"You heard nothing!" Hector growled, "Now get out of here!" Turning back towards Siobhan, he raised his fist, "You stupid girl!"

Keith grabbed his arm, "Don't you dare hit her."

Shoving Keith backwards, Hector snarled, "I said, get lost!"

"Hector!" Lilly stepped forward. "What are you doing?"

Casting a sympathetic gaze at Siobhan, he concocted a new deception, "You'll find out sooner or later." He sighed, "Though *I* didn't want to be the one to tell you."

Lilly asked hesitantly, "Tell me what?"

"William...had a little fun." He pointed towards Siobhan, "got her in the family way, so she came to me for help."

"Hector!" She laughed, "That's ridiculous. He'd ne'er do that."

"Take that back snake!" Keith rallied, "You'll not sully William's good name," he glared at Siobhan, "either of ye."

"It's true!" Siobhan looked frightened. "I know you think he's a goody-goody, but..." She continued, "William's not who you think he is!"

"Siobhan, I don't believe you, not for one moment." Lilly chided, "I see clearly now; it's you who've been chasing him!"

"Well Cinderella!" Siobhan glared back, "Whilst you were doodling notes on Skye, Prince Charming and his magic cross were doodling something else! Now he's pretending nothing happened, so just be thankful he didn't do it to you!" Glancing between Lilly and Keith, she waited for their reaction.

"How'd you know about my notes?" Lilly stammered.

Siobhan snorted, "William told me."

Keith demanded, "Then why was Hector about to hit you?"

"He was..." Hector grinned as Siobhan put a hand to her forehead, faking a breathless swoon. "catching me. Sometimes it makes me faint."

Keith huffed, shaking his head as Huw and I rounded the corner.

"Everything okay?" I asked.

Siobhan sauntered to my side, "Tis now that you're here, Will."

"Look, Siobhan," I stepped back. "Once and for all, stop this! I don't know what you're on about. Seriously, the only girl I've ever cared for is standing right here, and her name is Lilly Alcott!" I smiled, knowing she had finally heard my heart, but Lilly pointed to Siobhan, who stood beside me, rubbing her tummy. After a strained silence, I became puzzled, "What? What's wrong with everyone?"

"They know the truth, Will...about us." Siobhan purred, "It's no use pretending anymore."

"The only truth here," I insisted, "is whatever comes from your lips is a lie! You stole a kiss at the Ceilidh, that's all. There's nothing between us; there never has been and there never will be!"

"But William," Lilly's face was bathed in tears. "Siobhan's going to have a baby!"

The treacherous one pawed my arm, "Your baby, William!"

"What?" I laughed, "That...that's ridiculous!"

Siobhan sobbed, "You said you loved me! Was that an act?"

Thunderstruck by her emotional display, I sputtered, "Ye've got to be kidding me!" Siobhan started to wail uncontrollably, as I shook my head. "Och! This is rubbish; an utter, disgusting lie from the pit, and you know it!"

"Rubbish?" She dabbed her tears. "Come on, babe, you wouldn't want to offend God by lying anymore!"

Twas a nightmare, one I couldn't wake from, and the more I protested, the thicker and more condemning their lies became.

Hector sneered, "Just goes to show, these holy rollers cannae be trusted."

"Or is it only when it's convenient for you, Will?" Siobhan cried, "What am I supposed to do now?"

My friends shook their heads listening to lie after lie until Keith reeled in disgust, "William! How could you?"

I stared in horror, for nothing I could say or do would set them straight. In despair, I fled, their lies swirling in my head as I ran home, weeping great sobs of grief till Da caught me in the lane, "Will! What on earth is wrong?"

Mum went ghastly pale as Da confirmed, "The girl from the Ceilidh?"

I nodded.

He let out a long, heavy sigh. "I'm sorry I have to ask, but is there any truth to this... at all?"

"No, Da! Absolutely not!" I sobbed, "I've barely spoken to Siobhan till the Ceilidh, and by e'ry thing I hold dear, I wish I'd never danced with her! Now everyone believes her and Hector. Even worse, it brings shame on God, and unless I can prove she's lying, my life is ruined!"

"Try to be calm," Da comforted, "the truth will come to light."

"But, Da, she was asking Hector for money to..." I covered my face. "I cannae even say it."

Though stunned, Da kept his wits: "When a baby's born, a test can prove who the father is."

"Great! But what do I do in the meantime?"

Da grabbed my shoulders. "Ye've nothing to fear. We've seen the Lord, move time and time again, protecting us and disproving false claims." Reeling from my distress, his brow furrowed. "We will sort this out."

Mum offered a cool flannel to wipe my face and a hot cuppa, but I had neither appetite, nor thirst. I spent the next hour staring into the fire over and over, hearing Keith's accusation, seeing Lilly's tear stained face, and wondering how life got so messed up.

My scrambled thoughts tortured, awash in deep distress. Mum drew me close and whispered, "You're my warrior, William! Don't be surprised at the fiery trials when they come to test you."

"But Mum! What can I do?"

"Pray." I listened to her wisdom, "The battle belongs to the Lord, and He will deliver you!"

While the situation seemed overwhelming, as King David did, I fell to my knees and pleaded, trusting the Lord to intervene. But things only grew worse, and vicious rumours began circulating through school. So I kept my head down, avoiding eye contact, though that didn't shield me from cheeky comments. And to my absolute horror, Seth slapped me on the back, snickering, "Well done, holy man!"

If only I could vanish. How, I wondered, would I make it through this day? Under watchful eyes, I slipped behind my desk and began to sweat. Class began, yet I heard nothing of the lesson, remaining the proverbial elephant in the room. Thankfully, a tap at the door promised relief as I rose to answer a summons to our headmaster's office. But the click of the latch set off an explosion of chatter behind me, stealing away any solace an empty corridor might have provided.

"Tut, tut, tut." Looking over tortoise rimmed glasses, Mr. Baffle shook his head. "William Ridley, I am astounded. Yes, astounded at what you and Siobhan MacDoone are caught up in."

"Mr. Baffle..."

"Tut!" He silenced with a hand, "I've known you since you were a lad... I know your parents. Who'd ever believe such a thing? Yet Siobhan is going to have a baby."

Rising from his desk, he crossed to the window and stared across the courtyard. Then, drawing in a deep breath, he turned, "I'll speak plainly. While the facts are not yet clear, this... situation has caused disruption in nearly every classroom. I can't allow that." I nodded as he continued, "Until further notice, you and Siobhan will complete your assignments from home."

"But Mr. Baffle," I protested. "That's punishing me for a crime I didn't commit! By sending me away, you're saying you believe her too."

"William wait."

"No! I must speak. You know, if there were *any* truth in this, I'd admit it and do the right thing, but it's just not true! And though I cannae prove it, Hector Menteith is behind this, guaranteed!"

Locking eyes, Mr. Baffle sighed, "That remains to be seen, William... No, I've already sent Siobhan home, so you'll need to respect my decision as well."

Da offered an arm to steady me as we made our way to the car. It would be a week complete before the MacDoones could clear their schedule for a conference, and while Mum and Da did their best to keep my spirits up, that day couldn't arrive soon enough.

32

The Light of Day

I woke before dawn and prayed in earnest, fully trusting that God would deliver me from this present darkness. I'd still heard nothing from my friends, but with Mum and Da by my side, I headed into battle.

We were led into an imposing room of polished mahogany, boasting a library of leather-bound books on shelves that stretched from floor to ceiling. The soft glow from Mr. Baffle's desk lamp seeped through thick glass windows into the dreich morning, and closing the heavy wooden door, he sighed. "Sad business this day."

"Sad indeed," Da nodded, "for everyone."

Clearing his throat, Mr. Baffle tightened his gaze, "William, one thing I'd like to ask before the others arrive."

"Anything!"

"Do you have scars?"

"What?"

"A birthmark, scar, something that wouldn't show," he probed, "say unless you'd... taken your shirt off."

"Oh." Comprehending his meaning, I lifted my shirt, revealing the marred flesh of my torso: "From my fall at the lighthouse."

Mum winced. "It's never really healed."

"Anyone else know about this?"

I shrugged, "Huw and Keith."

"Very well." He noted, "Cover up."

Over the intercom, his secretary announced, "The MacDoones are here, sir."

"Ah, thank you. Send them in, please."

We stood to meet Siobhan and her parents, but bypassing Da's extended hand, Mr. MacDoone strode over and spat in my face.

Inserting himself between us, Mr. Baffle growled, "You will refrain yourself sir!"

"More courtesy than he deserves!" Siobhan's da sneered.

Mum handed me a tissue, and wiping away his spit, I stared, shocked, unsettled, but mostly feeling sorry for this family.

As they seated themselves, Mr. Baffle began, "Siobhan, you've brought a serious accusation against William."

"My daughter's pregnant; what more proof do you need?" Her da barked.

"A simple test," Da stated, "when the baby's born."

"Who's to say it'll go that far?" A stormy look crossed Mr. MacDoone's brow as he glared at Da.

"Gentleman!" Mr. Baffle commanded, "This situation bears heavy consequences for these young people." Siobhan looked surprised as he stressed, "I'm not suggesting anyone's lying, but there's a child to consider, so let's sort this out. Shall we?" We nodded as he prompted, "Siobhan, why don't you begin?"

Looking towards her Da, who continued glaring at me, she began spinning her tale, "Well...I guess it started the 5th of July. William invited me to Tantallon...the day Lilly left for Skye."

"And what happened next?"

"Well," she rolled her eyes, snorting, "do I really have to explain?"

"This is serious, young lady," Mr. Baffle reprimanded, "so I suggest you answer with a little less cheek."

"Go on, lass," her da encouraged. "Tell him what the swine did to you."

"He...um," she gulped, "William showed me around the castle, spouted some historical stuff, names, dates, and things like that, then totally gobsmacked me, saying he loved me! Really sweet, ye know? Then he showed me that cross he always wears and said," She mocked my voice, " '*God drew us together...*' then he kissed me. I didn't expect it would go further, but we..." She looked away, "We were together."

"Just like that?"

She nodded, "*Just* like that."

Ignoring my indignant gasp, Mr. Baffle asked, "Was that the only time?"

"Oh no!" She grinned wide, "He insisted several more times."

Mr. MacDoone slammed his fist on the arm of the chair as I shook my head in protest. "Siobhan, you're lying!"

She flashed a wide-eyed, innocent look as Mr. Baffle chided, "Hush! You'll have your turn..."

"May I clarify something?" Da interrupted, drawing a consenting nod from Mr. Baffle, "Siobhan, did you say it was the day Lilly left for Skye?"

"Aye, the very same. Will said with her gone, he'd finally be able to spend time with me. He seemed sincere."

Mum looked at Da, then asked, "Do you remember what time that was?"

"Three in the afternoon, exactly!" She chirped, "Will tells time by where the sun is in the sky, so he put his arm around my waist, then pointed out over the Firth. It was kinda cosy."

Siobhan had clearly used her time to concoct a believable story, but Da countered, "You're positive twas the afternoon Lilly left?"

Mr. MacDoone interjected, "She said so twice, are you deaf?"

"It's just," Mum added, "William and his friends were quite dejected that afternoon. We took them all to the cinema."

"That's right!" I added, "Huw'll have the tickets; he saves every one."

Mr. MacDoone sneered, "You people would lie about anything!"

Say almost anything about Da, and he'd keep his cool, but come against his family, and he defended like a wild bear, "My family doesn't lie, and I challenge anyone who says otherwise to prove it, or retract that statement!"

Both Da and Mr. MacDoone jumped to their feet, but Siobhan cried, "Alright! Alright! It could have been the day after, but we were there. *Please*! Don't fight."

"Gentleman, anger is hardly helpful." As the men resumed their seats, Mum took Da's hand, and Mr. Baffle asked, "How long have you known about the baby?"

"Since the Ceilidh. I told William that night, but he acted like it never happened. That's why I slapped him on the dance floor."

While I shook my head in protest, Mr. Baffle nodded. "I remember. So, did you go home right after?"

"What?" She reeled, "Why do you want to know that?"

"Details are important." Siobhan went silent, so he prompted, "Don't you remember?"

Her eyes darted around the room as though searching for an answer, "No, I... I left with friends."

"Male or female?"

"What are you suggesting?" Her da grumbled.

Mr. Baffle crossed his arms, waiting for his answer.

"It's okay, Da," she offered. "I went to a party with male and female friends."

"Right." He added, "So, if the Ceilidh ended at midnight, do you mind telling us when you arrived home?"

She whispered, "Later that morning."

"Mr. MacDoone?" Mr. Baffle redirected, "Are you in the habit of allowing your daughter to stay out all night, unchaperoned?"

His face grew red with anger. "I'm not even going to answer you on that!"

Mr. Baffle drew a deep breath. "Siobhan, I've known you and William, since you were weans, and honestly find it shocking either of you are here under these circumstances."

"I know Mr. Baffle," she cooed, "but these things, unfortunately, do happen."

Crossing the room, he stood before her. "Then tell me the absolute truth. Is William the father of your baby?" Wide-eyed, she remained silent. "Or, is it possible, something else happened?"

"Now wait just a minute," Mr. MacDoone spewed.

"It's alright, dear," Mrs. MacDoone spoke, "we've nothing to hide." Petting her daughter's head, she said, "Answer Mr. Baffle, Siobhan."

Her face turned deathly white, then she started to sob, turning towards the window. Stepping back, Mr. Baffle softened, "I understand this is difficult to talk about, but if what you say is true, you'll need to answer a few more questions. Okay?"

With deep furrows in her brow, she nodded.

"When you were *with* William these several times, did he take his shirt off?"

"Are you daft, man?" Mr. MacDoone bellowed.

Ignoring the outburst, Mr. Baffle asked again, "Siobhan?"

"Aye, of course he did," she added with a grin, "you don't rush these things!"

"Than you would know...if William has scars, correct?"

Her eyes grew wide as she stammered, "Ye can't expect me to remember that!"

"My dear girl! I may be an antique to your thinking, but I

remember everything about my wedding night. My Lucy has two scars, and I know exactly how and when she got them. So, I'd like an answer. Does William have a scar," he paused, "or not?"

Siobhan looked at me, then started to cry, "I don't know. I don't know!"

"Siobhan," I pleaded, "Please, *please* tell them the truth."

She started to shake, and her Da prompted, "Siobhan?"

Looking from her Da to me, then Mr. Baffle, she gurgled, "Ah! The party, after the Ceilidh. Hector's friends gave me a drink. One minute we were talking and laughing; the next, I must have passed out."

Her Da launched to his feet and began pacing.

"I've ne'er done anything like that, honest! When I woke up, I couldn't find my shirt, and then..." She trembled, "I saw what they'd done to me."

Siobhan crumpled, wailing uncontrollably, and Mum and Mrs. MacDoone began to weep as well. "Och," she soothed, pulling her daughter close, "my darlin lass."

"Siobhan!" Her Da gasped, "Why didn't you tell us?"

"I was terrified, Da!" She sobbed, "Hector said it was my fault, but I couldn't remember, and I knew you'd be angry."

He stammered, "What on earth were you doing there?"

"Hector promised me twenty quid to dance with William and do something shocking to make Lilly mad... so he'd have a chance with her." She softened, "I didn't mind. I like ye, William."

I struggled to comprehend how she could think that possible.

"He said he'd pay me at that party; else I'd ne'er have gone." The room fell silent, then Siobhan's voice cracked, "How'd ye know?"

"I didn't." Mr. Baffle answered. "Only heard a rumour."

"But Siobhan," I tensed, "you've made everyone believe I did this to you! Why?"

"Hector started it! And I was so frightened, I couldn't see any other way out. Please forgive me, William. I am so, so sorry."

Stunned, Mrs. MacDoone raised a hand to her mouth as Siobhan's whole body began to tremble. She looked up at her da, who exploded, "I've heard enough!" He spat his words, "I can't even look at you right now!"

"Da! Please..." Siobhan whimpered, "I need your help."

But her cries fell on deaf ears as he stormed out, slamming the door so hard, it shook on its hinges.

"William," Mr. Baffle pressed, "how would you like to proceed?"

The enormous weight of her deception had tortured me, and till now, I'd not even been allowed to defend myself. Rising in anger, I began pacing, words stinging in my mouth: "You've caused such grief, Siobhan, to me, to our families. *And* you've driven Lilly into Hector's arms!"

This crafty, opinionated, accusatory, devastating liar of a tear-stained girl looked so fragile, leaning on her mum. Then striding towards the window, wrestling between anger and pity, I stared out at the dismal day. Shockingly, I discovered the bitter, raging face staring back from the glass was my own. In that sobering moment, I whispered, "God forgive me."

As I drew breath, a ray of sunlight pierced the gloom, shimmering over my cross. Grasping it, I turned to her, "I am truly sorry for what happened to you, Siobhan, but after today, I don't ever want to think about this again." Crossing the room, I took her hand, looked into her tear-filled eyes, and said, "I forgive you."

Looking up, she mouthed the words rather than spoke, "Thank you, William."

"Your forgiveness," Mr. Baffle broke the silence, "is commendable; unfortunately, school policy is not. I'm afraid your time at Berwick has come to an end, Siobhan."

She grasped her mother's hand, pleading, "Please, Mr. Baffle. I made a horrible mistake, but I said I'm sorry. Please don't make me leave."

"I too am abhorred at what's been done to you; it's unconscionable. And I promise to do everything in my power to help, starting with a call to the police, but in your condition, I've no choice."

She received his decision with a solemn nod of resolution.

Siobhan had nearly destroyed my life, yet I couldn't help but pity her. Yes, she'd made a mistake, along with an outrageous lie, but her innocence had been stolen, and her life had been forever altered. Plus, when she needed her da most, he abandoned her. A casualty of this sinful world, but at the very least, she had Mr. Baffle's help to count on.

I too had been tested by fire, but through prayer and patience, God delivered me. Then, like a rusty wheel set back in motion, I got on with my studies. There were still whispers and snickers in the hallways, but I had my life back.

Immediately, Keith apologised, "Even after knowing you all these years, Will, Hector and Siobhan were so convincing and knew things they shouldn't have. I'm sorry I doubted you. Really, really sorry!"

My voice cracked with emotion as I nodded, "Thank you."

Huw added, "I'm ashamed to say I believed them too. And, when you needed a friend most, Will, we weren't there for you. Can you forgive us?"

Releasing a sigh, I smiled, "Aye! I forgive you numpties for being so thick!"

For the first time in weeks, we laughed, then Keith added, "What a horrid thing to do! Don't know what I'd have done in your place, Will."

"What did you do?" Huw asked.

"Honestly? I wept. Then I prayed. Then Mum and Da prayed with me. There really is a battle between good and evil, and if not for the Lord, I'd have been destroyed, but He delivered me!"

Keith chimed, "That's some serious faith!"

"No." I corrected, "That's a mighty serious God!"

Meanwhile, Hector scrambled to regain Lilly's favor, "Look, I was just as duped by Siobhan as everyone else! Honest Lil."

"What about paying her to dance with William?"

"The girl's a born liar! She made us believe she was dating him! Come on," he simpered, "ye cannae blame me for that?"

With smooth words and a puppy dog smile, Hector found forgiveness, while I remained at a distance. My emotions were too raw to say anything at present. One could simply say I was jealous, but 'Two steps behind' kept ringing in my ears. The same way I heard 'Walk away!' at the Ceilidh, I sensed Lilly was in danger. But things between us were different, and she'd been seeing Hector. So I retreated until our paths crossed between classes.

Staring for a moment, I said, "Hello!"

"Hey, Will," she offered with a wave.

I spoke without thinking, "How's your boyfriend?"

A crushed look covered Lilly's face.

"Look, that was rude. I'm sorry." We stared for a moment, then I added, "Honest, if Hector makes you happy, I'll say no more, but you're dearer to me than I can say, Huw and Keith too, and we don't want to see you get hurt."

Hope shimmered in her eyes. "No, Will, I'm sorry. You were all so right. It's just since the Ceilidh; I thought you were with Siobhan, and this...thing is not at all what I wanted. Hector's not like you, he, he..."

Fear covered Lilly's face as Hector rounded the corner, grabbed and pressed her into a kiss. Wrestling against him, he chided, "What's the matter, Lil? You didn't mind last night!"

"Stop it, Hector!" She wiped away the stolen kiss. "And don't you ever do that again!"

Placing a hand on his shoulder, I warned, "Let her go!"

Hector scoffed, "Mind your own business, preacher boy!"

Seeing Mr. Baffle heading our way and pleased with his conquest, Hector winked, then disappeared into a sea of chatty students.

I wiped a tear from her cheek. "Ye alright?"

"Oh, William," she covered her face, "this is my mess. You can't help me."

"Of course I can, Lil," I pleaded, "anything, just ask."

"No," she began to cry, "ye can't. Please don't try!"

As she ran down the hall, Mr. Baffle appeared. "What happened lad?"

"Hector's got some kind of hold over Lilly," I sighed, "and she won't even let me help."

Our headmaster furrowed his brow. "Give it time lad."

The only thing I could do was wait. I could almost hear Papa G saying, *"Prayer and patience!"* His words echoed as I attempted to bury my concerns in study. Mum tutored Huw and me on our upcoming math exam, and while some problems were easily solved, others remained a complicated puzzle, a most welcome distraction. Yet when my brain was too full of integers, calculations, and equations, I walked by the sea, letting the freshness of the air wash away the fog in my brain. Then, in the quiet of the day, I'd allow myself to think of and pray for Lilly.

33

It's all in the Dance

While Jimmy, Huw and I frantically studied our notes before the exam, Keith leaned back, yawning. "Easy peasy, lads."

"If it's so easy," Huw countered, "whoever aces this can buy us all curry chips!"

"Och Huw!" Jimmy groaned, "If my tummy rumbles during the exam, tis yer fault!"

"Hey," I asked, "do ye hear that?"

"What, my stomach?" Jimmy smiled.

"No." Keith stood up, "Someone's crying."

"That's Lilly!" I shouted, running for the door.

Gripping her arm, Hector shoved her into a corner. "You cannae break up with me, you're mine!"

"You don't own me, Hector," Lilly returned, "and let go; you're hurting me!"

Racing over, Huw and Jimmy spun Hector around, while Keith and I grabbed his wrists. Gritting my teeth, I seethed, "About time you picked on someone your own size!"

The curious gathered as we restrained him, but with height and weight on his side, Hector twisted round, pummeling Keith's shoulder, then grazed my chin with a jab.

Raising my fist to return the favour, Lilly screamed, "William, no!"

Her terrified cry diverted my attention, allowing Hector to seize me by the throat. "Where's yer Jesus now, preacher boy?" Toying with my cross, he taunted, "Maybe I just need one of these, so I can be all *holy* too!"

"That would mean repenting!"

He snorted, "It's about power, you twit! And in the end," he tightened his grip, hissing, "I win!"

"No Hector!" I choked, "In the end, we all die...Where'll you spend eternity?"

Struggling against each other, he balled his fist, "Ugh...enough!"

"Break it up!" Mr. Baffle pushed between us, "This instant!"

Expelling a dark sinister laugh, Hector released his grip, but as a token of malice, he spat in Mr. Baffle's face.

Rarely had we seen our headmaster's ire but fully kindled, he growled, "Young man, into my office. Now!"

For a moment, he only stared, then lightning fast, Hector pulled back his arm and, with one mighty punch, sent our headmaster and I into a heap against the wall.

He snarled at the crowd, "Anyone else want a go?"

Jumping up, I scrambled towards him, but he grabbed Lilly around the neck, using her as a shield. Students scattered, screaming, till amid the chaos, Mr. Tinley intercepted from behind. Freeing Lilly, he wrestled Hector to the ground, and finally, North Berwick had endured enough of Hector Menteith.

As he was led away spewing obscenities, he threatened, "You'll regret this preacher boy!"

Rubbing his shoulder, Keith and I helped Mr. Baffle to his feet.

"Ye alright, sir?" I asked.

"Och, all but my dignity," he dusted off. "Ye lads alright?"

We nodded, "Aye, but more importantly," I pointed, "is Lilly okay?"

Surrounded by a clutch of lassies, they pressed her towards the girl's room, clucking.

"You're safe now, Lil!"

"Hector's a beast!"

I wanted to rush to her side, hold her, comfort her, but Mr. Baffle patted my shoulder, "Not yet lad, not yet."

He spoke the truth. These past few months, our entire world had been turned upside down, then by each clarifying event, set right side up again. Lilly was going to need plenty of time to recover without pressure from me. Siobhan moved away to her auntie's awaiting the baby, and Mr. Baffle discovered Seth had been the one who assaulted her. He and Hector were sent to a residential centre, and the rest of us got on with our lives, awaiting the great healer of time to render us more like ourselves.

"Hey," after class, Keith nudged me, "We're away to the chippy. Ye coming?"

"Aye." I returned, "Be right there."

"Don't be long." Huw groaned, "We're hungry!"

After a few minutes, still deep in thought, I gathered my notes in the quiet room, then stepped into the hall. At the same moment, Lilly came bounding down the corridor, doing a twirling leap. There was no stopping our collision, and books and papers went flying in every direction. Stunned and sprawled out on the floor, we stared, breathless.

"You alright?"

Lilly nodded, then we burst into laughter. Quickly she defended, "I'm so sorry, I'm learning ballet."

"Och! And they say my family's rubbish at the dance!"

We laughed again, and looking into her deep blue eyes, for a moment, I beheld the Lilly I used to know. "Oh, how I've missed your laughter, Lil."

Staring a moment, she breathed, "I'm so sorry, William. I've not been myself since... well, you know, but things are getting better."

I offered a hand to help her up. "It's braw to see you again!"

"You too!"

Our pleasantries faded into an awkward silence, so I asked, "How's your mum?"

"She starts a new job this week. And we've plans to hike Glen Nevis this summer. It's..." Suddenly self-conscious, she stopped, then looked away.

"Beautiful!" I encouraged, "And easier to hike than the Ben, with waterfalls all along the Reiver's trails."

"Aye, I believe you're right."

"But I don't know how to break it to ye, Lil."

She looked concerned. "Break what?"

I whispered, "There're no hogs there."

Throwing her head back, we laughed again. "Well, we'll see about that."

"And yer da?"

"Oh...em," she shrugged. "He's Da, you know? I miss his stories, but lately he's only interested in his bevvy."

"I'm sorry."

"He doesn't mean to!" She blurted.

"I know, just wish I could help someway."

"You're so kind, William." She touched my sleeve, "I admire that."

"And I admire you, Lil," I encouraged, "for many reasons."

"Really?" She challenged, "Like what?"

"You're strong yet delicate, an amazing artist, and more adventurous than any lad I know!"

"That, I get from Da!" She brushed back a strand of hair. "Ye know, we don't have the perfect family, but I am thankful for them."

"No one has a perfect family, Lil! And there's goodness in your folks. I remember yer da waiting, probably overnight, till we got back from the Bass."

"Aye, I'm sure he did. He was ill a complete week after! But," she paused, "what you have with your folks, and Mr. Ramsay, that's rare. I'm so glad we spent that time together."

"Me too, Lil ...me too."

Our eyes locked, then she whispered, "William?"

"Aye?"

Mirroring where my cross sat, she gave her neck a gentle touch, "Ye know how ye talk about God's love— that He's always with you, protecting and guiding you?"

I nodded, "He is!"

"Do you think...Do you think God could love me like that? I mean..." She stammered, "I've done bad things, and maybe that's why all this stuff happened."

"Lilly," I gushed, "Yer the sweetest, kindest lass I know."

"I'm serious, Will! You may hate me when I tell you, but I was so angry, I told Hector things that Siobhan used against you. I didn't know. I'm so sorry." Her eyes welled up with tears.

"Hey! Tis okay." I breathed, "That's over."

"But, it was wrong, Will!"

Soothing her worry, I explained, "We all do bad stuff; God calls it sin. When we do or say something we shouldn't, relationships get strained until we apologize. Yet, with Jesus, no matter what we've done, if we're truly sorry, He forgives and removes the burden because He's God! Unlike any human, Jesus washes us clean, renews our soul, wraps us in His righteousness, and loves us...forever!"

"Is that really true?" Her eyes glistened.

"If it wasn't Lil, God would be a liar, but He's not. Though I don't know everything, I know He's good, and I know He loves you, dearly."

"That's good." She stared a moment, then diverted, "I em, heard about your intensive math studies. How'd ye lads do on exams?"

"Not bad... Mum's tutoring'll get us promoted. Which reminds me, the musketeers miss your company."

"I can't imagine why." She huffed, "I've been so horrible to you all. But I have missed our conversations... Especially yours!"

"You're always welcome, Lil, anytime." I stammered, "I've missed you too."

Lilly averted her gaze as a few students shuffled past, then lifted her eyes. "Did you really mean what you said behind the school?"

"What's that?"

"That I was the *only* girl you'd ever cared for?"

"Aye!" I smiled, "With all my heart. I think it started the day you shared about your Da in class. And it's long overdue, but I'm so very, very sorry about the Ceilidh. I never should have danced with Siobhan, and I'm sorry she made up those horrible lies and how it hurt you."

Tears began spilling down her cheeks.

"Please don't cry, Lil! I'm so sorry my stupidity caused you pain."

"No silly, these are happy tears." She caught her breath. "I'm sorry too. Sorry, I believed Siobhan and Hector. And..." she let out a disgusted, "Ugh! That I let him rub my feet. I was trying to make you jealous, but it backfired, big time!"

"It's okay, Lil."

"No, it's not okay!" She scolded herself, "If I'd only been patient, things would ne'er have gone the way they did."

I took her hand in mine. "We all bungled a bit, but that's in the past now."

She nodded. "There's something...I've wanted to tell you."

I interrupted, wiping another tear from her flushed cheek, "I don't ever want to cause you sadness, Lil."

"I told you, these are happy tears." She waved her hands, "It's all my emotions spilling out, because what I wanted to say is..." she struggled, "and I know I'm being impatient and should probably wait for you to say this first, but..." She breathed, "I love you. I love you, William Ridley!"

I stared, fearing I'd not heard correctly.

"From that very first day at the castle. You and the lads welcomed me, made me part of your family, and though we all had lovely adventures, twas always you I loved."

Afraid to breathe in case the moment should vanish, I squeezed her hand, drawing it near with a kiss, then looking into her eyes, I declared, "Oh Lilly, ye've no idea how long I've wanted to tell you... I love you too. I'm sure I always have, and from now on, I'm going to take care of you."

Without hesitation, she threw her arms around my neck, and we spun round and round, laughing and crying, when Mr. Baffle came round the corner.

"Everything alright here?"

Setting her down, we beamed with joy, replying in tandem, "*Brilliant! Just brilliant!*"

34

Last Breath

The weeks to follow were the happiest of my life. Lilly and I spent every possible moment together, laughing with Keith and Huw, who immediately reprised their choral arrangement of "William and Lilly sitting in a tree..." Nice to know, some things ne'er change. And atop Tantallon's windy ramparts, we dissected every aspect of Hector and Siobhan's betrayal.

Keith seethed, "How can ye not be angry, Will?"

"For a time I was, but eventually, ye have to let go."

Pointing a finger, "I tell ye, if it was me..." he stopped mid-sentence, "Why're ye smiling?"

"Century upon century of intrigues and betrayals have left their scars upon these walls." I motioned, "Yet, here they stand...as do we."

"So," Lilly grinned, "yer saying we're scarred?"

"More like weathered." I took her hand, "A storm changes people, and this... made us stronger."

"Storm?" Keith sputtered, "More like a tsunami swept through!"

"Aye," Huw sighed, "leaving a horrible stench in its wake. I just hope they get what's coming to them!"

"We'd all be in a sorry state if we got what we deserved, Huw."

"Och!" He rolled his eyes. "Here he goes again, Mr. Biblical!"

"Lilly's safe now," I reminded, "plus Hector and Siobhan are getting help."

"How gallant of you, Will!" Keith mocked.

"I think lads," Lilly added, "if William can forgive them, so should we."

Though tested by fire, we agreed to speak no more of the troublesome two, concentrating rather on a new adventure... a trip to the Bass!

It was to be a welcome reunion, but the morning of our excursion, Huw and Keith were called in to work. Then a short time later, Lilly hurried up the drive, falling into my arms like a flower bearing up against the wind.

"I'm so, so sorry, William!"

"Hey lass. What's the matter?"

She stood back, taking a deep breath. "You know I've been looking forward to seeing everyone, but...Gran just called. She's on her way, and she'll be off her head if I'm not here when she arrives."

"Oh, Lil!" The mention of Gran dampened my spirits. "Mr. Ramsay, and especially Abi'll be disappointed."

"Uh!" Crossing her arms, she stamped her foot. "But you're not?"

Wrapping her in a hug, I swung her around, "I'm missing you already, Lil...or don't you know that by now?" She giggled as I set her down. "Come on," I tugged her hand. "Ye can fare us well with Mum."

"Aw," she tugged back. "I can't do that either. There's a thousand things to do before she arrives. I just...wanted to remind ye." Looking down, she grew quiet.

I lifted her chin. "Remind me of what beautiful?"

"That I love you, William Ridley! Always remember that."

The sun streaming through the poplars haloed her lovely red tresses, and I smiled, "I will, lovely, angelic Lilly Alcott."

"Yer daft Will!" She tossed her head. "But ye know I love that too."

Taking her hands in mine, I whispered, "Mo anam cara. You and none other."

Biting her lip, she whispered back, "My very own *Braveheart!*"

"Hi ya, Lilly!" Mum waved as she and Da stepped from the cottage. "Looking forward to the Bass?"

"I was." She lamented.

"Eh? What's this?" Da asked.

Lilly sighed, "I just told William, Gran's coming today...so I can't go."

"Oh, that's a shame." Mom looked sad, "But I do know how ye feel."

"Now don't be fretting, my lovelies." Da took Mum's hand, "Ye'll both come along next time for sure."

"Thanks, Mr. Ridley, and please tell Abi I said hi!" Watching my parents walk hand in hand up the path to Tantallon, Lilly sighed again, "That'll be us in twenty years."

Shooting her a smile, I remembered my conversation with Da, knowing without a doubt, Lilly was my forever girl. "Ye know, I was just thinking the very same thing!"

Raising up on tiptoe, she placed a whisper soft kiss on my cheek, and I caught the scent of lavender she was fond of wearing. Drinking it in, as she retreated, I gazed into her deep blue eyes. Then, ever so softly, her lips brushed mine, causing us both to catch our breath. Twasn't a kiss, but there beneath the poplars twas the promise of one to come.

I exhaled, "I'll see ya later then?"

Stepping back, she groaned, "William?"

"Aye, what's wrong?"

Her eyes filled with wonder. "Are ye e'er gonna kiss me?"

"Oh, Lil!" I stepped back. "*That* is a most powerful temptation."

"So..." she stared, "that's a no then?"

She shook her head, turning to go, but I caught her hand. "I know that seems the natural thing to do, but it's because I love ye, that I'd ne'er want to compromise your honour."

"But it's just a kiss, Will."

"Still, a huge temptation, and if you feel half as much as I do, well..." I sighed, "A very wise man once said, dinnae awaken love before its time."

Studying my face, she replied, "I can't say I'm not disappointed, but... I get it. And I'm honoured." She wrinkled her brow, "Which will take some getting used to."

"I promise, Lil, the day we get engaged..."

"Engaged? We're not even out of school yet!"

"Exactly!" I added, "There'll be a time for kissing; it's just not yet."

"Well then, I shall wait with great," she chewed on the word "anticipation!"

Reluctantly, we let go of each other's hand, and my lovely, fairest Lilly turned and skipped down the lane.

With a fair wind at our backs, Da motored up alongside the Bass. Its formidable size dwarfed our vessel and the dock where Andy and Drew lay basking, toes dipping in the chilly water. Despite appearances, these lads were always ready to tote provisions, then after the heavy lifting, ready for food.

Quite near to delivering her bundle of joy, Abi had prepared a hearty meal, and if a woman could glow, she did! She was secure that Drew would provide for and protect their growing family and approached motherhood with radiant, joyful expectation, the way it was meant to be. But as she gushed about the baby, I remembered Siobhan and how differently her situation turned out. Then silently, I offered a prayer for all of them.

"Something on yer mind, lad?" Mr. Ramsay enquired.

"I was just thinking," I sat back, "how Abi's transformed this place."

She giggled in response, "I hope ye mean for the better sprite!"

"Indeed, I do!"

Raising his cuppa, Mr. Ramsay chimed, "I'll drink tae that!"

Grabbing the basket of Mum's fresh baked scones, Andy, the younger touted, "Well, soon as I find a wife who bakes this good, I'm away off this rock."

Drew spouted, "Ye'd have to learn some manners first."

"Och! What's that tae mean?" Andy pouted.

"A woman wants a man," he retorted, "she can show off in polite society."

Mr. Ramsay snickered, "That leaves the likes of us out!"

"Hush lads," Abi giggled. "Any lass'd be blessed to have either of ye!"

"My wife," Drew motioned, "the consummate optimist."

"And a very good cook for an eye doctor!"

Bestowing a thump to the back of Andy's head, Drew amended, "I said optimist, not optometrist!"

Shaking his head at their silliness, Mr. Ramsay enquired, "How's our dear AnnaLee?"

"Oh, I miss her so much." Abi's voice trailed off.

"She was awfully sorry she couldn't come today. Says she misses you all..." Da added, "Especially Abi, but sends her love, and of course that basket of goodies in her stead."

Andy replied with a big, "Ummmm!"

Mr. Ramsay rolled his eyes, asking, "And your bonnie lass Will? Everything patched up since the Ceilidh?"

Taking a deep breath, the story was related in full, till Da rumbled, "Enough! God protected William and Lilly, and for that, we give Him thanks and praise!"

"Aye!" Mr. Ramsay nodded.

"If I e'er catch sight of Hector," Andy sniped, "I'll teach him a lesson he'll nae soon forget!"

"Nae Andy." I defended, "He needs help and he's somewhere he can find it."

"Well," he conceded, "yer more forgiving than I'd be."

"That's what Keith and Huw said."

"So where are these young folk?" Mr. Ramsay chirped, "Thought they'd be joining ye today."

"The lads had to work, and Lilly's Gran arrives today."

"Well, I'm sorry for that," Mr. Ramsay cheered, "but that's all the more biscuits for us!"

While Da, Andy, and Drew tended the lighthouse, Mr. Ramsay and I took to the highest point of the Bass. The wind off the Firth was cold, but the sunshine was warm, making our walk about quite enjoyable, plus, a surprise awaited!

Nearing the cliff, we got down on our bellies and crawled towards the edge. Pointing to a nest tucked behind a crevice, Mr. Ramsay whispered, "Look there! See the shape of the bill, the colouring of the cap feathers? I believe...this may be a brand-new species!"

Truth be told, I couldn't tell one bird from another, but it delighted me to see Mr. Ramsay taking so much pleasure in his discovery.

Watching the bird take flight, joining the swirl of others scouring the waves for fish, I commented, "I'll take this as a sign."

"Eh?" Mr. Ramsay replied.

"That life is coming back to order."

Standing up, he smiled, "All things in their time, lad."

"Mr. Ramsay?"

Brushing off, he replied, "Um?"

"Ye ever get lonely out here on the Bass? Think of moving ashore?"

"Och, sometimes. I certainly enjoyed coming o'er for the wedding. But with Andy and Drew, who make turmoil enough, plus Abi, we've our own wee family...currently on the verge of expansion!" We chuckled, gazing upon the swirl of feathered creatures, then haloed by the sun, he concluded, "No, lad, this is where I belong, till the good Lord takes me to that glorious home He's preparing. Then, there'll be plenty of company and conversation, I should imagine!"

Mr. Ramsay was not only wise; he was content with where life had taken him. Be it a roomful of conversation or sharing a cuppa, silently admiring the view, he was satisfied, and I admired that.

"William, lad," as we turned for the cottage, he grew serious, "you look after Lilly. She'll be needing yer strength."

"Especially with her Gran visiting again!" I shook my head. "I'm praying she won't cause more trouble."

Mr. Ramsay drew in a deep breath, "I'm afraid this old hermit has little wisdom there. Birds act as they ought, but people, they're unpredictable. You just keep Lilly close, be the man she can respect, leave the rest in God's hands."

Contemplating his words and watching the Bass grow smaller and smaller over our stern, Da sighed, "'Tis like another world out there."

"Aye," I nodded. "'Tis."

We continued deep in thought, till halfway across the Firth, our engine began to sputter, then stalled. After yanking the starter cord several times, Da turned, "Did ye fuel the engine before we left?"

"No, I..." I stammered, "I thought you did!"

Floating with the tide, staring blankly, we burst into laughter.

"Right then!" With a shake of his head, Da rolled his eyes, then took up the oars. After a time, he passed them to me and before long, we were back ashore.

Together, we hefted the dinghy onto its stand, inhaling a deep breath of sea air. Stretching our arms skyward, we marvelled at the sunset casting golden hues upon the chilly waters and blushing the sandstone walls of Tantallon. Delightful yes, but never enticing enough to keep Da from something of much greater significance.

"Don't be long, son!" He patted my back, then hurried up the steep path to assure Mum we were safely home. Personally, I think he just couldn't bear to be parted from her that long.

As the sun dipped beneath the waves, Da disappeared beyond the castle walls, glistening in the ebbing rays of light. The cooling wind provided incentive to hurry the completion of my task, along with the tasty supper Mum'd have waiting, and my stomach growled in anticipation. Still, like a man addicted, I turned back to the sea.

With a full heart, I gave thanks to God, lifting my voice in song...

"Amazing grace, how sweet the sound, that saved a wretch like me.

I once was lost but now am found, was blind, but now I see..."

Across the Firth, the keepers had lit the beacon, and the golden light swirled out across the water. Stars emerged from heavenly hiding places, dazzling the cerulean sky, and I blew into my cupped hands, allowing the warmth to restore flexibility. Whilst the incoming tide provided a tranquil accompaniment, I began casting straps across the keel when suddenly I heard strange laughter.

The din erupted from a cluster of lads approaching at high speed. Everything inside me screamed, "Edward! Berwick! Flee!" In an instant, they surrounded me.

"Hector, Seth." I spoke with calm clarity, "Yer back."

"Aye, and we brought a few friends."

"I see. So...what do ye want?"

"What do I want?" He snarled, slurring his words as he repeated them over and over. Circling, he eyed me as I weighed what might come next.

"Are you alright?"

He began to laugh, a dark guttural sound, then without warning, he lunged, landing a fist in my stomach. Immediately, my knees buckled, and I fell, gasping on the sea-drenched shore. Standing a full 6 feet over me, Hector snarled, "God's little warrior boy! I'll tell ye what I want. I want ye dead!"

Catching my breath, I spouted, "Hector, stop!"

"Aw, stop it, Hector." Seth mocked. "Don't be so mean!"

A bottomless hatred burnt in his eyes as he drew close, hissing in my ear, "You'll regret crossing me."

"I've only tried to help you."

"Yeah," he spat his words, "you and yer bonnie wee wench!"

I exploded, "You leave Lilly be!"

He jumped backwards, "Oh, I intend to... when I'm done with her!" His hideous laughter rang in my ears as he balled up his fist, "Let's see God protect you from real live demons!"

Despite dodging sideways, his punch landed hard in my ribs, then the others joined in, punching and kicking. There were too many to defend myself, and they beat me, pummeling every part of my body.

As I cried out in pain, someone smashed a bottle o'er my head, glass exploding in every direction, then all went momentarily black. My sudden stillness halted their attack until Hector yanked me upright.

Life seemed to be moving in slow motion; faces mouthed indistinct words, warm blood running down my face blurred my vision, open wounds stung from icy salt spray, then a heavy fist connected with my cheek.

Collapsing on the beach, the chill of the Firth soaked into my bones. Then dropping beside me, Hector wrapped his fist around my cross, pressing his knuckles into my throat.

"I just want to be friends!" He mocked, "Here, let's take this heavy burden off your chest!"

Before he could rip it away, the dinghy crashed down beside us, and Hector rolled away just in time. Righting himself, they circled like a school of blood crazed sharks, when an evil smile curled across Hector's chiselled face. They huddled, then hefting the keel up craft, with a mighty force they drilled its heavy frame into the sand o'er the top of me.

Jumping aloft, Hector and his crew slammed thunderous blows

upon the hull, ranting a frenzy of indistinct words. In that eerie darkness, the incoming tide seeped in, higher and higher, till my body began to shake uncontrollably. Twas clear: this vessel that had been the source of so many happy adventures was about to become a seafarer's tomb.

But as I embraced the thought of my own death, something unexpected happened. A pale blue light filled the space beneath the boat, washing over me with a warmth and peace I couldn't explain. The beating on the hull and shouts faded, the shivering stopped, and I lay completely still... I wasn't alone!

35

The Other Side

There was no fear or sense of dying, just awareness of a brilliant white light, not travelling through it or towards it, but being wrapped in it, like a cloak of glorious, peaceful, unconditional, all sustaining love. Passing through a gossamer veil, I could see the hem of a linen robe billowing in an almost nonexistent breeze...and then came the sound of His voice...

"William, go back; it's not time yet..."

Immediately, I knew I was in the presence of Jesus! A fathomless love emanated from my Saviour, and overcome with awe, I marvelled that He knew my name! So many people I'd met demanded signs and wonders, physical proof that God exists or they'd nae believe. But God's not a genie in a bottle granting wishes, and sometimes there's no human explanation for the miracles He performs. Yet occasionally, He offers a glimpse of His glory, and nothing on earth, in the sea, or in the heavens compares to the awesomeness of standing in the presence of Jesus!

I had no fear, and I didn't want to leave, but at His command, I turned, releasing a wee sigh, "Aye. Okay."

Gasping, a deep rush of air filled my lungs, awakening the full force of pain now surging through my broken body. My head ached beyond comprehension, and in the wake of the glorious freedom my soul had just experienced, my shattered earthly shell disgusted me. Twas as though I'd showered, put on clean garments, then dove headlong into a stinking pool of sewage! My immediate response was a repugnant, "Ugh!"

Da, Mum, Papa G, Miss Norah, and a handful of folks who'd been praying over me gasped, their collective surprise providing a welcome distraction from that putrid sensation. Squeezing my hand, Mum's eyes brimmed with tears, and Da's strong hand rested firmly on my shoulder.

Mum's voice quaked, "We thought you were dead!"

I forced a smile, "Not yet!"

Our friends erupted with joy, and for one brief moment, I thought I saw...

"Lilly?"

"Shh," Mum calmed.

So many questions raced through my aching head. I tried to sit up, but Da pressed me back into bed, "Rest now, son. You've been through an awful lot."

My spirit was overwhelmed by this outpouring of love, yet it paled in comparison to what I'd just experienced. The God who'd answered the prayers of these dear folks had called me by name and, for reasons yet to be revealed, sent me back to earth and all its trials.

How different this felt from when He spoke to me at the castle. As a child, I told anyone who would listen about Jesus and my Celtic Cross, including the ponies in the far pasture. But this... this was far too personal and rudely interrupted by Inspector McFayden.

Pushing his way into the room, Nestor McFayden sported bushy sideburns, the colour of ash, around his mid-forties temples. Tall and proud, he'd spent his life on the force with hopes of, as he said, "Solving the big one!" Yet, serious crime had rarely, if ever, darkened the borders of our wee village, so an opportunity to prove his crime fighting prowess enlivened him. Ushering everyone, save for Mum and Da, out, he took centre stage like a Shakespearean actor, "Right then, let's get to the bottom of this!"

"Later!" Da directed, "William's only just opened his eyes."

McFayden ignored him, scribbling something in his notebook, then commenced firing off questions. While drifting in and out, I explained, "Twas Hector, Seth, and some lads I didn't recognise."

"Might you..." his words dripped with sarcasm, "have provoked them?"

Before Da could react, Mum roared, nose to nose with McFayden, "Are ye out of yer mind?"

He squealed, "Just gathering data, ma'am!"

Da stepped in-between, "You'd best leave now."

Backpedalling, McFayden peered over his notebook, "Tis customary to get a statement from the injured, soon as they're able, so we'll not miss details with bearing on the case, to locate the guilty party..." He soothed, "You see?"

Da cleared his throat as McFayden continued, "Now, William, I'll try not to tire you, but how em," stressing the word, "*intimately* do you know a Miss..." pausing to find her name, "em, Lilly Aeellcot?"

"Alcott," I corrected. "Lilly has nothing to do with this."

"A-hah!" McFayden passed a knowing look between himself and his aide, "She has more to do with this than you know."

I gasped, "Hector threatened her! Is she alright?"

"That, laddie, is what I'm trying to decipher."

"What do you mean?" Da restrained me from sitting up.

"She's gone missing, and *you* were last to see her." I gasped again as the inspector glared, "A bit suspicious, possibly why these lads jumped ye?"

"For Pete sakes, McFayden!" Da ordered, "Yer done!"

"Not just yet!" The room swirled as he probed for answers I didn't have, "If you're innocent, ye've nothing..."

"Inspector McFayden!" Mum stopped him. "As servant of the Crown, you are duty bound to find the lads who nearly *killed our son* and find that darling lass. Now he needs rest, and you, sir, need a reality check." He glared as she finished, "Until you've fulfilled that duty..." Her lip quivered, "Get out!"

Grabbing him by the scruff of the neck, Da ushered him towards the door. If not for the seriousness of the situation, I might've laughed, but then a desolate figure blocked the doorway.

Grasping McFayden's arm to steady herself, Rose Alcott tumbled into the room. The stark flourescent lighting magnified the discoloration of bruises swelling up on her face and torn clothes, stained with blood. Recoiling, McFayden dropped his notebook as Da helped her to a tweedy chair where she slumped like a tattered rag doll.

"Stay here, Rose," Da patted her hand. "I'll get a doctor."

"No," She waved him off, "that'll wait." Taking in a laboured breath, she began with calm resolve, "Inspector, it's, it's Lilly..."

Composing himself, McFayden sneered, "Yes, yes, as you see, I'm on the case. Though, from the looks of it, you've had another domestic!" Mum gasped as he retrieved his notebook, wincing, "You should get those bruises looked at, but since you're here, you can see how it's done."

"You were already done, McFayden!" Da rebuked, "Now, I'll not ask ye again. You'll get answers when William and Rose are well enough, in the presence of your superior, who'll hear about your insolence! Meantime, I suggest you get out there and look for Lilly!"

As McFayden and his aide began slinking out the door, Rose cried out, "No! Lilly's..."

Turning back, he snapped, "What? Have ye sent me on a wild goose chase?"

Mrs. Alcott looked horrified. I wanted to reach out, comfort her, but as she tried to speak, her eyes rolled back in her head, and she collapsed. The room exploded with noise. Da shouted down the hall for a doctor, then a scurry of medics raced in and wheeled Mrs. Alcott away on a trolley.

Amidst the turmoil, I drifted into a fog, not awake nor asleep. Faces appeared over my bed, some smiling, then Gran sneering. I heard voices calling my name, taunting, growing louder and louder, until finally this horrible swirl of noise ceased with a ray of light and a smile from my dearest Lilly, then I woke to a new day.

"Mum?"

"I'm here, Will!" She soothed my brow. "Da's gone for coffee, but we've been here the whole time, praying."

My voice was hoarse. "How long have I been out?"

"Three days, lad." The doctor who'd been checking my chart answered, "How're ye feeling?"

"Okay, I think..." Trying to sit up, I groaned, "Uh, my head hurts!"

"Not surprising," he added, "ye've 28 stitches up there."

The smell of coffee mixed with the familiar scent of Da's cologne wafted in, sweeping away the cobwebs. "Da?"

"Will!" He gushed, setting down the cups.

Reality caused me to remember, and I struggled to sit up. "Where's Lilly?"

"Not now, son." Da pressed me back onto the bed, "You need rest."

"But Da," I pleaded, "How can I rest if Lilly's in trouble?" It took all my strength to get the words out, then I drifted back into that dreamlike place.

At times I was aware of people speaking, reading Bible verses and praying, the steady sound of an IV dripping, machines beeping, clocks ticking and footsteps in the hall. Once, I even imagined hearing the sun rise. Somehow, those tiny awakenings kept me tethered to the earth, as my body pressed on through the healing process.

When I woke again, snow swirled past the window, and Huw and Keith were arguing in the corner. I wondered if I might be dreaming, when unable to stifle a yawn, they rushed to my side.

"William!" Huw shouted.

Mum and Da arrived seconds after Keith blurted, "You're awake!"

"Excellent deduction, Holmes!" We laughed until my ribs caused me to groan in pain. Mum soothed my forehead, and everyone, including Da, were moved to tears. Rolling my eyes, the only thing that didn't seem to hurt, I said, "This is gonna take some time, I imagine."

"Your body's done some healing," Da encouraged, "but aye, it'll be awhile before you can row us to the Bass again."

All I could do was nod, "Um." I drew in a deep breath, "It's good to see you, Da... I heard you and Mum singing."

She smoothed the hair from my forehead. "We were singing, dear." Her voice faltered. "We were so worried..."

"Aw, Mum, please don't cry." I gripped her hand, then remembered, "Did the inspector find Lilly?"

"Aye son." Da answered, but Mum turned away, "He found her."

"Oh, thank God!" I breathed, then managed, "And Mrs. Alcott? Is she alright?"

"Better now, Will." Da calmed, "She'll be in...when you're up to it."

"Now's good." I asked, more than said, "I think I've been asleep a very long time."

Exchanging glances, Mum and Da exited while Huw kept chatting, "We were shocked, Will!" He added, "Hector and Seth should've been at that centre."

"Shh!" Huw poked his side, "Everyone at school is hoping ye get better soon."

"Even the lads who shove us into the walls?" My friend's expressions looked strained, but they cracked a smile, and I added, "You've to thank em for me."

Huw released a pensive sigh, "You had us scared, Will. For a while," his voice cracked, "it didn't look like you were gonna make it."

"Och! Ye cannae get rid of me that easy!"

"No Will! You don't understand." Keith insisted, "Your heart stopped. That machine over there..."

My friends brows were etched with fear, then Huw clarified, "They called it flat-lining."

"I'm so sorry... Sorry that frightened you, but everything's going to be fine."

"You don't know that, Will." Keith shook his head. "You keep drifting back out!"

I smiled, "I saw Jesus!"

"What?" Keith snapped.

"He said it wasn't time yet."

Keith snorted, "It's the morphine," while Huw's eyes filled with tears.

"No!" I assured, "Heard his voice as clear as we hear each other right now!"

Da returned with his arm about Mum, who'd been crying.

"Mum? What's wrong?"

Looking from face to face, no one said a word, save the nurse wheeling Mrs. Alcott, "Someone to see you sleepyhead!"

Her face had been battered, and she looked so frail, whispering, "Heard you'd been asking for me."

"Aye," I managed. "How are you feeling?"

"Tolerable," she wobbled her head. "Well, not really. The important thing is you're back with us." I studied her face, so like Lilly's, when she added, "Ye strong enough for a visit?"

"Aye." Even in my pitiful state, I felt deep concern. "But what about you? What happened?" A painful look crossed her face, so I added, "Tis, if you don't mind me asking."

"Twasn't Gerald, dear." She touched her face, "He'd ne'er do this."

Was she defending him the way Lilly defended Hector, or, I asked, "Were you in an accident?" She shook her head, and still, no one addressed the one thing I ached to know. "Where's Lilly? Is she okay?"

"She'd be here if she could, William." Mrs. Alcott trembled, her face contorted, and big tears began streaming down her face. Mum rushed to her side as she covered her face. "Oh lad," she sobbed. "How do I tell ye?" Pausing, her eyes met mine. "Lilly's dead!"

"Wha...No!" I wailed, "No! That cannae be!" But her tear stained face confirmed the horrible truth. "How?"

Da gripped my shoulder while Mum held Rose's hand as she poured out her grief. "Lilly was so disappointed not to go with ye to the Bass. Then Mum's car broke down, and while Ger and I went to help, Lilly went out, said she'd be back soon."

"Where'd she go?" I pressed.

"Hector tricked her." Mrs. Alcott winced at his name, "Said he felt horrible about what happened and wanted to make it up to her."

"No..." I gasped.

"You know her nature; she thinks... thought the best of everyone. He tried to kiss her, but she refused, told him she loved you, so he tied her up." She sobbed, "He battered my poor lass."

Tears stung as they poured o'er my bruised face, "Oh, Lord, this is my fault!"

"Twas nae your fault, William! No one knew he'd come back, and somehow, in that twisted head, he believed he loved Lilly. She reasoned, someone who loves you wouldn't beat you, but Hector flew into a rage, then went looking for you."

My mind was reeling; I couldn't; I wouldn't let myself believe this was real. "I don't understand! Why? Why would God let this happen?"

My head fell backwards on the pillow as Da grasped my hand. "I don't know, son. I don't know."

"God didn't fail her, William. There's more..." Rose seemed determined to complete this wretched story, as though by telling it, she might make sense of what she felt, and I could only stare back as she spoke.

"Lilly was ne'er religious you know, but she told me she prayed, and a pale blue light filled the shed. She felt a warmth around her wrists and ankles, then the tethers fell away and she ran home. I was so relieved, I just held her, dried her tears. I should've called the police right then." She sobbed, "Oh, why didn't I?"

"Rose," Mum soothed. "Ye'd no way of knowing, no more than we did."

She nodded. "Lilly needed a doctor, but when I opened the door, Hector pushed in. Ger started to phone the police, but they wrestled, Hector battered him till he stopped moving."

"Rose," Da intervened, "you don't have to do this."

"William needs to hear it all." She lowered her voice. "I want him to hate Hector as much as I do. So when he's recovered, he can return the favour!"

Her tale was brutal, and she was right; I needed to hear every last detail, not to fuel hate but instead to find a shred of hope, a glimmer of light in this abyss of darkness.

"Then what happened?"

She breathed heavily. "I stood between them, told Lilly to run, but Hector shoved me and grabbed a bottle... There was blood everywhere. I tried to stop him, but I couldn't; I just couldn't. I can still hear her screams!"

"No!" I sobbed.

"I threw myself over her." Rose shook her head. "So much hatred; he never noticed; he just kept punching... blow after blow after blow. When I came to, Lilly was across the room, terribly quiet. I crawled o'er, wrapped her in my arms, and rocked her like a wee bairn until she smiled, so beautiful...she said, 'I love you, Mum.' I smoothed the bloody hair from her face, then she looked up and whispered, 'Oh, Jesus, you are beautiful!' Then she closed her eyes and breathed her last."

"Lilly!" I could barely breathe! Hot tears streamed down my battered face as I cried, "My dear, sweet Lilly!" Awash in tears, Mum held Mrs. Alcott while Da, Huw, and Keith grasped my hands, and we wept.

Stepping from the corridor, Inspector McFayden wiped a tear. "I am so, so sorry. To all of you. I'd always hoped for some fantastic case to solve, but ne'er," his voice broke, "not in a million years would I have wanted this." Moving closer, he grasped Rose's hand, "You've my word, Rose; whatever it takes, Hector will come to justice!"

As he dashed from the room, we hesitated to say another word. There were no words. Nothing could come close to expressing my grief for the vast chasm separating me from my beautiful Lilly.

36

Hope!

There's no reset button on life. You can't go back and change what's been; retrace your steps and do it over. You can only pick up the pieces and, by God's grace, live one day at a time in His comfort and strength.

Days, then weeks, washed over me like rolling waves while I nursed broken ribs and several fractures in my right leg. Though the physical pain began to ease, my heart ached with grief and regrets. What if instead of heading to the Bass that day, I'd stayed behind with her? Oh, if only... but this proved pointless. My beloved Lilly was gone, and my only solace was knowing she was in God's glorious presence... no fear, no pain, just rejoicing in ways I couldn't even begin to imagine.

"But why Magnus? Why did God let this happen?" From the pit of his grief, Mr. Alcott groaned, "Why would God hurt my Lilly? Twas me who spent life a drunken waste. Is that what caused God to punish me so?"

"Gerald," Da took him by the shoulders, "God's not punishing you!

He didn't do this; Hector did!"

"But why?" he repeated.

"Truth is, we live in a sinful world. Bad things happen to everyone. Jesus doesn't single us out because we fail him. If that were true, He'd have taken me out years ago!"

Mr. Alcott snorted, "You Magnus?"

"Aye! Shames me to remember, but no human is sinless. Well, only one, but He was God in the doin' of it because He knew we couldn't. That's why Christ's grace is so powerful. He took our punishment; all He asks is, we acknowledge our sin and need of His forgiveness." Gerald's countenance softened as Da continued, "A relationship with the Living God is what carries us through our trials. So, even in the depths of sorrow, we have hope for the glorious eternity to come, where Lilly's waiting... Will ye trust Him, Gerald?"

"I... I can't explain it, but something inside is sayin', take this chance!" Grasping his wife's hand, Mr. Alcott dropped to his knees. "I am a sinful man; have been, and I have such need of forgiveness. Sweet Jesus, take this broken life and make it worth something." Tears were streaming down his cheeks. "And till I can hold my Lilly in my arms again, tell her how sorry, how very, very sorry...and how flippin much I love her and miss her!"

As he wept, we gathered round and prayed, but Mr. Alcott wasn't the only one with questions. I wondered too. Why? Why help Lilly escape, only to die a few hours later? Did Jesus allow her murder to bring her da to a saving faith? Or so we'd find comfort in her final words? And what about Hector still skulking around out there?

From the window seat, I stared at Tantallon, gripping the cross that had come to me years ago. After a long while, Mum sat beside me.

"What's my brave warrior thinking?"

"How is it possible," I croaked, "to be a Defender of the Faith when I couldn't protect one beautiful, lovely, worthy girl? Oh, Mum...I loved her so much!"

"As she loved you, William." Tears welled in her eyes. "Some questions have no answers, but eternity matters, and you gave Lilly hope! You will see her again."

"I know, it just…" I sobbed, "hurts so much now."

Wrapping me in her arms, Mum rocked gently back and forth. "God ne'er intends for such evil to befall us, but somehow, in His sovereign plan, He allowed this." She stroked my face, "So, we'll grieve, and we'll stand alongside Rose and Gerald, giving as much encouragement as we can. And thank the Lord He spared you, William. There's a bigger plan; we just cannae see it yet."

Mum's words helped a great deal, but nights were tough. I'd lay awake wrestling with thoughts and regrets… the unseen demons you cannae banish easily. Plus, limping from class to class, everyone staring sad, empty looks reminded daily of the huge chasm in our world.

They meant well, some patting my shoulder, attempting to encourage, but others kindled embers of revenge, and no one, absolutely no one spoke her name. Straining beneath this collective wake of grief, Mr. Baffle called on Da to help.

Twas Thursday. The squeak of wooden chairs being occupied pierced the heavy hush in the assembly room as students filed in. I'd never seen so many young people gathered in sombre silence. We knew why we were here; we just didn't know how to do life the same since Lilly left us.

Looking out among our sad faces, Da began,

> *"As for me, I am poor and needy,*
>> *but Lord you take thought for me.*
> *You are my help and my deliverer;*
>> *do not delay, O my God!"* ~ Psalm 40:17

"These ancient words from King David echo our great need of heavenly comfort… Lilly Alcott twas a dear, lovely lass whom we loved, each of us in our own way. So, aye, there's a huge hole in our hearts, and we'll nae see her make the travels and adventures she spoke so fondly of, but *there is hope!*

"Though our grief is heavy...death does not have the final word! Because of her faith in Christ, Lilly *is* alive, not only in our hearts but in heaven, where Jesus is enjoying the laughter she so often shared with us."

Aisling responded softly, "Lilly's in a better place!"

"Aye lass, and I pray ye'll take comfort in that."

Instantly, Keith yelled out, "And may Hector rot in hell forever!"

"Amen to that!" Jimmy shouted, and chaos erupted.

Mr. Baffle drew back, horrified, as Da tried to halt the anger sweeping across the room.

"I know yer angry... " He shouted over the noise, "I'm angry too! It's right to be outraged by this! Only... don't offer your hearts as soil for wrath and bitterness, for their roots consume, like choking vines! Instead, pray it out, write it out," his voice broke. "Go to the ocean's edge and shout it out at the top of your lungs, and when ye've done all that and exhausted all the rage within, give it up to a mighty God and let Him deal with Hector as He will."

I hadn't planned on speaking, but limping forward, Da steadied me, and the rumble of voices hushed as I faced my grieving class-mates.

"I know I've not said much, and as most of ye know, there were some pretty turbulent days leading up to..." I paused, "None of us could have known. If we had, things would be different, but they're not..."

"I miss Lilly. I'll always miss Lilly, her laughter, her smile, her kind-ness, amazing artwork, and epic stories. She was good with a sword and knew *exactly* how to tease Huw and Keith. She made us dance the Snoopy song and planned on travelling to wonderful places.

"She smelled of lavender, and she shone like the sun. She touched our hearts in profound ways, and I would have you believe that she is even more radiant today than when she walked among us, within these rooms and corridors.

"And since our dearest shield maiden loved nothing better than a good story, let me tell you the last one I shared with her.

"Once there was a wealthy businessman named Horatio Spafford. With his wife Anna, they were raising five children, but in 1870, their only son died from scarlet fever. Then a year later, the great Chicago fire swept through their city, and they lost practically everything. Even so, they gave what little they had to help others who were suffering, and by 1873, Horatio had recovered enough financially to visit a friend in England, where they hoped to forget at least some of this tragedy.

"They got as far as New York when Horatio was delayed on business, so he sent his family ahead. Somewhere over the deep, blue Atlantic, an iron vessel struck their steamship, and in less than twelve minutes it vanished beneath the waves, and with it, over two hundred souls drowned.

"When Anna reached safety, she sent a telegram that read, *'Saved alone. What shall I do?'*

"Immediately, he sailed to comfort her. And as they passed over the spot where his four daughters had perished, overcome with grief, Horatio retired to his cabin. He had every reason to surrender to anger and despair, but above those waves, despite overwhelming tragedy, something...supernatural happened. He wrote a song of hope, declaring his trust in a Sovereign Lord and Saviour, Jesus Christ. I pray his words will comfort your hearts as they did for Lilly..."

With tears, I lifted up my voice...

> *'When peace like a river, attendeth my way*
> *When sorrows, like sea billows roll*
> *Whatever my lot, thou hast taught me to say*

It is well, It is well, with my soul…
Though Satan should buffet, though trials should come
Let this blest assurance control
That Christ hast regarded my helpless estate
And hath shed his own blood for my soul
It is well, It is well, it is well, it is well with my soul…'

Voices joined, raising delicate harmonies, then trailed off, leaving sweet peace in their wake.

"We've been shattered by the irreversible effects of sin!" I drew in a deep breath, "I know many of you don't like that word and think it's odd that I'm not angry. Believe me, it's a struggle! I loved Lilly and always will; I just ne'er told her near enough, and if not for the faith Jesus has given me, grief and anger would've destroyed me. But her murderer, who assaulted so many of us and sent me to the brink of death, will not escape justice. When Hector's days on earth are done, he'll stand before God, and unless he comes to a saving faith, he will pay eternally in Hell. If anything, he's to be pitied!"

"How can ye pity that monster Will?" Keith jumped to his feet. "He nearly killed you and murdered Lilly!"

"I'm wrestling with that, Keith, but if we let hatred consume us, we'll never heal!"

The room fell silent till Keith addressed my da, "So, what if, by some *small* chance, Hector hears the Gospel and asks God to forgive him. Will he not be punished?"

"Before I answer ye, Keith," Da responded, "may I ask you a question?"

"Aye."

"Have ye ever taken something that wasn't yours?"

"I suppose," he looked down, shuffling his feet, "that depends on what ye mean by wasn't yours!"

The heaviness lifted a touch as we giggled, even Da gave a wee grin then asked, "Have ye ever disobeyed yer Da, been cheeky to yer

Mum, pinched a plate of cookies or," looking about the room, "had an impure thought about one of your fairer classmates?"

Looking stunned, Keith reasoned, "Och! No one's perfect, but still, that's not murder!"

"No," Da replied, "but the Lord counts it all the same; it's sin, which will send us to Hell if we don't repent."

"So, in answer to yer question... If God truly changes Hector's heart, aye, he'll be saved. Mind ye, it's not saying a prayer that saves us, but Christ alone, who paid dearly for murderers, fornicators, drunkards, sloths, as well as the tyke who pinched a cookie from the jar... Something we should be grateful for.

"Losing someone we love tis a wretched thing. Our hearts'll ache for some time, but this life is not the end; tis only a steppingstone. So, if, like Lilly, we trust Jesus to save us from God's wrath, we'll see her again, more joyful than you've ever known her, and more importantly, spend eternity in a place where there's no sorrow, no sickness, no tears, just absolute, overwhelming joy in the presence of our precious Lord and Saviour! This, each and every one of you can put your hope in!"

As Da's words echoed, a brilliant sunbeam burst through the etched windows, cloaking the inhabitants in a warmth we hadn't felt in weeks. Then lifting our faces to the light, we spent the afternoon sharing memories of Lilly, her quirky humour that came out in funny things she said or did, and times we spent together, sorrowful we weren't able to help but grateful for the opportunity to put a voice to our grief.

It wasn't till that afternoon, the heaviness began to lift from my soul, and I fully comprehended a healing truth: Lilly's death wasn't my fault! It happened, and had there been a way to save her, I surely would have.

Twas Autumn again, and for the first time since the incident, I ventured down to the shore and sat beside the upturned dinghy.

Placing a hand upon its aged timbers, I thought of the Ark and God bringing Noah and his family through the flood...to start again.

Bitter as it seemed, twas time now for me to start again.

I sat for a long time...gazing towards the Bass, allowing the tranquil sound of the Firth lapping the rocks to quell a bit of my sorrow. Then, drawing in a deep breath, I thanked the Lord for His mercy, and He responded with a salty breeze, whisking the shaggy hair from my eyes to reveal a glorious pearlescent glow in the sky.

To my beloved, I whispered, "Dearest Lilly! My beautiful Mo Anam Cara! I'll ne'er forget you. Wherever I go, you'll be right here with me...till we meet again!"

Then, as she had done so many times, I pressed my fingers to the Celtic Cross, wondering once more at the hand of God. What might He ask of me next, and if this was preparation, would I be strong enough to endure it?

At the tender age of 16, with a "Voice of Democracy" speech award in hand, Connie (Stroedecke) MacLeod set out to change the world for the better. However, the strain and stress of school and home life resulted in a bout of pneumonia... so severe, she flat-lined. Not being raised in a Christian home, she knew little of God, but that's when Jesus introduced Himself, saying, "Connie. Go back. It's not time yet!"

Knowing God was real and that He cared for her birthed the unmistakable expression of joy she exudes and a new outlet, music. Turning her hand to songwriting, she traveled the world with her guitar, playing self penned tunes and encouraging songs, recording with award winning engineer John Blanche. But upon releasing her sophomore album, "I Wish You Well," tragedy struck!

An unrelated surgery took away her singing voice. Having identified as a singer/songwriter all her life, this devastating blow made her wonder, "Did I let God down? Was He mad at me, punishing me?"

The answer was a gargantuan, resounding, "NO!"

It was the start of God molding her, remaking her, and reminding her that she was not just a singer/songwriter...she was His child, beloved and adored by the God who created the universe and everything in it!

With a Bachelors Degree in Radio and Television Communications, Connie wrote copy, articles, and feature stories, along with award winning photography featured in newspapers, global magazines, newsletters, and web blogs, as well as producing promotions for radio and television.

Following a calling, she and her husband Roddy moved to the wild bush of Kenya, living with the Samburu tribe. While sharing the love of Christ, each day was akin to an Indiana Jones movie, outrunning danger, spitting cobras, brush fires, and tribal warfare, but despite the mortal danger, God held them in the palm of His mighty hand.

The spiritual warfare was fierce, but as you'll learn from William's story and Connie's ongoing story, Jesus is our defender, protector, and deliverer, who proves daily that He is mighty and He is in control. By trusting in Christ, when He calls us to something, He makes a way in the wilderness and changes the impossible to possible!

Today, Connie and Roddy reside in Scotland, where together they continue sharing the Gospel, the Good News, that through repentance and forgiveness, Jesus Christ rescues sinners and will lavish upon them the gift of eternal life...Salvation!